Servile Disobedience

"You can have everything you desire if you come with me," I told them. "No one will be able to hurt you. You can do as you want, when you want, when you're free, like I am."

Vanais gasped out loud. "You *should* be punished. I'm getting our mistress."

She approached me, but I blocked her from going through the door. It was like pushing against a bundle of dry sticks.

"I have money," I insisted. "A great wealth, enough for you all to prosper. I can show you how. We can find a place even better than this. You only have to follow me."

Vanais tried to struggle past me again, but I pushed her away. She went down on her knees, scraping them in her awkward fall. Her outraged look pained me.

"You're leaving Montplaire?" Bene asked.

"Yes, this very moment."

Their frightened, angry expressions spoke louder than words. "We'd die on the streets," one girl protested, while a boy agreed. "They'll catch you if you try." Two of the younger girls pulled their blankets over their heads as if they couldn't hear such disobedience.

"Come with me, Bene," I urged, hoping if he agreed that the others would follow.

Vanais was furious. "You *can't* go anywhere," she demanded, her voice rising.

"Claim the life you dreamed of when you came here," I called to the others as Bene quickly donned his tunic and leggings, tying on his boots. "You can be free—"

Suddenly Vanais slipped away and wiggled past me. She flung the door open and started down the stairs, crying out for the master and mistress. . . .

A Pound of Flesh

Susan Wright

A ROC BOOK

ROC

Published by New American Library, a division of
Penguin Group (USA) Inc., 375 Hudson Street,
New York, New York 10014, USA
Penguin Group (Canada), 90 Eglinton Avenue East, Suite 700, Toronto,
Ontario M4P 2Y3, Canada (a division of Pearson Penguin Canada Inc.)
Penguin Books Ltd., 80 Strand, London WC2R 0RL, England
Penguin Ireland, 25 St. Stephen's Green, Dublin 2,
Ireland (a division of Penguin Books Ltd.)
Penguin Group (Australia), 250 Camberwell Road, Camberwell, Victoria 3124,
Australia (a division of Pearson Australia Group Pty. Ltd.)
Penguin Books India Pvt. Ltd., 11 Community Centre, Panchsheel Park,
New Delhi - 110 017, India
Penguin Group (NZ), 67 Apollo Drive, Mairangi Bay,
Auckland 1310, New Zealand (a division of Pearson New Zealand Ltd.)
Penguin Books (South Africa) (Pty.) Ltd., 24 Sturdee Avenue,
Rosebank, Johannesburg 2196, South Africa

Penguin Books Ltd., Registered Offices:
80 Strand, London WC2R 0RL, England

First published by Roc, an imprint of New American Library,
a division of Penguin Group (USA) Inc.

First Printing, February 2007
10 9 8 7 6 5 4 3 2 1

Copyright © Susan Wright, 2007
All rights reserved

 REGISTERED TRADEMARK—MARCA REGISTRADA

LIBRARY OF CONGRESS CATALOGING-IN-PUBLICATION DATA:
Wright, Susan (Laurie Susan)
A pound of flesh : a novel of fantasy / Susan Wright.
p. cm.
ISBN-13: 978-0-451-46127-8
ISBN-10: 0-451-46127-4
1. Slavery—Fiction. 2. Slaveholders—Fiction. 3. Sexual dominance and submission—Fiction.
I. Title.
PS3623.R5656P68 2007
813'.54—dc22   2006024987

Set in Bembo
Designed by Spring Hoteling

Printed in the United States of America

PUBLISHER'S NOTE
This is a work of fiction. Names, characters, places, and incidents either are the product of the author's imagination or are used fictitiously, and any resemblance to actual persons, living or dead, business establishments, events, or locales is entirely coincidental.

The publisher does not have any control over and does not assume any responsibility for author or third-party Web sites or their content.

Acknowledgments

Liz Scheier, my editor at Roc, and Lucienne Diver, my agent
at Spectrum Literary Agency, for their exceptional
guidance and support.

A Pound of Flesh

1

With my first step onto the ruddy sand of the beach, the evil spirits infesting Vidaris pressed in on me. Clinging wisps of foul air snaked along the ground, drawing closer to suck at my strength and muddle my mind. My instincts cried out for me to flee before they found a way to seep inside.

The native Thule who had brought Lexander and me back to Vidaris also sensed the demons. The dark-skinned warriors gathered close, silently supporting each other's *inua*. They left everything in the round-bottomed *umiaks* except for their spears and bows. Even the two wounded men readied their weapons, making the warband a full score strong. They had come to free Qamaniq, the granddaughter of Nerriviq, who had been lured away by Lexander to become a pleasure slave.

There would be no rest—Lexander planned to attack Vidaris at once.

The sliver of moon cast barely enough light through the clouds to reveal the sheer red cliffs of Fjardemano Island. On top of the cliff there was something new: a rough wooden tower rose next to the gate in the palisade, overlooking the ocean. I urged the merry *olfs* to rise up the cliff face to illuminate the tower. There was no sentry in sight.

Lexander could see through the darkness even without the

olfs' light. "I hear one freeman on watch." He tilted his head. "He's snoring."

I didn't doubt Lexander's uncanny ability, though the crashing of the waves nearly drowned out the howling of the wind through the forest trees above. "Helanas built it?" I asked.

His golden eyes shone much brighter than those of the Thule. "She intended to be forewarned of my return."

I shivered at his tone. "What will you do?"

"That is my concern." Lexander turned away so I couldn't see his face.

Nerriviq approached, his distrust for Lexander evident in his watchful eyes. "My granddaughter waits."

Lexander gave Nerriviq a curt nod. "Stay with me, Marja."

He led the Thule to the mouth of the river that followed a crevice in the line of cliffs. Vidaris had been Lexander's estate for nearly two decades, and he knew every step up the winding path.

As we climbed inland, twisty little demons—mere puffs of smoke—whipped branches into my face, seeking to tear out my eyes. The Thule chanted in low voices, begging the *olfs* to aid us. Those faithful creatures gathered around us, surrounding us in a warm glow and warding off the malevolent spirits.

Some *olfs* flew ahead to light our way, while others dabbled in the dreams of those sleeping in Vidaris. A fussing baby was lulled by the gentle singing of a pair of *olfs*. Even the animals sighed and drowsed.

We ducked under the bridge for the wagons and not far beyond was a ravine. One by one we pushed through the brush that filled the bottom of the gully, then climbed the crumbling sides into the fields. The oats were nearly ready for harvest, the heads of the stalks glowing golden in the moonlight. Insects buzzed around us.

When we finally reached the *haushold,* I was panting from withstanding the malicious pressure that was building around me. I feared one of the demons would wake Helanas and warn her about us.

The servants had gone home to their own cots, so the kitchen was empty. Lexander lit a handful of candles from the rack and conferred briefly with Nerriviq. The Thule split up, going in opposite directions to block any possibility of Helanas' escape.

I followed Lexander into the fire hall. Everything was achingly familiar, from the red brick walls to the padded benches set before the hearth.

Nerriviq and his son followed us, stepping cautiously over the cool bricks and warily watched the towering ceiling far above them. My mam's people were attuned to the spirits like no others, so they could sense what had happened here, like echoes of the pleas we pleasure slaves had made for mercy. I could almost hear Sverker's cries as Helanas bound him too tightly and his wicked laugh as his cruelty fed the demons, taking his pleasure in penetrating me, making me cry out as he repeatedly forced his fat *tarse* into me . . .

Lexander motioned for the Thule to wait while he entered the smaller slave hall. Sleeping ledges lined both walls, but there were only six slaves now where once there had been a dozen.

"Wake up," Lexander called out softly, "but don't be frightened. I've come to take you away."

I lifted my candle higher to see Niels sitting up, rubbing his eyes. The two Skraeling sisters huddled together, their long dark hair tousled and their narrow eyes fearful at the reappearance of Lexander. Torngasoak was brave enough to put an arm around each of them. The two blond brothers from Fylkeran were confused, but in the scant few moons they had been in Vidaris, they had learned not to ask questions.

Lexander went to check the other door. Niels stood hunched over as if expecting to be hit, whispering, "Marja, is that really you? Where are Sverker and Rosarin?"

I was pained by the thought of what my slave-mates suffered now in the hands of Lexander's people. He had saved me from that fate, but they had not been so fortunate.

Lexander returned. "Quiet, or you'll wake Helanas."

The slaves went very still at her name. At our gentle urging, they followed us into the fire hall, scurrying in fear when they saw the Skraelings waiting for us. They clung to each other, including the Skraeling slaves who surely recognized the Thule as a northern clan.

"Where's Qamaniq?" Lexander asked.

"She was summoned to Helanas' chamber," Niels offered.

Lexander gestured to me. "Take them to the bathhouse, Marja. Stay there until I come for you."

He sounded much like the master of Vidaris that I remembered, though he had freed me himself a few days ago, before the battle of Tillfallvik.

Lexander took Nerriviq through the courtyard. I paused in the doorway to the kitchen, the slaves close behind me. "Niels," I ordered, "take the others and go to the bathhouse."

"What about you?"

"I'll be there soon. Now *go*."

He gasped, shocked that I would defy our master. But he was accustomed to obedience and left without another word of protest. The baths were familiar. The slaves would be safe there.

I went through the courtyard, and was surprised to see Lexander's chamber was open. He appeared holding a long sword. It had an ornate guard on the handle, yet he held it lightly as if its weight were no burden.

He glared when he saw me. "Go away!" he insisted under his breath.

I set my lips and shook my head.

He hesitated but could not take time to argue. The Thule blocked the hallway on either side of us, their spears pointing inward.

Lexander handed the heavy casket to me, opening the top to pull out a key. With a motion of his hand to stay back, he threw open the door to Helanas' chamber, rushing inside with the Thule warriors behind him. My candle shook as I followed, casting wild shadows on the flowered tapestries that hung on the walls.

Someone screeched in protest. I wasn't sure if it was Helanas or

Qamaniq. Then I saw the Skraeling woman on the floor, her dark hair a tangled mess and her body limp. I knew that Qamaniq was beyond suffering right now.

Nerriviq's kin picked up Qamaniq, exclaiming over her naked form. But I had eyes only for Helanas. My mistress was on her feet, a knife in her hand.

Lexander caught her with the point of his sword against her throat. Her shapely body was bare. Many times had I caressed those generous curves and stroked my mistress until she writhed in pleasure. Yet Helanas had never smiled when she took her satisfaction, preferring to glower and furiously taunt the slave who served her even as she climaxed.

With two steps, Lexander drove Helanas back against the tapestry until she could go no farther. "Drop your knife!"

Helanas hesitated, her eyes taking in the Skraelings in the room. She sneered when she saw me. "That sly bitch! She's seduced you from your duty, Lexander. You will live to rue the day you found her—"

"Silence!" Lexander demanded.

There was an edge to his voice that I had never heard. Perhaps Helanas was right: someday he would regret the choice he had made to leave Vidaris and abandon the ways of his own people. Perhaps he feared that fate more than anything else.

"You drove him to it," I told Helanas. "If only you had not been so cruel—"

"You will *not* look at me, slave." Her hand tightened on the knife. *"Gesig!"*

My knees buckled in an unreasoning compulsion to obey. But I fought my trained reflexes and stayed on my feet, clutching the heavy casket tighter. The brass studs dug into my flesh, piercing the demon-roiled cloud that threatened to overcome me.

Disgust twisted Helanas' face, marring her satiny skin and perfect features. "Think of what you've done, Lexander! You can still rectify this terrible mistake. Stay here in Vidaris. I won't tell Saaladet—"

Helanas hardly shifted, but suddenly her knife slashed up.

I gasped as Lexander blocked it with his arm. The blade bit in deep as he thrust it away. The knife flew into the tapestry and clattered to the floor.

Lexander hadn't moved the sword from her throat. Nay, it pressed in, and a line of blood trickled down to the hollow of her throat.

"You're hurt," I cried. But Lexander didn't even glance at his bleeding arm where the sleeve flapped open.

Helanas went quite still. Now her eyes were very wide and I saw my mistress's fear for the first time. "You don't have to kill me, Lexander. Take what you want and go. I've done nothing to you."

"Did you send word to Stanbulin that I left?"

Her eyes shifted. "Naturally! By merchant ship. But I could fix it for you. I could tell them I made a mistake. Without me, you are renegade—and will suffer the consequences."

I couldn't see Lexander's face, but hers was eloquent. She was gloating, even with his sword at her throat. She would get her way, as she always did.

"You lie," Lexander said quietly. "You were never able to fool me, Helanas. Never."

Her expression grew more guarded. "You don't think you—"

Helanas didn't finish. Lexander leaned in, driving the point through her neck. Helanas clutched at the sword as if to stop it, the sharp edge slicing into her fingers. She gurgled as blood welled over the blade and poured down her chest.

When Lexander withdrew the sword, her arms flailed. Then he brought the sword slashing across her neck.

I dropped the candle and ran from the room. Helanas' body was too beautiful, too flawless to be ripped apart. And Lexander's expression was . . . inhuman.

Lexander appeared in the doorway, glaring at me. "You insisted on seeing that."

I clutched the heavy casket to my chest. "Why . . . Lexander, why?"

"It was the only way to stop her."

A high-pitched wail began to rise, making my ears ring. The evil spirits that had been drawn by the slaves' terror and pain had grown strong over the decades. They had fed on Helanas' misdeeds, and would not disperse easily. I was buffeted by their swirling presence.

"Something terrible is happening," I gasped.

"We have to get out of here." Lexander still held on to the bloody sword. "Come!"

The sky was growing brighter with the approaching dawn. I swallowed hard when I saw the blood staining the sword and the long cut in Lexander's forearm.

The Thule carried Qamaniq's bruised and battered body out of the *haushold*. Nerriviq's eyes blazed with anger. Only the sight of Lexander slaying Helanas stayed his hand from striking down the man who had enslaved his granddaughter.

Evil spirits careened around us, and I realized there was heat welling up from below. The Thule felt it, too.

"What is it?" I asked.

"When a master is killed in our own house, retribution follows." Lexander ran down the gravel path toward the bathhouse, where the slaves huddled. "Hurry," he ordered then. "We must get away from the *haushold*."

They followed us meekly. In the morning light, I saw that Niels had lost his childlike beauty. His face was thin, lined by despair and weariness like a shriveled old man.

We had not yet reached the gate in the palisade when the earth shook beneath my feet. I stumbled into Lexander, who supported me. I glanced back to see the walls of the *haushold* split apart as flames roared through the peaked roof. Everyone ducked as bricks went flying high into the air.

Lexander leaned over me, trying to protect me from the falling debris. We were far enough away that most of it missed us. But the estate lit up like daylight from the fire that roared into the sky.

I marveled at the force it took to destroy the *haushold*. Lexander's people truly wielded power far beyond our own.

"So it is done." Lexander watched his home burn, his face lit eerily by the orange glow.

2

As the *haushold* burned, I followed Lexander like a shadow. He settled the slaves in the crude sentry tower. The freeman who had been asleep on his watch had fled in the face of the fire.

Nerriviq returned from the *umiaks* where they had taken Qamaniq. "My granddaughter lives, though we have no assurance her spirit is intact. That is for the shaman to determine."

"Don't leave yet," Lexander urged. "Help me raze Vidaris so this place can't be used to enslave your people again."

We were joined by half a dozen Thule carrying their spears and bows. I was concerned about the slaves, so I asked a few *olfs* to stay behind in the tower to alert me if they needed me.

The blood on Lexander's sleeve was beginning to brown, but he shrugged me off, refusing to allow me to tend to the cut. I had seen the terrible wound Ketil Grimsson had given him when he won Silveta's right to speak to the chieftains in Issland. That blow would have maimed another man, but Lexander had healed in one night. His people had powers greater than ours; they were godlings in their own right.

Lexander went to each of the longhouses on his estate, ordering his people to abandon Vidaris. An outcry went up as the servants were told they must leave their homes. The freemen stared in shock at the burning *haushold* while their wives and children wept. They had always had a prosperous life on the estate, with everything they needed at hand. They implored Lexander to have mercy and let them stay in Vidaris.

Lexander simply repeated, "Gather your belongings, and take the grain and livestock with you. You'll have plenty to make homes for yourselves elsewhere."

Even stout Hallgerd, for so long in absolute charge of the kitchen, could not disobey his command. The scullery maid who had taunted me during my training was reduced to a shivering, broken child. It was not what I would have wished on them, but surely it was better than living in the maw of evil.

Lexander relented only with a handful of field hands who had also served as oarsmen. He quietly directed them to take their possessions to the longship and wait for him there.

The protests of the others were cut short by the presence of the Thule, their weapons held ready. Lexander's people had been raised on tales of Skraeling attacks that had destroyed entire settlements, and the sight of them was too much. Tears flowing freely, they hastily packed their carts and barrows full of their belongings. Casks of wine, baskets of ripe fruit, and bags of grain were piled up high. They tethered the fat cattle to their carts while youngsters herded the sheep and geese with sticks. The dogs barked joyfully, adding to the commotion.

They set off into the rising sun, which cast a pallid light through the oily black smoke that hung over the estate. As each longhouse was emptied, Lexander set fire to it, letting the thatch blaze brightly. The former inhabitants hurried away, glancing over their shoulders at the madman who used to be their master. I wondered what tales they would spread about the fall of Vidaris.

Lexander didn't speak to me throughout the exodus. It was a brutal contrast—the stark destruction he wrought on land that was flush with late-summer abundance. The trees hung heavy with fruit and the thick grass waved in the meadows. It seemed a place destined to prosper. But I could feel how the life was seeping away day by day as the benevolent spirits were kept at bay by the demons.

After the servants and freemen were gone, Lexander walked the edge of the fields, setting fire to the crops that were ready to be harvested. The wind picked up the blaze and spread it rapidly. He also burned the rows of vines hung with clusters of grapes that were made into fine Vidaris wine. The plume of smoke that went up could likely be seen as far as Brianda on the other side of Fjardemano Island.

Nerriviq was finally appeased by Lexander's all-consuming wrath. They were united in their desire to destroy Vidaris, and the Thule could have done it no more thoroughly than Lexander.

My only relief came from watching the *olfs* dancing in the flames. Fire was the best way to banish the evil spirits. With nothing to cling to, the demons drifted off with the smoke right before my eyes. I knew that soon the trees would retake the fields and grass would cover the scars left by the burned homes. The land would become whole again.

When there was nothing left to set ablaze, Lexander returned to the *haushold*. The smoldering rubble sent streamers of smoke into the sky. Lexander wandered around the broken walls as if searching for something.

Only one fragment of a wall still stood, reaching not quite to my chin. It had once supported the storage platform. My mistress had delighted in using the hook high in the wall to string up the slaves by our wrists, leaving us with our heels scraping against these bricks, trying to find purchase. I had come closest to dying here, despite everything else since, when Helanas had tied me around the neck and forced me to stand on my toes. As my feet gradually gave out, I couldn't breathe and blackness hovered over me. Lexander had released me, as he so often had, though he had never tried to stop Helanas from hurting us . . .

I jerked my hand away from the rough brick—*he had never tried to stop her.*

Warily I glanced over at Lexander, pacing through the rubble. He bent down to pick up something, then let it drop again.

I went over to the white bit of stone. It was a tiny figure of the Norogod Baldr, the god of light, from the *hneftaf* game. Lexander had taught me to play *hneftaf* last winter, and we had spent many an evening moving the figurines about the board as he told me about all the places he had been. I clutched the tiny sculpture in my fist, not wanting to let it go. In the midst of the wretchedness, there had been some good in Vidaris.

Finally, I asked, "How did you set fire to the *haushold*?"

He looked at me as if he had forgotten I was following him. His face and smooth head were sooty, reminding me of my da, the village smithy, who had sold me to him.

"I released the fire by killing Helanas," he finally said. "It's a protection my people place within our houses. We've gained a reputation of being difficult to kill, and those who try usually perish with us."

Now I knew where Lexander had learned his ruthlessness. It must have shown on my face.

"For nearly twenty years," Lexander said, "Helanas was my consort."

"Do you regret killing her?" I had to ask.

Lexander frowned. "Never. I only wish I had done it the night I saved you."

I was sure there was more to be said, but he turned and walked off.

When we returned to the tower where the slaves had been left, they were wrapped in the blankets left behind. Niels had been crying again. They hastily got to their feet, watching Lexander warily.

"You'll be fine now," I assured them. They looked wrung to near exhaustion, but none had been tainted by the evil spirits.

"I hereby free you all," Lexander said heavily.

The slaves looked dazed. I wasn't sure the Skraelings understood, so I explained it to them in my mam's tongue.

"I should never have brought you here," Lexander admitted stiffly. It was as close to an apology as he could give them.

"Is it true?" one of the brothers asked. "We can go home now?"

"Yes," Lexander assured him. "We'll sail to Tillfallvik first. From there I'll send you to Hop."

Niels asked faintly, "Tillfallvik is in Markland, where you're from, Marja?"

"Yes, and 'tis the best of lands," I assured him. "You will be safe there."

The Skraeling sisters were even more frightened at the thought of going to another Noroland. But Torngasoak kept his arms around them, holding them firmly.

The six former slaves followed us down the long flight of steps to the beach at the base of the red cliff. Lexander carried his casket under one arm, and the others kept the blankets around their shoulders to ward off the chill wind. I still clutched the figurine of Baldr in my fist.

The stench of smoke filled the air even with the ocean breeze in my face. The sun was lowering, casting long shadows across the beach. I was eager to leave Vidaris before darkness fell. The vicious spirits that roamed the woods at night, bloodsucking *adlets* and packs of *qiqirn,* would be drawn by the void left by the demons.

Farther down the beach, the Thule were dragging their *umiaks* into the surf. It was a daunting task to row across the Nauga Sea. They had not slept since we left Tillfallvik, but they would not linger here. Their wounded were being tended carefully to make sure that no evil could seep into them while they were weakened.

Without a word, Lexander and I went over to the Thule, the slaves trailing behind us. I didn't see Qamaniq until we drew nigh. She was wrapped in furs, lying prone on the red sand. Nerriviq sat next to her, murmuring a healing chant.

Lexander went straight to her side, kneeling down. "Is she . . . well?"

Nerriviq glared at him. "She will recover if the gods are good to us."

I stood where I could see Lexander's face. I had been sorely jealous of Qamaniq from the moment Lexander had acquired her. Her regal bearing and sumptuous figure had enchanted him.

"Qamaniq," he said tenderly, "it's me, Lexander."

My hands tightened into fists at the way he said her name.

"Lexander?" Qamaniq murmured, turning toward him.

I drew in my breath at her ravaged face, worn with weariness and sorrow. Helanas must have tried to grind her into dust to bring about such a transformation. Probably because Qamaniq was a favorite of Lexander's, as I had been.

"Master," Qamaniq said more strongly, "it's you."

"Forgive me, Qamaniq," Lexander said stiffly. "I should never have convinced you to leave the Thule. They are far more merciful than I."

For a moment I thought Lexander would atone by offering to take care of her, as he had cared for me.

But Qamaniq's face crumpled. "The gods themselves could not forgive one such as you."

Lexander drew back. "No, indeed," he quietly agreed. "The gods themselves could not."

Nerriviq tried to soothe Qamaniq. "Go, Vidaris. I've got what I demanded, but do not risk my anger a moment longer."

I tugged at Lexander's arm, seeing the truth in Nerriviq's words as his kin began to gather closer. Their fury was clear. Lexander hesitated, as if willing to endure whatever sacrifice they required.

I gestured to the Skraelings on the sand behind us. "Lexander, the other slaves are waiting. We must get them to safety."

But Torngasoak stepped forward to address Nerriviq. "Honored Elder, please take us home. The sisters will come to my clan, where they will be safe. They have agreed to join me."

Lexander had brought the Skraeling sisters to Vidaris shortly before me, and they would have gone to Stanbulin in the winged ship when it next arrived. Though Torngasoak was little more than a youth, the terror he had endured had made a man of him. He would be able to care for the sisters as they deserved.

"Yes, join us," Nerriviq agreed. It would make their journey longer to go to the Beothuk lands, but he could not refuse the young Skraeling's plea.

Nerriviq picked up his granddaughter still wrapped in the furs. Torngasoak put an arm around each of the Skraeling sisters and followed the Thule to the *umiaks*. The sisters were still hunched over as if they would forever be afraid.

A crease appeared between Lexander's eyes. Perhaps the others took it for anger, but I knew he was distressed. Niels and the brothers from Hop waited for us.

"It's not enough," he said roughly. "There are other masters like Helanas, some even worse. I must stop them."

He had spoken of the other pleasure houses from time to time. Before Vidaris, Lexander had been master of the house in Veneto, in the Auldland. "How many houses are there?" I asked.

"I don't know. We are ordered to maintain secrecy, even amongst ourselves. But there must be dozens."

My eyes widened in horror. Lexander gently took my hand. "This is nothing we need to speak of now." We headed back to the three young men waiting for us. "We'll set sail immediately. 'Tis the last you shall have to see of this accursed place."

3

With only five men to row, Lexander had to take an oar while I leaned into the tiller to steer the longship. The last time I had manned the tiller, we were fleeing from Birgir after he had killed the old chieftain and seized Silveta's estate.

The cliffs behind us were lit up by the burning of the palisade. Lexander was determined that nothing remain of his estate, so he had set fire to the fence and hastily built sentry tower. The flames formed a line along the top of the cliffs, and even the steps down to the beach were burning. There would be nothing left of Vidaris but ashes when the winged ship arrived.

Soon enough the lurid blaze disappeared into the fog. The water was a darker version of the gray sky, with the lowering clouds touching the sea around us.

The wind had died with nightfall, forcing the oarsmen to row incessantly. The two brothers were useless, though they tried to take an oar. They kept tangling with the others and Lexander impatiently told them to desist. Niels huddled near me, too frail to even try to help.

I couldn't touch the water, so I used the feel of the currents pushing against the rudder to reach out to the sea spirits. In their slow, watery way, they responded to my plea for help in reaching Tillfallvik. In exchange, they wanted to know what had happened in Vidaris.

But I could not satisfy them. I was a mass of confusion. I had never seen Lexander so fierce, so heartless. I could not forget the sight of him slashing the sword across Helanas' slender, elegant neck, yet I could not face it either. The sea spirits disliked my uncertainty and withdrew from my touch.

I slumped over the tiller, appreciating the warmth of Niels against my legs.

We finally reached Tillfallvik as the sun began to rise, casting a feeble light through the intermittent drizzle. Lexander's forehead was creased thoughtfully, though he seemed not at all tired. The oarsmen were fatigued to the breaking point, and had been taking breaks in pairs, flinging themselves down on a bench and gasping for breath.

I helped Niels and the brothers onto the dock while Lexander spoke to the oarsmen, cautioning them not to mention Vidaris. He donned a fur cap to disguise his smooth head, to keep others from recognizing him as the notorious slave master.

Niels held my hand tightly. He had never seen the hilly town of Tillfallvik and he must have thought it was a crude place compared to his beloved city in Viinland.

I bent to pick up a broken bit of arrow lying on the dock—the chipped stone was bound to a broken-off shaft. It was a remnant of the fierce fighting that had taken place only a few days ago. I clutched it as a talisman of my beloved Thule. Before we had left Vidaris, I had buried the figurine of Baldr from the *hneftaf* game at the base of the cliff, covering it with rocks. I would have liked to keep it to remind me of pleasant evenings with Lexander, but my sacrifice would help heal the land.

When we reached the end of the dock, we were accosted by a few women bundled in knitted shawls. They cried and pleaded on their knees, holding up their hands in supplication for any coins we could spare. Bedraggled children crouched alongside them, reaching out their tiny hands.

"What's this?" I exclaimed in surprise. I had never seen beggars in Tillfallvik before. "Does Silveta know you are in need?"

"That she-devil!" A woman with gray stringy hair and a dirt-caked face spat onto the docks. "Silveta threw us into the streets. Birgir Barfoot was slain by her paramour and now we have no homes, no food, nothing!"

I took a step backward. "You are mistaken," I breathed. "Birgir was destroying our land—"

"He was our savior! Without him we are doomed," the old woman wailed.

Lexander appeared by my side, his hand going to the heavy sword on his belt. The huddled women backed away, their cries growing louder. "Come, Marja," he told me. "We must be out of here."

These women didn't know that we were responsible for Birgir's downfall. If they knew, they would probably descend on us, scratching with their ragged fingernails and screeching like crows. I hurried away, pulling Niels and the brothers along.

"All they knew was the everlasting fighting in Danelaw until Birgir brought them here," Lexander explained. "Markland must have seemed like a paradise until he was slain."

Tillfallvik was not the same town as I remembered, when the streets had been crowded by working men and every woman carried a full basket on her hip. Donkeys, goats, and chickens had thronged in the open yards, while pigs rooted in the mud near each house. But those animals had been seized by Birgir's men to feed his warriors, and the gardens had been picked down to stubs.

There were some signs of renewed life. We made our way through the marketplace, where a dozen carts and makeshift stands sold produce, bread, and ale mainly to the mercenaries who had arrived with Jens to help vanquish Birgir. The first time I had come to Tillfallvik, the merry noise and smells of the market had overwhelmed me. Now the loudest voices were those of the castoff remnants of Birgir's rule: women and children clustered near the stalls begging for food.

As we climbed up to the estate, some mercenaries were busy removing the boards from the windows and doors of houses, taking possession. Too many of the men in Tillfallvik had died fighting Birgir before Silveta and I could return with our Skraeling warband. Silveta had asked two score of Jens' mercenaries to remain as her own bondsmen, and likely she was gifting these houses to them to seal their bond.

When we arrived at the estate, repairs were well underway. The main gates were standing once again, constructed of fresh yellow pine and smelling of sticky sap. There were two crossbars in place where once there had been one.

After what I had seen on the docks, I feared opposition would rise against Silveta's rule. My slave-mates also looked concerned—this war-torn place was not what they had expected.

The estate was like a barracks with many men wearing leather armor, their helms ready to be donned at a moment's notice. They spoke in booming voices and made rude comments to one another, jesting as only fighting men could do after a successful battle. Most were idling about in clumps, but some were reinforcing the scaffolding that had been used so effectively by Birgir's men in repelling our attack.

The stench and death cries from the battle still hung in the air. I shied away from the dark stains where blood had spilled. The demon that had infested Birgir had dissipated, leaving behind a raw wound in the land. The *inua* of the slain warriors had already gone to the Otherworld, but the violence had torn the fabric of life. Little wonder the cheerful *olfs* avoided the estate. I wanted to flee as well, leaving place to heal in peace.

We went straight to the fire hall, which sat on the crest of the hill. It bristled with the horned skulls of bulls that Ejegod's family had sacrificed to the gods throughout generations of their rule. The latest addition was nailed directly to one of the huge doors—Silveta's sacrifice to celebrate our victory over Birgir. Shredded pieces of pink flesh still clung to it, and flies buzzed around eagerly.

Inside the fire hall, several women were embroidering banners with Silveta's new signet, the bull quartered with a seabird to honor Jens. Others were sewing the dress Silveta would wear at their wedding.

Aside from the empty rafters, stained black with smoke and age, the hall had looked much the same under Silveta's first husband, Chieftain Ejegod. The women were cleaning the trestle tables after the morning meal, and a trace of tinkling laughter could be heard through the kitchen doors under the solar. The servants were pleased by the return of their *freya*. Life under Birgir had been brutal, and many of the servants had escaped the estate. There were a few women who went about with their heads bowed, unable to meet anyone's eyes, traumatized by what they had seen and been forced to do.

Silveta was seated on the chieftain's chair made of walrus tusks, cushioned with snow lynx fur. Jens had not disputed her right to it. Silveta's betrothed would likely become chieftain, as befitted the conquering hero, but his wife would run the estate bequeathed to her in her marriage contract with Ejegod. She had fought hard for that right and would not likely give it up to anyone, not even to her beloved Jens.

The candles on the high table lit Silveta's yellow hair, braided into a crown around her head. She had woven the strands with pink and lavender crystals. Her immaculate dress was embroidered with tiny violets on the neckline and wide sleeves. She was the embodiment of the goddess Freya herself. But Silveta always looked regal, even when she had been crouched in an open *knaar* crossing the ocean.

When Silveta saw us approach the dais, she put down her *stilo*. "Well, was it a success?"

"Vidaris is no more," Lexander answered.

"And your consort?" Silveta asked delicately.

"She is no longer a concern." He reminded her, "I must leave it to you to ensure that no other pleasure house is established here."

Silveta nodded, glancing at me. She had despised my subservience from the moment we met, but she had still used me to serve her own purpose. "I would hate to ever see another pleasure house in any of the western maritime lands. Jens will have to convince the overlord, but I'll make it a key point when I send my trade delegation to Kebec."

"I must speak to Jens, then," Lexander decided. "I'll be leaving immediately. There are other houses I must tend to in the Auldland before word spreads of what I've done. But be forewarned, the ship from Stanbulin will arrive within another moon. They will track down the servants, and someone is bound to report that I came here. You must never admit to seeing me this summer."

"So you cannot stay," she agreed thoughtfully. "But surely you will be able to return soon?"

"Next summer." Lexander touched my cheek. "I can stay away from Marja no longer than that."

I raised my brows. "But I'm going with you."

"No, it's far too dangerous," Lexander said with a sad smile. "I will be able to move faster and more safely without you. And I'll not risk having you near other masters."

"Definitely not, Marja," Silveta agreed, more vehemently than Lexander. "I can tell how much you hate what just happened in Vidaris. Stay here with me. I need you to deal with the Thule as they settle the northern coast. You're the only one who can translate for me."

Lexander nodded, pleased by Silveta's support. I inclined my head rather than argue with them; the most important thing now was to help the Vidaris slaves. Niels was sniffling and trying to hide behind me. The two brothers were leaning against each other to keep from falling down.

I gestured to them. "Can you help my former slave-mates, Silveta? They're from Viinland."

"The mercenaries are heading south today. These three can go along, if they wish," Silveta offered. "Jens just took the lot of them down to the docks."

"Many thanks, Silveta," Lexander said quietly. "That will fulfill my last obligation to them."

But I had one more concern. "Why do those women beg at the waterfront, Silveta? Surely there is enough for all."

Her mouth pursed in annoyance. "I couldn't very well let them stay in the estate, Marja. They're Birgir's people, and they saw their men die yesterday. Jens says they're a risk to both of us."

I remembered the tearstained faces of the children. "They're not to blame for Birgir's deeds."

"They were eager enough to take the homes of our bondsmen who were slain by that butcher," Silveta retorted. "We have no room for them here, nor have I any desire to succor such folk in my bosom. I've given them the land where they first settled on their arrival, across the bay. Jens has ordered some of his men to build longhouses for them."

"But . . . 'twill be a terribly cold, wind-blown place in the winter. I can't imagine children living there."

Silveta waved off my sympathy. "Any mercenary who swears as my bondsman can take a wife from among them, if that's his wish. As to the others, they are not my people and never have been. My responsibility is to my own, Marja."

Silveta exchanged an exasperated glance with Lexander. They thought I was unreasonable for being concerned about everyone who crossed my path. But how could I ignore the misery before my eyes?

We hurried back down to the waterfront to see Jens. It was much busier than when we had first arrived, with the mercenaries now thronging the wooden docks. It was a fearsome sight, and I was glad they were merely preparing to return to their homes rather than readying for another fight.

Jens was easy to find because of his banner carried on a tall pole by a bearer. Usually a grinning *olf* sat on the bobbing crossbar, but today there were none to be seen. The crimson banner was quartered by the crest of his father, the Overlord of Viinland, while the upper half held his personal signet. The white seabird was a fitting symbol for the boy who had grown up on a rocky isle in the midst of Straumsey Bay.

Jens was a young man still, for all that he had accomplished. He looked quite boyish without his helm, his auburn hair flying freely about. His eager, sun-kissed face was beardless and showed the enthusiasm of youth, yet the mercenaries treated him with the utmost respect, as a victorious leader deserved.

When Jens saw us approach, he broke away from the cluster of mercenaries who were receiving their pay. "I saw your longship and knew you had returned." His voice lowered. "How did you fare?"

Lexander answered, "The estate is no more, but another pleasure house will be built unless you can convince the overlord to forbid it."

"Ah, I will make sure of that." He glanced at me. "I always felt sorry for the pleasure slaves who were brought to the bastion to tempt my father."

"Jedvard never invited Vidaris to entertain in his house," Lexander reminded him. "So likely you'll find him receptive."

The brothers from Hop were much more awake now, excited by the hubbub of mercenaries preparing to depart. But Niels was panic-stricken, darting glances from side to side as if fearing he would be trampled at any moment.

"These young men are former slaves of mine," Lexander explained. "They need to go back to their families in Hop. Would they travel safely in the company of your mercenaries?"

"I have a good man I can entrust them to," Jens said. "The boys will not be harmed under his charge."

Jens began searching for the men he had in mind, seemingly not realizing that he was the same age as "the boys."

I asked them, "Are you sure you want to return to Hop?"

"Yes," the brothers said as one.

But Niels' face crumpled. "What's wrong?" I urged. "Tell me, Niels."

"My father will beat me for failing. I know it." His hands twisted in the hem of his short tunic.

"Then you'll stay here," Lexander declared, as if the matter was settled. He ushered the brothers after Jens without glancing back at Niels. They quickly disappeared into the sea of mercenaries.

I thought it was done too hastily. Niels, not Lexander, should have decided his own fate. Niels took hold of my hand in a tight grip. "What am I to do, Marja?"

It was too late now. I would have to make sure Niels would be cared for properly. "Come, Niels. I have an idea."

We climbed back up the steep streets of Tillfallvik, trying to avoid the mud churned by the mercenaries' boots. I was pleased to smell baking and hear the voices of children playing again. The *olfs* were much more plentiful in town than down on the waterfront among the mercenaries or on the estate, where the fiercest fighting had taken place.

Niels silently followed without questioning my intent. He would do whatever I told him without a thought for himself. He had always been overly dependent.

I went straight to the fire hall, where Silveta had not moved from her post. She was writing furiously, and a pile of papers covered the table before her. "I'm recalling all the magnates to Tillfallvik. Not only is there the wedding, but we need to settle this matter of chieftain. Has Jens sent off the mercenaries yet?"

"Soon," I assured her. "He's finishing his payments to them now."

She frowned slightly at the thought of the expense, but quickly shook that off. "It is well worth it. We have an abundant land."

"There's something I must ask of you." I drew Niels forward. "This is Niels. He needs a place where he can be useful and protected. He could serve you well, Silveta, since he writes with a fine hand and can read for you."

Her raised brow of skepticism changed to interest. "He can write? I didn't realize Lexander taught his slaves the finer arts of knowledge."

"Niels learned before coming to Vidaris," I explained. "He assisted Lexander from time to time as a scribe."

Silveta glanced at the pile of parchment. "I do need someone to copy this letter for me, and to write what I dictate." She looked down at Niels. "Can you do that for me?"

"Oh yes, *freya!*" Niels' eyes were shining at the thought of serving such a fine lady. "I will please you, I swear."

Silveta smiled at his eagerness. "Then go to the kitchens and tell them you're to be given some proper clothes. I can't have you working in that," she said with a laugh, pointing at his brief tunic.

For a moment I worried about the brothers from Hop. But surely Lexander would not send them home wearing only their short tunics and blankets around their shoulders. I nodded to Niels, who waited eagerly for my permission to go. "You serve Silveta now, Niels. But remember, you're not her slave."

"Certainly not!" Silveta agreed with a slight shudder. "I've a mind to free all the slaves in Markland."

Niels ran off to the kitchens, the first spark of joy in his face that I had seen in a very long time. "Thank you, Silveta. You'll be the saving of him, for he will always be a child at heart."

"I'll make sure he's cared for," Silveta agreed seriously. "But, Marja, why do you ask for nothing for yourself?"

I took a deep breath. "I have one request."

"Name it, and you shall have it."

I met her eyes firmly. "I can't stay here while there are other slaves who need my help. Look at Niels! He would have been lost without me."

"But the Thule—"

"You'll have to find someone else to translate for you," I interrupted. "Send for one of my siblings in Jarnby, if you like."

Silveta was not accustomed to being rebuffed. "I only want you to be safe, Marja. You've come to mean so much to me."

"I've helped you in every way I can," I reminded her. "Our land is safe because of it. But now it's time for me to leave."

Silveta toyed with the *stilo,* tapping it on the table. At last, she had to agree. "If that is what you wish, Marja."

4

I was not the only one who requested a boon of Silveta that day. Lexander returned from the waterfront and formally petitioned the use of one of the ocean-going *knaars* that had brought Birgir and his people to Markland. In exchange for his passage to Danelaw, Lexander agreed to broker a trade of Silveta's surplus goods for luxury items that could be obtained only in the Auldland.

Silveta discussed the arrangements with Lexander for some time while I watched Niels happily run errands for her and commence the copying of the letters to the magnates. On his way out, Lexander caressed my cheek, his fingers so gentle and loving that I closed my eyes in contentment. He was too reserved to often be affectionate, and rarely before others. His simple touch was a sign of his much deeper feelings.

"I'll come with you to help make the arrangements," I offered.

But Lexander wouldn't let me rise. "It's dirty, heavy work, loading a ship—not meant for you."

He strode off, determined keep me away. I had resolved to go, but little could be gained from pressing my point now.

So I watched Lexander's progress from the hilltop in front of the estate. Lexander rowed among the *knaars* of Birgir's fleet and selected

the sturdiest craft. With help from the oarsmen from Vidaris, they unfurled the yellow-striped sail to make sure it was sound. Then they
rowed the heavy ship into the deepest dock to load it with supplies
and trade goods.

The *olfs* were merry at the renewed bustle. With the mercenaries departed, they were free to indulge in their antics on the docks,
though they continued to shy away from Lexander as if shunning a
dark void.

I held on to the Thule arrowhead until I knew its curves and sharp
edges like my own hand. At sunset, when day and night were about to
touch, I returned to the estate. I went to the meadow Silveta and I had
run on the night we escaped from Birgir. The old fence on that side
had been torn down and replaced by the much taller palisade.

I knelt down and dug a deep hole near where we had gone over
the fence. I opened myself to the land as the wet dirt shifted through
my fingers. There were still sickening reverberations left behind by
Birgir's demon.

I took the tip of the Thule arrowhead and pressed it into the soft
flesh of my arm, just below the crease of my elbow. Taking a deep
breath, I thought of those who had given their last drop of blood
to preserve this land, both Thule and Noromenn. The gods had not
demanded my blood, so in return, I freely gave what was not spilled
in battle.

The sharp tip bit into my skin. Blood welled up, and I smeared it
onto the arrowhead. Then I buried it there in the soft soil.

Now a tiny piece of my spirit would always remain, even after I
had left. It was a fitting sacrifice for a new beginning.

I cleaned the mud caked beneath my fingernails and attended the
evening meal at the high table, wearing the crimson dress Silveta had
given me. Lexander never appeared. He was busy on the docks, bar-
gaining for oarsmen to accompany him to the Auldland. He would
have to pay a premium because of the shortage of men in town. But
magnates were beginning to arrive from around Markland, having

heard of Birgir's demise, so there were enough willing men for the journey.

During the meal, Niels grinned shyly and accepted some light-hearted ribbing from members of the noble entourage. With Silveta's approbation, her bondsmen and servants were beginning to accept young Niels. In truth, he was so eager to please everyone that they could hardly resent his presence.

That night, I retired alone to Silveta's old sleeping closet. The dark wooden walls and ceiling reminded me of Birgir; it was here that he had raped and beaten me. It was here that I could have killed Birgir, if I had been more ruthless, forestalling the horror of the recent battle.

The bed and table were the same, but Silveta's embossed chests and caskets were gone, likely moved to the solar she now shared with Jens. But the familiar fur blanket beckoned me, and I crawled in grate-fully as I had done the first night I had slept here at Silveta's behest.

Lexander returned very late, having made preparations to depart at sunrise. He did not tell me, but I knew the *knaar* was ready to go with all the oarsmen sleeping onboard to guard the cargo. Lexander had com-pleted everything with excessive haste, for reasons of his own.

The *olfs* drifted away when Lexander appeared, setting the candle in the wall. Seeing that I was awake, he pulled back the fur, revealing me naked and waiting for him. His eyes devoured me.

I had to tell him. "I'm going to the Auldland with you, Lexander."

"Let's not speak of that, Marja. Not now."

His lips met mine, softly at first, then urgently, as if he could never get enough. Flesh pressed against flesh, heating and moistening as we kissed. I caressed his smooth skin, pulling him down to lie against me. He was no longer my master, but I could let my submissive desires run free when we joined together. I could surrender to him completely, knowing that he would never hurt me.

I opened my mind and my emotions to him, as I did with the *olfs*. I hid nothing, exposing every part of my being. We merged together as he sank into me, to that very core of me that was always accepting, embracing whatever was desired.

He could see that I longed to please him, even if it meant disavowing my own wishes. And that satisfied him. For he was distraught at the thought of leaving me. I could feel it now, despite his outward certainty that I should stay behind. He longed to be with me, but he had yielded to a deep-seated fear that I couldn't penetrate.

We rocked together, rising to the highest pitch, losing ourselves in each other. I didn't know where I ended and he began as our passion weaved us together. We cried out, our voices mingling as one.

I forgot all else, sleeping in his arms. Lexander woke me by brushing the strands of hair from my face. The candle had burned out, leaving us in darkness. But as always, I felt the coming dawn.

There was the whisper softness of silk around my wrist, and then it tightened. "What?" I murmured, pulling against it.

"Hush," he whispered. "I must claim you as my own."

With a quick turn, he secured my wrist to the post at the head of the bed. My arm was outstretched, and tugging showed me that I was held fast. He quickly tied my other wrist to the other post.

He had never bound me in this way, and it sent a thrill through me. I was exposed, displayed for his delight. He caressed me with his hands, then kissed my face. Languidly, he moved lower, molding his full lips against every part of me. My neck, shoulders, breasts, and ribs, then lower to my belly and hips, down each leg to the tender flesh behind my knees. I lost myself in his lips.

Since I could not touch him, I could only feel what he did to me. I became pure sensation.

He spread my legs wide and kissed me there, where he entered me, licking slowly and surely, driving me to madness. I writhed and jerked against my bonds, but they held tight. I was forced to receive, only accept, and I surrendered to him again and again.

Lexander finally took his own satisfaction when I was limp and long past awareness of myself. He claimed me for himself, driving into me deeper and deeper.

When he was done, my body was thrumming. My mind was far away, gone astray in bliss.

He kissed my lips, and I responded with every fiber of my being. I had never felt such fulfillment, such abandon.

He tossed the fur over me, and the blessed warmth made me drowse. The clink of the lock on the door was a distant annoyance, to be ignored in my suffusion.

The clink of the lock . . .

I fought my languid contentment. A tug on my wrists showed me that I was still tied. And Lexander was gone.

Lexander had left without untying me. He would sail away in the *knaar* for the Auldland, leaving me here with Silveta.

"No! Lexander," I cried out.

He would give the key to Silveta with instructions to release me once he was safely gone. Would she come sooner, remembering her promise to me? Could she, when Lexander requested otherwise? During our long search for a warband, Silveta had served Lexander, relying on him and doing as he said. It was natural for Lexander to call out obedience in others. He always would have that power.

Silveta would obey him. I hated her for it, though I could not blame her.

I tugged at the bindings on my wrists, gasping as they refused to give. So soft, yet so strong. I strained against them, willing them to part. But Lexander knew his craft, and I was held fast.

Olfs appeared, responding to my need. Their soft glow lit the snug closet as they spun around the ceiling and bounced along the floor.

"Please," I pleaded with them. "Release me."

The *olfs* came closer, curious. They little understood physical constraints. Nothing could hold them, and they were puzzled by my struggle.

"The cloth is tied to the posts," I explained, shaking my wrist in emphasis. "Undo the knots, I beg of you."

Most of the *olfs* were useless, uncomprehending or taking mischievous pleasure in my thrashing. They liked to tease people, but I had no patience for their games now. I had nothing to bribe them with, no ripe fruit or shiny coin.

A tiny *olf* floated by my head. It had twiglike limbs and a comically distended belly. I focused on its sad, knowing eyes.

"Help me, little one, as only you can," I begged. "I helped rid your land of Birgir. Please help me now."

The tiny *olf* jogged up and down in indecision, then bounced over to one post. It cocked its head on its frail neck, looking at the knots.

"Yes, untie it," I urged. "The loose end must be threaded through from where it came."

Its delicate fingers plucked at the cloth. I poured good thoughts into the *olf,* encouraging it, adoring it, and promising to give it whatever it desired.

The knots parted and my wrist was finally free. "Bless you!" I said as I wrestled with the other binding. The little *olf* did somersaults in delight.

I ignored the crimson gown and snatched up my Thule parka and pants. They were made of caribou fur, waterproof yet soft against my skin. They would keep me warmer during the ocean crossing than any cloak. My boots were also fur-lined, repelling both water and ice.

There was no one in sight as I ran from the longhouse. The estate was sleeping in the twilight of the morning, darkened by clouds overhead. I rushed along the familiar paths to the gate.

I was gasping when I reached the bondsmen on guard. "Has a tall man left the estate?"

The bondsmen gaped at my Thule pants, but were even more surprised when they recognized me. "*Freya* Marja! Is something amiss? Nobody's left since we changed at daybreak."

Lexander could have left through the rear gate, but I knew he was still with Silveta, saying his farewells and giving her instructions to release me when he was gone.

My fingers tightened on the bondsman's arm. "Listen to me well. Let me through the gate, and do not speak of my departure to anyone, even if asked. Do you understand?"

The tone of command was foreign to me, but I had learned at Silveta's knee. The bondsman straightened to attention, snapping out,

"Yes, *freya*! It will be done." His eye strayed to his fellow sentry, as if to impress my order upon him.

They pushed the gate wide enough to let me through. They were intrigued, perhaps wondering what I was going to do next. I suppose anything could be expected of a girl who could summon a Skraeling warband.

A light sprinkle of rain began to fall. I ran through the streamers of fog toward the waterfront.

On the docks, I picked out the *knaar* with the yellow-striped sails. The oarsmen were still groaning and splashing the sleep from their eyes with buckets of water. Lexander had not yet arrived.

I climbed into the *knaar* and stood in the stern, with the *olfs* bounding around me. One of the older men called out, "Get off, girl! We're about to cast away."

"I'm going with you." I put my hands on my hips.

An oarsman who knew me from Vidaris quickly intervened. "Leave off, man. She belongs to the master."

Since that was enough to keep them from tossing me off the *knaar*, I didn't bother to correct him.

"We weren't told a woman was coming," the older man protested to the Vidaris freeman.

When Lexander arrived, surprise widened his eyes. He started to speak, then seemed to think better of it. He climbed into the large ship and the oarsmen pulled back and busied themselves at the sight of his frown.

"You've betrayed me, Lexander." My voice was low, but I didn't try to hide my anguish. "How could you?"

Lexander gestured down to the dock. "Get off this ship, Marja. You're staying here."

I repeated more slowly, "How could you?"

"I knew you weren't listening to me. I wish I could take you along, but it's not possible."

"Then I am your slave. And you're a slave master still."

He couldn't meet my eyes. "I won't have you at risk, Marja. Will you make me put you off myself?"

For a moment I thought he would pick me up and drop me over the side, just as easily as he had tied me up and walked out. "I'm going to help the other slaves, Lexander, even if I have to do it alone. I'll find another ship to take me to Danelaw without you."

"Marja!" he cried in frustration. "You can't."

"I'm going to the Auldland. There are other boys like Niels out there who are suffering and need me."

"How can you be so obstinate?" His eyes bore into me. "Would you kill my love for you?"

I drew in my breath. "You would threaten me with *that*?"

He paced back to the stern, shaking his head. He was distraught, but his words hurt just the same. How could he deny me so? We had never fought before. The clouds drifted just out of reach overhead, adding to the foreboding in the air.

After a few tense moments, I went close to him, lowering my voice. "You cannot stop me, and in good conscience you shouldn't try. We are here in Tillfallvik because I fulfilled my pledge to rid my homeland of Birgir. Have no doubt, Lexander; I will do as I say."

He sank his face into his hands. "Enough! Can I say nothing to prevent you from making this terrible mistake?"

"I made no mistake this day, except in trusting you." I turned away, pained by the very thought of it.

"Marja!" someone cried from the docks. "Marja!"

It was Silveta, running down the wooden palings. She clutched a bag to her chest.

I leaned over the rail. "Silveta, what are you doing here?"

She glanced at Lexander. "I had to make sure that you were all right. And what did I find but that you were gone!"

"I'm sorry I can't stay, Silveta. Please tell Niels farewell for me. I'll return as soon as I can."

She knew it was no use to protest. "You must take this, Marja. It's your dress and a cloak, and a few other things you'll need once you reach the Auldland. Take it, with my best wishes for your safety and happiness."

I was touched. "Silveta . . . how kind of you."

She lifted the bag to me. It felt heavy, stuffed full of good things as only Silveta could give. "Take care of yourself. You, too, Lexander."

Lexander curtly bid Silveta farewell; then he jumped across the benches to yell orders for the crew to depart. I exchanged a look with Silveta and we both smiled sadly. The last time we had set across the ocean, Silveta had been with us.

"Take care of Birgir's people, Silveta," I urged. "Give them a chance as you gave me."

Startled, she couldn't deny me. "If you think so, Marja."

"You won't regret it," I assured her.

I grasped her hand, our fingers tightening on one another. For once Silveta was straining to reach out to me.

"Come home soon," she said. Tears stood in her eyes.

As the mooring rope was tossed to the dock and the oarsmen took their seats, I reluctantly let go of her hand. Silveta waved her veil over her head for as long as I could see her. I didn't stop looking back until she was swallowed by the clouds.

5

Rain began to fall in earnest as we sailed from Tillfallvik Bay. The small islands that dotted the channel were ghostly sentinels draped in fog, emerging and disappearing as we passed by. The black and white seabirds were barking as they woke from their night's rest, but their water diving was concealed by the mist. I briefly closed my eyes and asked for Alanerk, sea god of the tides, to speed us on our way.

We sailed into a gray formless wall where water and sky merged together. Circles appeared on the waves as fat raindrops fell. In my Thule furs, I was warm and dry, but the oarsmen grumbled sourly at the dismal start to our journey.

The *olfs* who had lingered onboard disappeared one by one. I hoped desperately that at least one would accompany us to Danelaw. But they silently wafted away, and I knew it was because of Lexander. The *olfs* avoided him now, as they had avoided Helanas. Her deeds had echoed through the *inua* of the world, drawing evil to lap at her feet.

After the brutal ease with which Lexander had killed her . . . I couldn't blame the *olfs* for disappearing. I rubbed my wrists where my skin had chafed while trying to get free from Lexander's bonds.

As the rain fell and the waves grew higher, I resisted sinking into the sea spirits, though the rocking of the ship was hypnotic. The spirits were whispering to me, asking me to recount the battle of Tillfallvik and Lexander's revenge in Vidaris. But I couldn't stand to relive the horror, nor could I bear to think about Lexander. I had to refuse them.

My unease grew as Lexander avoided me. He returned only to set down a jug of mead and a loaf of bread stuffed with raisins and nuts. I said, "Please, we must try to—"

He merely turned and stepped over the benches to reach the prow, where he could watch the flow of the waves. An oarsman manned the tiller near me, but he huddled in his cloak and said not a word to me.

When the gloomy day began to turn to night, I crawled under the canvas protecting the trade goods and supplies. I rolled myself in the warm cloak Silveta had thoughtfully provided, and tried to sleep on the stacked blocks of beeswax. Yet whenever I dozed off, the dead tormented me—Birgir came out of the darkness to claw at me, gaunt and desperate, while Helanas screamed in anguish, her face too close to mine.

I kept waking suddenly as if I was falling. Eventually I gave up the effort of trying to sleep, and I swayed with the moving ship, wondering what the morrow would bring.

The rain turned into a gale that whipped the waves higher. By day's end, we were in a raging storm. The seasons were turning, and the tang of autumn was in the air.

The oarsmen were forced to lash the sail down to keep it from ripping into shreds. Their oars were useless, and they huddled under the canvas to avoid the icy waves that washed over the hull. They bailed continuously to keep us from swamping. Lexander endured the numbing cold at the tiller, guiding our foundering ship to keep us afloat.

When the oarsmen's prayers grew shrill, pleading with the Norogods for their lives, I knew our situation was grim. I finally sank into the sea spirits to beg them to take our ship away from the storm. But they slipped through my fingers and drifted away. I had refused to share my stories with them for too long, and they were unwilling to listen now, much less lend us their aid. I had been unwise to deny them.

Emerging from under the canvas, the wind whipped my face as I hung on to the ropes that lashed the goods to the deck. The dark clouds churned overhead. I had grown up on the fens watching the movements of the sky, and had learned how to rise above the ground to flow with the clouds, seeing everything passing below. But that couldn't happen in this lurching ship with the water rushing over the sides and salt stinging my eyes.

I saw no familiar patterns in the shifting clouds. This was no ordinary storm—an unseen hand was stirring the heavens. The flashing bolts came down all around us, staying with us as we were driven forward.

I doubted any of the oarsmen—or myself for that matter—interested the gods enough for them to put forth this effort. It had to be Lexander. The sea itself was rising up to stop him from reaching the Auldland.

Despite the howling wind and water washing over the sides, I climbed across the benches, clinging to the rope strung to the stern.

"Marja, get back!" Lexander cried when he saw me coming. "You'll be washed overboard—"

In a few moments, I reached him. Lexander was wedged into the stern with a rope tied to his waist. His arm closed tightly around me, holding me against the surges of seawater that washed by. The shock of his touch was stronger than the icy water that hit my face.

"If only you had stayed behind!" he cried, as the heavy *knaar* landed against a wave with a boom.

We both ducked down to avoid the spray. "There's something strange about this storm," I told him. "It's not right. Could your people be trying to stop you?"

"Impossible." Lexander strained to search through the driving rain to see what lay ahead, leaning on the tiller. "Only the most power-ful among us could cause a storm such as this, and they care nothing about me."

"But, Lexander, *you* could be causing it."

"I'm not . . . you can't think that I—" He broke off, his arm loos-ening from around me. "You don't know what you're saying!"

Water swelled over the side, rushing by and shifting me off my feet. I was nearly washed away with the water. Lexander's fingers dug into me, holding on. He dragged me back into his tight embrace, clutching me like a drowning man.

My face pressed against his chest as I hung on to him. His heart was beating fast and there was a catch in his breath. I was sheltered against him, and it suddenly felt as if the storm was far away.

"I'm sorry," he murmured into my hair. "Sorry for everything I've done to you. I never should have taken you from your family."

"Lexander!" I exclaimed, looking up at him. "You regret that?"

"You belong on the fens. Not here."

Despite the wind whipping away our words, my voice was low but clear. "You saved me, Lexander. You set me free. Now let me live."

His troubled brow showed his unease. "I fear I'll be the cause of your death."

I reached up to touch his face, straining to kiss him. Then his lips were on mine, making me flush hot. I could forgive his arrogance and overbearing ways when he opened himself to me like this. Through our touch, I felt his emotions roiling beneath his iron-clad control, going far deeper than his conflict with me. His vengeance ran too strong; his pain was too sharp.

"You're fighting yourself," I whispered.

His clasp tightened convulsively. "You know me too well."

"Because I love you," I murmured into his chest. I felt more than heard him say the same.

Finally he released me. As I pulled back, I realized the sound of the wind had lessened. The booming thunder was receding. Now our boat was riding the waves instead of pounding against them.

Lexander and I stayed together in the stern, holding on to each other. The danger had passed once Lexander had accepted the truth about himself.

When the rain finally eased and a break in the clouds was spied on the east, the oarsmen came out from the hold and cried out their gratitude to their gods. But I knew the cause, and our salvation, lay much closer.

We sailed on through intermittent squalls and downpours that punctuated the dreary days. At times the waves rose higher than our mast. Lexander didn't sleep except in the rare calms, staying close to the tiller to guide us through. Though we had smoothed over our conflict, I could not forget what he had done to me. I couldn't take pleasure in him, and he maintained the same careful reserve toward me.

The sight of land was welcomed by everyone onboard. As we passed by the sparsely wooded shoreline shrouded in mist, I was reminded of my homeland. Much of the coast was wild between the broad swaths of pasturage and fields. Though the air was moist and chill, it was no longer the bone-shattering cold of the ocean.

We stayed overnight in the mouth of a wide estuary. There were a good number of longships anchored in the calm of the river, just out of reach of the encroaching waves. All of the double-prow Noroships put me in mind of Tillfallvik.

Once we set sail again, going upriver, the salt water rode the tidal bore far inland. Busy yards and structures lined the riverbanks. People kept pointing to our *knaar*. Some waved in frantic welcome, as if we were returning kinsmen. Others fled at the sight of our square sail and the serpent rising from the bow.

An imposing fortress of stone marked the principle town of Londinium. From far downriver the round-topped turrets at each corner could be seen. The ground around it was scarred, and there was a rawness to the red and white stones, as if they had been freshly laid. The fortress was attached to an ancient gray wall, nearly as tall, with a round, crumbling top. Within the wall was a mass of pointed roofs with seemingly no room to walk between them. Londinium dwarfed every town I had seen in Viinland.

Then directly ahead appeared an incredible structure—a wooden building spanned the mighty river from one bank to the other. It was a bridge, built on as large a scale as the fortress and town wall. It was supported by thick posts that disappeared into the swirling brown water. People and horse-drawn carts crossed it, ignoring the churning water rushing below.

Our mast was too tall to go underneath, so the oarsmen struck the sail and rowed us to a wharf that jutted far into the river. Of the other large ships docked there, few were Noroships like ours. Most had two masts, with big-bellied hulls pierced by small round windows. A few were sleek with triangular sails, exactly like the winged ship that had come from Stanbulin to take away my slave-mates. I swallowed my apprehension, unwilling to let Lexander know how the sight of them unnerved me.

A commotion was raised as we pulled in. On the dock, several men waved their arms as if to ward us off, while at least two dozen more arrived on the run brandishing broadswords and round shields. Lexander ordered the oarsmen to hold as he called out to them.

The warriors were concerned that we might be loyal to a northern Noroking called Swegn. Lexander assured them we were from Viinland, which had no allegiances in the Auldland. Eventually we were allowed to berth. But we were treated suspiciously, the warriors remaining on guard along the wharf.

As we docked, Lexander turned to me. "I must deal with these men. I will do better if I know you are safe here. Will you stay in the *knaar,* Marja?"

"Yes, I'll stay."

Lexander's expression softened in a smile. I longed to set foot on land, but it gave me a secret thrill to be able to please him.

Lexander jumped onto the wide wharf, and I settled down to wait with much more equanimity than the oarsmen. The warriors kept them from disembarking, and they muttered amongst themselves at this inauspicious greeting.

I was reassured by the number of *olfs* flitting from place to place. There were a remarkable range of sizes and shapes, from *olfs* so fat and squat that they looked like bubbles with hands and feet, to tiny sprites that were no bigger than my little finger. The sprites buzzed together in clouds, descending on whatever intrigued them. Soon I was laughing out loud at their antics, grateful to return safely to land.

After more discussions among the officials, several of the warriors returned with Lexander and they poked underneath the canvas, examining the blocks of translucent wax. I stayed out of the way and didn't say a word. Before they returned to the wharf again, Lexander gave orders for half the oarsmen to go ashore for the evening. The other half were to stay onboard and protect the goods. It had been a weary journey, and they all longed for some good ale and women. Those left behind would get the next day off, but they grumbled so loudly that I wouldn't have been heard if I had rebelled. Among those remaining behind were several of the Vidaris freemen. Lexander had ordered them to protect me with their lives.

I leaned on the side of the ship, watching everything on the waterfront. The tall bridge cut off most of my view upriver, but the town lay before me. The surrounding wall of gray rock, smoothed with age, stood higher than most of the wooden structures within.

The construction yard in front of the fortress was busy with movement as the tower was completed. The fortress was a massive square block with a few narrow windows here and there in the formidable facade. The top was lined with square battlements where men could crouch and take aim at any warband that tried to invade the town.

The ground was very flat, so I could see only the road along the river and the roofs and chimneys of buildings beyond. There were workshops of every description lining the riverfront, mostly one story but some with two. Women poked their heads out from the upper floors, shaking out cloths or dumping basins directly into the street.

The pot-bellied ship beside us was briskly selling casks of wine from its hold. The shipmaster rapped out a continuous spiel about the wine—both new and old—and the price per cask. The shipmaster mostly spoke in the Noromenn's tongue as a steady stream of buyers queued on the water-logged dock. They wore knee-length tunics with *braies,* wide-bottomed breeches. The wealthier ones fastened a mantle to their shoulders with decorative brooches. Their hair was long and they had full beards and mustaches like my father's kin.

The men in armor guarding the docks were different. They spoke the Frankish language amongst themselves, and were clean-shaven with close-clipped hair. Though they weren't large in stature, they were well formed from hard work. Their snug tunics were very short and their leggings were tight, their swords fastened to low-slung belts. One squat warrior in a leather jerkin sewn all over with lozenge-shaped metal plates ordered four casks of wine and hired some hunched, servile porters to carry them back to his own ship.

There were also some men whose heads were shaved in a round circle on top, leaving a fringe of greasy strands hanging all around. Their robes were long, reaching to their feet, and were invariably black as night. Some carried long staves to swipe at the urchins and beggars who gathered round them. I guessed from their garb that they were clerics of Kristna. They reminded me of Issland, where the numerous Kristna followers had denounced all otherworldly spirits, harming the fragile ground. Yet despite the prevalence of Kristna followers here, the *olfs* and sprites didn't seem to be in the least imperiled.

I received a number of curious looks, and eventually I realized it was my Skraeling parka and pants that were drawing attention. No other woman wore form-fitting pants as I did.

I withdrew under the canvas, letting it drop for privacy, and pulled out the bag Silveta had given me. The crimson dress was wrinkled from its long confinement, but I cared not about that. Silveta had also provided a brush, which I used to untangle my long, snarled locks. I braided my hair in one plait down my back as was customary here, and tied it with a bright red ribbon torn from the sleeve.

Silveta had also tucked in her own purse, full of coins. I tied it to my waist, under the skirt, where it would not be tempting. The final gift was a gold-linked chain with teardrops sparkling along its length. I wrapped the chain several times about my waist, then looped it in a knot and let the ends dangle between my legs. All the women were girdled so, and I thought it best to try to adhere to the customs of the place. It felt odd to have my dress held so close around my hips, but it did show off my figure to good advantage.

I emerged from under the canvas to appreciative stares from the oarsmen. The air was chill, so I put the cloak around my shoulders, glad to hide the swell of my bosom from the hungry eyes of the men. The freemen of Vidaris planted themselves between me and the rest of the crew, clearly anxious for Lexander's return.

I was determined to give Lexander no cause for concern. I ignored the men, and quietly played finger games with the sprites, letting them jump between my hands, while *olfs* took turns swinging from my long plait and trying to undo the ribbon. I sang songs to them, and hummed under my breath.

I opened myself to them as I did with the *olfs* in my homeland. As the day wore on, I realized that somehow I was already familiar to them. Time and distance meant little to the *olfs,* who were connected by other means.

Meanwhile the town lay tempting, just out of hand's reach. The great fortress that loomed over us was like a magnet, pulling me toward it. Perhaps Lexander was inside right now. I wanted to follow him, but I had agreed to wait.

Bells pealed through the town at regular intervals, including the night, ticking off several days as Lexander traded the goods we had brought from Markland. Merchants came to our *knaar* and surveyed our hold. Then ivory and wax were off-loaded by the oarsmen while bags of cloth, spices, precious dyes and barrels of olive oil arrived.

I tried to be invisible throughout, but too many of the merchants licked their lips at the sight of me. It made Lexander even more tense than he already was.

The fog was usually thick in the mornings and evenings, blanking out the sight of the houses along the waterfront, burning off only at midday. Sometimes I couldn't see the fortress, and at its worst, the ship next to us became a hulking shadow.

We had some trouble with our oarsmen. Two didn't return once they ventured out, and at first Lexander thought they had abandoned their posts without the pay they had been promised. But one eventually reappeared with knife wounds from fighting robbers. Others suffered beatings and blackened eyes.

When I showed Lexander the purse of coins Silveta had given me, he took it, his fingers tantalizingly grazing my palm. "The best way for me to get inside Becksbury is to be exactly who I am—a master whose house has been destroyed. It will give me a chance to find out what they know about the other houses in the Auldland, and to determine the best way to destroy Becksbury so another pleasure house will never be raised in this town."

"Then I must be your slave. I certainly know how."

"It will be dangerous, Marja. Think of Helanas. I can do only so much to protect you without alerting them."

I was nodding. "I think it's best. That way I can speak to the slaves."

"You mustn't tell anyone the truth. If we're discovered, then we both are in grave danger."

"You trained me well, Master." I couldn't help smiling slightly as I said it.

But Lexander was not amused. "They will read your eyes, Marja. They will know you love me, as Helanas knew, and that will make them suspicious."

"As you wish," I said obediently, the perfect slave.

He was not satisfied, but I would not be denied.

I was more than ready when the morning finally came to bid our faithful oarsmen farewell. We stood on the dock watching as the *knaar* pulled out, the yellow sail freshly mended for the return voyage home.

Lexander and I set out, leaving the waterfront behind. The smells and sounds grew overwhelming. The predominant odor was no longer dead fish, but rotting offal, burned wood, and the acrid stench of hides being cured. The fog soaked everything—my clothes and hair, the thatch on the houses, and the slippery cobblestones underfoot.

Each street was dedicated to a particular trade—candle making, bread baking, ironworks, carpentry, and weaving. On every corner was a public cookshop selling roasts and stews of birds and fish. The vegetables and roots sold from carts were rather wizened and small. There were no cattle, but a great many pigs rooted in tiny pens and searched for tidbits in the center ditch of the road. Most of the meat I saw butchered, hanging in haunches and full-bodied, came from pigs that had been smoked or spitted.

We passed one row of houses that had recently burned to the ground. People shifted through the piles of blackened beams to find iron pots and kettles. Some carried off the timbers to use in their own buildings. All of the dwellings looked so flimsy that a strong wind threatened to blow them over. They were mostly of wood with only a few stone houses here and there, decorated with pointed crenellations along the eaves and the round-arched windows and doors. The stonework was rough, done with pick and ax.

The most impressive structures were the Kristna sanctuaries, usually surrounded by a fenced yard or protected by a thorn hedge. When I asked what the stone and wood markers were for, Lexander said the dead Kristna followers were not cleanly burned but were placed underground with the worms and bugs. That had been Birgir's fate, and in my homeland burial was only for the dishonored.

There were countless people in Londinium, and too many without homes or means of livelihood. Some unfortunates had sores marring their skin, and they held their hands out and lamented for the lack of a meal. I saw legs missing and eyes filmed white or sunken and scabbed over. The cripples and beggars gathered around the finer buildings as if drawn like flies to a venison haunch.

Lexander ignored them, sometimes clearing a path for me by pushing them aside with an iron-tipped stave he had acquired.

We could hardly get past a huge crowd gathered in front of the blacksmith's shop. At the sound of a piercing scream, I leaped in fright. The crowd let out a cry of victory.

A hard-eyed man held something aloft, dripping bright red. It was a hand chopped off at the wrist. With a shout of glee, he drove a nail through it, pinning it to the door. Blood streamed down the boards, and through the shifting crowd, I could see a man on his knees, clutching the stump of his arm. His broken cries went on unheeded.

"No . . ." I breathed, my knees weakening.

Lexander put his arm protectively around my shoulders. "'Tis a moneylender who made bad coins. That is the punishment for stinting on silver in pennies in Danelaw."

"It can't be." It was too dreadful.

"This is not your homeland, Marja. You little know how civilized your people are compared to those in the Auldland." His expression was grim as he ushered me along. "I wanted to protect you from this."

I could not forget those white fingers clutching at nothing as the life force poured out. I swallowed hard, trying to force my stomach to settle.

We continued on streets that twisted until I didn't know our direction in the fog. At times I thought we were heading to the river, but Lexander knew exactly where to go. He must have assessed the Danelaw pleasure house in the past few days, though he hadn't spoken to me about it.

Indeed, the massive town wall rose at the end of the street. "We are almost at Becksbury." He released my arm.

"Yes, Master," I replied obediently.

Lexander looked pained, so I could not indulge my secret titillation. I followed him like a good pleasure slave, clasping my hands together and keeping my eyes on his heels.

We reached a round-arched gate in a stone wall that was taller than

Lexander. He rang the bell, and almost immediately it was opened by a servile old man.

"Take me to your master," Lexander demanded imperiously.

The old man bobbed without daring to answer in return. He used a large handbell to summon the *huscarl,* a sharp man of mature years, who asked Lexander, "What is your business, sir?"

"I'm an old friend of your master's from Stanbulin," Lexander said impatiently, looking around the courtyard at the outbuildings and a barn that were hulking shadows in the fog.

The *huscarl* treated Lexander with utmost respect as he led us through the courtyard. Two modest timber halls stood at right angles to each other.

There were few *olfs,* and I knew that boded ill for us. I would have to guard myself well, or I could inadvertently reveal everything.

The *huscarl* showed us into the larger hall. Inside, rough tree trunks served as pillars and heavier crossbeams supported the pitched roof. It was smaller than the fire hall on Silveta's estate, but still it felt drafty and echoingly empty. Tapestries were hung on the walls, some faded or grimed by soot. The ceiling was clouded with smoke from the fire that burned fitfully in the center of the floor. Ponderous irons held the logs while the coals drifted in a pile below. The only light came through narrow slits high in the pointed eaves that let the smoke out.

Not far from the fire were several *settles*—long, high-backed benches that were cushioned in blue pillows. A man and a woman were lolling there, looking bored. The man had sparse pale stubble on his head and his face was without beard, as Lexander's naturally was. But this man looked older, with skin the color of aged bronze and deep grooves on either side of his mouth.

He was suspicious at the first sight of us. But when Lexander removed his peaked cap revealing his smooth head and sparkling amber eyes, the man leaped to his feet. "You bring word from Saaladet?"

Lexander glanced at the *huscarl,* and the master impatiently dismissed his servant with a silent wave. "I am Lexander of Vidaris, in Viinland," Lexander explained. "I'm on my way to Stanbulin."

The eager light in the man's eyes faded as if he had suffered a mighty disappointment. He slumped back down, deliberately turning his head to stare into the shadows.

But the woman rose from the *settle,* unfolding herself as languidly as if emerging from a bath. "Viinland, you say? Surely that is on the other side of the world."

Her eyes ran over Lexander as she appraised him. She was a tall, fine mistress, much like Helanas in her pleasing form. But she had ice-blue eyes and her fine white hair brushed her forehead and neck in pretty wisps.

Lexander did not smile in return. "Vidaris was attacked and burned to the ground by raiders. My consort died in the conflagration, and all my slaves were stolen except for this one."

The mistress cast a negligent glance at me. I could see through my lashes that she cared not what had brought Lexander here, only that he was a pleasant diversion. "I am Drucelli of Becksbury. You are welcome, Lexander."

But the master was not pleased. Perhaps it was the interest Drucelli displayed in Lexander, or perhaps it was merely his nature. "You lost your house?" he sneered. "And now you slink back to Stanbulin?"

Drucelli tossed her head disdainfully. "That's Ukerald. He's been stuck too long in this backwater village that the dogs fight over like a bone. He hoped you brought word that he would be relieved of his burden."

Lexander nodded shortly. "I will convey a message, if you wish, Ukerald. I will be on my way as soon as passage can be arranged."

Drucelli placed her hand on his arm, drawing Lexander to the *settle.* I remained where I was, my hands clasped before me.

"There are many who are waiting for passage, and they will continue to languish here for some time." Her eyes caressed his face, and her hand still rested on his arm. He did not try to dislodge it. "The conqueror himself won't travel with the seas filled with Noromenn. Swegn has laid claim to Danelaw, and he has many loyal warriors."

"I had no trouble when I arrived."

Drucelli let out a breathy giggle, leaning closer. "Coming from Viinland, you were in a Noroship, yes? Naturally they wouldn't try to stop you, but no one else can get through. The ship from Stanbulin is weeks overdue."

I suddenly realized Ukerald was watching *me*. He saw my distress at the way his consort charmed my master.

In confusion, I averted my eyes and noticed a girl in the shadows. She was naked and crouching in the rushes, her fingers digging into the dirt floor. There was a clinking sound as she shifted—a chain attached to the collar around her neck was fastened to a nearby pillar. I couldn't see much in the dim light, but her eyes were as brown as her hair, while her skin was exceedingly fair.

Drucelli stroked Lexander's arm. "The Noroking will arrive any day to take back what is rightfully his. It's a wonder the Frankish conqueror has held Danelaw for so long. We've secured the house and taken in supplies enough to withstand any siege. You'll be safe here with us."

Ukerald looked more annoyed than not, but he didn't protest. Lexander graciously inclined his head.

I was afraid that getting out of Becksbury would be a lot more difficult than entering it.

6

⟨⟩⟨⟩⟨⟩

erhaps I was still in shock from seeing the blacksmith strike off the moneylender's hand. I did not want to destroy this pleasure house or these masters. Yet it was clear from the girl in chains that things were amiss here.

Ukerald made a motion, and a boy appeared. He wasn't much younger than I, but he still had the awkward limbs of youth. He wore an unflattering tunic and baggy leggings.

"Take her to the slave hall," Ukerald ordered.

My last look at Lexander must have been clear to both Drucelli and Ukerald. I couldn't help but lock eyes with him. I saw a flicker of anguish, and yes, of anger that I had insisted on coming here. Yet I doubted either Drucelli or Ukerald could tell. He was the master once again, detached and in complete control of himself.

I followed the boy to the adjacent hall. The walkway was covered by a pointed roof, but the sides were open to the muddy yard still shrouded in fog.

The slave hall was smaller, but it had the same wooden pillars and pitched ceiling, with a fire in the center. Two trestle tables were pushed against one wall with the benches upturned on top. It was as dark as the other hall, with a feeble light slanting through slits high above us. The walls were hung with tapestries, though these were far more threadbare and had been chewed into ragged holes along the edges.

There were no *olfs*.

The pleasure slaves were sitting in various positions on the dirt floor or crouching near the fire to get warm. They looked at me intently, as if they weren't accustomed to anyone entering their hall. From my splendid attire, they assumed I was not a slave. They wore loose leggings and bulky tunics. The colors were dark—brown, rust, green, and gray.

I didn't know how to explain myself. The boy who had brought me retreated in silence, and I could see from their wary glances that they were reluctant to question him in front of me.

I remained standing, my hands clasped and eyes downcast. I did not take the *vordna* pose of deference because it was not proper for a slave to bow to other slaves.

Ukerald arrived not long afterward, alone. The other slaves instantly knelt where they were, facing him. I remained standing since I had not been given an order. I refrained from looking at him directly, stealing glimpses. Ukerald had remarkably light russet eyes with the same bewitching kaleidoscope depths as Lexander's.

Ukerald carried a thin, pale stick. "Take off those clothes," he ordered. He swiped the cane through the air, making a whistling sound.

I had prepared myself to acquiesce to anything. I gracefully unwound the chain from my waist and looped it over my wrist. Then I undid the cloak and pulled off my dress. I draped the garments over my arm, then bent to remove my fur-lined Thule boots.

Ukerald gestured for the closest slave to take everything from me. I didn't see which chest my garments were placed in, as the master commanded, "Take your positions."

The slaves shifted into straight lines, three abreast. There were eleven so I took the open space farthest away from the fire. It did not surprise me that this severe master had not ordered clothes to be brought for me. I remained naked.

Imitating the others, I knelt in *lydnad,* straight up on my knees with my head bent in obedience. I did my best not to shiver though I was already chilled.

"*Anbud!*" Ukerald ordered.

I dropped my hands to the dirt in front of me, pressing my face against them as I raised my buttocks high in the air. The pose presented my nether parts in full display. Ukerald walked among the slaves, muttering orders. I couldn't see much but the boy in front of me, the one who had brought me here. His leggings stretched over his raised buttocks.

Ukerald prodded the boy sharply in the back with his cane. "A deeper curve, Matteus."

Matteus flinched at the point of the cane, and he thrust his hips higher. The master examined him critically, stepping around him until he turned to face me.

I went very still as Ukerald approached. His boots were near my plait, which curved down to the ground, still tied with the gay red ribbon. My toes were pointed correctly and barely touched, as Helanas had demanded.

Ukerald stepped behind me where I couldn't see him. I tried to breathe slowly.

Without warning, the cane whistled through the air behind me. I felt a slash of burning fire rip across my hind cheeks. I gulped back a cry, letting out a strangled squeak. But the agony grew worse, spreading as my body shuddered, threatening to collapse to the ground.

Then his hands were on my hips, and I felt him prodding me from behind. The wound left by the cane flared in agony at every touch. Ukerald shoved his thickened *tarse* into me, forcing me to open for him.

It was too sudden, too humiliating to be used in this way. But even as I silently fought against him, my body began to respond.

His harsh breathing was the only sound in the hall other than the popping of the wet wood in the fire. Not a word spoken as he took me in front of the slaves. I was accustomed to Helanas' whims, but this went beyond even her talent for persecution.

Even so, his pleasure had more to do with Lexander than me. I could almost see Ukerald sitting next to my master, toying with himself as he thought about violating me. He would use me to prod Lexander into revealing more than he intended.

Ukerald suddenly pulled away, as if knowing my mind had wandered to another man. I tensed at the sound of the cane slicing through the air. I couldn't keep a cry from escaping. The pain seemed too terrible to endure, but the feeling spread and intensified, like my flesh was splitting. I longed to touch my skin to see if I was still intact, but I knew I would be punished for it. Each slight movement was torture.

"*Gesig!*" Ukerald ordered.

The other slaves rose up, sitting back on their heels. I followed a slight beat behind. Ribbons of fire blossomed as my abused flesh rested on my heels. Though I had been shivering from the cold, sweat now glistened on my skin.

Ukerald continued giving commands, taking us through a vigorous training that Helanas herself would have admired. We performed each pose several times, moving from kneeling to standing and bending poses, then back to kneeling ones. I felt the lash of the cane a few more times because I had difficulty holding the poses for long. I was sorely out of practice.

Ukerald pulled down the leggings of several slaves to strike them across their bare buttocks or to briefly use them for his pleasure. He struck others over the leggings, which must have lessened the pain. His long *tarse* hung out the front of his *braies* the entire time. He barely spoke, but there was an undercurrent of menace in his taut gestures. The slaves were terrified.

When we were again in the *anbud* pose, he returned to me. I thought he would take me again, making my wounds sting more harshly.

But he abruptly knocked me over. I sprawled on my side, looking up in astonishment. His boot went to my throat, pushing me down on my back.

I couldn't help myself; my hands went to his boot, as he pressed against my neck. I couldn't breathe. I writhed underneath him, scrabbling at his foot.

"You will unhand me!" Ukerald ordered.

It was impossible. My throat was being crushed. Blackness descended as I gurgled. He would kill me.

I forced myself to release his boot, forced myself to clench my hands to my chest, trying to relax, to not fight the inevitable. Yet it was done too quickly and I couldn't find that place of utter submission in the face of his assault. I had fought for my life against Birgir and would fight to save myself always.

I was near blacking out when he finally lifted his boot. I choked and curled on my side, coughing and trying to draw a breath. My hands clutched my throat.

Ukerald jerked my hair, ripping the red ribbon from my braid.

I'm not sure when he left or how long I stayed there in the dirt. I only knew that I had to survive.

Later, the morning meal was served to the slaves. My throat was swollen and I could hardly eat the hard rye bread and bland cheese. I had to stand because I couldn't bear to sit on the rough bench.

I used the water bucket to wash my skin, twisting to see the bruises on either side of the raw stripes left by the cane. The wounds seeped, but thankfully there wasn't much blood.

Since I was naked, I could not sprawl on the ground as the others did because it would press dirt into my wounds.

The slaves stayed away from me, too fearful to reach out. I understood and did not resent their silence. Several of them departed at the tinkle of a bell attached to a cord on the wall. One of the eldest, a big blond man who reminded me of the Sigurdssons merchant family, returned with a naked girl. It was the slave who had been chained in the main hall. She looked like she had been through even worse than me.

It seemed like a miracle when an *olf* followed them in. The *olf* responded to my burst of surprise and delight, darting over. It was such a relief to feel its soft light shining on me. Its chubby face was concerned, unusually so for such careless creatures. It pulsed in sympathy with my throbbing buttocks.

"No," the girl demanded. She was looking directly at me. "I want you here."

It was the first time any of the slaves had spoken to me. Curious, I started toward her.

The girl shook her head, making her fine brown hair fall into her eyes. "Not you! Him," she insisted, pointing to a spot near my head.

I realized she was talking about the *olf*. "You can see it?" I exclaimed in disbelief. Skraelings talked to the *olfs*, but I had never met a Noromann who could.

"Come to me," she insisted to the *olf*, stamping her foot slightly against the ground. She had swelling breasts, yet she was still boyish in the waist and hips. Her dark eyes looked up slyly from side to side as she kept her chin tucked down.

The big blond slave shook his head in exasperation. "Don't pay any attention to Olvid," he said as he passed me. "Her mind has come undone."

Olvid put her hands on her hips, jerking her chin. "*She* knows what I mean."

I would not deny her. But my kinsfolk in Jarnby had thought me touched in the head because I spoke with the *olfs*. Surely I should not court that reputation here.

So I turned to the male slave. "Who are you?"

"Rimbert," he replied with the obedience of a well-trained slave.

"And the others?" I asked. Rimbert began to introduce the slaves, distracted from Olvid as I had intended.

At last some began talking as they told me how they had come to Becksbury. Most were Noromenn, but Drucelli had recently lured in several short Frankish boys who had followed the conqueror's warband to Danelaw. Rimbert had grown up in Londinium while others had run away to come to town, only to find it nearly impossible to survive. I had struggled on the streets of the port of Brianda and could heartily sympathize. They had come to this house when Drucelli offered them food and a warm place to stay, often in exchange for some minor sexual favor. Once here, they were enslaved.

Barissa, the prettiest girl, had been sought out by Ukerald and seduced into leaving her home with promises much like those Lexander had made to me—a life of exotic adventure and high status as a companion to kings and emperors. But none of these slaves believed that anymore. The spirit had been beaten out of them, and most sat in dejected silence, unable to summon the will to describe the horror of their lives.

It was much like Vidaris, yet worse. I tried to ignore my pain, shivering continually in the damp cold. Now I understood why they wore such cumbersome wool garments.

Then Drucelli arrived for our afternoon training session. She strolled in, her silver girdle emphasizing the swing of her hips beneath her sky-blue dress. For a wonder, she smiled at us, much like an *olf* who had just eaten a bowl of cream. I wondered if she had been with Lexander and, unbidden, I could imagine him kissing this perfect woman, her head tilting back as he tasted her neck and cleavage. I hoped it was a fantasy born of my feverish state.

I joined the slaves in kneeling, facing Drucelli. Olvid was right next to the mistress, having not moved far from the door. The *olf* hovered over her, but Drucelli seemed not to notice it.

"You know what to do," Drucelli purred.

The slaves fetched a bundle from a chest and spread it out on the floor. It was heavy canvas, like the material of a sail, but was worn soft with use. I helped pull it out flat, but Olvid only pretended to take part. She was still preoccupied with the *olf,* looking up to one side, her lips moving as she spoke to it.

Drucelli also carried a cane, but hers was longer and more flexible than Ukerald's. She enjoyed swishing it through the air, making that distinctive whistling sound. I cringed with the other slaves every time. Ukerald's blows were still ringing in my flesh.

The slaves disrobed and deposited their garments on the upturned benches on the tables. It was time for the arts of sensual pleasure.

Drucelli announced, "The girls on Olvid, and the boys on Matteus."

We separated into groups and I followed the girls. Their expressions of disgust were clear as they approached Olvid's dirty body. Perhaps that's why Drucelli had ordered it. Barissa began to kiss Olvid. With Barissa's beautiful heart-shaped face and voluptuous body, I wouldn't have minded having her lips on mine, but Olvid remained impassive.

Two girls each took a breast and began to mouth her nipples. Drucelli flicked her cane against another girl's back, leaving a short mark. It was not the terrible full-armed swing that Ukerald gave us, but it was enough to make her flinch. The girl quickly crouched between Olvid's thighs and began to lick her crotch. Her eyes were closed.

That left me without a traditional position to take. Before Drucelli could chastise me with her cane, I knelt at Olvid's feet and lifted one in my hands. They were as dirty as the rest of her, but I had no choice. I lowered my lips to kiss her toes. I tried to brush the worst of the dirt away when I could, but was forced to lick, then gag when Drucelli wasn't watching. Olvid hardly moved.

Despite Olvid's disinterest, the girls slowly brought her to climax. They began to shift and exchange glances as Olvid started to twitch, then flung her arms up as if to stop the girls. They held her down as she writhed beneath them. I clutched her ankle to keep her from kicking me.

The *olf* grew increasingly agitated as Olvid burst out of control. My silent, desperate questions were answered by the *olf* in a vision of Ukerald standing over her—he slammed his fist into the side of Olvid's head and she went flying across the room. As she lay on the ground, her limbs began to twitch uncontrollably.

The horrifying sight disappeared along with the *olf* in a puff of white vapor.

Olvid convulsed, her thrashing and guttural cries going on and on. I noticed the boys kept on pleasantly tormenting Matteus, who was responding despite Olvid's fit happening not an arm's length away.

Drucelli never took her eyes off us. It sickened me. Ukerald had done this to Olvid and Drucelli enjoyed it.

If I could have gathered every slave and walked out right then, I would have done it. It seemed impossible to bear it a moment longer.

But I had to endure. It wasn't enough to free these poor slaves; we had to make sure that Ukerald and Drucelli were stopped for good. I would do whatever it took to burn this house to the ground.

Drucelli called for us to each take a partner, and I was paired with a well-endowed young man with a strapping chest whose name I had forgotten. At his first tentative touch, I almost shrugged him off, too shaken to desire any intimacy.

But Drucelli's eyes were hard and appraising. I would have to be a slave for a little while longer. I had to abandon my freedom, even in my own mind.

So as my partner stroked my body, I concentrated on making it pleasurable for him. Likely he had little enough enjoyment in his life. I lost myself in his fine body, becoming mesmerized by his well-defined chest and the hard muscles in his arms. He responded vigorously, taking his time to stimulate me into passion before he took me.

As his body pressed into me, his desire purely driven, I relaxed and finally sank into my most submissive state. I rested in that deep place inside of me that was always accepting, always molding myself to the needs of the moment.

As I stopped struggling, it was easier to bear. Paring away everything else but the pleasure, I found myself again. My gift would carry me through even this.

Barissa was summoned that evening to the main hall to serve Lexander. The last time Lexander had joined with me had been in Tillfallvik, so it wasn't just the stabs of pain from my welts that kept me up that night.

My one consolation was that I was finally given leggings and a tunic to wear, so I was much warmer. The cloth was thick, matted wool, beaten and shrunk, then clipped to a velvety texture. My tunic was dark gray, with maroon sleeves and leggings. Our bedding was a thin blanket for each slave, and we slept on the ground.

I woke with the cacophony of bells ringing periodically throughout the night from the Kristna sanctuaries, calling the followers to prayers. I kept starting up, fearing there was a fire, but the other slaves ignored it. Somehow, the bells had not been as frightening when I was sleeping on the *knaar*.

Barissa didn't return until long after dawn. She was satiated and pleased with herself. The loose tunic showed reddened marks on the curve of her neck. Going closer, I saw she had been bitten several times, probably during a sound rutting with Lexander.

My fists clenched in jealousy. Lexander may have intended to taunt his hosts by so visibly marking their prize slave, but he must have known I would see it, too. I was reminded unpleasantly of my competition with Qamaniq for Lexander's attention. Yet I also knew that I would be safer if he didn't show interest in me. Ukerald would enjoy exploiting that.

Then we suffered through another pose session with Ukerald. He didn't hesitate to expose my buttocks and back to administer more lashes. He also rutted with me again, though I couldn't tell what pleasure he got from it. He didn't peak with me or any of the other slaves.

I endured it better now because I gained satisfaction from mere acceptance. It was a simple joy, but real nonetheless.

It sustained me through another day without Lexander. My opinion of Ukerald and Drucelli was confirmed by their many cruelties, both mean and petty. I suspected that Ukerald was drawing evil spirits to Becksbury, much like Helanas had done. Their foul miasma crept along the ground, repelling most of the *olfs*.

So I was grateful when the *huscarl* appeared and announced my name to help serve the evening meal. I eagerly followed the other two slaves, taking deep breaths of fresh air. After the dingy hall with only the privy walls for variation, it was a wonder the slaves had not gone mad.

My first sight of Lexander made my heart leap, but I forced myself not to reveal one bit of emotion. I carried a platter of flat bread high and set it on the table between Drucelli and Ukerald, then retreated to the kitchen for another burden.

It was only on my return that I noticed Lexander was wearing new garments in the Danelaw style. The cloth of his tunic was brightly embroidered, while his mantle was a vibrant yellow. The brooch on his shoulder sparkled with colored jewels. The style suited him. Outwardly he appeared relaxed, but a line appeared between his brows.

"How is she compared to your slaves?" Lexander asked casually, leaning over to carve a hunk of meat off a spitted bird.

"She does well enough," Ukerald said grudgingly.

Lexander shrugged. "I should attend one of your training sessions to see your technique."

I quailed at the thought of Lexander watching Ukerald abuse me. But the master lowered his eyelids, the closest he came to a nod.

Drucelli trilled a laugh, and agreed. "It would be enlightening, I'm sure."

Lexander held his goblet for me to fill with wine. I poured without spilling a drop. I wanted to touch his hand, to feel his skin against mine if only for a moment, but I dared not.

I knelt behind him, my knees crunching on bones and bits of food they had tossed on the floor for the dogs. The conversation fell around me like water on parched ground. Lexander asked a good many questions about the situation in Danelaw and the Frankish lands across the strait. Ukerald was not talkative, but Drucelli was eager to please him. She explained that the people of Danelaw did not desire a Frankish overlord, and some were organizing a revolt under Swegn, king of northern Auldland. The conqueror had bestowed huge sections of Danelaw on his half brothers and friends, usurping the true *jarls*. In some places, the conqueror had taken members of the gentry hostage to ensure their families' obedience. That was why Birgir and his warband had come to Markland, fleeing Danelaw after it had been taken over by the Frankish invaders.

"But I understand these Franks," Drucelli assured him. "Before I came here, I was mistress of Montplaire. In the Twelve Towns of Lutece—have you been there?"

"No," Lexander demurred. "But the Frankish lands are said to be charming."

With his encouragement, Drucelli poured out all she knew as they drank the wine. I increasingly struggled to follow their words. My body ached from the unaccustomed use, and fatigue was setting in. Being so close to Lexander made me feel safe, so the edge of terror that had kept me alert began to wane.

My hand slipped from my thigh and I lurched to one side. I realized I had almost dozed off. I righted myself, looking at Lexander, of course. But it was Ukerald who beckoned me to stand.

I went to him, avoiding Lexander's eyes. Ukerald didn't say a word as he pushed me over the table and pulled down my leggings. I was thankful that it was too dim for Lexander to see the welts that crossed my skin.

Ukerald remained seated as he swished the cane through the air. As it landed, I did everything I could to keep from crying out. I didn't want Lexander to see how badly it hurt. My fingers clutched at the wood slats of the table, feeling the crumbs and spilled liquid from their feast. All I could see for a moment were red spots.

"Return to your position," Ukerald ordered, setting down the cane.

I pulled up my leggings and turned. Lexander barely moved his lips. "That's an unusual form of chastisement."

Ukerald shrugged, but he was watching Lexander closely. I was a pawn being played between them. Lexander's hand was clenched, the only outward sign of his distress.

Drucelli laughed and leaned over Lexander, squeezing his arm. "Ukerald is harsher with the slaves than I. They are always eager to please *me*."

I gingerly settled down on my heels. Now there was no risk of dozing off, not with this new lash throbbing.

I didn't have to last for long. Soon after, Lexander set down his goblet, ignoring several hints from Drucelli that they should adjourn to her private chamber in the rear of the hall. Ukerald merely watched them.

"Marja, you'll accompany me," Lexander announced as he pushed back from the table.

I stood up demurely, hiding my elation. I wouldn't have to face Ukerald tonight. Drucelli pouted, clearly annoyed.

I followed two paces behind as Lexander left, lighting his way through the misty night with a candle. He entered a small house I had not seen in the rear of the compound. It had one narrow room, with a fire in the center hearth and a bed tucked under the slanting ceiling. The moist air seeped through the chinks in the wall.

Lexander put down the latch and placed a crossbar over the door. There were no windows. He stirred the fire and added two more logs.

His voice was low to keep anyone outside from hearing. "What have they done to you, Marja?"

"We've had training sessions in the poses and sensual arts. Other than that, we're left alone in the slave hall."

Lexander stepped closer. "He's been striking you?"

I lifted one shoulder reluctantly. "Surely you've seen Ukerald use the cane."

"Only once. I thought it was for a serious infraction."

" 'Twas nothing I could not bear. But we must save these slaves, Lexander. Ukerald and Drucelli are worse even than Helanas."

His eyes narrowed, and he turned me so my back was to the flames. He raised my tunic and pulled down my leggings.

"No!" he cried out in a strangled voice.

The welts looked ugly on the other slaves. The vivid red lines were edged with blue and purple bruises on either side. I had a dozen deep marks by now, and some crossed. Where that had happened, my flesh stung with every movement. Some still oozed, with bits of fuzz from my leggings sticking to the wounds.

In the silence, his fingers brushed against my skin. I could sense his worry and fear boiling to the surface. I suddenly felt powerless and small, consumed by a long-familiar rage at my own weakness. It took a few moments before I realized these were Lexander's feelings, not mine.

"I didn't know," Lexander swore. He picked me up and carried me to his bed, where he eased me down, facing away from him. He carefully washed my back, the cloth stroking every welt, sending fire sizzling through me. The marks on my lower back and thighs were the worst. "I thought those canes were an affectation, used for intimidation. Not this, never this . . ."

He fetched a jar of salve from a shelf and dabbed it on me. The cool gel made me sigh as it soothed the burning. Then he wrapped me in a sheet of finely woven cloth and pulled the fur coverlet over me.

His touch was so sweet that I almost drifted off. But muffled sounds roused me.

I blinked in the low ruddy light. Lexander was on the floor, resting his head on the bed. His shoulders were shaking.

"No, Lexander," I murmured, caressing his head. "I was willing. We had to see how they treated their slaves."

He raised his face, wet with tears. It was a shock. Once before I had seen a tear fall from his golden eyes, but he had sought to hide it from me. Now he cried outright, overflowing with grief.

I sat up, putting my arms around him. He clutched my waist, his head in my lap, as he struggled to stop.

It tore my heart to see his agony. I stroked him, murmuring endearments.

With his voice cracking, Lexander insisted, "I must take you away now, tonight, Marja."

"No!" I cried. "These masters must be stopped, Lexander. You've not seen the worst of it. Ukerald hit Olvid so hard that now she falls into fits. And Matteus can hardly speak, he's so terrified."

He raised his face, letting me see how he could not abide it. "I cannot watch them hurt you, Marja. I cannot . . ."

He dropped his head in my lap, and I could do nothing but stroke him, holding on as tightly as I could. With a terrible foreboding, I realized I was asking too much of him.

7

I slept that night in his arms, and the knot of fear that had taken root inside of me began to ease. Lexander's touch told me that he would not let Ukerald hurt me again.

By the early-morning bells there were several *olfs* clustered in the room with us. They responded to the purity of our feelings for each other, despite their reluctance to be near Lexander. Indeed, I could hardly believe that he had shown his anguish to me. It made me love him all the more.

Lexander waited until I woke before gently pulling away. He dressed quickly.

I smiled up at him, but something had shifted inside of him. The *olfs* disappeared even as I recognized it—his eyes were hard and the multicolored flecks glittered brightly within the gold. He had looked the same after he had cut off Helanas' head with the sword he was now buckling to his waist.

"You're going to kill him." I sat up, letting the blanket slip from my bare shoulders.

"Of that, there is no doubt." He considered me. "But if I slew them both now, other masters would be sent in their place. I must devise a way to destroy this house completely, so another will not be raised."

I was pleased to see his fury checked by forethought, though even greater destruction was his goal. "I agree."

"And you'll not suffer anymore," he said sharply.

It was not his words but the thought of how he had cried last night that stopped my protest. In truth, I didn't have to share in the slaves' agony in order to help them. "I'll not leave Becksbury. There must be some way I can remain here with you."

"Perhaps, but no master should be possessive of their slaves. That is our cardinal rule, for we are training you for others. Yet I cannot allow Ukerald to dominate me through you."

"I thought that was his intent."

"I shall respond in kind, and use you against him." Lexander came over and sat down beside me. His arm braced my back, and I gingerly leaned into him, looking up.

His fingers touched my face, stroking me lightly, as if to truly caress me would make him lose control again. I could feel the desire, but he was holding back for fear of being overwhelmed by loving me.

I kissed his fingertips. "I will do whatever I must," I murmured.

His arms tightened on me. I thrilled to his possessive hold, and he responded. He pulled my head back, his breath on my cheek. "My own beloved . . ."

I leaned up to meet his lips and we clung to each other.

"Are you ready?" Lexander asked me. "You must display no emotion, no matter what happens."

I took a deep breath. "Yes."

We were finally united in our purpose. He gave me a kiss on the top of my head. I was startled by the gentle caress, the kind one would give a child. He was telling me without words that he would take care of me.

We left for the main hall in correct master-slave mode. The table was littered with the remains of the morning meal for Ukerald and Drucelli. Poor Olvid was naked and chained to the post as she was each night. She had still not bathed, so the grime on her was even thicker. Two of the house dogs were lying nearby and she tried to reach out to them, mouthing words as she did with the *olfs*, despite their abrupt snarls and snaps at her hand. Several *olfs* drifted over and she shifted her attention to them.

Lexander marched down the hall and stood over the table with his hands on his hips. "Marja," he ordered. "Remove your clothes."

He had not told me what he intended, which was just as well. I gracefully removed my tunic and leggings and joined Lexander at his curt gesture.

"Turn around," he ordered. I obeyed so I faced away from Ukerald and Drucelli.

"So?" Ukerald drawled.

Drucelli hastened to explain away the beating. "Don't worry, Lexander. The marks fade much quicker than you expect. Even if the ship arrives tomorrow, she'll be perfectly healed by the time you reach Stanbulin."

"I needed her to be pristine *now*," Lexander insisted. "One or two welts I could countenance, but this makes her unappealing to all except the most confirmed sadist. Surely you're aware of that."

I stood in the *bojakna* pose, with one hip higher than the other, gazing down and off to one side. They were behind me and I could only see Olvid. Feeling Ukerald's eyes on me made me shiver.

"Why do you want her to be unmarked?" Ukerald inquired.

"I intend to use this slave to bribe my way to Stanbulin. Coins are easily taken, but pleasure is far more powerful. As you've seen for yourself, she is of the highest quality."

"She is superior indeed," Drucelli smoothly reassured him. "An example for the other slaves."

Lexander continued, as if Drucelli hadn't spoken, "She will remain with me from now on."

"At all times?" Ukerald asked. "Surely that is excessive."

I remembered how Lexander had spoken as he challenged Ketil to a duel. He sounded the same way now—like a sword being unsheathed. "Perhaps that will prevent *excessive* marking of this slave."

He waited a few beats, as I held my breath. I couldn't hear

Drucelli and wondered if she was also holding her breath. The tension that swirled in the hall intensified. The *olfs* ricocheted from the walls to the ceiling, diving through the thatch to avoid the ill feelings.

Olvid suddenly cried out, her hands to her head. "Stop it, don't make them go! Please don't!"

She flopped down and began shaking in every limb. Her tongue protruded, and without the other slaves to hold her down, she thrashed uncontrollably. The dogs leaped up and began growling at her, their hackles raised.

The *olfs* couldn't take it. The last of them vanished, along with much of the light.

"That one should be put down," Ukerald said behind me.

Drucelli retorted, "But you enjoy toying with her so much."

They both did. Ukerald drew the demons to Becksbury, but Drucelli was hardly better in her disregard for everything but her own pleasure.

Olvid was still jerking and shaking, but her fit was starting to ease. I wished I could help her, even if it was only to stroke her hair to soothe her final tremors.

Lexander sounded perfectly at ease. "Come, Marja, I have an appointment to keep."

I refrained from glancing back at Ukerald as I followed, still holding my clothes. I couldn't keep up with Lexander's long-legged strides. Olvid lay unnoticed as the scrape of the bench against the ground indicated that Ukerald was done with his meal.

I didn't need to see Ukerald's expression to know that I could never bear to be alone with him again.

I accompanied Lexander back to his chamber, where he produced my crimson dress and Thule boots.

"Oh!" I cried out, clapping my hands. I had thought I would never see Silveta's gift again. I had refused to think about it. As a slave, nothing was my own.

Lexander's expression eased as I tore off the tunic and leggings and slid into the fine wool dress. "You are so easily pleased."

With that, he pulled out the chain with the gold teardrops along its length. He looped it around my waist, caressing my hips as he did.

I was so delighted that we were together again that I could have joined with him right then. But Lexander warded me off by handing me my cloak. "I'll explain what I've discovered on the way."

We left the manor, and Lexander lent me his arm as we made our way over the slippery cobblestones. "Ukerald may send one of his servants to follow us and report back on what we do. You must act as my slave at all times."

"I understand." I resisted the urge to look behind me.

"I'm hoping the blockade is broken soon so the ship from Stanbulin can arrive. The shipmaster would be able to tell me of a dozen houses, at least. Except for Drucelli's description of the Montplaire house, I've discovered little I didn't already know."

As we made our way through the meandering streets, Londinium reminded me of the overlord's bastion in Viinland, writ large. The shops and houses faced each other so closely there was barely room for a cart to maneuver between them. Through the occasional gate or alleyway, we could see yards beyond the walls, with gardens, trees, and outbuildings. Mist hung heavily in the air, muting the colors and making the outlines of everything seem fuzzy.

When we arrived at the waterfront, Lexander went straight to a bigbellied merchant ship that rode high on the water. It looked battered but serviceable. There were a number of *olfs* hanging about, examining the off-loaded cargo and tripping up people who were passing by.

The shipmaster emerged from a cabin belowdecks. He was a small man, nearly two heads shorter than Lexander. With his leathery skin and prominent nose, he was as spare as if he had been carved from a wooden post.

They had obviously talked before, because Lexander omitted any preamble. "When are you to sail?"

The shipmaster pushed at his short hair that was standing up in stiff locks. He spoke the Noromenn's tongue with a drawling accent. "There's no telling now. We've reports of *knaars* full of warriors blocking the mouth of the river. More than fifty all told."

"Massing to attack?" Lexander asked. "That's hardly enough to threaten the conqueror. Especially if he takes a stand in the fortress."

"They've shut down Londinium and blocked trade," the shipmaster said. "The conqueror will have to act to open the waterways, and soon."

I realized that the shipmaster was also Frankish, and therefore must be supportive of the new overlord.

Lexander nodded sympathetically. "I'm sure the residents are pressuring him for fear of what *vikingr* would do in Londinium."

"The town surrendered to the conqueror when he arrived to escape a burning," the shipmaster agreed with a short laugh. " 'Tis sure they'll not want to risk themselves in defending their new master. But if Swegn's warbands head upriver, we'll slip down along the shore so as not to be caught between them."

"In that case, I'll want passage for myself and my slave," Lexander said.

"If you're here when we depart, you can sail for the price we've agreed on," the shipmaster acknowledged. "But I can't be held waiting for you."

"Send the boy to Becksbury, but he's only to speak to me," Lexander replied. "No one else."

The shipmaster snorted in something that could be considered agreement. But I got the distinct impression that he cared little about passengers, and he wouldn't hesitate to flee without us if the need rose.

Indeed, Lexander frowned as we left the waterfront. I refrained from questioning him, because that would be out of character for a slave. A rough boy who I'd seen in the kitchens of Becksbury was hiding among barrels on the wharf watching us.

Lexander must have sensed my unease, because he quietly said, "Let's go to the fortress to see how the conqueror fares."

The riverfront was unusually busy, yet there was no sense of frantic haste or panic about the massing Noroships downriver. People were rude, shouting and shoving one another, but not violent. *Olfs* darted among them, cheerfully adding to the mayhem. Lexander tried to shelter me through the throngs, and it took some effort to reach the end of the street.

The fortress rose up in the fog before us, with a few windows facing over the river and the town. Men stood along the crenellated top peering down. The buttresses that ran up the sides were nearly as thick as the walls themselves, supporting the immense weight of stones and mortar.

The muddy ground from the ongoing construction was interspersed with clusters of sheds and barns. Among them were men enough for a dozen warbands, and the waterfront was crowded with their boats. Everyone was wearing leather armor and most were sharpening or mending their weapons. It certainly looked like a battle in the making to my appalled eyes.

Lexander cursed under his breath as he tried to withdraw, keeping ourselves from being pulled deeper into the fortress yard. I understood why—we had already seen the worst. There would be a fight, but whether it took place in town or on the river remained to be seen. And in the midst of so many short, dark-haired Franks, Lexander was at risk. He looked like a Noromann because of his height.

Lexander pushed our way out, heading back into town. We followed a wide thoroughfare away from the waterfront. It was filled with people and carts, some pulled by donkeys or small horses.

The close-packed buildings opened into a large muddy square. A market was briskly underway on the far side.

I kept a watch out for the Becksbury kitchen boy, but we must have lost him in the crowd by the fortress. Lexander relaxed as if pressure had been lifted from him, giving me a brief smile.

In one corner of the market stood a stone structure, not as massive as the fortress but on a similar scale. The pale gray walls rose several times higher than the houses around us, solid and powerful, with only a single row of arched windows near the roof. A tall pointed tower rose at one end, with a cluster of slender points thrusting into the sky around it.

"What is it?" I asked.

"A Kristna sanctuary," Lexander replied.

I gaped up at it, astonished at the size. In Issland, the land had been ravaged because the people had turned away from the gods to worship Kristna alone. But here, the *olfs* had no compunction at popping into the sanctuary itself and swinging from the decorative carvings around the door.

I extended myself into the *olfs* to try to understand. Many generations of people had lived on this riverbank, weaving their *inua* into the fabric of the world. They had always given abundant praise to the sun and the wind and the rain, so the *olfs* prospered. Perhaps if Silveta had kept her bargain with Issland and brought clerics to my homeland, Kristna would not have subsumed everything else. But as I took another look up the towering walls, I still doubted. Why did a god need a sanctuary second only in might to the conqueror's fortress?

Lexander saw my curiosity, and with a quirked lip, he led me up the steps. It was brighter inside than I had expected, and my gaze was drawn up to the arched ceiling far overhead. It was so high that it seemed a place fitting for a god. Slender columns marched the length of the sanctuary, with the arches between them leading to narrow corridors that ran the length of the building.

The clean, chiseled stone reflected every sound, echoing voices into a finely sustained, high-pitched tone, like the walls themselves were humming.

It wasn't until Lexander drew me down the side corridor that my tension eased. I couldn't feel the presence of Kristna in this place, but there was no mass worship underway as I had observed in Issland.

My feet scuffed over the carved runes in some of the floor stones. Each wall niche was brightly painted with ingenious scenes of miniature buildings and people. They were veritable windows into distant places, much like the visions the sea spirits showed me. It was quite beguiling, but I was still not tempted to let a god take up residence inside of me as the Kristna followers did.

"Kristna holds great power here," I murmured.

"Not as much as in the Holy Empire, but certainly Kristna followers here have a great deal of wealth. The conqueror is a supporter of Kristna, as many Frankish people are, so likely the influence of the clerics will grow—" He stopped as if struck, staring up at a scene of a naked man and woman. "It's said the conqueror brought a new bishop to Danelaw, one of his own loyal men."

I was not surprised that the dreaded conqueror was also a Kristna follower. Surely he would be eager to share the piece of god inside of him with everyone here. I only hoped the *olfs* could withstand such a siege.

Lexander gestured to the scene on the wall. The unclothed man and woman were standing among the trees, reaching out their hands to each other. Their dreamy expressions made it seem as if they were about to kiss. "This scene shows the Kristna legend of when men were once godlings, and how they lost that part of themselves."

"So that's why they allow Kristna inside them," I exclaimed. "They believe that he belongs there."

"They claim it was a woman's fault that they lost Kristna. She used her sensual wiles to tempt her mate into forsaking the godly part of themselves. They flaunted their freedom and lured others into their abandoned state. That's why Kristna clerics are celibate. They believe it's the only way to avoid the temptation of this earthly realm."

My mouth fell open. There was nothing the *olfs* loved more than a good rutting. I could not believe any god would reject that life-building force.

"How do you know this?" I asked.

"I spent two decades in the Veneto house. We were surrounded by the Holy Empire on every shore, so I had to learn the ways of Kristna." His hands tightened into fists. "I can use Kristna to bring down Becksbury. If we can make the bishop fear for his eternal salvation, he will muster all of his power against the pleasure house."

"But I thought Becksbury was a great manor, like Vidaris."

"Ukerald has isolated himself," Lexander explained. "He's made no ties with the leading families. How could he when there have been three claimants on Danelaw in the past decade? If Becksbury is not aligned with anyone, they cannot be brought down by their opposition. But that is also a weakness."

"They have no allies," I agreed.

"Not among the ruling class. But from what I can tell, they take in many more slaves than they send to Stanbulin. They must be selling the slaves who are not fit to the gentry, perhaps even to merchants."

My heart ached for the poor children they'd pulled off the streets and tortured into oblivion. Someone like Olvid would surely be sold here in Danelaw, rather than sent to Stanbulin with the more polished slaves. Perhaps the other failures became the slaves I had seen around Becksbury, like the collared gatekeeper. "Do you really think Kristna will help us save them?"

Lexander actually smiled. "You seduce the bishop, Marja, and I'll take care of the rest."

8

⟞≡⟋●⟍≡⟝

The bishop's residence was next to the great sanctuary, an imposing house made of the same pale gray stone. The entryway was capped by a small spire just like the one over the door of the sanctuary.

Lexander announced his need to see the bishop with such authority that he wasn't challenged. Inside, one archway led to an altar. A statuette of a robed woman stood in a niche in the wall. There were other signs of worship—kneelers on the floor and several crystal and silver chalices on a wooden shelf. An *olf* or two drifted inside, watching us curiously. But most darted off to the market throng, where they could filch bits of food and drink.

Lexander took my cloak along with his own and handed it to a servant. The bishop arrived soon enough. He was a man in middle years with pronounced round cheeks and a swelling belly. His florid health reminded me of Birgir, but the bishop was dark where Birgir was pale. For a Frankish man, he was quite imposing.

He went to the ornate chair in the center of the room and sat down, his movements deliberately slow. I was reminded of Jedvard, the Viinland overlord, for a moment.

Lexander wasted no time in coming to the point. "I am Lexander of Becksbury. I've come to negotiate for asylum for my house."

"Asylum?" the bishop countered. "From whom do you flee?"

Lexander raised one brow. "Noromenn warriors are preparing to invade Londinium. Surely you must be aware of the fleet that has gathered at the mouth of the river?"

Lexander's sneer was so open that my eyes widened. 'Twas most unlike him to reveal disdain for other people. He had treated even Helanas with courtesy.

"One could say that sentiment is treason," the bishop retorted. His hands were in constant motion, fiddling with his robe. He had left his homeland to ally himself with the conqueror; he must have some unsatisfied ambitions.

"We all must take precautions," Lexander said. "The conqueror has built a fortress for himself. I'm sure he wouldn't be surprised to see the town in flames by morning."

"Do you doubt the might of the conqueror?" the bishop demanded.

Lexander ignored the obvious signs of his displeasure, stepping forward conspiratorially. "Come, my man, let us be reasonable. You have sacred ground on which few would step. I need to protect myself and my cohorts, along with our slaves. By staying here, we need not fear looters and raiders."

Lexander let his eyes wander up, indicating he expected to be housed in the bishop's own home. It was audacious, verging on insulting. Hospitality was given, not demanded.

The bishop glared at Lexander. He was a proud man, but his post was newly gained. "I've heard something of Becksbury," he declared flatly. "Surely you know your trade is an abomination in the eyes of any man who follows Kristna."

"So you say," Lexander said with a wink. "But any man would agree that he is well paid when he receives gold coins and the delight of a warmed bed at night."

Lexander glanced at me. *Seduce him,* had been his order.

I went forward, lowering myself as I approached, letting the bishop see how willing I was to abase myself. On my knees before him, I kept my head bowed as I lifted my hands to my breasts to offer myself to him. The low-cut gown girdled tightly at my waist showed off the flare of my hips. I moved slowly, sinuously, as if I could weave my way into his very *inua* and make him desire me.

When I finally gazed up at him, his nostrils flared in resentment. I let my eyes linger, knowing this man wanted to strike back, to battle my allure, to ultimately conquer me.

I slipped the neck of my dress off my shoulders, letting it slide slowly down over my breasts. With a slight breath, my nipples pulled free, tightening in the chill, moist air.

For a moment, he wanted me fiercely. Then rage took over. His hand swung back, and I flinched, knowing he was going to hit me.

Lexander stepped in, blocking the bishop's arm. His voice was remarkably light. "Now, Bishop, you can do whatever you fancy with her. But first I must have your agreement that my house can take up residence with you until this crisis has passed."

"Never!" the bishop shouted. He stood up and thrust Lexander's hand off him. "You dare insult me on ground consecrated to Kristna! Becksbury will rue the day you thought to tempt *me.*"

Lexander pulled me up, shaking me as if I was on display. "*This* is what men want, Bishop. You and every other man. We supply pleasure, and even you cannot do without that."

The bishop was red in the face. "I call upon you always to dread the Day of Judgment and every day to have before your eyes the moment of your death! Consider the condition in which you are seen in the eyes of our God."

I wondered if Lexander had gone too far and the bishop would have us seized as blasphemers.

Lexander inclined his head. "If that is your last word, then I will trouble you no further."

I pulled up my dress as he accepted our cloaks from a wide-eyed servant. From the bishop's reaction, I was certain he did not forgo the delights of sensual pleasure. He had responded to me, desiring me with a dark intensity that would have made me tremble if I'd had to bed him. But the servant thought his master truly lived without women.

Back outside with the sanctuary looming over us, Lexander kept his pose of the perfect master as he murmured, "Well done, Marja. Now let's complete the task and force it into the open. He won't be able to ignore Becksbury for long when we've gone to every sanctuary in town and made them a similar offer."

We spent the next two days visiting Kristna sanctuaries. Lexander insulted everyone we encountered, astutely judging the best way to irritate each man.

Indeed, they were all men. We saw few women among those who served the Kristna clerics. Yet, in spite of the belief that women were responsible for the loss of their god, some clerics lived with consorts and had begotten large families. These men were not averse to helping the pleasure house. One cleric who watched over a humble shack not far from Becksbury was very interested in me, reaching out to stroke my hand. I drew closer, sitting on his lap and pressing my thigh against his thickened *tarse*.

Lexander was hard-pressed to insult this cleric, who was willing to take both coins and flesh in return for giving us shelter during the coming crisis. But Lexander dismissed the man's house as a hovel, and declared the only suitable place for the Becksbury gentry was in the bishop's home. He gave the man enough to wet his greed, but not enough to satisfy him, insisting that he convince the bishop to help them.

We also ventured outside the town walls and visited a Kristna abbey where the followers had chosen to live in seclusion, devoting themselves entirely to the worship of their god. The cleric who ran the abbey drew back at the first sight of me, hardly able to bear my presence, as if his religious convictions had subsumed his reason.

When Lexander saw that, he began to treat the abbot as if he were a lover of men, standing too close and reaching out to touch the man's arm as he spoke. The abbot hardly gave Lexander a moment's hearing before clerics in hooded black robes were ushering us out. Their faces were forbidding as we were escorted directly to the gate.

To all, Lexander intimated that the bishop was open to our bribe, including a roll or two with me, but he was not being flexible enough in his negotiations. It ensured that our uncouth efforts would reach the man with the power to destroy Becksbury.

Lexander paid a handful of boys to watch the sanctuary and the fortress to keep him informed. They reported in periodically at the cookshops and taverns we frequented. Too many Becksbury servants were seen in the same vicinity, indicating Ukerald was keeping a watch on our doings. We avoided him by taking our meals outside the manor, leaving early and returning late.

But by the third morning, as we woke in each other's arms, Lexander murmured, "It's time to face Ukerald."

I nodded, having expected it. "When do you think the bishop will act against Becksbury?"

"It depends on how determined Swegn is. If nothing is happening on that front, then the conqueror may lend his support to the bishop."

"And if the Noromenn do invade Londinium?" I asked.

"Then we shall be in the midst of a war. I shall waste no more time on Ukerald and Drucelli."

I shuddered at that. "We'll have to take the slaves with us. They would be lost before they knew they were free."

Lexander nodded, adding, "Saaladet will try to establish another pleasure house here, but they will find it more difficult than they anticipated after our hard work. At worst, I can return in a few seasons to clean them out again."

He felt me trembling, and with a light kiss, he rolled out of bed. We talked about it all except the one thing that silenced me—his ruthlessness. I could not speak of it because I was not blameless. I was helping to incite the wrath of the bishop and the conqueror against Becksbury. How many more deaths would I have to bring about before the *olfs* kept their distance from me as they did with Lexander?

Though no *olfs* would come inside his chamber unless we were rutting, by day we were accompanied by a revolving troupe of mischievous creatures. They lived in the moment, never thinking of what would come, so they enjoyed the clerics' confusion and heightened emotions. I'm sure they filched small items from the various sanctuaries we visited.

Since I would have to face Ukerald and Drucelli, I dressed that morning in my bulky slave tunic. I actually welcomed its warmth after so many chill, damp days. We arrived in the main hall with a few curious *olfs* right after the master and mistress sat down to the morning meal.

"Another trencher," Ukerald ordered Rimbert when we came in. "We thought you had left for Stanbulin."

I knelt behind Lexander as he sat down at the table. Olvid was chained to the pillar as usual. The *olfs* went over to coo at the poor girl to try to cheer her up.

Rimbert returned with the porridge and a trencher of bread and set it down. Lexander tossed me a hunk of bread without a break in his expression.

Drucelli's exquisite face was petulant. "You couldn't have avoided us more if we were lepers."

Last night, after our lovemaking, Lexander had finally confessed that he had succumbed to her seductions. He claimed he had taken her to irk Ukerald, but I could tell he had been truly tempted by Drucelli.

Now he barely glanced at Drucelli as he accepted a goblet of wine from Rimbert. "I must reach Stanbulin in all haste so I can return to Vidaris with reinforcements. Trying to get around this blockade is nothing but a cursed nuisance."

Ukerald's pale brown eyes flashed. "Apparently Becksbury is not secure enough for you."

Lexander laughed out loud. "Don't be as simple-minded as these yokels, Ukerald. It doesn't become you."

Drucelli raised her brows in surprise. "Do you dare insult your host, Lexander?"

"He insults my intelligence by making such a claim."

Ukerald narrowed his eyes. "I'm waiting for an explanation of why you interfere in my affairs."

Lexander picked up a knife and cut the smoked sausage. "To ensure that the blockade is removed, I have incited panic among the Kristna sanctuaries, knowing the new bishop has the ear of the conqueror. If the bishop puts pressure on the conqueror to end this useless stalemate, then I will be free to leave."

Ukerald leaned forward, uncomfortably close to Lexander. "This is my territory. You have no right to stir up trouble."

Lexander shot Drucelli a glance. "*Your* territory, Ukerald? It seems to me you've done little to protect Becksbury during these upheavals."

"You've brought this house to the attention of the Kristna clerics. You know we're an anathema to them."

"That is why I went to them and not the merchants," Lexander responded coolly. "Becksbury has nothing to do with Kristna, so I haven't infringed on any of your prior agreements. And frankly, I think your lack of cultivating the clerics is unwise. Kristna followers must be placated and flattered from time to time."

"That is not for you to decide!" Ukerald was finally getting heated, pounding one fist on the table. He was so accustomed to making everyone quake before him that Lexander's casual dismissal was infuriating. "You are a guest in this house and I forbid you to interact with the people here."

The dogs rose slowly and began to growl, responding to their master's fury.

"You forget yourself, Ukerald." His amusement was clear. "You have no power over me."

Drucelli grew shrill. "We can deny you our table and the bed you sleep in at night!"

I was ready to leap to my feet at Lexander's signal. But I was not sure Ukerald would let us go so easily.

The dogs began to bark, running toward the door to the courtyard. The *huscarl* appeared, ushering in a young boy. I recognized him as one of Lexander's messengers. The boy hesitantly started forward, nodding to Lexander. "A warband, sirà."

Ukerald shoved his bench back with a harsh scrape. "Come here!"

Lexander leaped to his feet, demanding, "Which way do they march, boy? To the ships or the sanctuary?"

"The sanctuary," the boy stammered, keeping a wary eye on Ukerald.

The dogs were making such a din that I silently begged the *olfs* to descend on them. We were all at risk as long as Ukerald could order his dogs to attack. I promised the *olfs* the first bites of my meals for the rest of the season. They darted over to cloud the dogs' eyes, driving them out the door.

Ukerald ordered, "Fetch them, Rimbert!"

Rimbert hurried toward the door as if glad to escape. I silently begged the *olfs* to goad the dogs across the compound, taking the slave with them.

Meanwhile, Lexander tossed the boy a coin, which he caught in midair. "Begone, quickly."

Ukerald roared out, "Stop! You'll go nowhere until this is explained."

The *huscarl* blocked the boy from leaving. His eyes were wide, and I feared he would spill everything he knew. I could barely remain on my knees.

Lexander turned to Ukerald, his voice deadly serious. "You've mismanaged everything, Ukerald. There's a growing sentiment against this house amongst the Kristna followers. I tried to create a rapport with them, but it was too late. Now we must escape before they arrive."

Ukerald's face contorted. "What have you done?"

"This boy has brought warning that a warband under the bishop is marching on Becksbury." Lexander gestured to the messenger boy to go. The *huscarl* was retreating in horror.

"Go, bar the gates!" Ukerald ordered. At his sharp gesture the *huscarl* fled.

"You've been caught unawares," Lexander insisted. "I've got a way out, but we must hurry."

Drucelli had her hand to her mouth. "It can't be true! We've done nothing to these people."

"You've created no alliances," Lexander said. "No bonds with any of the local *jarls* or gentry of Londinium. You left yourselves exposed."

"The situation has been unstable for decades," Ukerald insisted. "The conqueror could be ousted tomorrow, and a Noroking placed here instead."

"*Today* you are being attacked," Lexander said flatly.

"What do we do?" Drucelli cried out.

Lexander turned to her. "Go get your valuables and put them in a bag. Don't bring anything heavy. We have to go over the town wall."

"What about the slaves?" Drucelli asked. My eyes went to Olvid chained to the post.

"We'll take them with us," Lexander declared. "Get your things, then fetch them here."

Drucelli looked over at Ukerald for a moment. He didn't believe Lexander, but he didn't protest. She saw his indecision, rare for Ukerald, and that made up her mind. She hurried to her chamber in a rustle of skirts.

Lexander turned away as if to follow her. That's when I saw the knife he had kept hidden in his hand the entire time.

Ukerald reached out to stop him. "You did this! How did you provoke them?"

Lexander shifted as if to tell him, leaning in confidentially. But instead he thrust his knife into Ukerald's side. He pushed hard, driving the point deep into his chest.

Ukerald cried out, and his feet kicked, sending the bench tumbling across the ground. Lexander pulled out his knife and Ukerald gasped, trying to draw another breath. The godling's strength was prodigious; a man would have been crushed. Lexander wrestled with him for a moment, then slashed the edge of the knife across his throat.

It was done too quickly, too expertly, as if Lexander was killing a bird for our evening meal.

He dropped Ukerald, who was left to writhe in his death throes right before me. The few *olfs* who remained bolted away.

Lexander hurried to the chambers in back. "No," I breathed, knowing what he intended.

I scrambled away from Ukerald, who was growing still. His eyes stared past me as the blood covered his neck and mouth, even flowing from his nose.

The door opened behind me and the sounds of a struggle followed. I tore my eyes away from Ukerald as Drucelli screamed. It didn't last long. Lexander reappeared in the doorway, his knife hand bloody to the elbow and a wild light in his eyes. There was a bag slung over his back.

"Is this what you planned?" I cried.

"What else?" he countered. "Hurry, Marja, the hall is starting to burn."

Olvid was crouching in terror by the pillar. I was surprised she hadn't fallen into a fit. "We have to take Olvid."

Lexander called, "Marja, don't!" but I ran to her. The chain was held closed by a peg. I hit it against the post to force it out. The girl was so simpleminded she had never realized escape was within her grasp.

"You'll be fine, Olvid," I tried to assure her. But she was staring at Ukerald sprawled on the ground. The air was growing hot and the pillars were smoldering.

I tried to guide her away, but she saw Lexander coming and jerked from my hands. She ran to the front, where the door was ajar to the courtyard. I started to follow, but Lexander shouted, "Marja, come here!"

Flames crackled up the walls, setting the tapestries on fire. We needed to leave from the back to reach the town wall. Olvid slipped out the front, so she was safe.

Lexander had the door open and was waiting for me when I dashed up. The thatch overhead sucked up the fire and burst into a smoky mass.

Hand in hand we ran toward the rear of the manor. We hadn't gone far when the ground shook with a low rumble, and the hall began to collapse. I went down into the grass, but Lexander pulled me back up. Somehow we kept going as the flames gained strength, shooting up from the collapsing timbers. People were rushing away in the forecourt to avoid the burning building.

"The slaves—" I started to say.

"They'll be all right," Lexander interrupted. "See, the servants let them out."

The pleasure slaves huddled together as the *huscarl* drove them away from the burning hall.

"We have to take them with us," I insisted.

Lexander was gazing through the smoke toward the gate. "It's too late. The bishop is here already."

Lexander pulled me across the open yard to the towering wall that surrounded Londinium. He was able to scramble to the top where the wall was broken down on the innermost layer. He reached down a hand for me, stretching as far as he could. I didn't think I could make it, but I willed myself to climb the near vertical side until he could grab me. Then he easily hauled me up, rolling me over him.

The top was uneven and layered with broken bits of gravel. Lexander motioned for me to stay down so we wouldn't be noticed from below. With the hall fallen in, we could see the gate, where a mass of men were entering. They met with no resistance.

"Look," Lexander pointed. "There's the bishop."

The imposing cleric was in the lead, his head shaved in a white circle fringed with dark hair. He and a few other tonsured men were the only ones wearing long robes instead of armor. But the bishop carried a broadsword. He hefted it as if accustomed to the feel of a weapon in his hand. I could imagine him on the battle-field with the conqueror, blessing his troops and praying over the martyred dead.

The flames flickered between us as the warriors fanned through the manor. The slave hall caught fire, but I was reassured by the sight of the pleasure slaves, nearly indistinguishable from the servants in their bulky garments.

"What's going to happen to them, Lexander?"

"They'll be fine. They're certainly better off than under Ukerald." Lexander was retrieving a coil of rope from a crack in the top of the wall. "I stored this here in case we needed to escape."

He began to tie one end to a projecting stone. Outside the wall spread a marsh that was fogged in. The sounds of frogs and trickling water were comfortingly familiar.

Smoke shifted to briefly block my view of the manor beyond the hall. It also gave us a temporary reprieve, keeping the warriors from seeing us.

But through the swirling vapors, Olvid was dragged forward. Naked, she squatted down in front of the clerics. The bishop silenced everyone, shouting something that was lost in the crackle of the fire.

"You go first," Lexander urged.

"But Olvid—" I started to say.

The girl jerked and fell heavily to the ground. The warriors pulled back in trepidation. Several made the horned sign, warding off the demon that infested her. It wasn't her fault that Ukerald had cracked her skull so the evil could get in.

"Marja, we have to get away," Lexander insisted.

The bishop held his sword in both hands, pointing downward, as he raised his arms. Olvid was beneath him. He plunged the sword into Olvid's chest, pinning her to the ground. With a final heave, her writhing abruptly stopped.

"He . . . he . . ." I gasped.

Lexander pulled on my arm. "Come, Marja. Or we'll face the same fate."

I felt as if I were choking. Olvid had been spitted in cold blood. Just like Lexander had slain Ukerald and Drucelli. I went numb, unable to feel it all at once.

Lexander dragged me to the outer edge of the wall. There, I grabbed on to the rope, noting there were knots along its length. I swung my leg over the side, reaching for the knots with my feet. The rope was rough, and my knuckles scraped against the stones.

I could think of nothing but Olvid—I had left her behind. I should have brought her with us. I should have made sure all of the slaves were freed before the bishop arrived. Would they be killed like Olvid?

I wasn't paying enough attention because my feet slid off the rope, and before I could regain my footing, my hands slipped, too. I fell the rest of the way, slamming along the mortared stones until I landed with a soggy splat in the icy marsh.

9

The next thing I felt was a slight swaying. My head was spinning and my stomach lurched from its moorings.

"Marja!" Lexander murmured close to my ear. "Thank the gods you're awake. . . ."

I was being held against his chest, his arms around me. I moaned, trying to form words to beg him to stop rocking me. But as I swam to consciousness, I realized we were both moving. We were in a small boat.

"Hush, now, Marja. There are people nearby. We mustn't be seen."

I relaxed, realizing it would sicken me if I fought the motion. I was far too groggy to reach out to the sea spirits, but simply knowing I was supported by their embrace eased me.

There was a tangle of bare branches around us. We were deep in a thicket along the shore, lying on the floor of the boat, where nobody could see us. The water was just on the other side of the wooden plank beneath my hip.

At first I thought it was early morning. Then I remembered that Londinium was bathed in haze through much of the day. That reminded me of Becksbury and scenes too bloody to bear.

I shuddered, and Lexander stroked my hair, murmuring, "We're safe now, Marja. When you fell so hard and didn't wake up, I feared . . . but I couldn't take you to a healer. All they would do is bleed you, weakening you further."

There was a pleading edge to his voice, as if he needed to believe that I wasn't badly hurt. But I felt pain in far too many places.

"I carried you through that godforsaken swamp. I thought we'd never get out. The ships are still in dock, and we cannot wait any longer for the conqueror to clear the river. Only a rowboat can get through the Noromenn blockade, so that's what I bought. We'll make it through, Marja, I swear it."

Sometime later, Lexander began rowing, using his uncanny vision to see through the darkness. There was not an *olf* in sight to help light the way. After Becksbury, I wasn't sure if the *olfs* would ever come near Lexander again.

"Where are we?" I murmured.

Lexander shushed my questions, and the pounding in my head drowned out everything else.

It was wet, cold, and dark for too long. Then the boat shifted abruptly, shaken by waves from the encroaching sea. Lexander was riding the outgoing tide. The fog grew so heavy that it turned into cold needles of rain against my skin.

A huge beast reared out of the blackness. It took a few wild moments for me to realize it was a ship lit by a lantern. The prow was carved in the shape of a dragon leaping into the air, its wings spreading behind it. The square sail meant there were Noromenn onboard.

I choked back my instinctive cry of welcome. These were not the Noromenn of my homeland but Birgir's kin from the cold north.

Lexander strained to silently pull us away from the circle of light cast by the lantern. I held my breath, fearing the worst.

But we slipped into the darkness again. The splash of waves beat against their hull, and the voices of men echoed over the water. Sentries must have been posted to watch for movement upriver. Somehow, Lexander had evaded them.

The rocking finally ceased. I wakened slowly, lying in the water in the bottom of the boat and staring up at the slowly brightening sky. I was alone.

I struggled to sit up, my head throbbing painfully with every heartbeat. The boat was beached on a crescent curve of white sand backed by low dunes. The ground rose higher into a rugged bluff beyond, but the drifting fog partly obscured it.

"Danelaw," I murmured, realizing we had not gotten far in our escape. Then again, perhaps the entire length and breadth of the Auldland was blanketed in clouds.

I collapsed back, wrapping the sodden cloak around me. I was chilled through despite my wool tunic and leggings.

A shadowy form approached out of the fog. I thought it was Lexander at first, but this man had a heavier step. I hunched down in the boat.

"What ho?" the man called out.

I forced myself to sit up again, though the world spun around. I could hardly see his face leaning over me. But to my everlasting gratitude, two *olfs* were hovering at his shoulders, sending out sparks of welcome. Their curiosity was like a warm burst of reassurance.

I smiled regardless of the ache in my head. The *olfs* didn't flee from me despite the terror I had helped bring down on the people of Becksbury. "I'm so glad to see you," I murmured to them, sinking back down in the boat.

"I've not heard that before." The man let go of the heavy bag he was dragging across the sand. He spoke the Noromenn tongue, but his words were odd and slurred. "Are you sick?"

"I'm waiting for my . . . Lexander. He brought me here."

The man stood up, looking one way then another. "I don't see anyone nearby."

"He'll be back for me soon." I put my hand to my head, wondering if I should try to sit up again.

"I can't leave you here," he declared. "Let me carry you up to the village."

I fended off his hands, though I could tell from the *olfs* that his intent was pure. "No, I must wait for Lexander."

But I was as weak as a kitten and couldn't resist. He lifted me up from the boat as if I weighed nothing. "You'll catch your death lying in the water, lass."

A shout went up and I recognized Lexander's voice. "Unhand her!"

"That's him," I said.

The man hastily laid me down on the sand. There was something wrong with my belly, which made sitting quite impossible. There was also a problem with my right leg, which sent sharp pangs into my groin.

Lexander appeared while the stranger backed off, taking the *olfs* with him. They were clearly avoiding Lexander.

"She smiled at me," the stranger said softly.

"Don't worry," I told Lexander, wishing everything was not so blurry. "This man will help us."

Lexander looked over at the hulking, silent man. "Marja, are you sure?"

I whispered, "Ask him and see."

Lexander carried me gently, but even that was too much for me to bear. I woke next in a dark place, lying on a blanket. I could feel the prickles of straw beneath the ticking. My head was ringing and I was burning hot.

Then I realized Lexander was speaking to me. "Wake up and drink this, Marja. Remember what I told you about your body needing water."

I swallowed. Lexander sounded calmer, not so anxious and rushed. That was all I needed to know.

Then one morning the pain receded. There was still an ache in my head caused, I now discovered, by a tender lump above my ear. As I gingerly stretched my arms and legs, the sharpest pangs were now mostly caused by the stiffness of inactivity.

I rolled over and saw Lexander lying on a blanket on the ground. The fire behind him had burned to coals. His face was turned toward me, shadowed. The crude wooden walls were close around us and the ceiling was low.

Lexander was sleeping. I so rarely saw him asleep that I held very still, gazing at the strong lines of his smooth cheek and jaw. I longed to touch him, but I also wanted to savor the sight of him so utterly at peace.

He looked very different when he killed without hesitation, without remorse.

A slight sigh escaped me, and his eyes opened. He was instantly aware of everything around him. It was one of his inhuman traits, like his luminous amber eyes.

"You're awake." He pushed himself up, his hand stroking the hair from my face. "Thank the gods, Marja, for I feared I would lose you."

I could hardly raise my hand. "Perhaps the Otherworld was calling, but I couldn't leave you."

He bent his head to kiss my hand, cupping it with his own. He seemed to fear jostling me, for he was very careful.

"Where are we?" I asked, looking up at the baskets and bags hung from the low ceiling.

"Porter is letting us use his cot. He's sleeping on his brother's floor." Lexander got up to stir the fire and put on another log. "He would have given us food, too, if we had been in need. I've rewarded him handsomely for his aid."

"Porter?" The time since we had left Becksbury was oddly shadowed.

"The man who found you on the beach. His family are all glaziers. We were fortunate he was collecting sand that morning rather than firewood." Lexander checked a pot that was sitting next to the coals on the stone hearth, and then poured the heated water into a cup.

I remembered the man accompanied by two *olfs*. "He lifted me from the boat."

"Yes, we came ashore north of the river." Lexander sat down next to me on the bed. He held the cup. "I had intended to go south to the port town, where we could get passage to the Frankish lands, but Swegn and the currents prevailed, so we landed here."

He helped me sit up so I could drink. The liquid was thick with herbs and tasted nutty. I realized how much he had cared for me while I was ill.

"Thank you, Lexander," I murmured between sips.

He heard all that I intended in those words. "I could not let you go."

When I was finished, I felt so weak that it was a relief to lie back down. I watched Lexander move carefully about the tiny cot, preparing a meal and grinding up more herbs until I fell asleep again.

It wasn't long before I pleaded to be taken outside. I needed to escape the narrow, smoke-stained walls. So Lexander carried me into the courtyard and laid me wrapped in a blanket on a pile of straw the glaziers used to pack their bottles.

It was a perfect, clear day before autumn turned to winter, when the air was pleased to recall summer. I breathed deep, glad that I had insisted on release.

Now I could see everything I had heard from inside the cot. The rhythmic thumping of the bellows beat through the glaziers' compound, seeming to never cease. The heat rose with the clear smoke from the large clay furnace in the center of the yard. Orange and blue flickers through the air holes showed a fire that burned much hotter than any natural flame.

Porter was bent over, stoking the outdoor furnace to blast the quartz sand into glass. I knew it was him by the way the *olfs* gathered round. When he saw that Lexander had brought me out, he shucked his thick gloves and ran a hand over his hair. The strands looked more gray than muddy brown from the loose bits of ash.

"Good day, Porter." I smiled up at him, also acknowledging the *olfs* that hovered nearby.

Lexander was seated on a bench not far away, but he tilted his head to listen.

Porter seemed eager yet wary, as if accustomed to being rebuffed. "You are better now?" His words were slurred, perhaps because his upper lip was split in the middle like a cat's mouth. If it was an injury, it had long ago healed.

"Yes, I'm sorry to have taken your bed for so long. I'll soon give it back. Your hospitality has given me strength."

His smile was achingly sweet. " 'Tis not much, not near good enough, lass."

One of the *olfs* was darting at me, trying to snatch a thread that had come loose on the cuff of my tunic. The *olf* had a tiny face on a rather puffed-up head, which I thought was endearing. I pulled out a dark red thread and held it up. The *olf* plucked it from my fingers and sailed away with it.

Porter's eyes widened. "Gift givers are always rewarded."

"You can see the *olfs*?" I asked.

"Oh, I think most people can, lass, but they don't think on it much. That's why they offer the pinch of sugar or salt as regular as their own meals, and lay out the wards to keep the mischief away."

I nodded. "So I've seen in my homeland."

Porter suddenly smiled. " 'Tis sure to be true everywhere. But I know only this—the *olfs* do brighten my day."

With that, he returned to the furnace. Most of the *olfs* went with him. They avoided the bench where Lexander sat, and I could tell they had not come into the cot because of him. It saddened me, but I was relieved they had no wish to avoid me.

I watched Porter work hard all day, cutting wood and pitching it into the bottom of the furnace with an expert eye. There was a brisk efficiency about the glass making. Inside a long shed, the two brothers used metal rods to blow the glass over the smaller hearths. They spun the molten globs, forming them into blue, green, and yellow bulbs. The bottles were cooled and stored on shelves until they were packed in crates filled with straw. Some of the *olfs* dived into the bottles, making them glow in brilliant colors. They delighted in leaping through the airholes, shooting through the furnace and out the top vents.

The *olfs* gathered round that evening when Porter opened the upper chamber of the furnace. He had transformed a pile of sparkling white sand into runnels of cloudy glass. While he collected the glass into a basket, the brothers retired to their houses at the end of the courtyard. I had heard their wives and children on the other side of the fence, tending the garden, pulling water from the well, and feeding the hens.

It was an ideal place for me to heal. The weather was mild, so I stayed outside as much as I could. It wasn't long before I knew everyone's name. They were artisans, much like my da. Their love of glass was infectious, but I needed little encouragement to admire the rows of brilliant bottles. Their invalid father took to hobbling over to my straw bed to talk about the craft, making the bottles in the air with his trembling, knobby hands.

Porter's mouth was shaped such that he couldn't blow through the pipe to form the glass. He did the hard work, carrying loads of firewood on his back morning and night, and hauling large bags of sand up the bluff from the beach. He pounded the dye to dust so his brothers could mix it with the remelted glass. I never heard Porter complain. He usually hummed to the *olfs*, going about his work. But occasionally I saw him stare at the bottles lit up by the playing *olfs,* and his expression was wistful.

One evening Porter came over and silently held something out. It was a globule of glass, a perfect oval, with swirls of white within. The bottom was slightly flattened and rough from the bricks it had rested on as it cooled.

"Ohh . . ." I exclaimed as he gave it to me. It felt slippery in my hand. "How beautiful!"

"The *olfs* carry off the tiny beads of glass," he explained. "But a big one like this doesn't happen very often." He smiled shyly. "Keep it, lass."

I reclined back in the straw—I was still as weak as a baby and could barely rise from the cot with Lexander's support. As Porter returned to the furnace, Lexander came over and sat down next to me. "It's time we talked about what happened in Becksbury, Marja."

I pushed myself up. "Yes, it's been preying on me, Lexander. We shouldn't have left the slaves behind. Olvid should be here with us now, alive."

Lexander slowly nodded. "This is why you can't come with me. You can't accept what must be done to destroy the houses."

I stared at him. "Are you going to tie me up and run away again?"

"No." He shook his head. "I need you to understand why I have to go on alone."

"Go where?" I demanded. "We should return to Londinium to help those poor slaves."

"It's too late. We'd never find them, Marja, and it's more likely we'd be discovered by the bishop's clerics. Do you think he'd hesitate to run *you* through with his sword? And me, as well. You can't even consider it."

I heard the finality in his tone. Lexander would not go back. Perhaps it was too dangerous, but Olvid's horrid death would haunt me forever. As would the fates of Matteus, Barissa, Rimbert, and the other slaves. I should have thought more of them, and less of simply following Lexander's lead.

"Marja, you almost died," he pointed out. "You're not strong enough for this, and I need to know that you're not in danger. I need to know you're not being beaten or raped. Is that too much to ask?"

"Someone could be raping Barissa right now. You didn't even try to save her."

"Believe me, Barissa can take care of herself." His wry tone reminded me of the bite marks he had left on her neck. "I do feel sorry for those slaves, Marja. Ukerald was loathsome. But the important thing is that they aren't suffering under him anymore."

"You gave me a chance to be free, Lexander. They deserved that chance, too."

Porter turned to look as my voice rang louder with determination. Lexander lifted me up and carried me back inside the cot to avoid the glazier's curious gaze. He sat on the bed, cradling me in his lap.

"I can wait no longer for you to recover," he told me. "The ship from Stanbulin could reach Londinium any day. My name is too clearly tied to what happened there. I must act now before the training masters realize I was the cause of both catastrophes and warn the pleasure houses against me."

I didn't want to let go of him. I thought if I just held on, he could not leave me behind. "You can't go without me, Lexander. It's not right. I'll be able to travel soon. I can feel it."

"You can't walk a dozen steps alone. Porter has promised to take care of you, and I have paid the glaziers well for it." Lexander tried to summon a smile. "Don't tell me you're not contented here. It's the best place for you to winter while you fully recover. I'll return in the spring, after I've destroyed a few more houses."

I wanted to rail at him, to make him see that the slaves needed my help.

But before I could protest, he touched my lips with his finger. Through his caress, I could feel him silently pleading with me, opening his sore heart to show me how much he loved me. He'd suffered untold agonies when I was tortured by his people.

But his touch revealed more than he realized: a dark, driving force buried deep inside of him, the thing that drove his killing rampage and excluded me at every turn.

I knew there was nothing I could say that would stop him.

He kissed the tears sliding down my cheek, holding me gently as if fearing how fragile I was. I had no desire to raise my lips to him.

"You deny me even a kiss?" Lexander asked, hurt by my rejection.

"I can't bid you farewell," I cried. "You're abandoning me, Lexander."

He laid me down on the bed, as tenderly as he always did. "This is a safe place for you to stay. I'll return for you as soon as I can, Marja."

10

Lexander gave me one lingering look, and then left. At first I thought he was coming back, that I would have another chance to convince him before he finished making the arrangements for his departure. But through the open door I watched the shadows in the yard lengthen in growing dread.

A curious *olf* was playing with a bag left on the tiny hearthstone. When it plucked out a coin and darted off, giggling, I realized Lexander had left the purse behind for me. It must have come from the goods Drucelli had packed before Lexander had killed her. He had planned this well.

My tears of frustration burned through me. In that moment something inside of me died; in truth, I could trust no one. I had only myself to rely on.

I had failed Olvid and the others because I had let Lexander make all the decisions in Becksbury. I should have made sure the slaves would be safely whisked away when the bishop arrived. From now on nobody, not even Lexander, was going to stop me.

It took far too long to stagger through the glaziers' compound to reach the top of the bluff. Once there, it was impossible for me to climb the trail down to the beach. I could barely see the village farther down the bluff, a cluster of peaked roofs behind a stone wall.

I waited for a long time, hoping Lexander would appear on the curve of beach below. But there was nothing but the wind and the fresh salty smell of the sea.

Porter eventually found me on the bluff and carried me back to the cot.

I could not leave my bed the next day because of my venture. But I concentrated on soaking up the healing glow from the *olfs*, and I drank the herb mixture Lexander had left for me every morning and evening. Porter brought me food and water at regular intervals, and supported me in walking about so I could get stronger.

All the while, I kept hoping Lexander would appear. It had happened too fast. He had run away rather than face me. Porter admitted that Lexander had asked if I could stay soon after we arrived. The glaziers' welcoming took on a new light when I realized they expected me to spend several moons with them.

I longed to return to Londinium to help Rimbert and the other slaves. But I had lain sick for so long that they were likely already scattered, bought by new masters or killed by the bishop once he realized they had been trained for seduction. There seemed little I could do to redeem my mistakes.

Lexander was surely going to Montplaire in the Frankish lands, where Drucelli had once been mistress. The only other house I knew of was in Veneto, somewhere in the Auldland. The Frankish lands were just across the strait, so that was my destination.

Porter soon brought word from the village that the long-awaited battle had taken place between King Swegn and the conqueror. The Noromenn had skirmished with the Frankish warriors in their boats just outside Londinium. On their retreat, Swegn's men had raided the homesteads along the river, taking supplies. Much of what they stole belonged to Noromenn settlers, which didn't help their cause. It was said the Noroships had departed for their cold northern homeland, and the conqueror was firmly in control of Danelaw at least for the winter.

Now I wouldn't have to sneak through an armada of Noromenn to reach the port town south of the river. The glaziers didn't own a boat, so I decided that the village was the best place to look for passage.

On market day when the glaziers prepared their bottles to be sold, I helped the eldest brother's wife pack the bottles into crates filled with straw. She showed me the trick of how to properly cushion the glass so none would break. Her two sons were not yet old enough to be trusted with the bottles, but they hung about the cart, their eyes huge.

Porter's brother, Daakon, came out to help us load the crates onto a handcart. Porter arrived smeared with black soot from cleaning the rendering oven. Daakon was wearing a fine tunic made of hunter-green wool with striped *braies*. He shook his head at his brother but didn't bother to reprove him. My older brothers had given me that same look when I had returned dirty and unkempt after a long day in the fens.

Porter noticed I was watching the antics of the *olfs* as they jostled for a spot on the handcart, and we exchanged a secret smile. I'd never seen him without an *olf*. Daakon didn't pay any attention to them.

Porter leaned his weight into the crossbar to pull the cart over a sandy path. The village of Ry was situated on top of the bluff at its highest point. The *olfs* swung from the rails of the cart, bouncing up and down during the bumpy ride.

I had to cling to the rail to keep from falling down in exhaustion. The village wasn't far, but it exceeded my strength.

Porter gave me an anxious look. "No need to tire yourself out, lass." He urged me onto the cart so I could ride at my ease. It appeared my weight hardly slowed him.

Our path met the main road into the village. We joined others from outlying homesteads and passed through the open gates. The town wall was made of stone, but most of the structures within were of rough-hewn wood. Each house had its own plank fencing around their sheds and barns. These folks must have suffered generations of raids and incursions—first the Noromenn, and more recently the Frankish invaders.

The road forked between the houses. Porter plunged straight ahead, dragging the wood-wheeled cart over the rocks that were embedded in the road.

"It's like a miniature Londinium," I exclaimed. Structures lined both sides of the road, some split in half with workshops and living quarters side by side. One long building housed a smith who was making bolts and hinges. The glow of the flames reminded me of the glaziers, but their compound was much larger. Likely the village had refused to allow the huge rendering furnace within their walls for fear of the fire spreading.

The talk I overheard mostly concerned the conqueror and the purges he was making among the leading families who had supported the Noroking. There was a new Frankish *jarl* who had been given a vast tract of land that included the village Ry. Many feared they would be forced to pay another tithe.

Porter pulled the cart into a dirt square next to a small Kristna sanctuary. There were a number of ramshackle booths and other carts selling their wares.

"Do you need to worship?" Daakon asked gruffly. "They're about to begin."

"You mean Kristna? No, he is not my god."

Daakon shrugged. "I say fire and the birth mother are the only two powers worth praise. They are stronger than any god fashioned in the form of a man."

He turned to help a merchant who was interested in bottles of various shapes and sizes. Porter grinned at me. The split in his upper lip was less noticeable when he was happy. I knew he would not accept the Kristna god inside of him. He could never forsake the *olfs*.

When his transaction with the merchant was completed, I asked Daakon, "Where might I go to find passage to the port town?"

"Why?" Porter protested. "You're staying the winter with us."

"No, I've recovered much faster than Lexander expected." That was certainly the truth, though not all of it. "I need to get to the Twelve Towns of Lutece."

"Now, there's no need to be hasty," Daakon cautioned, no doubt thinking of the rich payment Lexander had given him for my winter board.

"I'm leaving," I said simply. "And if you help me find passage to the port town, you can keep all the coins Lexander gave you."

Comprehension dawned as Daakon realized the amount he would save by not having to feed me for several moons.

But Porter was concerned. "You're very ill, lass. You should still be in bed, not pitched about in a boat."

"I'm well enough," I insisted. "I just need to get to the port town."

"That's fine by me," Daakon declared, glad to be quit of me with so little bother. "Go find a rowboat you can rent for the day, Porter. You can take her yourself." Under his brother's stern eye, Porter was forced to agree.

On my last evening in the cot, Porter handed me a bundle. "I got this for you today."

I opened it to find a gorgeous spill of fine felted wool. The cloth was woven of blue and black threads, with flecks of gray. I held it up and found it was a dress with long flared sleeves and a pretty neckline. The girdle was a knotted black cord strung with shell beads.

"It's beautiful!" I exclaimed.

"I thought you'd rather dress as a woman than a boy."

I remembered how the villagers in the market had stared at my tunic and leggings. Women in Danelaw always wore long skirts.

It was a thoughtful gift, and I couldn't help but consider my bene-factor. Porter was kind and a good provider. He was also quite strong from his hard work. I couldn't understand why a sturdy man like him didn't have a wife.

"Why are you unmarried, Porter?"

He shifted uncomfortably on his stool. I felt a pang of regret—

likely it involved some sort of heartache. What if his wife had died in childbirth?

"Forgive me," I said hastily.

"No matter. After all, what woman would want me thus?" he muttered, gesturing to his face.

I didn't understand for a moment, and then I realized he was speaking of his split lip. "Surely the girls here are not so blind."

He turned his head away. "Now you're teasing me, lass. Besides, what do I have to give a woman? This cot? A wife needs a proper home that she can be mistress of."

I remembered the neat timber and wattle structures in the village. Porter's brothers each had a house with hearths and lofts for sleeping.

It wasn't fair. Porter worked ceaselessly for so little. I had seen enough to know how separated he was from everyone else. He watched his young nieces and nephews play with a heart-wrenching expression. And he treated his brothers' wives with the same delicate respect as the glass bottles that he couldn't create.

"Surely you've had chances, Porter. A dalliance with a girl that didn't work out?"

"No, I've never . . ." he said hesitantly.

"Never what?"

He took a deep breath. "I've not kissed a woman."

My eyes widened at the implications of that. "You haven't?"

His fingers touched his mouth in a self-conscious way. He didn't have to say it—he thought it was enough reason for women to avoid him.

I went over and stood before him. It made him uneasy to have me so close. I put my hands on his shoulders as he sat on his bed.

"Look at me, Porter," I told him.

It took an effort, but he raised his head. His longing spoke louder than words—he desired me, but he struggled against it. I understood his connection with the *olfs* like no other, and our growing rapport meant everything to him.

"Listen to the *olfs*," I told him. "They see more clearly than anyone else, and they adore you."

I leaned down and kissed him. He tried to pull back in surprise,
but I held on to his shoulders. I caressed his lips with my own,
lightly, tenderly, wanting nothing else but to give him pleasure. He
responded, tentatively at first, then more eagerly.

When I had kissed him thoroughly I drew back to smile. His mild
eyes were shining.

Olfs were popping inside the cot, responding to our burst of exhilaration. He pulled me down onto the bed so we were sitting together.

"That's even better than I thought it would be," Porter said with
a sigh.

He made no move to kiss me again, but his hands were holding
on to mine tightly. Through our touch, his lifetime of longing flooded
me. He was always watching, forever alone. Porter was too kind to be
served that fate.

I leaned forward to kiss him again, more hungrily this time. I felt
his need and responded to him as naturally as I breathed. I wanted
him. How could I not? He had courage and strength to spare, and had
faced his struggles in the spirit of true acceptance. In that, we were
kindred spirits.

My hand caressed his face, and I felt him moan under my mouth.
He was breathing fast when I finally pulled away.

I couldn't help but feel his intent—he wanted more than one
night's pleasure. He was well on his way to falling in love with me.
It would be too cruel for me to bed him and leave tomorrow. Too
cruel . . .

Porter abruptly stood up and made his way to the door. "I'm so
grateful to you," he said brokenly.

"As I am to you," I reminded him.

He finally looked back, and his shy smile was sad. He did not return to the cot that night.

———

The next morning I put on the blue dress Porter had given me. When I stepped into the compound in the pearly morning light, his gaze lingered. Now that my eyes were opened, his adoration was clear.

But Porter was not like Lexander. He knew I had to leave; he could feel my resolve through the *olfs*.

It took him a few moments before he could speak. "I hope you find Lexander."

I wasn't going to explain my real purpose in going to Montplaire. "If I don't, then I'll be back next spring. That's when Lexander said he would return."

Porter seemed inordinately comforted to hear that. "Come back even if you do find him, Marja."

I silently gave Porter the purse with most of the coins Lexander had left behind. Porter had seen the pretty embroidered bag, but he seemed surprised at how heavy it was.

"Build yourself a house," I told him, pressing the purse into his hands. "Take a wife of your own. Choose the girl you want and go get her. Do you understand, Porter?"

He was bewildered by my insistence. He tried to give the purse back to me, but I left it on the bed. I had enough coins to reach Montplaire, and this small fortune would transform his life. It was what I should have done for the Becksbury slaves. I could almost see Porter tenderly caring for Olvid and giving her a comfortable home in spite of her illness. But I had spoiled that chance.

I tried not to let Porter see how winded I was by our walk down to the beach, even with him carrying my meager bundle of tunic and leggings. They reminded me of the Becksbury slaves, and at the last moment I couldn't bear to leave them behind.

Porter turned out to be quite competent with the small boat he had rented from a villager, deftly using the oars to maneuver us beyond the breakers. He rowed steadily down the coastline with the *olfs* drifting along with us. One *olf* hardly bigger than my hand clung to the oar the entire time, going up and down as Porter rowed.

At times I could see the marshy shore, while at others we were lost in a sea of gray. My rough leather cloak protected me from the clammy cold, but Porter stoically shrugged off the weather as mild.

I trailed my hand in the water, communing with the sea spirits. I held nothing back this time, pouring out everything that had happened in Becksbury, my own failures and my lingering illness. They felt my despair over Lexander's betrayal. I had forgiven him once before, but how could I ever trust him again?

We finally sighted our destination; a brown smear through the fog. Porter spoke so low that I almost couldn't hear him. "The *olfs* will show me what you do, Marja."

The thought of it warmed me. Though Porter would never go farther from Ry, he would be watching over my shoulder.

Porter beached the rowboat on the sandy shore above the town. I would have to walk downriver to reach the docks where the big ships were moored. There were people about, dragging out small fishing boats or lugging crates up to the carts on the road.

"You stay here," I told Porter. "Someone will take the boat if you leave it."

He glanced at the unsavory men who were loitering about. "You shouldn't go alone."

"I'll be fine," I assured him. I kept my battered hood up and my cloak closed. The bubble of glass Porter had given me was tucked into one corner of the bundle.

"Your house should be built by spring," I reminded him.

I looked back a few times to give him a wave of reassurance. The *olfs* stayed near him, bouncing among the boats. Porter stood watching me until I could see him no longer.

The port town was decrepit, the battered docks falling into the water. The houses were mere sheds patched with crate tops and driftwood. I passed three ale shops in a row filled with shipmasters and their crews jostling, drinking, and braying with exuberance at being on land.

By dint of asking everyone along the way, I found a passenger ferry waiting to cross the strait to the Frankish lands. But I wasn't allowed onboard because it was already overfull. People were sitting and lounging everywhere on deck, having waited for days for the weather to change.

I could find no other ships setting out for the Frankish lands, so I sat on a crate near the bow of the passenger ferry, hoping someone would give up and leave. I was determined to find passage.

When darkness fell, the situation on the ferry remained unchanged. The lantern on the bow burned a sickly yellow. I pulled my hood far over my face and huddled back against a wall where I could see the ship. It drizzled during the night, soaking the waterfront. Under the cloak, I wrapped my arms around my knees to try to keep warm. It was impossible to sleep.

When dawn broke with a muggy, gray light, my vigilance was not rewarded. Soon the ferry greeted the rising wind by pulling up its sails and tossing away the mooring ropes. I ran forward to try to bargain with the shipmaster, calling, "I'll give you every coin I have!"

But the ferry was overloaded already from the long wait. I was forced to stand there and watch them sail away.

11

On the wharf nearby, an old man with a round, creased face was coiling the mooring rope. He'd seen me haunting the ferry from his post in a large wooden box. There was barely enough room for him to sit inside and wait for ships to arrive. He chuckled quietly to himself at my dilemma.

"Tell me there's another ship crossing the strait," I said plaintively.

"No'um. You'll get to Frank faster by walking to Dorster. It's two days south on the coast. Most ships ply the strait from there."

I watched the *olfs* gaily swinging from the mooring ropes and masts, but it didn't make me feel any better. Certainly I could walk to Dorster, though there would be dangers on the road. The *olfs* would help me as they had when I had crossed Fjardemano Island to Brianda.

But there might be a faster way.

I had noticed an impressive two-masted ship down the wharf. It had the full-bellied look of a merchant vessel, and the hull was freshly painted. The foremast was nearly as long as the main and raked forward over the bow.

I'd seen the shipmaster going back and forth, speaking Frankish to his men. He was beardless and finely dressed, unlike most people on the waterfront. The short cut of his tunic and broadsword were of the warrior clan, yet there were several jewels set in his buckle and his cloak was lined with dark fur. He wore only black, and his appearance was somber despite his show of wealth.

"What about that ship?" I asked the old man.

The old man got a gleam in his eye as if he could read my mind. "She's carrying wool cloth. She crosses the strait once she's loaded with supplies. All the way to the Twelve Towns of Lutece."

The Montplaire pleasure house was in Lutece, far upriver in the heart of the Frankish lands. This fast merchant ship would likely reach the Twelve Towns within a few days. Lexander could hardly reach Montplaire that fast. Surely I would get there in time to make sure the slaves were taken care of.

I thanked the old man and wandered toward the merchant ship. The shipmaster was not in sight. The crew was busy unloading barrels from a cart drawn up on the wharf, then lowering them one by one through a hatch in the middle of the deck.

Olfs played among them, making the barrels swing until they bounced against the sides of the hatch. The crewmen swore and struggled to control their cargo. Then a youth who was already browned and wind-creased despite his tender age appeared with a handful of porridge oats, which he tossed onto the deck. The *olfs* jumped onto the bait, but the boy acted as if he couldn't see them. The crew laughed at him, but their loading went smoother after that.

When they were finished, two crewmen climbed down the rope ladder hung over the side. I pushed back my hood as the last one went by. "Pardon me," I said, using the Frankish words the *olfs* had helped me pick out of the patterns of speech. "Does this ship take passengers?"

"No," he replied, startled. Had I spoken the Frankish incorrectly? He hurried away, talking rapidly to the other two, who turned to look back at me.

Coins alone would apparently not be enough to get me onboard. But I had other things to barter. I started down the wharf to find a place to loosen my hair and clean my face.

But the shipmaster was coming toward me. The crewmen were right behind him. He had a purposeful air as if readying to leave. The shipmaster was asking about the cart of barrels that had just been unloaded.

As they approached, I pushed my cloak over my shoulders, revealing my clinging blue dress. "May I speak to you, Shipmaster?"

The shipmaster paused, but he waved the others on. They climbed the rope ladder with brisk efficiency meant to impress him.

"Yes, what is it?" His shrewd, dark eyes took my measure. We were nearly of a same height; he was powerful yet compact. His short hair stood up stiffly from the salt in the air.

"I must go to the Twelve Towns, and I'm told that's your port of call—"

"I don't take passengers," he interrupted, and tried to brush past me.

I stepped into his path. "I won't presume to offer coins to a man of your stature. But I can give you pleasure as you've never known before and my sincerest gratitude for conveying me to Lutece."

"Is this a jest?" he sneered. "Where are your people? You're not from here, not with that accent. Are you Frankish?"

"No," I said with a laugh, glad that I had confounded him. "I am from very far away, the western maritime lands across the ocean. I will tell you everything if you take me with you."

His eyes narrowed. "What kind of woman sells herself for passage?"

I shrugged slightly, moving my bosom enticingly. "I spent a moon last summer with a merchant prince and his wife, pleasuring them in exchange for transport. Besides," I added more seriously, "from the looks of that ferry, I would probably be raped by the crew or passengers. I would rather choose my partner and make it an agreeable journey for us both."

"I think a pretty maid makes for a nice trap, yes?" He returned to his ship, waving to a man on the forecastle. "Prepare to depart."

The shipmaster started up the rope ladder, and I followed right on his heels. "There's no harm I could do you. Indeed, I am the one at risk—for I'll be at your mercy. But I must get to Lutece right away."

He swung his legs over the railing, and then stood on the deck glaring down at me. I thought he was going to order me off the ladder.

I clung to the ropes, defying him to shake me off. I sensed this man wanted intensity. My urgent need resonated with something in him, whereas it would have made a milder man too wary.

The shipmaster stepped aside. He didn't smile as I climbed up, but I did. I stood against the sterncastle, keeping back as the crew hoisted the foresail to turn their great ship away from the dock.

They worked together with precision, and the ship was marvelously responsive. I could feel the delight of the sea spirits in the way she moved. I was thrilled to be off to Montplaire with so little effort.

I was surprised when two *olfs* stayed with the ship. They made it their home, which certainly boded well for me.

The crew also seemed quite cheery at their work. They slept in the two neat cabins in the stern that were lined with bunks. The forecastle covered the shipmaster's cabin. I was taken there by the shipmaster as soon as the main sail was hauled up and we were well on our way across the strait. The shipmaster sent his first mate to the top of the mast to keep watch for raiders.

I followed him down five steps into a triangular chamber with curved wooden walls and a low ceiling. A table hung from the hull on one side, and the bed on the other. The movement of the ship felt more pronounced under the deck.

One of the *olfs* followed us and amused itself by swinging on the unlit lantern. The *olf* had too many fingers and toes, and when it smiled, it also had too many teeth. I grinned back at it.

The shipmaster crossed his arms and examined me. "Now tell me why it's so urgent that you reach the Twelve Towns."

I could see him through the prism of the *olf's* eyes and could hear his need. This man had to be in absolute control. He would reject any attempts to manipulate him.

So I gave him honesty, as far as I could. "I am going to meet my lover. I had a bad fall and was ill, so I stayed with a friend. I recovered sooner than we thought, so I'm going to Lutece to meet him."

The shipmaster didn't believe me; he couldn't conceive that I would reveal my honest motive so easily. "Curious way of journeying to your lover, by giving yourself to another man."

"He trained me to please others when he was my master. But then he freed me, so now it is my own choice whom I please."

"Who is this man?" he demanded.

I didn't have to consider it. "A warrior."

"Whom does he serve? What nation is he from?"

"He serves no man," I said simply. "And he has not told me the name of his homeland."

The shipmaster was growing more suspicious, as if I presented a puzzle that he must unravel.

I could talk until my throat was raw, but nothing I said would convince him. And, in truth, it mattered not. We were on our way across the strait.

I yawned, having not slept since I left with Porter to journey to the port town. I eyed the bed longingly. "May I lie down? I sat in the rain all night waiting to get onto the ferry."

The shipmaster frowned, but he saw no reason to object. He nodded to the bed, taking a seat in the wooden chair. It was low to the floor so it wouldn't tip with the motion of the boat, and he stretched his legs out. The only light came through the small round portal over the table and in the door.

I removed my cloak and lay down on the bed. Overcome by exhaustion, I fell asleep, unconcerned by the shipmaster's speculative gaze.

I dreamed that I was rutting with the shipmaster, his forceful eyes staring into mine as we moved together. My hands were on his shoulders, pushing him away, but my fingertips dug in, wanting to pull him closer. It was pure sensation, without thought or feeling.

I came awake, but it was happening still. I was gasping as my eyes opened. My hands pushed at his shoulders, with the shipmaster on top of me rubbing his rigid *tarse* against my groin. My skirt was hiked up around my waist. Instinctively I lifted my hips, feeling him more fully. He was naked.

With our bodies grinding together, intensified by my dream, I was bathed in a burning heat. His eyes were defiant as he entered me, taking what he wanted, watching me closely. I shuddered over and over, accepting the ecstasy he gave me.

When he was through, he rolled away quickly. I lay limp on the soft bedding.

The shipmaster slipped on his black leggings, giving me a good look at him. His chest was lean but wiry, nearly as dark as his tanned face. It was difficult to tell how old he was—his third or fourth decade? He pulled on a white under-blouse, then his black tunic to cover it.

His expression was serious. "Are you satisfied?"

"Yes," I answered simply. He had taken me in a sneak attack, but I had enjoyed it too much to be upset. I was no timid bride that needed wooing, and I had made my bargain with him freely.

He waited as if he expected something more, but I had nothing else to say.

So he left in a gust of cold wind, carefully latching the door behind him. Outside he called for the crew, his words lost in the flapping of the sails and the relentless creaking of the hull.

I lay back, content to doze in bed. I had not asked his name, nor he mine.

It was extremely windy and cold during our passage across the strait. I mostly stayed in the cabin as there was no need for me to do anything. The crew praised the sea spirits and gave abundant sacrifices to the movement of life around them.

While the *olfs* kept watch for the shipmaster's return, I carefully examined the contents of his chests and caskets. In one was a razor, comb, and silver scissors. In a small bag were some coins and a couple of weights for weighing them. I put his possessions back exactly where I found them.

When we reached the Frankish lands and sailed into the wide river, the frigid wintry blasts were somewhat tempered. I sat on the forecastle, where few of the crew ventured, watching the banks and fields pass by. Even with midwinter fast approaching, the grass and leaves were emerald green. But the dismal rain was cold, eventually driving me back inside again.

The shipmaster took me whenever he wanted to, always without warning. I think he was trying to catch me off guard, to see if I was vulnerable in some way. I wasn't sure if he would have pounced on me if I faltered, or never touched me again. Regardless, his demands called out my submissive tendencies, and I was content to please him.

Indeed, the shipmaster did not understand me, and that fascinated him. He asked me questions at odd moments, very quickly, as if trying to catch me in deception. I kept only the names of Lexander and Vidaris secret and answered everything else without hesitation—from my childhood on the fens to my life as a pleasure slave, as well as the aid I gave Silveta in reclaiming my homeland from Birgir. He seemed to think I was spinning an elaborate fantasy for him, and was even more determined to discover the truth. But I wanted nothing more from him than a safe journey to Lutece.

When we reached the first of the Twelve Towns situated in the curve of the river, the banks were reinforced by stone walls rising out of the water. The flow widened out to become a lake, and one of the towns perched on an island in the center.

I expected us to dock to unload the cargo. I had stayed away from the hatches, knowing that any curiosity in that quarter would alarm the shipmaster. But the anchor was lowered and a rowboat was dropped over the side to take the shipmaster to deal with the port officials. There were a number of empty docks waiting.

The shipmaster had been possessive that morning, stroking my hair as I helped buckle his boots and holding my chin as he gazed at me. I had grown concerned about getting away from him. If he locked me in the cabin, his crew would certainly not interfere. I would have to hope someone heard my cries for help onshore and took pity on me—which was unlikely at best.

So I prepared myself and was waiting on the forecastle when the shipmaster returned in the rowboat. As he climbed up the rope ladder onto the deck, the crew readied to put into dock. They pulled up the anchor and lifted the sails, slowly turning toward the bank.

The shipmaster gestured for me to come down. He was accustomed to my obedience, so when I stayed on the forecastle he called to me, thinking I had misunderstood him. I turned away and went to the railing.

The shipmaster started up the wooden steps. His forehead was creased and his lips compressed as if he were prepared to face down a storm. I knew he intended to lock me up.

I unhooked the girdle, letting the shell beads tinkle as they fell to the deck. Then I leaped over the side of the ship.

The shock of the cold water was like a blow. I was instantly dragged under by my heavy skirts, and was afraid I'd made a terrible mistake.

I opened my hand, releasing the glass bubble Porter had given me. I silently pleaded with the river spirits to help me.

The spirits accepted my sacrifice, and with their aid, I slipped the dress over my head. Without the fabric weighing me down, I was free. Around my waist was tied an oilskin bag pilfered from the shipmaster's cabin that contained my slave tunic and leggings.

I burst to the surface with an agonized gasp. The ship was moving, but it hadn't gone far. The crew was rushing about on the deck looking for me. I dived down again. The spirits fair sped me along, and after a few more breaths, I was out of sight.

I spotted the shore, and struck off. The river spirits were beneath me, holding me up even as my limbs stiffened from the cold water. It was not the ending with the shipmaster that I had hoped for. But it had been worth the sacrifice.

12

I came ashore in the first of the Twelve Towns of Lutece. The houses were as compact as the Frankish people. The neat structures flowed up the hillside from the stone buttressing along the riverbanks. I asked a passerby how to reach Montplaire, and was pleased to discover that I had come to the right bank.

It was a fair walk upriver, through woods and past several mountainous hills until I reached my destination. I kept a watch out for the shipmaster because he knew I was going to Montplaire. But I doubted he would pursue me. My plunge into the river must have shown him I would not be taken easily.

After a serpentine walk up the hill, I came to a one-lane village lined by cottages, a few shops, and animal pens. Dotting the distant hillsides around us were the imposing stone buildings of manors. Unlike Danelaw, there weren't many walls here, mostly low stacks of stones strung along the pastures to keep the cattle in.

It was surpassingly lovely under the brilliant blue sky. Yet I dreaded that I would come upon a site of destruction like Becksbury or Vidaris.

I asked the way from a goose girl who was following her fat flock, brandishing a staff. She pointed carelessly up the lane, acting very much as if she was accustomed to directing strangers to Montplaire.

I climbed through another vineyard to some open pasturage. Crossing a slight rise, I saw a massive house. A tiny arched window under the eaves indicated there were three floors, and the sides were so tall that they were buttressed. Imposing trees grew next to it, nearly concealing a few smaller stone structures. The manor had a well-tended air, as if the land had been manicured by hand for generations, with each plant and furrow in place.

The friendly Frankish *olfs* were happy to obscure me from sight as I walked around the manor. I circled the great house, examining it from every vantage point. The orchards and fields rolled gently away from the house. Slender evergreens formed spires here and there in the meadows, while trees filled the dales. The fields lay fallow, the dirt rich and crumbling.

I saw no sign of Lexander. Either he had been delayed on his way here, or I had traveled much faster than him. Or he wasn't coming to Montplaire, but had decided to go to a different pleasure house.

Regardless, I would have to place myself among the slaves to find a way for us to escape the house together. I went straight to the great double doors and pulled on the bell cord. When the servant answered, I requested to see her mistress.

The servant led me into an imposing room. The house was even grander on the inside. I tried not to step on the tapestries woven in red, green, and purple patterns that were laid on the floor. The stone walls were packed with mortar and plastered until the surface was smooth.

From the luxurious furnishings to the fire crackling in the enormous wall hearth, it was very different from the dark, drafty hall in Becksbury. Several archways led to other parts of the house. The thickness of the walls was apparent in the wide, arched window at one end.

The tapping of heels sounded down one corridor. The mistress appeared, her fine, blond hair brushed straight back and cut severely at the nape of her neck. She had high cheekbones and full lips, like Lexander, and her eyes were an unusual silvery gray, full of sparkles.

"Yes?" she asked politely.

I would have to avoid all mention of Lexander to keep from getting our stories tangled. "My name is Marja, and I was sent by the Becksbury house in Londinium. There's been great unrest and our manor was set afire." I sounded properly frightened, as any slave would. "The *huscarl* sent me here to tell you—the master and mistress are dead."

The mistress's surprise was evident. One thing was certain: she had not heard of the fate of Becksbury.

"What happened?" she asked.

Her question gave me the impression that she was younger than other godlings I'd met.

"I know nothing but what the *huscarl* told me," I declared. If my threadbare tale contradicted Lexander's, I could always claim the *huscarl* had been mistaken. "He gave me coins so I could journey here." I untied the hem of my tunic and handed her my money. Thanks to the shipmaster, I had not spent a penny.

The mistress jingled the coins anxiously from one palm to the other. She was likely considering that she would have to notify Stanbulin of my news. Finally, she said, "You're a loyal slave to come all that way alone. Most would have taken the money and run away. Who were your masters?"

"Master Ukerald and Mistress Drucelli."

She grew doubtful again. "I never imagined Ukerald could inspire such devotion."

I froze. She knew Ukerald. I would have to tread very carefully. "I do as my master says," I declared. I rubbed my thigh slightly where it had been marked by the cane.

Her eyes narrowed.

"Very well, I'll take you upstairs," she agreed. "You may call me Canille."

The mistress took me down the corridor to another wing of the house and up an impressive wooden staircase. The large room was as fine as the first. The high ceiling was supported by a row of fat wooden beams. There was another wall hearth and the floor was tiled in terra-cotta squares. Several long tables were occupied by young men and women.

A tall, spare man was talking about the Noromenn and their settlements in a singsong tone. I'd grown fluent in the Frankish tongue under the shipmaster's constant questioning, and could easily understand.

Canille announced, "I must speak to you at once, Etien."

Etien scowled at the interruption, but he did as she requested. Only when he approached did I realize he was the master. His smooth head was hidden under a velvet cap, but his strong-boned face and mesmerizing eyes betrayed him.

The master and mistress left the room with a muffled thump of the arched door behind them. The pleasure slaves looked at me curiously. The girls wore pretty dresses that were cinched with laced bodices, while the boys had on short tunics and tight Frankish leggings. They each had a mop of dark brown curls falling into their eyes, and the girls wore theirs tied with brightly colored ribbons that dangled down the back.

Etien returned without Canille and launched back into a discussion of the map fastened to the easel. Without a word, the slaves moved over to give me room on the bench at one table. The master didn't notice.

It quickly became apparent that this was a formal training session, but it didn't involve poses or sensual allurements. I understood maps because Lexander had shown me, but he had not taught any of my slave-mates how to read them.

These slaves were well trained, answering the master's questions with quick precision. They were focused on the Noromenn lands in the north, and barely discussed the "harsh, cold clime" of Issland and

Gronland. My homeland wasn't even mentioned. It certainly showed me where we ranked in Frankish esteem.

When the map was at last rolled and stored with others in a large cupboard, the master continued with something he called "logic." It was a way of speaking that made no sense to me, but the others followed along as they compared men of different nations and the numbers of birds flying through the sky. I grew dazed and fidgety on the bench, but I was ignored.

Indeed, nothing was expected of me. That evening, we dined on a thick stew served in a round loaf of bread. It was the best thing I had eaten since I had left Silveta's estate. Once full, I followed the others up to the long narrow room under the massive peaked roof, with each beam as thick around as my hips. There was a row of beds, and the others kindly pointed out the one I could share with another girl. A few slaves were missing, busy serving the more formal meal for the master and mistress.

In the relaxed atmosphere of the slave hall, I found myself sitting cross-legged on my surprisingly soft bed and answering their questions. They were curious about my master and mistress in Danelaw.

"I'm so glad to be out of there," I told them, with the memory of Ukerald firmly in mind. "I never expected it would be like that . . . I hope your master and mistress are not as harsh."

The slaves exchanged glances as if they didn't understand. "They punish us," one of the curly haired boys agreed. "But I think the lessons are worse."

It was not at all what I had expected. Even sitting among them and talking so freely was something I had never experienced before. At Vidaris, the slaves had maintained a rigid hierarchy, the older slaves preying on the newer ones.

I would have to move slowly and reveal little until I understood the ways of Montplaire. I put an end to their questioning by declaring my exhaustion after my long journey.

I had to remove my tunic and leggings, and a sudden hush spread through the room. Even by the light of the one candle, the other slaves could see the remnants of Ukerald's beating. Most of the scabs had fallen off, leaving tender pink lines and peeling skin, but a few of the deeper wounds still puckered my skin.

Their revulsion was clear as they pulled back from me, murmuring among themselves.

"Have you never seen a slave beaten within the last breath of life?" I turned to give them all a good look. "Have no doubt—you could be next."

Canille took charge of us in the morning. We filed down to the large room where the slaves did their lessons. The tables were pushed against the wall and they removed their clothing before lining up in the customary manner to do the poses.

I took off my tunic and leggings and assumed the *lydnad* pose with the others. I was glad I had revealed myself last night because at least the ripple of curiosity among the slaves was no longer tinged with outright shock.

The tiles were clean and pleasantly warm from the fire. Canille paced between us, murmuring instructions and correcting our poses. The slaves in front were praised. Likely they were near the end of their training and would be sent to Stanbulin soon.

One of them caught my eye. He was a tall, slender youth with wild curly hair and merry brown eyes. As soon as Canille's back was turned, he shifted from the epitome of grace to exaggerating each pose. He lifted his chin to absurd heights or flattened himself in an effort to be perfectly straight. It made the other slaves smile and some shook with suppressed laughter.

Then Canille was standing next to me, and my pose was the only thing that mattered. I couldn't see the correction tool she carried.

"Nice," she commented with an edge of surprise in her voice. "But you need to release the tension here," she said, placing both her hands on my shoulders, drawing them slightly down and back.

Her hands were firm, adjusting my pose. She gave a slight stroke to my back on either side of my spine, and I felt a corresponding release. My pose was much better.

She must have seen and felt the wounds left by Ukerald's cane, but she didn't react. The distinctive marks proved my story better than words could.

Canille moved on to the next slave. Throughout the session, she used only her hands on us. The poses became something new—a calming experience as I focused on stretching my body into pleasing lines.

The only time I saw Canille strike a slave was when she realized the young man in the front row was playing the fool. "Stop that, Bene!" she commanded, smacking the top of his head hard enough to make the sound ring against the stone walls. After that he ceased his antics and concentrated on the poses.

I received more praise from the mistress and gentle corrections, but all in all she seemed impressed. Or perhaps she was astonished that Ukerald's technique had yielded one such as me.

After poses, we had a morning meal of bread and cheese. The bread was round and flat in both taste and form. But the cheese was as aromatic and full-bodied as those from home. I was glad to be rid of the bland Danelaw food.

After the meal, I was surprised when we were allowed to leave the house. I took one of the mantles hanging on the pegs that were used by the slaves. It was a clear day, chilly but not too cold. The slaves scattered, some heading down to a stream and others running to see the new horse in the paddock beside the barn.

Olfs were everywhere, diving into the wheel of the mill, playing among the trees in the orchards, and swinging from the mantles of the slaves. It was quiet without the regular cacophony of bells from the Kristna sanctuaries that had marked off the days in Becksbury in such a terrible, incessant march.

Only one girl stayed near the house. She silently practiced her poses on the flagstone terrace. She had been in the front row, so likely she was one of the elder slaves. Her long body was excessively thin, her bones jutting from her shoulders, hips, and narrow back. Her wide blue eyes had a glassy fervor.

She completed two full cycles of deliberate poses. I wondered if Canille had ordered her to do it. Perhaps the mistress's punishments were more arduous than blows.

I was finally driven to ask, "Why do you pose after the training is done?"

From her reclining position, she answered, "I do it to better myself."

"You do it perfectly already."

"I have high standards."

I sat down on a nearby wall. Stone steps led down to another terrace. On this side of the house there were a garden and a pretty walkway lined by hedges.

The slave smoothly went into another pose, rolling to her hands and knees, her toes pointed at precise angles.

"Aren't they afraid that we'll run off?" I asked. Becksbury had been a dangerous place to escape from, but I could slip away from Montplaire before they knew it.

She finally looked at me. "What kind of slave would do that?"

I raised my hands slightly. "There were some slaves in Becksbury who would have escaped. When people are in pain and frightened, they do things . . ."

She gazed at me uncomprehendingly, then went back to her poses. She tried to overcome the awkwardness of her knobby knees and sharp angles.

The saucy young man slowly approached, listening to us. I got up and walked around the house with Bene following me. "Anything you say to Vanais will be told to our mistress," he warned playfully. "Be careful."

I thought back over what I'd said, but I had stayed in my role.

Bene laughed. "I knew you had secrets. Your eyes are so different." He meant my almond-shaped Skraeling eyes. "And your hair is so bright. Does everyone in Danelaw look like you? We're all wildly curious."

Perhaps he was the one who carried tales. "There's mostly Noromenn in Londinium, but there's also lots of Franks now."

"You must have seen the fighting, didn't you?" he asked eagerly. "Do you think the conqueror will be able to hold the lands? I hear he's paying a gold coin to any man who goes to Londinium to fight by his side."

I raised my brows. "I think the fighting is over for the winter—"

The tinkling of a handbell sounded, and slaves came running back to the house. Bene grinned and took my hand. "Come on. It's time for our lessons."

I was expecting the usual instruction in bodily pleasure, but instead we were seated at the tables and lessons in rhetoric began. The slaves went up to stand next to Etien and recited off facts and figures about arcane subjects like Greek philosophy or the development of mathematics. Then another slave countered their assertions and they were given a chance to rebut.

I sat there with my mouth open. Even with the help of a few *olfs* hanging about, I couldn't understand what they were talking about. Eventually I fell into an absent daze, hearing only the buzz of words around me.

I couldn't understand why Etien went to such lengths with the slaves. Vidaris and Becksbury had only concerned themselves with our serving and pleasure skills. It must have fulfilled some purpose for Etien, for I could hardly believe Lexander's people had need of slaves with greater knowledge and understanding.

The next morning, we filed down to the lesson room and stripped naked again. But instead of poses, Canille ordered us into pairs to practice the art of stimulating each other with our lips and tongues. She grouped the slaves in twos and threes, ordering, "Bene, you take the new girl."

I reclined back like the others on the clean, warm tiles. Bene had a wonderful, sleek body, but he was just enough younger than I to make me feel protective of him.

Bene made an absurdly leering face as he pushed my legs apart and crawled closer. I could hardly stifle my giggle, it was so silly. If he was going to treat this like a game, then I could, too.

Bene bent his head and nuzzled my crotch with his nose and mouth. It felt good, very good. I relaxed and spread my legs wider, opening myself to him. As he began to flick his tongue against me, I tried to keep from groaning out loud.

After a moment he lifted his head. "Tell me what you like."

I realized the other receptive slaves were murmuring to their partners. "I . . . I'm not sure."

"Go on," he prodded, biting down on my tender flesh.

I writhed for a moment, and then he pressed harder. "That hurts," I gasped.

Bene released me and began to lick the offended spot. "Better?"

"Yes," I managed to get out. I wasn't used to thinking or speaking in the throes of lust. But he forced me to describe everything I felt and desired.

Canille walked up and down making comments. She wanted our positions to be as appealing as possible, while ensuring we were being properly pleasured. She urged Bene to use his fingers to tantalize me more.

I tried to resist the lure of climax. But as one after another of the slaves cried out and thrashed in ecstasy, I realized that was the only way it would end. Bene was relentless, holding onto my thighs so I couldn't wriggle away, his mouth never leaving my body.

So I gave in and let waves of satisfaction ripple through me. I cried out finally, letting go completely. My legs tightened around him as I shuddered in release.

Bene collapsed on my thighs, supporting his head on my belly. "Turnabout's fair play. Now you do me."

He must have thought I had purposely prolonged our scene, so he would hold off as long as he could. I let out something between a groan and a satisfied moan, knowing I would have to suck him until my jaw ached.

And I did. The silky black hair at his groin smelled fresh from the bath he'd taken the night before. I was looking forward to my turn in the tin tub that was set before the fire in the evenings.

I pleased Bene as mightily as he had pleased me. I used every trick I knew to make him spill faster, but he grimaced and resisted me.

Canille smiled when she realized what he was doing. "You look as if you're in pain, Bene."

He gave an incoherent cry, trying to hold on.

Canille leaned over him, sinking her fingers into his thick hair. Her breasts strained her bodice, nearly tumbling out. The rich smell of her wafted over us, making me wish she touched me instead of Bene.

He couldn't withstand her caress and he cried out in a frenzy of release.

That excited Canille. She whisked aside her skirts and mounted the last slave who had yet to climax, with the order, "I'll let you know when I've had my fill."

The rest of us lay where we were sprawled, watching them. I stroked Bene's sweaty skin, flushed and trembling from his feat. Thoroughly satiated, we cuddled together as Canille took her pleasure.

13

The days slipped by in Montplaire as quietly as leaves falling from a tree. Snow fell and blanketed the fallow fields. But a few days later it melted into the earth, leaving green grass behind. The *olfs* claimed the winter here would not get much colder than this.

Still Lexander didn't appear, and I wondered if he was somewhere out there in the twelve towns plotting the destruction of Montplaire. In that case, he should have made his presence known to me. But I began to believe that he had gone elsewhere.

I was somewhat at a loss, having come to Montplaire with the righteous intention of freeing the slaves. But these young people were in no way oppressed. They lived in luxury and were expanding their minds and emotions. They were smart, happy, and contented with their slavery. Etien and Canille were benevolent masters, taking in those who asked to be trained in the arts of pleasure. One girl claimed she had waited two years before she was at last accepted. Those who had been saved from the streets, like Bene, were even more grateful.

The other slaves kept their distance from me, and I was excluded from many of the routines of the house. I continued wearing the drab slave tunic and loose leggings, which was a peasant boy's attire in Frankish lands. And I was never summoned to serve the master and mistress. Etien clearly preferred boys rather than girls, and Canille never dallied with me even during our lessons, though she judged everything I did with a discerning eye. During our training, more often than not my partner was Bene. He was fascinated with me, and Canille indulged his desire to a remarkable degree.

I also didn't serve at table, so I had no reason to go into the kitchen with its massive chimney hung with copper pots. Once I used the help of the *olfs* to sneak downstairs to glimpse the elaborate dining ceremony. The slaves carried bowls of water for the master and mistress to wash their hands at every course, and white napkins on which to wipe them. In Vidaris, Lexander hadn't dined with Helanas unless there were guests. Usually he had eaten alone in his chamber with one slave in attendance.

I tried to explain the danger to the slaves in the evenings when we were free to talk and even rut together if we desired. The others would listen by the hour as I described the torture I had seen and endured. But beyond their titillated horror, my stories had no meaning for them. They had never felt the lash, so how could they truly understand? Canille would sooner cut her own hand off than hurt her slaves, while Etien used encouragement rather than punishments in his teaching.

Then one morning I woke from a dream with a start. The winged ship from Stanbulin was gliding toward me. At first it seemed like a nightmare, a manifestation of my greatest dread. But the *olfs* drifting overhead convinced me that a winged ship was sailing upriver to the Twelve Towns.

I sat up on my side of the bed. The girl I shared with protested sleepily as the cold air seeped under the blanket.

I went to the window under the sloped roof. The walls were so thick that I could sit on the sill. The river was hidden beyond the hillcrest.

The other slaves stirred and began to rise. I stayed in the window until I was forced to go downstairs for our lessons, all the while considering what to do. As Canille called out instructions, I went through the poses with a distracted air.

Eventually a servant appeared and announced a messenger had arrived. I almost panicked and ran from the room to escape. But Bene grinned through his legs at me, sticking out his tongue. He had completed his training, so he would be one of the slaves sent to Stanbulin next. I couldn't abandon him or the others.

I had a terrible fear that the slaves would summarily be gathered up and taken to the ship. But Canille dismissed us and the slaves happily ran downstairs for an extended outing.

I lingered behind. They would look for me outside, and Bene might come back to find me, but I had to risk it. I went down the steps without making a sound. At the end of the corridor was the fine hall. I kept close to the wall even though I was cloaked by an *olf,* creeping along quietly as I tried to listen.

There was a rustle of parchment as it was rolled. "Very well," Canille said, much louder than I expected. "We'll bring the cart at daybreak. You can tell him there will be five slaves this time."

The messenger boy muttered an acknowledgment; then the outer door creaked open. Canille appeared in the doorway, and I held my breath, pleading with the *olf* to conceal me.

Canille was mightily distracted, chewing on her lip and wringing her hands together. She passed by with a swish of skirts as I crouched under the *olf.* For a moment, I wondered if she would rebel as Lexander had, releasing her slaves rather than sacrifice them to her people.

But Canille encountered a servant at the staircase and told her to prepare baths for the slaves that evening. She was much too matter-of-fact to be contemplating a revolt.

I waited until they were both gone before I slipped out the side entrance, pulling the mantle around my shoulders.

Bene was waiting impatiently on the terrace. "Where have you been?"

"Did you see the messenger leave?"

He was instantly alert. "You've heard something. Tell me!"

"A ship has come. The cart will take us away in the morning."

"Our training is complete." He stared in the direction of the river. "No more maps and *stilos*! We'll finally get out of here and see everything we've learned about. I wonder who my new mistress will be."

I almost told Bene exactly what kind of monsters he would serve, but I bit my lip. "Tell me, Bene, what is the worst punishment you've seen here?"

He blinked a few times. "The worst? We usually have to stand facing a wall for a while. The mistress did make Filip sleep on the floor for the whole winter to break him of his talking back. And I'd have a lot more fun if there wasn't the threat of dish duty hanging over me."

I closed my eyes at the enormity of my task. These pampered slaves had no idea what faced them in Stanbulin. I couldn't imagine Bene being mistreated by a master like Ukerald.

"You must understand the danger you're in!" I grabbed his arms, giving him a slight shake. He laughed, thinking I was playing with him. "What's the worst thing that's ever happened to you, Bene? Imagine it happening every day, every moment of your life. Soul-wrenching, hopeless pain because you can't do anything to stop it—"

"That's what I got away from," he interrupted, extracting himself from my grip. "When I came here, everything was different."

"Yes, Montplaire is a veritable paradise," I said, sighing. "But we'll be given to vicious, heartless beings who care not whether we suffer and die. We have to get out of here."

"Even if it was true, there is nothing else for me," Bene insisted. "The only trade I know is farming, and I'd soon enough die than do that!"

It seemed there was no budging him. How could I frighten these slaves into leaving when Montplaire gave them everything they desired?

So instead, I proposed, "Don't tell the others about the messenger, Bene. Let it be our secret. They'll be surprised when they find out. You can laugh at them and say we knew all along."

Bene gave me a sharp look. He knew I had my own reasons, but it was just the sort of trick he liked to play. So he agreed and gave me a quick kiss on the cheek.

Etien taught the afternoon lessons as usual. Instead of struggling to understand or dozing in a bored haze, I considered what to do. I had to convince the slaves to leave tonight.

The four eldest slaves and I were bathed before the evening meal. Canille washed my hair herself, humming a haunting tune under her breath. I had grown accustomed to her gentle hands and no longer feared she would strike me.

I could only hope Canille regretted sending her slaves to Stanbu-lin. Certainly she sighed a great deal and was wistful even when Bene coaxed her to smile. The others didn't seem to suspect anything.

While the formal meal was served below, I went to the privy and used the chance to sneak into Canille's chamber. It was an airy room layered with embroidered pillows and drapes. I searched quickly and found a casket that held her jewels concealed within the window seat.

As my hands closed around the casket, a pang of guilt shot through me. I was no thief! But Canille was robbing these slaves of their lives, and the fortune they could get for these jewels would establish them elsewhere. I could imagine Vanais owning her own shop, ruling over it with an iron fist. Bene could travel and see all the exotic places he longed for.

I stashed the casket in a niche at the head of the staircase. It fit snugly next to a statue, so I was sure that it would escape notice for a while.

Then I returned to our attic chamber and waited anxiously for the slaves who were serving the meal to return. If any were taken to pleasure the master and mistress tonight, they would have to be left behind. I would use the help of the *olfs* to get them out later.

But they all returned, bringing with them a burst of talk and laughter as they undressed and slid under their blankets. I stayed near the door where the candle cast the brightest glow. Quietly, I called for silence. "Please listen to me one last time."

Some of them turned over or sat up at my announcement. Others ignored me.

"You've never truly understood," I continued. "You think that pain and suffering can never happen to you—"

"Our master and mistress have always been kind," Vanais interrupted, pushing aside her blanket.

I faced Vanais down. "They've lied to you. Slaves don't become companions to emperors and queens. A ship has come to take you away, to a place called Saaladet in Stanbulin. Dreadful things will be forced on you—rape and torture. They'll even make you hurt others. They'll use you until your spirit breaks—"

Vanais leaped to her feet, her face twisted. "You mustn't speak that way!" Several of the others were protesting as well.

Bene finally spoke up, "But the ship has come. I saw the messenger myself. Our training is complete and in the morning we shall leave."

The others were surprised, but Vanais protested. "Surely you don't believe these wild tales, Bene? Torture and rape, bah!"

His voice was low. "You wouldn't scoff if it had happened to you, Vanais. Perhaps you have yet to discover that not everyone is as kind as our masters . . ."

His somber expression, so unlike Bene, struck everyone. Now they were listening.

"You can have everything you desire if you come with me," I told them. "No one will be able to hurt you. You can do as you want, when you want, when you're free, like I am."

Vanais gasped out loud. "You *should* be punished! I'm getting our mistress."

She approached me, but I blocked her from going through the door. It was like pushing against a bundle of dry sticks. Vanais was unpleasant to rut with, the one time we had been paired in training. All I could feel were the bones beneath her taut skin.

"I have money," I insisted. "A great wealth, enough for you all to prosper. I can show you how. We can find a place even better than this. You only have to follow me."

Vanais tried to struggle past me again, but I pushed her away. She went down on her knees, scraping them in her awkward fall. Her outraged look pained me.

"You're leaving Montplaire?" Bene asked.

"Yes, this very moment."

Their frightened, angry expressions spoke louder than words. "We'd die on the streets," one girl protested, while a boy agreed. "They'll catch you if you try." Two of the younger girls pulled their blankets over their heads as if they couldn't bear to hear such disobedience.

"Come with me, Bene," I urged, hoping if he agreed that the others would follow.

He joined me by the door. "Are you serious?"

"Dead serious," I said flatly.

Vanais was furious. "You *can't* go anywhere!" she demanded, her voice rising.

That was the wrong thing to say to Bene. He was rebellious by nature, and only the plush surroundings had lured him into obedience. "I do what I want," he said flatly.

"You can't!" she shrilled. "You belong to our masters."

"Claim the life you dreamed of when you came here," I called to the others as Bene quickly donned his tunic and leggings, tying on his boots. "You can be free—"

But their clamoring cut me off, denying my words. Others were rising to help Vanais. She struggled with me at the door and I was hard-pressed to keep her inside.

Suddenly Vanais slipped away and twisted past me. She flung the door open and started to the stairs, blind in the darkness.

I grabbed Bene's hand. "Hurry!"

We followed down the stairs right on Vanais' heels. She was crying out for the master and mistress, but she hesitated in the archway leading to their chambers. She was too good a slave to go where she didn't have permission.

I ran past her, flying down the steps with the *olfs'* light to guide me. But Bene dragged at my arm, patting the wall to feel his way.

Suddenly I remembered the casket upstairs in the niche. Vanais was screaming to raise the entire house, and candlelight was flaring. I grabbed two mantles, thrusting one into Bene's arms. We ran out the side door as Etien's voice boomed out, "What is this?"

Outside, we paused on the gravel drive. "Now what?" Bene asked breathlessly.

"This way," I said much more confidently than I felt.

We struck off down the lane through the meadows. Canille would organize her freemen to search for us. Hopefully they would assume we had bolted into the Twelve Towns. But at the junction, Bene and I crossed over like cats in the dark, heading away from Lutece, as far from Montplaire as we could get.

14

Perhaps it would have served better to speak with each slave alone rather than all together. But even then I doubted my ability to persuade. When I was in training at Vidaris, nobody could have convinced me to abandon my master. Only Lexander could have sent me away as he did.

At least I had gotten Bene out.

We ran down the frosty road, trailing clouds with every breath. A handful of *olfs* followed along with us, lighting the countryside as bright as day for me. They loved the excitement.

"We're heading away from the river, aren't we?" I asked. The waterway was so serpentine that most roads didn't follow it.

Bene gave me an incredulous look that he didn't think I could see. "You don't know?"

I tried to remember the maps Etien showed us during the geography lessons, but I couldn't be sure. "We don't have time for games, Bene," I warned.

Chastised, he replied, "Yes, we're heading toward the rising sun."

I would rather have been going downriver, but that meant we would have to pass by Montplaire and the rest of the twelve towns. At least this direction was not as obvious.

I pushed myself at a great pace, refusing to stop to rest. Bene was in the flower of youth and he easily kept up with me, though he stumbled in the dark and swore occasionally.

The road was deserted, so when I heard a horse approaching from behind, I dragged Bene over a hedge and hunkered down in the mud. The horse's pace was a brisk trot, and the man had a lantern in one hand.

Bene froze. "The dog—" he started to murmur.

A mastiff hound began to bark, digging into the hedge on the other side. His baying alerted the man on the horse, who swung his lantern toward us.

"Run!" I grabbed Bene's hand and pulled him across the meadow away from the road.

We ran down the sharp incline, saved from being immediately savaged by the dog because of the thick hedge. But I knew it would get through soon enough.

At the bottom of the hill was a creek. I splashed into it and tugged Bene along over the rocks. He fell in, and then I slipped and wet my wool leggings to my hips. But I continued on, begging the water sprites to prevent the dog from smelling us.

We had no breath for talking as we struggled on. The creek splashed around us. The trees arching overhead cut off the faint moonshine, and I was grateful to the *olfs* for their light. There was no sound of pursuit by the dog or freeman.

When we had gone far upstream and my entire body was numb and shaking, we climbed out. But I wouldn't let Bene collapse on the ground. We had to keep moving. "They know where we are," I reminded him.

He was gasping from the exertion. "If I were still a slave, I'd be warm in my bed right now."

"We're not free yet," was all I could say through my chattering teeth.

We avoided several villages so we wouldn't been seen. There must have been a search party of freemen blanketing the area. We couldn't double back to the river, so I pushed us ever farther east. We lost one *olf*, and then as the sky began to brighten, the others disappeared, returning to the Montplaire pleasure house.

At sunrise we stumbled on a road. I wasn't sure if it came from the Twelve Towns, but Bene couldn't be dragged across the fields of dead stubble anymore. He managed to keep going, putting one foot stubbornly in front of the other as we plodded down the road. I wished we could stop in a barn somewhere to sleep, but I was afraid the manor folk would catch up to us.

More people began moving about, and every hoofbeat and shout could have heralded our doom. Bene and I pulled our mantles far over our faces. Splashed in mud and worse, we looked like a couple of day laborers. In my tunic and leggings, I was taken for a young man rather than a woman.

Bene and I paused by a stream to drink our fill. "Let's use some of your riches to get food and a place to sleep in the next village," Bene suggested. "We shouldn't be on the road where they can find us."

I sighed. "I'm sorry to say that I didn't fetch the casket. I left it behind."

Bene sat down hard on the ground. "You mean . . . we have nothing?"

"Don't worry," I quickly assured him. If Bene gave up, we would surely be caught. "I've found that coins are not always necessary."

"No? I've always found that the destitute starve." He shook his head as if reconsidering his decision to come with me. "How could you leave a fortune behind?"

"I was trying to save the other slaves. I didn't expect Vanais to raise the house. And in the rush to get out . . . I didn't think of it until it was too late." I hardened my tone. "But anything is better than being sent to Stanbulin, believe me. You're not meant to be a slave, Bene. Under any other master I've known, you'd have been beaten and punished until that wild nature of yours was broken."

Bene still refused to look at me. I had to pull him back to his feet, urging him onward. As we started down the road I began considering the men who passed by, wondering if I could proposition them for food. That would certainly improve Bene's outlook. But everyone looked as downtrodden and hungry as we.

Town walls rose in the valley ahead, nestled among the trees. We chanced discovery by going inside, hoping to barter for food.

Bene roused himself somewhat as we went under the arch in the wall, with the gates opened wide. A fat six-sided tower rose nearby with a parapet at the top. Two men gazed down on the surrounding countryside. Inside the walls, the twisty mud lanes were lined with stone and timber structures.

I followed the flow of people to the market. The busy square was swarming with people and spirits alike, as was the burial yard next to the Kristna sanctuary.

I shuddered at the sight, remembering how the bishop had killed Olvid. She had never harmed anyone, wanting only to be left alone to commune with her beloved *olfs*. I clung to Bene's hand tighter. I had failed to save Olvid, just as I had failed to convince the other slaves of Montplaire to escape.

Everything I'd said to the slaves would be relayed to Canille, and she would tell her superiors in Stanbulin about me. But I hoped they would continue to believe I was a Becksbury slave. Knowing Ukerald, my vehemence about torture and abuse would surely be understandable.

Then I caught sight of two freemen astride small horses typically used to pull carts. They were searching through the crowd in the market, looking at everyone's faces.

"I think those are Montplaire freemen." I led Bene behind booths and carts to avoid them.

We circled near the sanctuary. A cleric was standing on the porch with his arms raised over a group of people gathered below. Some were seated on mules, while others stood stoically holding long staffs. A few were well and fashionably dressed, but most wore long robes flowing down to their feet and cowls that covered their heads and shoulders that I had come to associate with followers of Kristna. They were surrounded by curious townsfolk.

Though the spirit of Kristna was flowing amongst the followers, I pushed deeper into the crowd. Bene kept glancing behind us, watching for our pursuers. The cleric was praying to Kristna to protect the *peregrini* before him, and to take his blessings with them on their journey. The *peregrini* raised their staffs in acknowledgment. With a lot of elaborate words in the vein of "go and be safe," the cleric finished with a flourish.

I was busy looking for the freemen from Montplaire, but the crowd shifted and moved. The townsfolk bid friends and relatives farewell and began to disperse as nine or ten travelers carrying their staffs headed out of the market square.

I pulled Bene into their midst, keeping far away from the searching freemen. Two women on mules provided the perfect cover when one beast kept shaking its head, frightening its rider.

"I'll guide him for you," I offered, putting a firm hand on the mule's neck. The poor animal didn't like the rider's uncertain seat. The mule calmed under my touch.

The girl on his back was very grateful. "Bless you, my dear," she told me, though I was surely older than she. "You shall be rewarded for your aid."

Bene followed behind me as we walked by the Montplaire freemen. They didn't bother to glance at the *peregrini*.

As we passed through the lanes back to the gate, I gave up hope of getting any food in town. It wasn't safe with the freemen looking for us.

So we continued on with the *peregrini*, going farther away from the great river. Though fatigue and hunger made my head spin, I was no longer worried that we would be discovered. We were well concealed in the midst of the *peregrini*. Some of them prayed as they walked, their staffs striking the ground with determined thuds. Others sang ordinary songs and stopped to wet their tongues with beer when we passed through a crossroads village.

Bene and I were saved when bread was handed to each of us at a modest sanctuary. The *peregrini* sat down to make a meal of it with fresh water from the well. Some of them had abundant coins in their fat purses, but they took what was freely offered.

"Why do they give us food?" I asked the girl whose mule I had continued to lead.

"It's decreed that all sanctuaries must help us on our way," she replied in a high-pitched, childish voice. I had discovered that one of the men on foot was her husband. "We traveled for three days to meet up with your group. Not many leave this time of year."

"And where are you going?" I asked.

"All the way to Ditalia. Surely you'll not be satisfied by the relics along the way? We must see the Holy City where Kristna rules."

Kristna followers claimed their god was cast in an earthly form, and I wondered if he walked among them in his city. But I was not eager to witness it myself. I had trouble enough with Lexander, a mere godling.

After Bene and I had eaten our fill, I considered leaving the *peregrini*. I wasn't comfortable in the midst of the Kristna followers, and I missed the *olfs,* who were avoiding the band of travelers. But we were safely hidden and were moving farther away from Montplaire. So I continued on with them.

Bene and I were fortunate that the days were short. As the sun lowered, we filed through the gates of a sanctuary compound and were shown up a ladder into a loft in the barn. There were mattresses stuffed with straw lain on the wooden slats. It was warm because of the animals below.

Bene fell asleep with crumbs of our evening ration of cheese clinging to his mouth. I snuggled up next to him for warmth, feeling as protective as a mother hen.

When I awoke refreshed the next morning, the *peregrini* began to stir. We received a bounty of hard bread from the cleric who tended the sanctuary.

It was difficult to feel victorious when we had barely escaped. It was already too late for Vanais and the other slaves who had been sent to Stanbulin on the ship.

"I had hoped to return to Montplaire," I told Bene. "To convince the other slaves to come with us."

"Sure, take me back to Montplaire. I'll stay there." He knocked the hard bread against the post in emphasis. "I only left because you said you were rich."

By his tone, he meant it. But I decided not to take his grumbling seriously unless he started walking back to Montplaire.

"We can't go back right now," I said. In truth, Montplaire would be fortified after our escape and the near theft of Canille's jewels. "We'll have to wait for a while until they let their guard down again."

"First you need to figure out how to convince the slaves to come with you," Bene told me. "Don't expect me to say this is better."

With Montplaire out of the question, the only other pleasure house I knew of was in Veneto, where Lexander had once been master. Doubtless he would take particular satisfaction in destroying it, like he did with Vidaris. Perhaps vengeance had driven him there after he had left me behind. In his current rage, he could even have gone straight to Stanbulin to directly challenge his people. But surely that would be suicide.

I wished I could be more hopeful that Lexander would free the slaves when he brought down a pleasure house, but I had serious doubts after Becksbury. Even one life saved, like Bene, was worth any price I had to pay.

I turned to Bene. "How far away is Veneto?"

"It's on the Azure Sea, south of here."

"Is it near Ditalia?" I asked.

"It's just beyond the Holy Empire."

I considered that. "So it would be quicker to sail there?"

Bene nodded, and I considered our options. To get to the river where we could find passage to the sea beyond, we would have to avoid the dedicated freemen who were searching for us. Or we could continue on foot to Ditalia with the *peregrini,* getting free food and lodging along the way. And no matter what else could be said of Kristna followers, their men had not tried to ravish us.

"We're going to become *peregrini,*" I decided.

"You're not a follower of Kristna," Bene protested. "And neither am I."

"There's no need to tell *them* that." I didn't want to explain my plan in case we were recaptured by Canille. "Trust me, Bene. You said you wanted to travel. This is as good a start as any."

Bene looked around at our companions. " 'Tis true, it's better than being a farmer. And perhaps the food will improve."

So our decision was made. The *peregrini* were curious about us—especially when they realized I was a woman, not a boy as my clothing indicated. They believed I dressed that way to protect myself on the road, and were vehement in their insistence that no one would dare trouble *peregrini* and bring Kristna's sentinels down on themselves.

When they asked why we had become *peregrini,* I replied honestly. "We were compelled to walk this path." They nodded approvingly.

The affluent *peregrini* rode mules so it was easy for us to overhear their conversation as we helped with their mounts. The young bride had a nervous temperament, and she made fervent prayers in every sanctuary for a child, having lost her babe with the harvest. I thought she and her older husband simply needed to rut for another year or two, but he was eager to get an heir for his vast holdings.

The other couple had a no-nonsense way about their devotions, belying their decision to leave their comfortable home and go vast distances to pay homage to Kristna. The matronly woman lolled on her mule, with her husband astride next to her. She chattered happily about her large brood of children left behind to anyone who would listen. I wondered if they had become *peregrini* simply as an excuse for a journey.

When her husband asked why we had no staffs, I admitted we hadn't a coin to buy them. The man was kind enough to pay a farthing for two of the stout staffs by which *peregrini* were known.

While the couples welcomed us, the squat Frankish clerics were all seriousness. They marched stoically through the rain, and set to begging before every sanctuary door. I suspected they had reserves of coins in their pouches because they often bought foodstuff in the markets we passed through. In contrast, there were three Danelaw clerics who maintained an austerity that was disquieting. They refused to wash themselves and ate only what the sanctuaries gave without begging for more. They rose at each bell to pray to their god, spending too much time on their knees before walking all day.

Because we were lodged close to sanctuaries, the bells woke me all through the night. I never truly slept, and it left me in a daze during the day. I longed to be able to commune with the *olfs* for rejuvenation, but all the otherworldly creatures avoided the *peregrini* because of the strong presence of Kristna among them.

Bene was thriving, always interested and exclaiming over something—an intricately carved bridge or a shining river snaking through a flat open valley. He wasn't suited to service, being much too mischievous and impulsive. He was happier flitting from place to place like an *olf*. So despite the hardships, he didn't really regret leaving Montplaire.

On one particularly harsh day, the rain turned to sleet and there was no convenient sanctuary nearby, forcing us to plod through the icy mud. That day Bene complained, but everyone did, including the Danelaw clerics who prayed loudly for Kristna to relieve their suffering.

When it became clear that Canille's freemen wouldn't find us, I began to confide in Bene. I told him about my homeland and that my mam was a native Skraeling. I explained that my own master had freed me, and that I was determined to free other pleasure slaves. Yet I never mentioned Lexander's name or that he was bent on destroying the houses.

The *peregrini* moved at a leisurely pace, pausing at each sanctuary and the various shrines to Kristna erected by natural springs and crossroads. Some of the sanctuaries held reliquaries that were said to cause miracles. At the sanctuary marking the entrance to the Holy Empire, the land of Kristna, there was a jewel-encrusted case that was said to hold the foot of a man who had walked with Kristna himself.

The *peregrini* knelt before the altar where the reliquary rested. I joined them, but instead of bowing my head, I stared up at the sparkling green and blue jewels, and the golden embroidery on the draperies of the altar. The cloth was so fine that the light shone through it. Two leather-bound books were embossed and dotted with pearls and rubies. The bronze candlesticks rose high, holding fat yellow candles that would take days to burn out.

At the rear of the altar was a carved ivory plaque hinged in three sections. It showed the tiny figures of men, some on horses, and the distinct outline of a Kristna sanctuary. A fancy bucket sat on a pedestal to one side. The *peregrini* were allowed to dip their hands into the water that had been blessed if they gave an oblation to the sanctuary. Even the clerics from Danelaw dug into their purses to hand over a coin.

Bene and I hung back. He was looking up at the stone carvings on the arches and columns—vines, leaves, and faces. Fat babies floated in the air on tiny wings, and I wondered if they were meant to depict *olfs*.

But no *olf* passed through the great bronze doors, cast in coffers like the arched ceiling. I was sorry because I thought they would like the wall paintings that showed Kristna followers, their mantles of bright color slung over their shoulders and hanging to their feet.

That day we passed by an edifice that was under construction.

The flimsy-looking scaffolding and pulleys rose higher than the unfinished wall. I heard one of the *peregrini* say it had once been a great sanctuary that had burned to the ground. It was being rebuilt taller and finer than before.

The Holy Empire surely belonged to Kristna. The spires of sanctuaries dotted the countryside, rising higher than the villages around them. The *olfs* were relegated to the kitchen hearths of the cottars or the wooded glades. It wasn't just because I was with the *peregrini*—there were decidedly far fewer spirits in the Holy Empire.

After too many days of walking without reprieve, I hoped we were nearing the end of our journey. But the *peregrini* settled into a rhythm that offered no hope of relief. As we arrived at a hospice, the last of the sun's rays shone under the blanket of clouds.

The wide valley was illuminated before me. It seemed to go on forever. At the other side was a line of mountains, with the undulating peaks shining white with snow. They extended far beyond sight.

"That must be the summits," Bene said in awe. He joined me on the slope near the hospice. "Etien said they're the tallest mountains in the Auldland."

"We're not going up there!" I protested.

"We'll have to cross them to get to Ditalia. From the other side we can head east to Veneto."

I stared at the mountains. "Is it possible?"

"So they say. At the rate we're going," Bene said thoughtfully, "it may take another moon to get there."

My expression must have been pure dismay. Bene began bouncing up and down on his toes. He wanted constant assurances from me. He had been trained to be subservient, and that was a hard habit to break.

There was no going back now, so I accepted the inevitable. I had misjudged the distance based on my travels at home.

When we stopped the next evening and the mountains appeared larger though not much closer, I realized we were truly in for a difficult time. What were these people thinking, crossing peaks like that in the heart of winter? The *peregrini* seemed confident that it could be done. But I also discovered the couples had left detailed instructions for the distribution of their property if they died along the way, which did not comfort me.

When we finally began the gradual assent into the outlying foot-hills, we came upon a village of stone in the midst of the trees. The sanctuary and tower belonged to a compound of Kristna followers. The village clung to its side like a burr.

The mountains rose up abruptly behind us. I'd seen mountains before, but never like this. The mass of rock loomed menacingly.

It was cold inside the hospice in the sanctuary compound. I hur-ried to the bed, but as soon as I touched it, tiny bugs sprang out. I tentatively pushed my hand into the blanket, and the black specks swarmed toward me, attracted by my warmth.

"I can't sleep here," I declared. My flesh had already been eaten raw.

Bene simply scratched and didn't seem to care. It made me won-der about his life before Montplaire. My family in Jarnby may have been poor, but we drank milk every morning and had our share of meat in the stew—and we had no biting bugs living in our furs.

There were simply too many people in the Auldland. The sheer number of villages, towns, and more villages was astonishing. Even our band of *peregrini* was growing as we picked up more clerics and followers. Most of the clerics avoided the women, but there were a few who watched us too closely, making me doubt their proclaimed celibacy.

I left the hospice to return to the barn. Bene followed me, as always. I couldn't go behind a tree to relieve myself without having him at my heels.

In the barn, we nestled into the clean straw stored for a fine herd of cattle. The sanctuary was prosperous, and it was said the clerics owned much of the surrounding land.

I snuggled up to Bene, lying on his mantle and wrapping mine over us. We were both shivering.

Since we were at last alone, I ventured to ask, "Why don't you ever speak of your family, Bene?"

"There's nothing to say," Bene mumbled. "I'm not from a distant land like you, where everything is different."

"Not so very different." I knew Bene was the son of a simple Frankish cottar. We had passed by hundreds of poor families living in shacks and eking out life from a muddy strip of land. "My family was poor, too. But I was never . . . raped."

He shifted uneasily.

"What happened, Bene?" I asked.

He had been trained to respond, though he didn't want to. "My older brothers used to take turns sleeping next to me and . . ."

Bene's arms loosened from around me as he began to draw away. I held him tightly. "Don't. We're just starting to warm up."

When he hugged me again, it was with a different intent. "Good idea to get away from the others," he murmured.

Bene rubbed his body against mine. It wasn't the first time, but I had discouraged his advances while we were in the midst of the Kristna clerics. They rejected sensual pleasure. The couples had refrained from rutting except for one or two notable occasions that had aggravated the clerics mightily.

Now, starting to feel warm and drowsy, I let Bene press his *tarse* into my hip. He grew turgid with excitement, and his hands pushed under my tunic to my bare skin.

It felt good, but somehow I could not enjoy it. Bene's urgency was born from more than a need to rut. It wasn't lust like we'd shared in Montplaire. Now there was something more he needed from me, just like Porter had briefly hoped that I would satisfy his unfulfilled longings for a wife.

I pushed at Bene's hands, trying to stop him from touching me. He was distracting me from my questions about his family. And even more, he wanted to be safe. For him, that meant pleasing whoever held the reins. He must have learned that from his brothers, and Canille and Etien had reinforced it.

"No, Bene, don't," I told him. "We can't."

He persisted, expecting me to give in. But I could feel no pleasure now, not when I knew what he was doing.

"Bene, stop it." I pulled away slightly, pushing on his shoulders and letting a blast of cold air under the mantle.

"Please, it feels so good," he urged, trying to pull me back.

"Bene, I'm not your mistress!" I snapped.

That penetrated his fog. He lay there breathing heavily. "We've rutted before, Marja. I don't understand why you don't want to."

"You can't rely on other people, Bene. I had to learn the hard way."

Stung, he asked, "What does that have to do with a harmless rut?"

I sighed. "You're trying to stay safe by pleasing me. But I'm help-ing you because I want you to be free, not because it serves me."

He lay there stiffly, unsure of what to do. I don't think he fully understood, but his silence was encouraging. Perhaps he was consid-ering it.

I pulled him closer, wrapping our mantles around us again and pressing my face against his shoulder. This time we melded together without any sensual sparks. That convinced me I was right. I had to give Bene the chance to become his own man.

We climbed into the mountains. The summits were not merely a line of peaks; beyond the first pass were even taller mountains with more ahead. I could only focus on the slippery path, beaten into packed snow. After we went into the summits, the blue sky disappeared for good, leaving only white clouds above. I couldn't stop staring at the vistas of conifers and snow-covered meadows before us.

The wind whipped against us, snaking through my mantle until I begged two thick blankets from a hospice so Bene and I wouldn't freeze. The young bride had a fur muff and a fur-lined cloak that looked very enticing. The clerics wore many robes of felted wool that kept out the frigid blasts.

When we crossed passes that went over the tree line, where there was only ice and gray rock, our pace slowed to a crawl. We were covering far less ground each day. Here water was frozen in ways I'd never seen before—in bubbles around springs, and long icicles hanging from exposed cliff faces, and frozen layers on top of softer snow that broke with each step.

We stopped every day in a different village tucked in the deep, narrow valleys. There were no walls here to keep out attackers—the mountains served that function.

Then we came to a town larger than most, situated on the edge of a long lake that was smoother than any ice I had ever seen. The cobbled streets were remarkably clean, with people walking about wearing bulky caps and striped wool cloaks, leading cattle and goats with shaggy coats.

The band decided to stop early because of the threatening black clouds pouring over the next pass. There was a special service in the Kristna sanctuary, celebrating a saint's day. Since it was too cold to explore the neat town, Bene and I went along.

The sanctuary was full of people, including a large number of *peregrini*. Bene and I stayed near the back so we would not be conscripted into their rites. Once I had accidentally let myself be pushed up to the altar, and I had to sip the sour wine from a large silver chalice. Bene partook from time to time, saying he wanted the wine, but the spirit of Kristna didn't lodge inside of him. He was free to choose for himself, but I would be sorry to see him accept the "one, true" god, thereby rejecting all others.

When the ritual was completed, we were told that the clerics would be given the last berths and there was no more room in the sanctuary hospice. Bene and I, along with the two couples, would have to stay at an inn.

Bene and I followed the couples. I had discovered that the young bride had lost two babes, born before their time, and she dwelled on it overmuch, anxious to be perfectly correct in her worship. The matronly woman, on the other hand, was quite pragmatic except for the day we drank from an icy, Kristna-blessed spring and her ring broke off. She was delighted, claiming the ring had been stuck on her plump finger for years and had caused her no end of trouble. I thought the silver ring broke because she struck it against the rock basin, but she said it was an intervention from Kristna himself.

The inn was a large stone house with a few arched windows and a tidy slate roof. Smoke puffed from the chimney. With the dark clouds lowering over our heads, I only hoped it was warm.

Inside the main room, lit by several lanterns and a large fire in the hearth, the other two couples bargained with the innkeeper in the Frankish tongue. Most people we had encountered in the Holy Empire spoke more than one dialect, perhaps because we were following the *peregrini* path to Ditalia.

There were several patrons seated at the trestle table eating a porridge of roasted oats. The central hearth was open to the kitchen beyond, where the iron pot hung near the flames. Two women saw us enter and began to gather more bowls.

"Two *pfenigs*," the bride told me. "For each couple."

"We have nothing to give," I said to the innkeeper. "We started this journey without any coins, as *peregrini* should."

The poorest clerics were disdainful of the wealth of the *peregrini,* who were supposed to give up everything in their journey to honor Kristna. Most of the clerics walked, refusing to ride the mules that carried their packs unless they were injured or sick. The bride's husband was also on foot to further humble himself before his god. But he wasn't above buying meat and vegetables in the markets to supplement the monotonous diet of hard cheese and bread.

The matron huffed as if ready to take offense at my words, but I held up a hand. "I make no boast, for we had no coins to start. Our journey would be easier if we did. But we don't ask for it to be easy, only to reach our destination in good health."

I was repeating phrases I had overheard from the clerics, but it mollified the others. "'Tis true," the bride's husband said. "Charity is supposed to be given to *peregrini* to aid us on our way. We can afford to pay, but these two cannot. I've seen it for myself—they've left no oblations in the sanctuaries, for they had none to give."

The innkeeper motioned for another *peregrine* to come inside. The man immediately agreed to pay for a bed. My heart began to sink at the thought of sleeping with the mules again on this bitter-cold night.

"Let my friend share with this man," I said to the innkeeper. "Surely I can sleep here by the fire."

The innkeeper shuffled his feet, pulling at his beard as if he wanted to refuse. But the *peregrine* was of our own band, and he was agreeable.

Bene protested. "I can't let you sleep on the floor while I have a bed."

"Better here than the barn."

He glanced at the strangers seated at the table. "It won't be safe for you alone. I'll stay down here with you."

The innkeeper turned away to show the *peregrine* upstairs, but the two couples lingered, listening to us argue. Bene's advances were becoming maddeningly insistent as I kept rebuffing him. He touched me in intimate ways and gazed at me longingly for all to see. Perhaps he thought he could wear me down until I finally ended up rutting with him.

From the kitchen door, the young woman called out, "You can share my bed, if you like, miss."

"Many thanks," I agreed quickly, so Bene couldn't protest. The girl smiled and went back into the kitchen. I thought at first that she was a servant, but her resemblance to the innkeeper's wife was too marked for her to be anything other than a daughter.

Bene was sulky as we sat down to eat the good, thick porridge. There was honey to pour on it, and the *peregrini* praised Kristna for the bounty. I was happy that several *olfs* made the inn their home, and they were elbow deep in every pot as well as rifling through the bags of the new arrivals. I hid my grin behind my hand, trying to not let anyone see my amusement. Silently I told the *olfs* that I had missed them exceedingly.

Fasia, the innkeeper's daughter, was grown enough to be wed. She kept filling our bowls when her father wasn't looking. The innkeeper and his wife were comfortable people who wanted for nothing in this mountaintop village, but he grumbled about the food we ate without paying. The bride's husband finally quieted him by giving him another farthing, calling it alms for the poor.

Bene touched me a few times during dinner as he was wont to do. He had been trained in the arts of allurement and he did it well. With a look or a brush of his fingertips, I could feel my flesh igniting. But he was not pursuing me out of desire. Lust, I could have countenanced.

His attentions escalated when he noticed that the innkeeper's daughter kept smiling at me. Fasia had round red cheeks and merry eyes. She was a sturdy girl, but I could see from her mother how she would grow plumper as she aged. Her blond braids were tied up in a kerchief.

Perhaps Fasia was simply reacting to my interest in her. I could not help myself. I felt all misty-eyed seeing a pretty blond girl again; she reminded me of home.

Bene was growing more upset by the moment, but I ignored him. Perhaps he didn't realize what he was doing, but I was tired of his manipulations. Perhaps Bene needed to be confronted by his own limitations.

So I smiled at Fasia in that secret way, and was pleased when she responded. Along with extra food, she heated water in the kitchen and carried it to her room so I could wash in the generous basin. Bene glared after us, but I simply bid him a good night.

I truly felt blessed to climb the stairs into the small nook next to the chimney, hidden behind a wooden door. The rising heat kept the room very warm. I was able to strip off my tunic and leggings for the first time since I had joined the *peregrini*. My body looked different—lean and hard from the constant effort of walking and climbing with barely enough food to sustain me. I scrubbed everywhere, removing layers of dirt.

I climbed naked into the bed, which was mercifully clean without a hint of a bug. I dozed off before Fasia finally came to bed.

She undressed and slid in beside me, smelling of warm flour and wood smoke. I was curled on my side facing her, so she matter-of-factly snuggled her back to me. I put my arm over her, and she moved even closer as if relaxing.

With such a wonderful armful of woman, I couldn't fall back to sleep. I pushed my hips into her slightly, feeling her rounded buttocks against my thighs.

If she was unwilling, she could have easily pulled away and I would have let her alone. But after a moment, she gently leaned back into me. Her hand took mine and placed it on her rounded belly.

I let out my breath in anticipation as I stroked the full curve of her hip. Her waist was smaller than I had expected, hidden under the bulky apron that fell straight to her knees. I squeezed her magnificent, plump breasts, rubbing her rosy nipples. She was pink and white, clean and hale. I couldn't believe this ripe woman had not yet been claimed by some man. It must have been by her choice that she was unwed.

She hissed and moaned, squirming under my hands. I held her close to me, stroking her rounded cheeks and strong thighs.

Fasia let me push her onto her back. Likely she had bedded plenty of girls who had passed through the inn, but she was not aggressive about her pleasure. I kissed her red lips, feeling her move beneath me. She was like a pliable doll that I could do with as I wanted.

My fingers eagerly excited her, rubbing as I watched her every reaction, and slipping inside to test her response. Then I did as Alga had taught me, rhythmically bumping her crotch with my thigh. She writhed with abandon, pressing the blanket into her mouth so no one would hear her. Bene would surely try to listen to us. But I didn't care even if the *peregrini* were offended.

In bringing Fasia to climax, I also peaked. I had been without pleasure for so long, resisting Bene's deft advances, that I almost screamed out loud. I had to bury my face in her mass of hair to stifle myself.

I collapsed on top of her, both of us glowing. We cuddled back together and drifted off to sleep.

15

When the blizzard kept us stranded at the inn for several days, Bene grew increasingly upset when each night I went to bed with Fasia and enjoyed her statuesque beauty. She was exactly the kind of girl that Lexander had once searched for—eager to enjoy herself and passive enough to be trained. But the thought of gentle Fasia being tormented by Helanas was unbearable.

It made me wonder if we had walked past other pleasure houses, leaving other slaves to suffer when I could have freed them. I whispered to Fasia one night after we were satiated, "Don't let yourself be taken away from here, my darling girl. There are those who would make you a slave and ruin your life."

She passed it off, assuring me, "I'll never leave my mother. Men have asked, but I always refuse."

"Let no woman take you away either," I warned, remembering Drucelli's charms.

Fasia giggled. "Man or woman, I could never leave Mama."

So other than Bene's barbed remarks about my enjoyment of Fasia, I enjoyed the enforced rest. I ate the abundant food and lay in front of the fire, soaking up the heat. I even washed my clothing and wore one of Fasia's dresses while the ugly maroon and gray tunic hung in the kitchen to dry."

Fasia was discreet when we weren't in her nook. Her parents didn't notice her preference, but Bene saw every glance we exchanged. He caught me alone by the privy and insisted, "If you can rut with that girl, then why not me?"

"Because you want something I can't give you," I retorted.

"I want you." He saw my doubt. "I *do*."

"You don't know what you want," I said kindly.

His hands clenched in anger. "What if I decided to stay here instead of leaving with you?"

I almost laughed. "It's a very nice place. I would make sure you were settled in and then I'd go on to Veneto."

"How could you leave me behind?" His dark eyes were accusing. "I would never leave you, not unless you told me to."

With a pang, I thought of Lexander. I quickly shook my head. "You are free to go anywhere I do, Bene. I'd much rather be together than have you struggle alone."

Bene rubbed his hands through his curly hair until it stood on end, frustrated and confused.

When we finally left the inn and I bid Fasia a fond farewell, Bene stayed far away from me, walking among the clerics. He took to leaving the *peregrini* whenever we reached a village, ducking down a side lane or taking an opposite turn when we passed through a market. I never said a word about it.

Once I saw him charming the matronly *peregrine* into giving him a fat sausage from the link she had purchased. She responded quite naturally to his flattery. I thought it was well that Bene used his skills to get what he needed. But he didn't have to do that with me.

Then one evening in a tiny village clinging to a barren, snow-swept cleft, Bene didn't return from his wanderings. I went searching for him in the fading light. There wasn't much beyond a few buildings, and I couldn't find him.

My heart was in my throat, fearing something terrible had happened to him. During the night, I lay awake in the hospice, imagining him hurt in a ditch or dying in the cold. I was afraid I had made a mistake in bringing him on the *peregrini* path in the dead of winter. I knew Lexander felt responsible for me in the same way.

Bene still hadn't returned by morning. The *peregrini* departed, fearing the weather would close in again before they crossed the next pass. The two couples were genuinely concerned about me and Bene, but they left anyway, claiming they couldn't lose the protection of the band.

Once the *peregrini* started off, *olfs* began to appear around me. They didn't mind the sanctuary hospice as long as the Kristna followers were gone.

Bene returned to the hospice that evening, defiant but watching me too closely, betraying his trepidation. He expected me to be angry with him.

It was an immense relief, and it made me laugh to realize how false my guilty feelings had been. It wasn't my responsibility to take care of Bene, just as it wasn't Lexander's responsibility to protect me.

I was lying down, letting an *olf* bounce on my leg. "Did you enjoy yourself?" I asked.

He considered it. "Yes, I did. I found the most accommodating woman with a great soft bed and lots of ale."

"That sounds good." I continued playing with the *olf*.

He looked around, realizing the others were gone. "They left without you?"

"There will be another group of *peregrini* through soon enough."

Bene was more confused than ever. He returned to the woman's house over the next few days, but when another band of *peregrini* arrived at the hospice, we continued with them.

The new band of *peregrini* was much smaller; six clerics who were intent upon their journey. They claimed to have left other *peregrini* behind who couldn't keep up, and they warned us about their prodigious pace.

Most of the clerics were of an age to be dandling children on their knees as they contemplated the work of the day. But instead they had dedicated their lives to worshiping their god. They were bundled up in drab layers of wool, revealing only their eyes, but even in the warmth of the hospices their shaved heads made them look the same. Of the two elder men, one was distinguishable by his large, hooked nose that came down in a point, while the other had collapsed lips where his teeth used to be.

I had been honed by my exertions so I was able to maintain their brisk pace. I had every need to reach Veneto quickly. Bene usually had energy to spare, so he didn't complain. Even when we caught up to our former band of *peregrini,* we continued on with the fast-moving clerics.

Then one day we surmounted a pass and instead of snow before us, I saw a verdant valley of luscious conifers. "We've reached the other side of the summits," I told Bene.

He looked around doubtfully. "I hope you're right."

It was not as bitterly cold, so I pushed back my hood as we walked. The clouded sky lifted ahead, showing a swath of blue.

It seemed the worst of our journey was over and that we had made it safely to Ditalia. But that night we learned that Veneto lay in the opposite direction from Kristna's Holy City. Soon we would have to leave the band of the clerics and strike out on our own.

We came down out of the summits onto the western coast of Ditalia. The brilliant blue sparkle of water beckoned us from the horizon. But the road forked and the *peregrini* continued down to the coast, while Bene and I turned inland. Veneto was off the eastern coast of the narrow peninsula of Ditalia.

We stayed in a sanctuary close to the fork in the road, hoping to meet up with *peregrini* going our way. But everyone was traveling to the Holy City.

Bene and I set off alone, and the *olfs* returned to bound along beside us. Bene didn't notice them, but I felt much better for their company. I started humming and singing to please them, and after his initial surprise, Bene joined in.

I realized I had to tell Bene about the *olfs,* otherwise he was going to think I had suddenly gone daft. He tried to laugh off my explanations at first, but when I began to describe their unseen antics— tickling a dog's nose to make it snap, tripping him up as he crossed a brook, and splashing water from puddles on us—he began to doubt.

I asked the *olfs* to obscure me from his sight, and when I disappeared before his eyes, he could no longer deny the truth. Indeed, he looked at me in awe, the way the followers gazed at the images of Kristna hung in every sanctuary.

That was certainly not my aim. "My mam and her people commune with the *olfs* every day. I've met people in the Auldland who do, as well."

In thanks for my open acknowlegment of them, the *olfs* led me to a smoker hung with meat from a freshly killed boar. It belonged to an estate that clearly lacked for nothing, so we feasted like kings. It was my first taste of meat in more than a moon. I began to feel foolishly optimistic.

But that afternoon we came upon a scene of devastation. A grand house had burned to the ground, and the cracked beams and utter collapse of the walls reminded me of Vidaris and Becksbury. A dozen men and women were gingerly poking the blackened mounds.

I looked for Lexander, but the headman stopped us from going closer with his soot-covered arm. "Hold up. What are you two doing here? We've claimed the salvage rights."

I understood him quite clearly from the *olfs,* but I stumbled in speaking the Ditalia language. "*Peregrini,*" I said, holding out my staff. His suspicion eased. "People die in fire?" I put my hands together piously, adding in Frankish, "We can pray for their souls."

"I've no oblation to give you," the man said bluntly. "And these folk would not want your prayers, not after Kristna's own has killed them. This was a pleasure house. The sentinels came two days ago and burned them out. The master and his consort must have been inside."

I had no doubt that Lexander was the instigator. "Slaves here, yes?"

He turned back to his work of shifting through the rubble. "Not anymore. They were taken to Chivasso to be sold."

My worst fears were realized. Lexander had brought down the fury of Kristna on this remote pleasure house, and the slaves were part of the wreckage. I grabbed Bene and ran without stopping to the town at the bottom of the valley. My only hope was that Lexander had purchased the slaves to free them.

I soon found the slave master and his cart in the marketplace. There were six pleasure slaves sitting in the straw, their wrists bound together in front of them. Their brief tunics looked much like the ones I'd worn in Vidaris.

I stopped a young servant boy and he told me about the excitement the previous day when all fourteen slaves had been put up for sale. The townsfolk had come to gawk at the slaves, pointing and shouting out lewd remarks until they were hustled along by the town sentries.

None of the slaves had escaped. A wailing cry filled my head—*How could Lexander allow this to happen?*

A fine wagon with tall wheels arrived, and a man in a fur-trimmed tunic peremptorily took charge of four slaves as if the sale had been previously made. A servant linked their wrists together with a rope and led them like a line of mules to the wagon. The slaves never looked up, their shoulders hunched wearily, as if they had suffered exceedingly before this latest trial.

I seized Bene's arm. "Please follow them! Find out where they go."

Startled, Bene asked, "Then what?"

"Come back here. I'm going to see what I can do about these other two."

The wagon drove away, and Bene ran off without questioning me. That was his training.

I circled around the marketplace to approach the cart from the rear. There were boys lurking about as I was, trying to get a look at the pleasure slaves. The sentries were making regular rounds, ordering loiterers off and swatting at them with their sticks.

I slipped under the wagon next to the slave master, hiding behind the wheel. A big donkey was in the traces of the slave master's cart, flicking its ears at the flies. There was no way to get the slaves out of the cart with the slave master on the other side. So I decided to take the whole thing.

Checking to be sure no sentries were nearby or urchins watching, I moved over by the donkey's rear legs. He was wearing hobbles. They made clinking sounds as I removed them. The donkey snorted and shifted when it realized it was being freed.

The slave master was at the back of the cart, leaning against it. Stealthily, I climbed into the front seat, picking up the short whip lying on the floor. As I gathered up the reins, I raised the whip to crack it, shouting out, "Yi!"

But the donkey was a staid old beast. My cries and the sound of the whip were not enough to startle it into a run. The cart jolted forward, then slowed. I gritted my teeth and lashed the donkey across the back, but by then it was too late. The slave master swung up into the seat and with one blow knocked me to the ground.

"Hold hard there, boy!" the slave master shouted at me. "Trying to steal my stock, are you?"

I scrambled under the wheels of the adjacent wagon as he came after me. My mantle caught on something, so I shrugged out of it and left it behind in my rush. The slave master was bellowing for sentries, as I scuttled around frantically trying to get away. I ended up panting behind a barrel with my head still ringing from the blow, when the slave master finally gave up and returned to his cart. I hoped the slaves had fled while they had the chance.

I cautiously made my way through the market. By the time I

returned, the slave girl was standing beside the cart. Her lush hair hung straight to her waist, hiding her bared breasts. The brief tunic was draped nearby, and a brawny man fondled her groin, examining her as he would a horse.

It made my blood run cold. Perhaps this was what Lexander felt when he killed his own kind.

The slave master seemed familiar with the girl, commenting on her docile nature. I wondered if he had been the *huscarl* of the pleasure house.

Their bargain was soon concluded and the man mounted his horse. The slave master put the girl on behind him. She clung to her new master as best she could, her legs bared to her hips.

I was ready to follow them, but the slave master got into his cart. He whipped the donkey and ambled off with the slave boy in the back. I ran after the cart, figuring it would move slower than the horse. But in the end I lost sight of the slave master as he turned onto an open road leading out of Chivasso.

Exhausted by my fruitless dash, I returned to the marketplace to find Bene had been searching for me. His fingers closed on my hand too tightly. "Where have you been? I thought I'd lost you!"

"I tried to follow the slave master. Did you see where the wagon went?"

Bene shook his head. "It left town, heading to the coast. I'm sorry, Marja, but I couldn't keep up."

"Neither could I. We failed them."

"It's not our fault," Bene protested. "They could have jumped off the cart—their legs weren't bound. But they just sat there."

"You can't blame the slaves, Bene. We're trained to yield. You wouldn't have escaped with me if Vanais hadn't goaded you into it."

He frowned at that, but still insisted, "We did all we could for them, Marja."

I remembered how I had used the *olfs'* concealment and stolen Canille's jewels. If I'd had more time, I could have taken what I needed to buy the slaves myself. The *olfs* would have surely helped.

One thing was certain—Lexander didn't care what happened to the slaves. He had only saved Niels and Qamaniq because he felt responsible for luring them into slavery.

I was not sure what we would find when we reached Veneto. I only hoped we got there before Lexander.

16

By the expedient of claiming we were going in the opposite direction, toward Kristna's Holy City, that night we were given shelter at a small sanctuary.

The kind cleric who oversaw the sanctuary gave us flat bread his wife had baked in a brick oven. He was the sort of cleric who did not shy away from women, making me feel more comfortable.

We were allowed to stay inside the sanctuary itself. Both of us had trouble sleeping, thinking of the slaves we had just missed saving. It was deep winter in my homeland, but here, even without a fire, the air was as mild as spring.

When I awoke in the morning, Bene was not beside me. He was sitting outside in the sun with our morning meal in hand. "I found a ride to Veneto for us. And the cleric gave me this," he offered, handing me the larger hunk of bread.

"A ride?" That news was more welcome than the food.

"I wondered why there were so few travelers on the road. They told me that trade goods are taken to Veneto by barge. We're near one of the feeder rivers, so I made a bargain with a barge master."

"But you can't speak to them," I protested.

He lowered his eyes and moved his shoulders in a suggestive manner. "Sometimes it doesn't take much talking. You know that."

I gave him a hug, beset by gratitude. "I hope you know what you're getting into," I murmured.

He patted my back. "Let me take care of this, Marja. It's about time I did something to help."

Bene handled everything. The barge master was a burly man who paid no attention to me, which was a relief. Bene stayed near him as if he genuinely liked the man. They spent each night under the canvas, rutting next to the large ceramic jars containing wine. Bene claimed it was easy to please him.

I lay on the deck in the sun, dwelling on what Lexander had done. I had never deceived myself about Lexander—he was ruthless. He was still very much the heartless master, to allow those slaves to be sold at market. He was blinded by his desire to destroy the masters, while I wanted to stop them from enslaving us.

So the days slowly passed with the rolling hillsides covered with vines and fields ripening despite the season. Under such mellow sunshine, it was odd to think that winter storms beat down on the summits and lands beyond. I felt disjointed, as if we had been transported to a place untouched by time.

Eventually we reached a vast marshland where the salt water sent its tendrils inland. I sensed the moment the river spirits gave way to the sea. I opened my eyes to see a city rising from the water before us. We were surrounded by rippling waves with the marshy grasslands behind us. At first I could see only the peaks of the tallest buildings, the distinct Kristna spires on round-topped towers. Then there were others, peaked and domed, crowding close together. Everything was bathed in a misty, golden light.

Bene appeared by my side, his own mouth opening in awe. The vibrant blue sky stretched impossibly far to the flat horizon, with the island city before us. Boats were approaching from every direction, crisscrossing the bay and heading to the sea beyond.

Even when we drew closer, the buildings seemed to float on the glassy surface. The water mirrored the flat sides, painted white, yellow, and green, creating a perfect wavering reflection of the walls.

"It's magic," Bene breathed.

From the clamoring of the sea spirits, they claimed this city as their own. I was overwhelmed in trying to respond.

The barge wound its way up a wide channel that undulated like a serpent through the city. Many channels branched off it, passing between structures that were partially submerged. The stone foundations descended deep into the murky green water.

Stonecutters filled the air with the sound of saws and chisels, making blocks from the large slabs resting on barges. Boats were being constructed in shipyards from logs of wood corralled on the water. An enormous hull with three towering masts was supported in scaffolding. Other ships equally as large were moored at docks and wharfs lining the channel.

A floating city was beyond my wildest dreams. Yet the drawling phrases sounded comfortingly familiar, and I soon realized the sea spirits had acquired some of their fondest tales here.

When the barge was docked, Bene bounded away from the barge master with hardly a farewell. He didn't have to deal with any of the messy possessiveness that the Frankish shipmaster had shown for me.

I quickly discovered it was nearly impossible to travel around Veneto without asking the way. A shopkeeper pointed us toward the pleasure house, Castropiero, but a curving maze lay between us and our goal. The narrow alleys between the stone walls twisted and turned, ending abruptly at waterways. At each open square, usually the site of a public well, we asked directions so we didn't have to search for the footbridges over the channels.

There were boats moored everywhere, sometimes several deep along the stone quays. Where there were no wooden bridges arching over the water or a walkway alongside the canal, we got into a boat and stepped from it to another, and in that way passed between cobbled lanes.

Bene and I both tried to beg rides from passing boats. Most people made a gesture with their fingers, asking how much coin we could give. But we had none. So we scurried along in the gutters along with the numerous rats.

In this manner we finally came to Castropiero, the pleasure house of Veneto. To my everlasting relief, it stood intact.

The great square house was situated on a wide channel among other imposing mansions. I counted eight windows with rounded arches on each of the upper two floors. The lowest level had only two small windows and a double door that opened onto the channel. The high waterline was clearly marked above the threshold.

An alleyway ran along the side of the house, ending at the channel. The facade of the mansion was highly ornate, but even the back had numerous windows. The rear entrance was up a wide flight of steps to the second floor, where a balcony stretched. A marble urn carved with grapevines sat in the center of a tiny courtyard. A row of modest houses was across the lane.

A boy hurried out from under the arches that led to the first floor. I could tell at a glance that he was not a pleasure slave. He didn't have that smooth grace instilled by the poses. He ran down the alleyway and jumped into one of the narrow boats moored there. Other servants called to each other and occasionally opened the windows to toss refuse into the channel.

I stayed and watched the house until the sun started lowering in the sky, striking the flat stones and turning them red and orange as if they were on fire. Bene returned from his ventures up the lanes, taking advantage of the help Kristna followers gave him because of his *peregrini* staff.

"We shall have to cross three bridges to get to the sanctuary," Bene told me. He had begged for food, and as the prize, he proudly handed me a slightly withered pear. I seized it with delight, desperate for a taste of fruit. I ate it right there, chewing it down to the core as if I could consume the sunshine it had basked in.

To please the *olfs*, I gave them the core. Sea spirits liked sacrifices of food, but they adored stories even more. I had much to tell after our long journey over the summits, but I decided to dole out my tales carefully to get the information I needed from them.

I followed Bene through the maze of the city to the sanctuary. As it grew darker, the lanterns hanging from the boats lit our way.

When we arrived in the open square of the sanctuary, I was impressed by the majesty of the colonnades down both sides, with slender columns supporting round arches. The wide facade of the sanctuary was a series of arches decoratively carved around the edges. Slender towers made entirely of columns rose from the upper level.

Some clerics noticed our staffs and we were quickly ushered up to the altar. We were asked for an oblation, but had nothing to give. The clerics did not believe us at first, but our battered, hungry appearance lent credence to our claim that we had walked all the way from the Frankish lands without a coin. After that, we were celebrated for our feat, and received much praise. I got enough food to fill me for the first time since Fasia had surreptitiously refilled my bowl at the inn.

I pretended to understand less than I did to avoid answering why we had chosen their sanctuary as our destination rather than the Holy City. We joined in their prayer session to show our goodwill, and eventually were taken downstairs into a vaulted hall where some of the clerics slept. The walls curved into the low ceiling, forming a long tunnel. I could feel the sea spirits through the layer of mud and a retaining wall holding back the sea, and hear their echoes in the trickle of moisture that ran down the curved walls.

After our first evening, we were accepted as members of the fellowship. We received exactly the same food that the clerics ate in the morning. I never saw them take an evening meal, and indeed some of the men were so thin they were near to starving. They scattered throughout the city by day, begging for food and oblations.

I returned to the pleasure house every day. Bene begged or stole food, and scrupulously brought me half of what he acquired. He told me about the things he saw, and quickly picked up the words he needed to get by. I stayed near Castropiero and learned the rhythms of the house.

The mistress was statuesque with a strong-boned face, like all of her race. With a fetching cleft in her chin, I would have thought Renata was beautiful, but her pale green eyes were rather fixed and flat despite their inhuman glitter. The master, Tomaz, overindulged in rich food and the ceaseless attentions of his slaves. He was a sour-faced, bloated man, torpid from satisfaction.

A large number of guests came under cover of darkness, mostly men whose equipage and dress indicated they were very wealthy. Shadows passed before the windows that glowed with lights. During the day, the servants moved about cleaning and bringing in supplies for the revelries.

There was no sign of Lexander.

One night I woke in the pitch-black vault of the sanctuary. The dripping of the water carried the sea spirits' voices. I pulled the blanket over my head for warmth, thinking it had nothing to do with me.

But they were calling Bene's name.

I sat up as the bells began ringing, summoning the clerics to prayers. The clerics were stirring around me as I reached over to Bene's cot. It was empty.

I got up as the clerics lit their few candles, casting black shadows against the curve of the vault. They buried their hands in their sleeves and pulled their cowls far over their heads.

I stumbled past them, up the steps to the door. In the corridor that led to the sanctuary, I saw Bene. He was kneeling in front of a cleric.

The young cleric's face was strained and his hands were buried in Bene's hair, pulling the strands as if to tear them out. His jaw clenched, and with as much passion as anger, he shouted, "Damn you!"

Then he saw me, and froze in his confusion. Bene turned, his mouth wet and the cleric's fat *tarse* clutched in his fist. The creamy seed spilled from it as I watched, and the cleric flushed near purple in apoplexy.

The other clerics were emerging from the vault behind me. They exclaimed in shock as the cleric hastily covered himself.

Bene leaped to his feet, protesting his innocence. But the clerics were denouncing Bene and their fellow, and my heart sank. The man who had been pleasured by Bene knew he was caught and he desperately confessed the deed. He fell to his knees, crying for forgiveness.

The clerics were incensed. All I could think about was the bishop in Danelaw piercing Olvid with his sword.

"Come," I ordered Bene, pulling him after me. The only way out was through the sanctuary.

Bene didn't need to be told twice. He ran with me, leaving the startled clerics behind in the corridor. The sanctuary was filling with shuffling men, most still half asleep as they appeared for prayers. Some knelt on the stone floor and began rocking slightly as they chanted the ritual words.

Bene and I ran down the aisle, making them glance up in bewilderment. Then we were out the doors and on the wide plaza. The moon was shining down on the clear, chilly night. The lap, lap, lapping of the water echoed in the stillness.

"I'm so sorry," Bene panted as we ran down a side street. "I didn't mean—"

I stopped, putting my hand on his arm to listen. There was no sound of pursuit. "Don't be sorry. Do whatever you want, Bene."

He tilted his head. "I should have known you wouldn't be upset. You realize we can't go back there?"

"Definitely not." I shuddered slightly. "We took from Kristna for far too long without giving him worship. He's shown a generosity of spirit in waiting until now to cast us out." Kristna was a dangerous god, patient in seducing his followers, lingering until they turned to him in need and accepted him into their heart.

Bene looked around with interest. "Where will we go?"

"Where we need to be," I retorted. "Near Castropiero."

17

That night we found a rickety bridge that we could sleep under. As it turned out, doxies haunted the bridges offering themselves to each passerby. We needed to rent a room, so I would have to earn some coins.

I soon gathered patrons from those walking over the bridge. My first was a working man who gave us his day meal in exchange for a quick suck under the bridge. He was fairly clean, and soon I discovered the city folk washed more than most. Living on the water, they thought nothing of stripping off their clothing and dashing buckets of water over themselves. Indeed, the mild days encouraged such bathing.

Perhaps it was having Bene nearby or maybe it was the mellow air, but the streets of Veneto were nothing like my desperate stay in Brianda. There I had been harried from place to place, ending up on the docks, where I had to serve the rough oarsmen.

I didn't ask Bene to help, but he was eager to service a merchant or two and any lady who showed interest in him. Bene was not being satisfied by me, and his passionate drive was too intense for him to remain celibate like the clerics.

When I had an adequate stash of coins in hand, we returned to

Castropiero. I went from one house to the next, asking if there was a
room available. Our new prosperity bought us an undesirable cellar
down a flight of steps. The perpetual damp left mold on the walls and
our garments had to be hung up at night or they turned white with
mildew by morning.

I sacrificed a great deal of food to the *olfs* in exchange for their
concealment as I peered through the windows of Castropiero and
listened to the servants. The slaves trained, ate, and slept in their chamber on the uppermost floor, and were brought out only when they
serviced the masters or a patron. One of the slaves had gotten pregnant despite the potion used to suppress our fertility for a full turn of
seasons. She was forced to engage in the training despite her distended
belly, and was sold to the highest bidder at night for games she sorely
loathed to play.

Tomaz used the slaves for all sorts of personal care, ordering them
to wash him and tend to his copious excretory needs while he lounged
in the hall. Renata didn't pay much attention to the slaves, but she
was vicious from sheer carelessness, leaving a slave bound too long or
locked on display inside a cage until he wept. I didn't see Renata rutting with any slaves, but she did take a patron to her chamber. Judging
by his abundance of jewels and loud, bragging voice, he appeared to
be an influential man.

When he left Castropiero with the dawning light, I followed him.
A boatman was waiting for him, and they rapidly melded into the
darkness. I woke the boy I had paid to wait in a skiff, and with silent
pushes of his pole, we trailed the councillor to his grand palazzo. By
following Castropiero guests home, I got to see many great houses of
Veneto. It usually didn't take much for the serving boys to start talking
to me about their masters.

When I returned to our cellar with the dawning, sleepy and ready
for bed, I suddenly found what I had been looking for around every
corner.

Lexander was striding down the lane toward the pleasure house.
I had mistaken men for Lexander before in my desire to see him,

but I was always disappointed. The tall man with a smooth head inevitably turned out to be a stranger.

"Lexander!" I called out, my voice quavering.

He turned, and it was indeed Lexander. For a moment, he didn't recognize me. He had never imagined finding me in Veneto. "Marja?"

Through my tears and my laughter, we rushed together. Lexander's arms went around me, wiping everything from my mind.

"Marja, how can this be?" he breathed in pure delight.

I opened myself to him in my elation, as I did with the spirits, and I could sense his feelings—euphoria, confusion, passion, and something else . . . a slow-rising anger.

I could hardly speak. My fingers dug in, trying to hold on to him.

He glanced over at the imposing mansion. "Come, we must be away from here."

I stopped him from retreating back up the lane, and led him down the steps to our cellar. Bene was sitting on the cot, rubbing his eyes as if he had just awoken to find me gone.

"Bene, this is Lexander." I gave him a glance. "He was my master."

Bene's eyes widened, partly in fear. "The one who freed you?"

Lexander was looking around in frank disgust. The dirt floor was stained from decades of use, and the wet stench was overpowering. "What are you doing here, Marja?"

"I couldn't stay in Danelaw. I came to help the slaves." I gestured. "I rescued Bene from Montplaire."

Lexander closed the distance between us, seizing my shoulders. "You went to Montplaire? Tell me, Marja, what did you do?"

"Less than I intended," I admitted. "The ship from Stanbulin arrived and I tried to convince the other slaves to flee with me. Bene was the only one who did."

"What about Canille?" Lexander demanded.

Through his fervent grip and the last tendrils of our connection,

I suddenly understood. I should have known; Canille was once Lexander's consort. She was very much like him, and she had probably recognized his training in me. That was why she had watched me so curiously.

"Was Canille your consort when you lived in Veneto?" I asked.

"Yes." He released me. "When I saw that she was mistress of Montplaire . . . I could not bring myself to destroy it."

"You passed by," I said tightly. "But I got Bene out. I was too late to save the slaves you abandoned in Chivasso."

"Chivasso? You were there, too? What are you thinking, Marja? You nearly died getting out of Becksbury!"

Lexander glared at me, then at Bene, who was unusually silent. Bene had not expected an angry master to descend on us. Lexander advanced on him. "Tell me what happened in Montplaire! How did you get here? Be truthful or I will know you lie."

Bene scrambled out of the cot we shared and backed into the corner despite the slick walls.

"Don't scare Bene!" I demanded. "We didn't do anything to Montplaire. We ran away and walked here."

He stared at me. "You couldn't have."

"We traveled with the *peregrini* over the summits. The sanctuaries gave us food and a place to sleep."

"But you abhor Kristna." His expression darkened. "Marja, you cannot deny this is pure folly!"

"Ask Bene," I retorted. "Would you rather be a slave?"

"No," Bene retorted, blinking a few times at his own vehemence.

Lexander refused to look at Bene. "I won't let you get involved in this, Marja. It's far too dangerous."

"I don't take orders from you!"

We glared at each other. Then Lexander gestured curtly to Bene. "You, boy. Come with me."

Bene pressed his hands against his chest. I protested, "What do you want with Bene?"

"I won't harm you," Lexander told Bene impatiently. "I only want to talk." He shot me a glance. "Away from her."

He had never been so dismissive of me. I sat down on the bed and crossed my arms. I should have known it would be this way, with us split asunder. "Bene, you don't have to go with him. But if you do, he won't hurt you."

Bene hesitated, then stepped forward, as if he felt compelled to obey. I wondered if he would bolt the moment he reached the top of the steps. I almost hoped he would.

Lexander refused to look back as they left. I hurried to the door and up the steps to see where they went. They walked down the lane, receding at a measured pace. Lexander's hand was on Bene's shoulder as he spoke to him.

I sat down on the steps to wait for their return.

I grew very hungry as the morning passed, but I remained on the steps. When Lexander and Bene returned, something was different. I could tell as they approached that Bene wasn't frightened anymore. He had a bounce in his step, and was excited and happy. Lexander also looked more at ease, and he held a bag slung over his shoulder.

They brushed past me to go down into the cellar. Lexander pulled some flat bread and a jug from the bag and placed them on the table. "Perhaps you haven't eaten," he said curtly.

Bene knew we had given our last coins to the lady upstairs to pay for the cellar for another handful of days. We had planned on going out early to earn our meal.

Bene was trying not to grin, but he wasn't succeeding.

Lexander's golden eyes were unreadable. "I'll come by in a few days to check on you."

My hands were shaking. "Where are you going?"

"Into Castropiero. I'm taking Bene with me."

"No, Lexander!" I exclaimed. "These slaves are kept locked up all the time unless they're being used." I went to Bene, clutching his arm. "What are you doing?"

Bene glanced at Lexander, who nodded. "Lexander is going to pose as an assessor from Stanbulin, here to inspect the masters' training methods. I'll be his body servant."

My heart sank when I realized that Bene had already cleaved to Lexander. I had refused him for too long. Now he was determined to please Lexander.

And Lexander was manipulating him exactly as a slave master should. He was once more in complete control. "Bene is the right age and status to be my servant. That way he'll be safe from the masters in the house, while I'll have the benefit of his eyes in the lower halls."

I didn't care that Bene could hear. "You'll ruin everything I've tried to do with him, Lexander, if you use him this way."

Lexander gestured. "Bene?"

Bene replied obediently, "I want to do it, Marja."

"Surely you can't argue with that," Lexander said flatly. He threw some coins onto the table. "This should be enough for you to live without selling your body. It won't be safe without Bene to stand guard for you."

It sounded as if Bene had told him everything.

Lexander turned to look at me one last time as they left. He meant to chastise me without a word, showing by his pained expression how much I had disappointed him.

When he was gone, I fell facedown on the bed, too empty to even cry. Once I would have sworn that nothing could come between us. How very wrong I had been.

18

I spent the next day sitting at the end of the alleyway with my feet in the channel, communing with the sea spirits. They showed me fleets of ships that massed and fought far to the south, near the end of the Ditalia peninsula. Some of the sailors who were killed were from Veneto, and their death cries rang through the water with astonishing clarity. Venetians were people of the sea and were attuned to it like no other.

The *olfs* who dared to enter Castropiero told me some of what happened there. Tomaz lolled in his chair, barking orders at the servants designed to impress their visitor from Stanbulin. In their upper chamber, Renata put the slaves through their poses while Lexander paced among them, judging their ability. According to one *olf,* he encouraged a lovely girl with dusky skin and black eyes to please him with her mouth, and though he offered suggestions to improve her technique, on the whole he thoroughly enjoyed himself.

Late that afternoon, Lexander departed the house in a narrow boat propelled by a servant. He was facing away as he helped Renata sit down. Now he was dressed in high Veneto fashion with a short cape over his shoulder and tight leggings that revealed his strong thighs and the curve of his buttocks. My rebellious heart leaped at the sight of him.

After a long wait, the boat returned with its passengers. Lexander was leaning close to the mistress, listening to her. Renata gestured, her nervous hands moving too abruptly to be graceful. Their attitude was so intimate that I instinctively drew back.

The sun was very low, glinting off the water and the windows of the pleasure house. Soon the night would come and patrons would arrive for the entertainment. Lexander would doubtless partake of the slaves to maintain his role as an assessor.

Lexander courteously helped Renata from the boat onto the ledge of the doorway. Her movements made the boat tilt, and she laughed uneasily. She was trying to be alluring with her sidelong looks and shy smiles. Surely Lexander saw through her artifice. But he responded by holding her hand longer than was necessary, and gazing appreciatively at her.

As Renata entered the house, Lexander caught sight of me. I had pulled back to crouch in a niche between a rain barrel and the buttress of the neighboring house. In the shadows, he could only see the pale oval of my face.

Without a flicker of acknowledgment, he followed Renata. His light comment about the beauty of the evening carried to my ears. Then they disappeared into Castropiero.

The next morning Lexander returned to my cellar. He entered with a waft of spicy scent. I took a deep breath, realizing it was the smell of the pleasure house.

I stood up and met his eyes. He crossed his arms and gazed down at me. There was an odd constraint between us, as we stood stiffly away from each other. I wanted to touch him, and show him my heart wordlessly so he would understand. But he wouldn't allow that, not now.

"What are you going to do?" I asked.

"I used the Kristna followers to destroy a house in Iberia as well as the one you saw in Ditalia. Unlike Becksbury, those bishops had no need to prove themselves to the clerics, but it was not difficult to inflame and disgust the locals. I made sure they'll never allow a pleasure house to rise there again. I will be more difficult in Veneto, but it can be done."

"But you forget about the slaves."

"They aren't sent to Stanbulin, which is more than enough. I'll deal with Saaladet soon . . ."

His tone sent a chill through me. I should have known it from the start. His quest for vengeance would not be satisfied by anything less. He would destroy all of the masters.

He dropped a dozen coins on the table. "You can stop lurking about, Marja. The servants have noticed you. It's only a matter of time before it's brought to Renata's attention, and she'll snap you up."

"I know what I'm doing—"

He shot me a dark look. "Don't think for a moment I'll let you enter Castropiero. I shall carry you out myself if you try."

Lexander stalked from the room, not bothering to hear my retort.

The weeping walls seemed to close in on me. During those long nights on my journey here, wondering what would happen when we met again, I had never imagined this.

But I wouldn't let Lexander stop me. The sea spirits had given me the information I needed, and I was determined to set my plan in motion.

All power in Veneto was centered on the sea, so that was how I found myself standing naked on the railing of a bridge. I was attracting quite a large crowd of passersby, all wondering why I was exposing myself. A man tried to grab my leg to pull me back, but I shook him off as I sighted my quarry.

An elaborate vessel was being propelled by a boatman down the channel. It had a low, curving hull with carving on the upturned prow and stern, like a miniature Noroship. But this boat had no sails, only a cushion in the center covered by a canopy edged in gold fringe.

Seated under the canopy was Domen Silvo, the Doj of Veneto. The *doj* had supreme authority over the city—commanding the defense fleet and militia, conducting foreign affairs, dispensing justice, and supervising the administration of services. According to the doxies on the streets, the *doj*'s various councillors performed the actual work in consultation with men from the highest-ranking families in the city. But the *doj* had the final say in everything.

I had heard stories about the grand *doj* from the first day we had arrived in Veneto. On the death of the previous *doj,* the people of Veneto had gathered around his palace to mourn and pray to the gods to give them a worthy successor. The name of Domen Silvo was suddenly called from the crowd and had been shouted out by all the spectators, and thus by general acclaim he had become their next ruler.

I was aiming high, I admit it. I could have chosen one of the *doj*'s councillors, and I almost settled on the admiral of the fleet, since I could rely on the sea spirits for information. But the *olfs* who went into the admiral's palace showed me that he kept two lusty wives who much occupied him with piquant pleasure. I would have a difficult time gaining a personal hold in that house.

The *doj,* on the other hand, was a solitary man. According to gossip, Silvo's wife was overly concerned with matters of the nursery. The *doj* had visited Castropiero every few days, which meant he would be amiable to my arts. The worst I had seen him do inside the pleasure house was to clench a slave's hair as he pulled her head back. His expression had been oddly remote, as if he was unaffected even in the throes of pleasure.

As the boat approached the bridge, the *doj* reclined back even after he saw me. I stretched up, holding my hands high and arching my back. I waited until the boat had nearly reached me and the *doj* lifted a brow in appreciation.

With a final plea for the sea spirits to aid me, I leaped off the bridge. I stretched out, diving into the canal right before the *doj*'s prow. The water hit me like a slap in the face, making my entire body tingle.

I was blinded by the murkiness, but the sea spirits warned me of the hull of the boat above and the silt below. Without their help I would have plowed into the bottom. I turned and surfaced by the side of the boat exactly where the *doj* was looking down.

I smiled up at him as the water streamed off my face and hair. I drew on the force of my *inua,* letting it shine through my eyes. There was a commotion on the bridge as people pointed to me, exclaiming over my dive.

"Fine day for a swim," the *doj* commented. He had the sort of face you pass by on the street, with plain, regular features. His shock of dark hair was tied back, and there was no ostentation in his dress or manner. Yet there was something remarkable in his confidence, as if he conversed with naked women in the water every day.

I treaded closer. "I've come to share a secret of the sea with you."

Domen Silvo grimaced, clearly doubtful of my sanity. People were still watching from the bridge, and he shifted irritably at being forced into this public situation. He raised his hand to urge his boatman to push on.

"Two days ago there was a battle at sea," I told him. "The Veneto fleet suffered many losses and now flees back to the city. Ships are pursuing them, harrying any that lag."

Silvo's voice was deadly. "Who are you?"

I held his gaze. "I am but a servant, a voice for the sea spirits who wish to help the great Doj of Veneto protect his water city."

"I see. What do you expect me to do about this . . . news?"

"I don't know," I replied honestly. "I merely provide the knowledge you desire."

He was intrigued, and he didn't tell the boatman to push on. But the *doj* was a cynical man and would not make the mistake of trusting me easily.

But I was only a naked girl, so what danger could I afford him? I gave him a smile that I hoped conveyed my amusement at his dilemma. I could not show him how much I needed him to respond.

"Come," Silvo ordered. "Get in."

The *doj* and his boatman shifted their weight so I could pull myself inside. People were still pointing at the boat, having recognized the *doj*. He gestured to a velvet lap robe, and I gratefully pulled it around my shoulders. The boat was propelled forward under the bridge and down the channel. I was on my way.

The *doj* took me to his palatial residence. The three levels were fronted by colonnades of arches. Rows of sparkling windows backed the balconies that ran the length of the extensive building. The bricks had been laid in delicate patterns of red and white diamonds.

The palace was busy with freemen and slaves performing administrative duties. The *doj's* reception chamber was on the uppermost level. The height of the large room was broken by the loft across the back, its dark wooden beams and spindle railing contrasting with the creamy white walls.

Silvo went to a metal casket and unlocked it. He placed a folded parchment inside and turned the key. Then he consulted a few stiff papers that had been placed on a table.

I waited, exhilarated that I had caught his attention. Now I needed to use my wiles to win his confidence. I kept the velvet lap robe tightly around my shoulders, knowing this was not the time to try to seduce him.

"So you claim to know where my perimeter fleet is now," he finally said.

I nodded. "If you have a map, I can show you."

With a sardonic shrug, Silvo removed a scroll from the shelf and unfurled it. I carefully followed the lines, having seen similar maps in Montplaire. But this one confused me at first because it showed only the Veneto Bay, a long finger of water. Then I realized the land along the western edge was the peninsula of Ditalia.

I closed my eyes and tried to reach out to the sea spirits through the sound of lapping water drifting in the window. The images that came of the retreating Veneto fleet were of a hulking mass of land to the west but nothing more distinct.

"I need to touch the water to know exactly where they are," I declared.

The *doj* shook his head impatiently, but he took me down a private staircase to the interior boat launch. Double gates were opened to allow the boats in and out. I thrust one hand into the water and let the other move over the map that I had brought along. The sea spirits guided me, and I placed my finger in a certain spot about halfway down the bay.

"Little more than a day away," the *doj* said sharply. "They're supposed to be—"

He broke off, examining me. He thought I was a charlatan, at best, or perhaps mad. But he asked, "How many of my ships are there?"

The number came to me instantly. "Six."

He didn't believe me. "And you claim they're being pursued?"

"Yes, by at least a dozen vessels." I closed my eyes and described the shape of the boats and the swarthy men with flashing white teeth who manned them.

He tapped the map briefly. "What is it you expect me to do?"

"Whatever you think is best."

He considered that. "I want you to say here until I find out more about this."

I smiled. "If that is your wish."

With a slight bow of my head in respect to the *doj,* I followed the servant he summoned to a cramped room on the lower level. There were no windows. Two fat candles illuminated a simple bed, a table, and two chairs.

When the door closed behind the servant, I wasn't surprised to hear the latch fall shut with a click. I tested the door and found I was locked in. I could have called an *olf* to open the door for me, but I was exactly where I wanted to be.

I sat down and began to wait.

I didn't see the *doj* for two days. The servant brought me food and a plain shift to wear, but refused to tell me anything. I couldn't speak

to the sea spirits from the enclosed room, so I had no way of knowing what was happening to the Veneto fleet. The *olfs* that popped in
and out were more preoccupied with what had been served at the
expansive table rather than discussions of fleet movements by the
councillors.

I wondered what Lexander would think when he came to the
cellar and found me gone. Likely he'd believe I was out wandering in
the city.

Then the door creaked open and the *doj* finally appeared. I blinked at the addition of two more candles, brightening my room. Then
he sent the servants out, shutting the door behind them.

From the intense interest in his face, I knew. "Your ships have
returned."

"Yes. My perimeter fleet was cut to a third of its size by the Cileans
in a lightning raid. Nobody could have returned faster with word
of it." His eyes narrowed. "If I had not sent ships to meet them, the
Cileans might have challenged the defenses of the home fleet, as well.
But in the battle that ensued, the enemy lost two ships and was driven
off. How did you know?"

"I told you, the sea spirits speak to me." He still didn't believe me,
so I added, "What does it matter, if my information is sound?"

"Perhaps." Silvo gestured and we each sat in one of the chairs.
With my hair demurely coiled at my neck, I must have looked like
one of his servants. No wonder he was perplexed by me.

"Who are your people?" Silvo asked. "You speak like a native of
Veneto, but you're far too fair."

"I came a great distance to get here. I followed the *peregrini* path
across the summits to reach your city. When I arrived, I knew that I had
not been called here by Kristna. The sea spirits spoke to me instead."

"A young woman traveling alone in winter? Have you no family,
no one who can guarantee your word?"

"My companion was a young man," I said. "We stayed in the sanctuary here until . . . he was caught rutting with one of the clerics. As I
said, we were not called by Kristna."

Silvo raised one brow. "Where is this companion?"

I could not mention Castropiero. "I know not. He disappeared into the streets a few days ago. I can only hope he has found a patron worthy of him."

Silvo nodded, obviously prepared to check my assertions with the clerics at the sanctuary. "What else have you foreseen for my city?"

"I can hear nothing from the sea locked in this room," I countered. "I need my freedom in order to speak to the spirits."

He nodded shortly. "You can go wherever you desire. What else do you want?"

I stood up, knowing it was not what he expected. I went to the door and found it open. On the other side was a long corridor with rooms opening off of it. There were many voices and people hurrying about.

I turned and smiled at him. "First, I would like to bathe. Then I would like to join you at this evening's meal."

19

1 spent the afternoon swathed in luxury like nothing I had experienced before. I was shown into a cool, spacious chamber filled with a dappled reflected light from the channel. The tub of hammered silver held frothing hot water that soothed me down to the bones. The servants were quick to fetch anything I desired, bathing me as expertly as Helanas could have wished and rubbing me with fine scented creams. Several beautiful dresses were brought for my approval. I chose a gown of supple weave that clung to my body and flowed in an amber swirl to my feet.

When I was dressed in my finery, I returned to the boat launch. I pulled back the flared sleeve and plunged my hand into the water. A servant had followed me, and likely would report everything I did to the *doj*.

I sank into the rhythms of the sea, feeling the spirits welcoming me. They showed ships plying the waters near and far. Many were winged ships skimming the waves, while the heavier merchant vessels plowed through the water with stately majesty. It was difficult separating the images, but at length I settled on a pirate ship putting into a cove. The landmarks were distinctive, and I envisioned the map the *doj* had shown me, moving my finger down the imaginary line of the bay. The spirits indicated which island the pirates used to resupply their ships.

It was something that might or might not interest the *doj,* but that was not my concern. My intent was to become a veritable fountain of information flowing from the sea.

When the *doj* joined me at the table, he said not a word about Bene or the Kristna sanctuary. Yet he must have verified my tale with the clerics. If Bene had still been with me, I would not have risked it for fear they would try to punish him for seducing the cleric. But I had not done anything amiss.

I maintained my status as guest, while deftly serving the *doj* during our meal. I held the bowl of water for him to wash his fingers after every course, and then wiped his hands with the white napkins. I trusted the mix of intimacy and mystery would be intoxicating.

He asked about my travels and I told him of the beauty of the frozen mountains and the clean, rosy-cheeked people who lived there. He had sailed to many parts of the great Azure Sea, but he had never ventured inland to the heights of the summits.

Etien's lessons served me well with the *doj.* He was a political man, accustomed to thinking about trade with nations and expanding Veneto's authority. Thanks to Montplaire, I understood the fundamentals of the regimes of the Auldland.

Olfs played on the table throughout the meal, once snatching a bit of food from the *doj's* fingers. He didn't see the *olf,* but he noticed me watching him closely when he sprinkled a few drops of wine on the tile floor, his lips moving as he made the customary offering. The *olfs* clearly approved of the city's ruler. Yet I had discovered from Overlord Jedvard that a sovereign could be ruthless in upholding his benevolent rule. The *doj's* interests coincided with mine at the moment, but I had no doubt that he would be merciless in defending his city, at my expense if need be.

I set out to intrigue the *doj,* but slowly I became captivated. I admired his subtle questions and assertions, so unlike the brazen ways of most men. He quietly received my attentions like he was accustomed to being served. When I told him about the pirates' lair, he nodded graciously.

Silvo was certainly a dominant man. It gave me a secret thrill to feel his appraising gaze. He picked out the choicest pieces of meat and the ripest fruit for me, urging me to eat and concerned about my slender form, worn from my long journey. He made sure I wanted for nothing and was quick to anticipate my needs. His address was ever courteous.

It reminded me of how Lexander used to treat me ... but now was not the moment to be distracted. I needed the *doj* to desire me. I was excited by him, went flushed and heated when he looked at me. Yet I remained demure, lowering my eyes and touching him lightly only while serving him.

I found myself wondering why Silvo's consort avoided his company. But the *olfs* whispered to me that she was preparing to pass through to the Otherworld. They could feel her *inua* very strongly, though I got the impression from them of a wasted body, her yellowed skin stretched like gauze.

My gasp made the *doj* lift a brow. "Yes?"

I could not lie. "Your consort . . . she is very ill."

He avoided my eyes. "All of Veneto knows how she has suffered. Some say it was bearing too many children. But she loves the babes so."

His consort and their children lived in the other end of the mansion. I couldn't tell if he felt sorry for her or was repulsed by her illness.

After we had partaken of the ices at the end of the meal, I made a show of rising. "Thank you for your hospitality, Domen Silvo."

"You're leaving?" His quick glance was shrewd. He understood gratitude and was comfortable being the provider, so it bothered him that I had asked for so little.

I smiled. "You said I was free to go as I will."

"Yes, certainly you may. But must you?" Silvo stood up and joined me, taking my hand. "I can give you a chamber to use as your own."

"With a guard at the door?" I teased. In truth, I would rather not return to the cellar.

Silvo gave a shrug. "If you wish to leave, I will accompany you to the boat that will convey you to your destination."

I raised his hand to my lips, kissing him with fervent appreciation. "Thank you, my *doj*. You have been most . . . kind."

My lips caressed the back of his hand. Impulsively, I turned it, lightly kissing and stroking his strong, square palm. He had the roughened hands of a man who had sailed ships and hauled goods. His great-uncle had been *doj* two generations ago, but Silvo had not rested on the reputation of his family. It was said he had made his fortune for himself.

Silvo caressed my face lightly, drawing me back to his side to kiss me. I responded with delight. He was fascinated, true, but in his touch he revealed his eagerness to gain mastery over me.

He pushed me down on the cushioned bench, and I laid my head against the gold pillow where his arm had rested during our meal. As Silvo leaned over me, his hand on my waist, a servant entered and removed our plates. The servant's gaze shifted away when he met my eyes.

Silvo ignored the man as he kissed me. I didn't protest as he gradually pulled my dress down the curve of my shoulders. The servant saw it, slowing to watch. Silvo must have noticed.

He hesitated, expecting me to object, but when I kissed him harder, he tugged until my bosom was exposed.

Another servant entered and put out several of the candles. When he was through, he waited by the door, staring inward where he couldn't help but watch as Silvo dragged up my skirt to reveal my long legs.

Perhaps for some women the humiliation of being taken before the servants would not be pleasurable, but it added to my excitement. I had always been watched during my training, and found it heightened my sensations. Perhaps that's why Silvo enjoyed the pleasure house, where he could rut with compliant women in front of others.

Silvo grew eager at my uninhibited response, baring his teeth as if he would devour me. When he spread my legs, I was ready for him. He was still clothed with only his *tarse* exposed. The servant licked his lips as Silvo took me.

Other servants, men and women both, entered while Silvo thrust into me. They removed dishes and poured more wine, acting as if nothing was happening. I moaned in abandon.

Silvo was caught up in the waves of pleasure that wrenched my body and could not withhold his own climax. But when I thought it was over, he continued pumping into me, still rigid. It carried me higher and further than before. He kept plunging into me until another burst of passion made him cry out. I lay fully replete beneath him.

The days that followed were surpassingly pleasant, the sort of life that could be mine with help from the sea spirits. But I was not one to seek the finer things for their own sake.

I'm sure the *doj* sensed that in me. He probed me ever deeper, both in flesh and mind. In doing so, I naturally came to know him better. He was the eldest son of an impoverished line of his family. He had fought hard to elevate himself and never forgot that he had been given nothing. There was an inherent roughness in his blunt speech and lack of pretension, as if his polish was only a veneer. I saw him do nothing deceitful, but I felt sure he would bend the law to suit his needs.

So I reached out to that part of him, the wild young Domen Silvo inside the *doj*. Though he was the ruler of Veneto, I spoke to him frankly, without elaborate honorifics or compliments.

I didn't mind it when he corrected me, whether it was my ignorance or a mistaken notion, and that puzzled him. I thoroughly enjoyed all of his efforts to gain control of me, knowing that even he could not plumb the depths of my submissive nature.

Yet at times Silvo knew I was preoccupied by something . . . or someone. I claimed that my abstraction was part of my ability to speak to the spirits, that meditative part of me, but he remained suspicious just the same.

I left the palace each day, taking long walks through the city. The *doj* had me followed sometimes, but with the *olfs'* help I eluded the servants. Whenever I returned to the cellar, I changed things in the room so Lexander would know I was still in the city. More coins were occasionally left behind, and the owner of the house said my fee had been paid for the next moon.

I waited in the cellar one afternoon, since that was when Lexander had come before. I even slept there one night, hoping he would appear in the morning. But he didn't. It was just as well since I could not give him what he desired. But I wanted to warn him about my plan.

From the *doj's* palace, I often asked the *olfs* to go into the pleasure house to see what happened there, but they were reluctant to enter. One *olf* did tell me that Bene had been rutting with Lexander. Afterward, Bene fell asleep with his head on Lexander's chest. I could almost see the sheets wound around them, revealing Bene's shapely buttocks and slender beauty.

What hurt the most was the *olf's* impression of Lexander's contentment. I wanted Lexander to care for me as he once did. But instead, he was satisfying himself at Bene's expense.

I wasn't sure what Lexander would think of my efforts to gain the trust of the most powerful man in Veneto. I only hoped he would heed my warning when it came time to get out of Castropiero. So far he had refused to listen to me.

That evening I whispered to the *doj* that his councillor of trade was using city ships for his own business. The *doj* listened intently, stroking my hair during our meal, more pleased with me than usual. He pressed the delicacies on me, urging me to eat more.

I basked in his adoration. But I wondered if Silvo would grow ever more possessive and try to impose his will on me. I appreciated that he was a domineering and forceful lover, but I would not allow him to command me in other ways. The fact that he was *doj* made it near certain he would try.

As we were finishing our ices, the servant announced, "The house of Castropiero, your grace."

Renata walked in first, followed by Lexander. The *doj* was not surprised, so he must have invited them. I should have known Silvo would be brazen enough about his appetites to bring them here.

Lexander was superb. His eyes widened in surprise at seeing me by the *doj*'s side, but he quickly recovered. Silvo was watching him closely, as he did everyone.

Two pleasure slaves followed Renata and Lexander, kneeling at their feet, *gesig*. I knew the pose of surrender would appeal to Silvo. One of them was a particularly stunning, auburn-haired woman.

I sipped my wine and casually followed their greetings. Renata was filled with nervous energy, twisting her fingers together and chattering too fast. I was not concerned that she would recognize me as the waif in the ragged leggings who had briefly haunted their courtyard. My face was enhanced with cosmetics as the *doj* preferred, and my hair hung loose and tousled. The wide neckline of my dress kept slipping off my shoulders, exposing far more bosom than was usual even in Veneto.

The *doj* spoke to Lexander as if they were acquainted, which meant Silvo must have gone to Castropiero since we had met. The man was insatiable!

I smiled as the *doj* introduced Lexander and Renata. Lexander's eyes were shuttered tight as he nodded to me. My heart called to him, standing there so fine. But his rigid stance revealed his anger and shock, reminding me of the distance between us.

"Where have you been hiding?" Renata cooed to the *doj*. She came close to the table as if her intimacy with Silvo was assured. "I don't think we've ever gone this long without seeing you."

The *doj* looked away as if bored by her presumption.

"We are pleased you allowed us to come tonight," Renata hastened to add. "We brought two of our best slaves. I believe they're your current favorites . . ."

Perhaps she said it to make me jealous, but it had the opposite effect. I would much rather see Silvo rutting with the pretty slaves than Lexander.

But Silvo declined with a bland expression. "Many thanks, but no. I have quite enough to tend to." His hand slipped into the neck of my dress. I gasped as his fingers tweaked my nipple hard.

I leaned closer to him, as he expected. I couldn't even glance at Lexander. The tension in the room quickly rose.

Renata drawled, "I'm glad to see you've been well entertained."

Silvo touched my chin, lifting my face. He licked me lightly on the cheek. "Delicious!"

Renata's hands were clenched, when she should have laughed it off. She wanted more from the *doj,* something beyond his patronage. Could it be that she lusted for him? I had never seen Silvo visit Renata's chamber, and he was not likely to rut with her unless it was in front of the others.

Renata shifted back and forth as if unsure of what to say, eyeing me sharply.

Silvo was more decisive. He pushed my head down to his groin.

I stiffened, a rare moment of resistance. We struggled for just an instant, until I gave in and began to nuzzle the velvet over his *tarse.*

"Suck on it," Silvo ordered in low voice.

It was not how I intended for Lexander to find out what I was doing. But it made the situation pretty clear. I unlaced Silvo's pants and dove in, licking and drawing his thickening *tarse* out.

"We will leave you to your pleasure," Lexander suddenly announced. It sounded as if his jaw was clenched.

Perhaps Silvo heard his fury, but he would assume it was a reaction to his insult—taunting the pleasure masters with a toy more worthy than theirs.

Renata ordered the slaves to follow, bidding the *doj* a falsely affectionate farewell.

Then they were gone and I had to focus on the task at hand,

confirming Silvo's assertion that I was preferable to the attentions of two well-trained pleasure slaves.

The next day when I arrived at the cellar, Lexander was waiting for me. "Marja, have you gone mad?"

I removed the silk brocade cloak Silvo had given me. "I've made an ally of the *doj*."

"You brought yourself to Renata's attention. Now she will not rest until she owns you." He ran a hand over his smooth head, a rare gesture of despair. "They rely on the *doj* to grant export of pleasure slaves from Veneto, but the tariffs are high. They've been trying to ease the burden by making him reliant on them. Then you appear!"

"I have influence over him," I reminded him.

"Only until Renata offers him something he wants more. She was annoyed enough after that display, flaunting his attention elsewhere."

I shook my head. "I give Silvo things he can't get—"

"Pleasure is fleeting, Marja. And even your ability to submit is not enough."

"I rely on the spirits, as well as my own nature," I insisted. "I can save the slaves and destroy Castropiero at the same time."

Lexander's tone was harsh. "I should take you away from here before it's too late. If I go fetch Bene, will you wait here until I return?"

"No. But you should send Bene to me. I'm afraid that your toying with him is hurting him. He doesn't need another master, Lexander."

"Then you refuse to leave with me?" he demanded. "I think you *have* gone mad. The *doj* is nobody to trifle with, Marja."

I took a deep breath. "Please, Lexander, when I send you a message to leave Castropiero, get Bene out immediately. Otherwise I'll have to rescue you both from the *doj*'s prison."

I turned and left the cellar. I had never walked away from Lexander before. But now I hurried from Castropiero and everything that love had once meant to me.

———

I avoided Castropiero after that. I couldn't bear to see Lexander again.

The *doj,* on the other hand, showered me with gifts in the hope of making me dependent on him. He persisted even though I cared not for such things. I traded one ring with a fiery stone for the use of a room in a boarding house. It was on the western end of Veneto where the sun lowered over the bay. I could sit in the window and touch the water when I reached down with my hand.

I gave the sea spirits everything in exchange for their images. The distant ship movements were confusing, the images jumbled and fragmented, a string of instants preserved in watery echoes by the spirits. Some things didn't make sense to me or the *doj.* Sometimes the passing of time brought clarity. But there was enough of interest to keep the *doj* fascinated beyond the visceral delight I could give him.

Every scrap of information had the potential to be the key I could use to free the pleasure slaves. I concentrated on the ships since most of the waterside activities were too mundane—fishermen in humble villages, women collecting shellfish in the tidal plains, and busy shopkeepers along the Veneto channels going about their business.

Very late one night, I was considering the montage the sea spirits were showing me when it all came together. The Cilean ships were returning stealthily, alone and in pairs. They had caught my eye for days because similar ships had attacked the Veneto perimeter fleet not long ago. But I hadn't noticed until now that they were moving ever northward toward the water city despite their seemingly east-west tack.

The fact that they had not yet drawn together was deceptive. Likely the merchant shipmasters who had seen them were also not alarmed.

The first line of Veneto defense, the perimeter fleet, had been destroyed while the remnants were in the repair docks. For the moment, Veneto was vulnerable to just such a furtive approach by an enemy fleet.

I gathered all the information I could, knowing that something inconsequential could tip the balance in convincing the *doj*. I could not show any undue eagerness. I readied for bed, prepared to launch my attack against Castropiero after I had warned Lexander and Bene to get out.

I asked an *olf* to go into Castropiero for the first time in days. When it returned, the *olf's* puffy face was crumpled in pain.

Going closer, I murmured assurances, hoping it wouldn't simply disappear. "What did you see?" I breathed, holding out my hands for the *olf* to rest on.

The *olf* whispered, *"The game has ended."*

My heart twisted—Renata must have discovered Lexander was not an assessor. But I couldn't react, not with the *olf* ready to vanish at any moment.

"What's happened to them?" I asked. "Are they still . . . alive?"

The *olf* was trembling, but I coaxed everything out, forcing myself to remain calm despite every revelation. Lexander had been thrown into a cellar and was lying unconscious. Bene had been beaten and questioned by Renata until he was insensible. The agony in his torn back flared red-hot through the *olf*. I had no doubt that Bene had told the mistress everything he knew.

The *olf* disappeared in a blue flash, and I nearly toppled off the windowsill trying to stop it. But I had heard enough. Renata knew Lexander was renegade. She would send both of them to Stanbulin as soon as passage could be arranged.

20

At first light, I returned to the palace and went to the *doj*'s anteroom. The sentries wouldn't let anyone into Silvo's private chambers unless he specifically ordered it, and no one would dare wake him unless it was an emergency.

Anything out of the ordinary might arouse the *doj*'s suspicions, so I waited patiently in the anteroom. I couldn't take any interest in the information I brought him. Yet I would have to carefully orchestrate what I told him in order to prompt him to move against Castropiero.

When the *doj* appeared, I was curled up on the divan in one of the low-cut, elegant dresses he favored. Petitioners usually waited in the anteroom to see him on business, but if anyone else had been present, I wouldn't have dared take such a provocative pose. It was Silvo's choice to whom he exposed me.

"Early again, Marja?" He gestured for me to follow him into his private chamber with the mezzanine. The round tables were stacked with new documents.

"The spirits showed me there are Cilean ships in the bay," I told him. "Some are traveling in pairs."

"Where?" Silvo demanded.

I shook my head. "It's confusing because they keep changing course. But there's at least three score of them."

Silvo was scowling down at a paper. "That is more than I was told. The Cileans would not likely send reinforcements when my scouts report they have retreated."

I sat down, tucking my legs beneath me. Idly gazing out the glass, I said, "Oh, no, they're heading toward Veneto."

He looked up at that. I set my chin dreamily on the back of my hand and watched the birds flying to their tiny nests in the carved eaves of the palace. I emptied my mind of everything but the sky and the giddy *olfs* bouncing on the steps up to the mezzanine.

"Do you have any idea how close they are?" he pressed.

"No," I said. "But I could ask, if you wish."

"Do that." His tone was grim, as if already pondering how to proceed. He would likely send out more scouts. But the Cileans could turn and retreat at any time. I needed to be sure they would continue advancing to be able to use them effectively against Castropiero.

From the anteroom beyond came the rising voices of councillors and petitioners who had arrived to see the *doj*. I left through the private door and went down the spiral staircase.

Going to my usual spot in the boat launch, I knelt by the water and steadied myself, reaching out to the sea spirits. Some of the Cilean ships were joining together as they neared Veneto. I was surprised to find they were little more than a day away, much closer than when I had first seen them. Time was always tricky with the spirits—the past and the present sometimes merged in odd ways.

"The *doj* wants to see you," a servant said behind me. They treated me with the utmost politeness despite having seen me in the most compromising positions.

I followed the servant up the back stairs to the *doj*'s chamber. The voices of the men in the anteroom were louder, as if he had sent them away to admit me.

"Well?" he demanded.

"The ships are much closer than I thought. Only a day's sail from Veneto."

"I've just received word. My councilors believe the destruction of our perimeter fleet was the first phase in their plan to sack Veneto. The Cileans waited just long enough for us to let our guard down."

"The spirits say the Cileans know your ship deployments," I told him. "That's how they ambushed your perimeter fleet and avoided the notice of merchant shipping as they approached."

"Who told them?" he demanded.

"The house of Castropiero gives information to Cilean spies."

The *doj* straightened abruptly, putting it together as I had hoped. Nearly all of his councillors visited Castropiero, often arranging to meet there. Surely the great men talked as if the pleasure slaves were nothing. But the slaves could report what they heard to Renata and Tomaz, and if the masters were in sympathy with the Cileans, they would be able to divulge the inner workings of the city.

"That new man . . . Lexander," Silvo ventured.

"Renata has done away with him," I lied smoothly. "He discovered their association with the Cileans and intended to expose them."

Silvo shook his head. "Then it was Renata herself involved in this. Who is her contact?"

"That's all they've shown me." I went to the window, watching the birds again. *I want nothing,* I chanted silently to myself. I imagined myself as a reed being swayed by flowing water, moving only at the behest of the spirits.

"But you must know more," Silvo said, expressing a rare frustration.

I took a few deep breaths, then said, "The loudest call I hear is from my belly."

I smiled at him, then quietly left the room. I had done it a dozen times before in just the same way.

The servants soon heard that the Cileans were bearing down on Veneto. I unobtrusively pilfered some food as their talk grew louder, anxious about their safety. When I left, a servant was right on my heels. Silvo must have given him special orders because he stayed very close, determined not to lose sight of me. But the *olfs* turned him around on a footbridge and he was heading back the way he came before he realized his mistake.

The lanes filled with people as news spread of the approaching Cilean fleet. I had to fight my way through city folk rushing to secure their homes and a flood of sailors who were suddenly called to duty.

When I reached the cellar, I crouched on the slimy bottom step in the doorway. It wasn't long before the tramp of feet echoing down the cobbled lane grew louder and a dozen sentries appeared. They wore the *doj*'s colors, so I ducked inside the cellar to avoid being recognized.

Some of the sentries stood guard as the others climbed up the steps to the double doors of Castropiero. The gatekeeper had no choice but to let them in when they showed their orders from the *doj*. As they disappeared inside, I asked an *olf* to follow them.

There were plenty of *olfs* curious about the commotion and they eagerly bounced among the sentries. The frightened servants did as they were ordered and led the sentries directly to the masters' chambers. Both were still asleep when they were routed from their beds.

The sentries took Renata and Tomaz into custody. With the Cileans coming, the *doj* would try to get information about the plan of attack from them.

The sentries placed Renata and Tomaz in a palanquin that had a bolt on the door. It infuriated Renata and confused Tomaz to be confined. Renata was nervously twisting the ends of her veil around her fingers, tearing the delicate tissue.

As soon as the sentries disappeared with the master and mistress of Castropiero, a young boy slipped out the side door and scurried down the lane. I could hear the raised voices as the other servants panicked. The streets were also getting louder as criers gave warning that the Cilean marauders were coming.

I marched across the courtyard to the kitchen door. I didn't try the main door on the second level because the old doorkeeper was not likely to admit anyone until his master and mistress returned. But the kitchen was wide open. The cook had locked herself in the pantry when the sentries had arrived and was refusing the other servants' entreaties to come out.

The demons who had taken root in Castropiero pricked at me, trying to frighten me away from their lair by showing me all the ways my plan could go awry—Renata talking her way out of custody, or the *doj* catching me in the act. But I didn't hesitate.

I announced in a ringing voice, "Your master and mistress are traitors to Veneto! They have conspired with the Cilean fleet that now threatens our city. The *doj* has taken them prisoner and will punish them as they deserve. As he will punish anyone who assisted them in this terrible deed . . ."

I glared all around threateningly. The girls put their hands to their mouths, and one flung her apron over her head and burst into tears.

I strode through the inner door to the stairs to the next level. I knew exactly where to go to reach the slaves' chamber despite the doubts laid by the evil spirits in my mind. At the top of a narrower flight of stairs was a door secured by a latch.

The scrape of the hook being lifted was loud. I wondered how many of the slaves listened for that sound in dread. Some must have been locked in this one dreary room for moons on end.

I flung the door open. A feeble light came through the cloudy white glass of the round window high in the wall. The slaves were rising up in their cots at the sound of my entry. Before I could say a word, they tumbled from their beds and knelt, *gesig*. A few swiped at their faces furtively, still bleary from sleep.

"Stand!" I declared. "I've taken Castropiero to set you free. Your master and mistress are traitors to Veneto and have been seized by the *doj*'s sentries. They won't be returning to this house again."

In truth, Renata might indeed be able to convince the *doj* of her innocence, but I intended to be gone by then. Along with the slaves.

They stirred and glanced at one another, but they didn't understand.

"I was a pleasure slave once, but I was set free." I lifted my arm, letting the cloak slide back to reveal my satin dress. It gleamed richly even in the dim light.

A wiry young man scrambled to his feet and approached me cautiously. He wore a brief tunic like the others, revealing his arms and legs. "You say our master and mistress are gone? They were arrested?"

This lad must be a kindred spirit to Bene. I pushed the door open to show them there was no servant or master lurking behind me. "Come see for yourself. You've longed to escape, and this is your chance."

"What about the servants?" the auburn-haired girl cried. "We'll be punished."

The young man's dark eyes burned with an eager light. "We shall see about that."

He started down the steps. I gestured urgently for the others to follow. "Come, it's not safe to remain here. Stay together!"

They followed us down the stairs, clutching each other and stepping tentatively. The pregnant woman was among them, her distended belly pushing out her skimpy tunic. Her legs looked very thin by comparison. I noticed that the girl with auburn hair was hanging on the arm of the burliest slave, looking to him for protection.

The boy who reminded me of Bene led the way, avoiding the doorkeeper's post and going down another flight of stairs to the side exit on the lowest level. It opened on the alleyway. He pushed the door wide and saw there was nothing preventing his escape. With a flashing grin at the other slaves, he ran off. His bare legs looked strong enough to carry him far.

"Take a cloak with you!" I called after him, but he was gone. I closed the door, hoping he would be all right in that tunic, without a coin in hand.

The others were shocked. "He can't do that," one of them protested.

"You can do whatever you want. You don't serve Renata and Tomaz anymore."

"What will happen to us?" the auburn-haired girl cried. Another whimpered, "Where will we go? How will we survive?"

"Take what you need from Castropiero," I told them. "There are clothes to wear and plenty of silver in the candlesticks and plate. Look for caskets holding coins and jewels."

Some of the slaves were scandalized, and I had to remember when I was in training in Vidaris, accustomed to doing exactly as I was told. "Go," I ordered. "Gather whatever you can find. Bring it back here, and you can leave with me. I'll show you what to do."

"I can't," the pregnant girl sniffled, tears running down her cheeks. "What if mistress returns? Or the servants?"

My heart ached for her. "There's a cellar across the lane. You can wait there, if you'd like."

Most of the slaves had already run back upstairs to pilfer through Renata's and Tomaz's belongings. I could hear doors slamming all over the house. Some of the servants had undoubtedly had the same idea.

I showed the pregnant girl and her friend across the lane to the cellar. They were taken aback by the streams of people, and cries of "Cileans!" on everyone's lips. Even the slaves' scanty attire drew little attention.

I left them there and returned to the pleasure house. The slaves had dived into their pillaging with childlike delight. Some of the boys were wearing Tomaz's fine clothing, the generous cut ballooning on their slender bodies. The girls had pulled out dozens of luxurious dresses in velvet and satin from Renata's chests.

I returned just as the doorkeeper tried to stop them, appearing in a mighty wrath to drag the slaves from his master's chamber. Still holding the candlesticks and jewel-covered cases they had found, they fell back in fear. Renata had rewarded the doorkeeper's loyalty in hiding Castropiero's many secrets by giving him the use of the slaves on regular occasions. The vile old man had terrorized them.

I leaped forward, accusing him, "*You* are the traitor! *You* conspired with the Cilean spies, and *you* will answer to the *doj.*"

He grabbed my wrist, nearly crushing it in panic. I pummeled his face with my fist, calling to the slaves, "Help me!"

The doorkeeper let go of me. "Stop at once! I'll put the lot of you in the well—"

Emboldened by my example, the slaves surged forward. They hardly looked threatening, but the doorkeeper fled back to his closet, slamming the doors shut. I stuck a poker through the handles so he couldn't get out.

With the remnants of my ragged warband behind me, I finally reached Bene. He was delirious with pain, lying on the floor. His clothes had been torn off and his back was flecked with blood and welts. There was a coiled whip lying on the table.

In dismay, I asked the slaves to help move him to a bed. One solemn girl with delicate, pointed features and sun-bronzed skin fetched a basin of water and some ointments. She remained calm as she tended Bene, and I soon trusted that he was safe in her capable fingers.

I soothed poor Bene, whispering in his ear, "I'm sorry I was too late, Bene. I came as soon as I could."

His eyes opened, fastening on mine. He recognized me, his hand clenching convulsively on mine. Then he drifted away again.

Tears threatened, but I could not break down now.

The demons sensed my weakness and whispered to feed my fears. They told me that Lexander was already dead and that the Cileans were at the door.

As the solemn-eyed girl, Eshter, smoothed the balm she had found onto Bene's back, I asked, "What happened to that other master— Lexander?"

She averted her head. "I haven't seen him in days."

I put my hand on her arm. "I know you can't trust anyone, Eshter, but this is vital. I must know what happened to him."

With her eyes fastened on Bene's torn back, she said flatly, "There's an old well in the cellar that they put us in to punish us. We have to stand in the water that rises and falls with the tide. Vido was in the well yesterday, and he says he heard the master talking in one of the cells. But why would a master be down there?"

"Which one is Vido?" I demanded.

"He's the boy who ran off."

I looked down at Bene. He was in no condition to be moved. "Will you stay here with Bene? We need to get out of here, but there's something I must do first."

Eshter responded as she had been trained. "I won't leave his side. You can rely on me."

I was not so sure, but I had little choice in the matter. I hurried back downstairs. There were only four slaves at the door waiting for me; the others had fled with their spoils. I sent two of the slaves up to stay with Eshter to help with Bene. The others carried all of the goods they had gathered across the lane to wait in the cellar. People were running in outright panic in every direction, similarly laden down.

I wanted to hurry down to the cellars to find Lexander, but the channel beckoned at the end of the alleyway. I had to find out what was happening with the Cilean fleet.

The waterway was crowded by boats, everyone shouting at one another as they tried to force their way through the narrow passageways. I dipped my hand in the water and saw the reason why. My warning had not come soon enough for the *doj*'s home fleet to intercept the Cileans. Too many of the invading ships had slipped through the last defense line and were rapidly approaching Veneto. The gentry and wealthy merchants were abandoning the city in their own ships, taking their families to safety. The less fortunate fought over smaller boats, fleeing to the mainland to take refuge in the Holy Empire.

The bulk of the Cilean fleet would reach the city by daybreak. The *doj*'s ships were already skirmishing with them in several places. Flames devoured the canvas sail on one ship. Other shipmasters had realized what was happening and were rapidly retreating to Veneto to try to cut off the Cileans. Unless the sea spirits and wind favored them, the Cileans would get here first.

I ran to tell the *doj*.

21

I no longer tried to feign nonchalance. I burst into the *doj*'s chamber without caring that it was filled with men. "The Cileans are coming!" I cried out. "Their ships have slipped past your defense fleet."

Silvo looked up from the sea maps spread across the tables. "No . . . it cannot be."

His councillors were busy quarreling with one another, but those who heard me looked up in alarm.

"They'll be here by sunrise." I went over and placed the tiny wooden ships where the spirits had shown me. "There's fighting there." I pointed to the places where I had seen the men in the ships drawn close, brandishing spears. "The water runs red with blood."

The councillors were shaking their heads and arguing, trying to drown me out with their raised voices. To them I was the *doj*'s doxy, not to be taken seriously. But the *doj* had heard the truth from me too often. His eyes lingered on the ships I had moved, trying to determine how he could win such a battle.

The *doj* asked a few questions of his councillors, and one gestured contemptuously at my display, claiming, "It's preposterous! Even if we recalled the fleet to defend our very shores, they wouldn't get here in time."

"I'll not have my city sacked," the *doj* declared furiously.

I drew back as the councillors shouted over the dilemma. They had no soldiers, no more ships, no way to stop the Cileans.

The *doj* knew it, too. His fist clenched as he glanced at me; then he quickly gestured with his chin toward the private door.

I waited in the curve of the stairs. He appeared only a few moments after me, as if fearing I would vanish again.

He took hold of my arm. "How can I save Veneto?"

"Have you any gods who favor you?"

He stared at me. "They say Kristna is strong, but he is not the patron of my city."

I wrung my hands. "I wish I had seen them sooner! The Cileans must have offered great sacrifices to the sea spirits to hide their approach."

His fingers tightened on me. "I will give these spirits anything they desire. Even if it's the lives of my people. Tell me what you want."

I could hear his suspicion, even now. He feared I would betray him into his enemy's hands.

But perhaps I could help him. "If you are serious about this, you may be able to sway the spirits. But they demand the most we can give, so you would have to reveal yourself to them with complete honesty."

"I'll do whatever is necessary." His narrowed eyes said he still doubted me.

"Then come to the boat launch. You'll have to speak to the spirits through me. Hurry, there's not much time."

He held on to my arm as we went down the stairs. At the boat launch, the sky glowed through the open doors in brilliant pink and orange flames, tinting the clouds. The day had gone far too fast. Several sentries stood armed and ready at the doors guarding the water gate.

"You'll have to give them a story about yourself, something powerful," I explained. "Only the most significant sacrifice of a secret long held will be enough to convince them to save Veneto. If they honor your revelation, they may change the currents in the waters and turn the wind against the Cileans. They alone can keep your enemies at bay."

"You can't be serious," Silvo told me in a low voice. "You want me to tell you a secret? Something incriminating?"

"This is your only chance to avert disaster," I said sternly. "They must hear you clearly to understand, and for that you need me. I know this will be hard for you because you conceal yourself so well. But the spirits demand that we give of ourselves when we ask for a miracle."

"You're not giving anything," he retorted.

"The spirits know everything about me." I clasped my hands between my breasts. "Please don't let this city burn."

He considered my plea, pacing away a few steps. Then he glanced up as if thinking of the councillors in his chambers who were growing increasingly frantic. Indeed, he had no other option. But he was a deeply pragmatic man, and things of the spirit had no hold over him.

"Get out!" he ordered the sentries, making them withdraw. "No one is to disturb us."

When they were gone, I sat on the smooth brick and curled my legs beneath me, placing my hand in the water. "Come, sit beside me. You must try to touch them, but don't be concerned if you feel nothing. I'll convey your story to them, but they must feel your presence in the water."

The *doj* was uncomfortable as he copied me, dipping his hand in. I took his other hand and held it firmly. Then I drew a deep breath, reaching out to the spirits.

Gradually I sank into the motion of the water. The sea spirits were fascinated by the *doj* because he ruled their favorite city. A sacrifice directly from him could be enough to quell their support for the Cileans. Silvo must reveal his heart, and at the heart of the *doj* was his grasp of power.

"What made you the man you are?" I asked. "You are from a noble family, but you had humble beginnings, did you not? What has driven your rise to rule?"

"I was the boy my parents birthed, and the man my shipmates made me."

"You weren't always this way," I protested. "Not when you were a child."

He hesitated. "No. My father was an artisan, but early on I realized I was destined for a life at sea. I worked as a cabin boy first, then sailor and shipmaster. I suppose I was a happy boy."

"Yes, the spirits have watched you." Their images ranged from a grinning, round-faced youth who knew little about ropes and ballast weights, to Silvo's steely-eyed reign over a merchant ship. The spirits clamored for more. "Why did you leave the sea?"

Silvo didn't want to reveal himself; he doubted me. But he had come too far already. He took a deep breath, averting his eyes from mine. "The sea had few comforts, but that was not important to me. Even after my father died, I returned to my mother's home little changed. I was a youth; what did I know about the cares of a widow with several children at home?"

I conveyed every nuance to the sea spirits. "I understand," I assured him. "Your mother must have struggled mightily."

He briefly met my eyes. "One time I came home to find her cousin there. My father's side of the family had fallen away from wealth and influence in Veneto. But Loranzo was thriving from his wise investments. I assumed he was simply visiting, but he stayed too long and it was apparent he knew the ways of the house. The children were banished to the upper level and my mother tried to send me out as well. But I resisted, feeling that I was the man of the house and must stay. I was naive; my mother was his mistress."

"How did you find out?"

He clenched his teeth at the thought of it. "She took him to her bed that night, the bed my father had shared with her. When Loranzo was done, he left without a word. I tried to challenge him in the hallway, but my mother intervened. Loranzo shoved me aside as if I were his own serving boy." Silvo shook his head briefly. "I swore I would put a stop to it, but my mother . . . she insisted that she had to feed the children and clothe herself, and there was no money to do so. I gave her all I had, but it was nothing, nothing compared to her needs. It would be many years before I gained a post that would allow me to provide for her, and meanwhile there were my brothers and sisters to be cared for. My mother claimed that Loranzo supported them. He maintained our home and sent my brothers to school. But every time I returned and Loranzo took her to bed, I wanted to kill him."

The sea spirits were greedily absorbing all he said. But I couldn't understand the depths of his anger. "Why?" I had to ask. "It was her choice to take Loranzo as her lover—"

"She was forced to it!" Silvo insisted. "If my father had survived, she would never have been brought so low. She wore the clothing he gave her, and received him at any hour he desired. She even entertained his friends in our home, and cultivated women for their willingness to please his guests. She was no longer welcome in polite society."

His fingers dabbled in the water, and he avoided my eyes again. "I left the defense fleet as soon as I could and joined the service of a shipping merchant, intending to make my fortune to help her. I discovered later that Loranzo had recommended me so that I would not come home as much. I gained status through the years until I became a shipmaster. But my mother died not long afterwards. My siblings were settled, and my dealings with Loranzo seemed at an end. My employer was a councillor to the *doj,* and I learned everything I could from him of politics and diplomacy, as well as shipping. My travels served me well because I had visited many of the cities that Veneto deals with. I also knew men as others did not, having had my eyes opened at a tender age. But by the time I could protect my mother, she was no longer alive."

It still pained him deeply. I wanted to offer solace, but the spirits were clamoring louder, sensing there was something more. "What about Loranzo?"

"As he grew older, his status decreased. I had something to do with that later, but he could not have sustained his rise. It was dependent on one man, a bad gamble, which was a lesson I learned from his downfall. I let him know I had a hand in it, and I didn't hide my disdain for him. I also toyed with his granddaughter, spoiling her maidenhood. But it was an empty gesture in the end, when she married well." He stared into the water. "I went to see Loranzo before he died. He told me it would have been better if I had not opposed him because then my mother's lover would have been a great man instead of a pauper. In the end, my mother was nothing but the debauched mistress of a failed man."

I waited, but he had no more to say. "Is there nothing that can give you ease?"

"As long as I am *doj* and my city is prospering, I can ask for nothing more. Does that satisfy your sea spirits?"

The spirits were humming with approval. They had seen some of the things he had described and they were pleased to have the story that weaved everything together. "Now tell them why you want them to save Veneto from the Cileans."

He closed his eyes and murmured like a prayer, "I am bound by the sea, as my city is bound by the sea. Who else lets the water fill the streets and come inside their very homes as we do? We are yours to protect, and I beg that you save us from the Cileans."

In his fervor, the spirits heard him. I added my humble plea that they stop the Cileans from coming to Veneto. The rape and pillage that would ensue was too horrifying to contemplate.

The spirits washed through us before finally withdrawing. "Yes," I said, removing my hand from the water. "I think they are satisfied. But I cannot know for certain. We shall have to wait and see what they do."

"You don't know if we'll be saved?" he demanded.

"The sea moves slowly and the ways of the spirits are difficult to understand." I tried to smile at him. "But you've done all you can, of that I'm sure. They've heard you. The rest lies with them."

The *doj* got to his feet. His hand was on his knife, and his face was drawn. By morning he could be fighting for his life, at best to be imprisoned until he was ransomed by his ravaged people.

"I'll do whatever I can," I assured him. "I'll return when I hear more."

"Stay here, Marja." His voice hardened, as if he needed my obedience. Perhaps he felt vulnerable after revealing so much of himself.

But I had to return to Castropiero. "Remember our agreement? I must be able to come and go, or I cannot help you." I held his gaze as the implied threat hung between us. I would remove my support and his sacrifice would come to naught without me.

He almost refused, but he could not part with his last shred of hope. "Go, then!"

Without another word, he turned and strode back into the palace.

The streets of Veneto were emptying as twilight fell. Everyone carried baskets or pulled handcarts piled with goods. Some were abandoning the city while others were taking their precious belongings elsewhere for safekeeping. But nowhere in Veneto would be safe if the Cileans landed.

In Castropiero, the cook was snoring loudly in the pantry and the doorkeeper remained blocked inside his closet. The rest of the servants were gone.

I went straight to the cellar. By the time I reached the bottom step, I was choking from the thick miasma of evil spirits. The narrow tunnel and dripping ceilings were dreadful. I had to take deep, calming breaths to be able to force myself to continue on.

I found the well that Eshter had told me about beneath a round wooden cover. To my everlasting relief, there wasn't anyone inside. I couldn't imagine standing in that inky blackness, the cold water at my knees as I struggled to stay upright.

I pushed open several doors, until I found one that had a heavy crossbar locking it shut. The bar was difficult to remove, but I managed to slide it out.

The space inside was so low I had to duck my head. Lexander lay on the crude bench, apparently collapsed in utter weariness. The rise and fall of his chest made me cry out in relief.

I knelt down beside him. In repose, he seemed much younger. Yet he was older than the oldest man alive. Perhaps to him, my life was but a blink of his eye.

I stroked his cheek. "Lexander?"

He stirred under my hand instead of waking instantly. He moved with great difficulty, as if his limbs were very heavy. His eyelids opened and shut again. His hands flexed slightly.

"You must wake up, Lexander," I urged. "We need to get out of here."

He tried to focus on me, but his golden eyes were sightless.

It was shocking to see him this way. "What did they do to you?"

But he was too far gone to hear. His lips were parched despite the damp air. I lifted the ladle from the water bucket, but there was something odd about the smell. It stung my nose when I sniffed it. The demons urged me to give it to him, to save his life by letting him drink the water—

I shut them from my mind and ran upstairs to fetch fresh water. I splashed some in his face, and when I tilted the bowl to his mouth, he drank with desperate gulps. I kept giving him more water until it slowly began to revive him. His eyes finally opened and he saw it was me.

"*Marja* . . ." he murmured.

When I heard the love and longing in his voice, I wanted to cry. He had been angry for so long.

"Yes, it's me, Lexander." I kept giving him water, wishing he would recover faster. "Is there anything I can do to help you?"

He gestured to the water, drinking more. "Where is Renata?" he managed to ask.

"She and the master were arrested by the *doj*."

"That was your doing, I suppose." Lexander shifted and groaned in pain.

"Are you injured?" I asked.

"No, but it will take some days for the poison to leave my body. The water helps flush it away."

He gradually pieced together what had happened to him. Renata must have dosed his cup at the evening meal a few days ago. Once he was in the cell, he drank the water to survive even though it was drugged as well. "Saaladet must have alerted them about me," he mumbled.

"Lexander, we have to go." Not only were the Cileans approaching, but the *doj*'s sentries could return at any time. I couldn't risk having Silvo discover me in Castropiero. Then he would know I had an ulterior motive in denouncing them. I also worried that Renata would somehow break free. The demons were pressing on me urgently; I needed to gather everyone and get out.

Lexander pulled on my hand so he could sit up, swaying with light-headedness. The shock of touching him shot through me.

He grimaced at his own weakness. "Where are we going?"

"The cellar across the lane, if that's all you can manage. But if you can walk, I have a safer place not too far away. It has a strong door that we can secure."

"I can walk." He leaned on me, trying to find his feet. I had not realized how heavy he was. He had always been careful not to crush me, but now with him slumped onto my shoulders, I felt his full weight.

We got up the steps somehow, and I began to think the cellar would have to do. Lexander could barely put one foot in front of the other. I left him sitting slumped near the side door, then raced upstairs to get Bene.

Eshter woke groggily, on guard. There was an unsheathed sword next to her.

"Eshter, it's me," I told her. "It's time for us to go."

Eshter sat up, confused for a moment about where she was. The other slaves were asleep.

"Come on," I insisted. "Wake the others, and make sure to bring all the bedding."

I gently tried to rouse Bene, running my hand through his hair. "Bene, you must get up. How has he been?"

Eshter was leaning over the two sleepy slaves. "I put more balm on his back when it sank in, and he ate some of that almond paste the others found."

"Bene, listen to me," I urged.

He turned his head and smiled when he saw it was me. Then the pain hit. He let out his breath in an agonized rush.

"I know," I told him, feeling dreadful about his wounds. "But we have to leave. You must try to walk."

By the time I got everyone moving, with Bene supported by Eshter and another slave, I was definitely leaning toward the cellar, horribly crowded and damp though it would be.

When the slaves saw Lexander waiting near the door, they started up in alarm, trying to retreat. No wonder—he had not been particularly kind to them as he played his role as Stanbulin assessor.

"What's *he* doing here?" Eshter exclaimed fearfully.

I kept them from backing out. "It's not what you think—Lexander intended to destroy this house. That's why Renata put him in the cellar."

Bene was nodding and muttering to himself. He must have told Renata everything he knew.

"But . . . he's a master," Eshter insisted.

Lexander could hardly hold himself up. I couldn't imagine anything less threatening, but they saw it differently.

"I can explain later. I swear he's no danger to you. You have to help me." I ordered the young man who wasn't with Bene to take Lexander's other side.

The slaves had been conditioned to obey, and the most compliant ones had waited for me while the others had fled. Before I knew it, we had crossed the lane and I decided to try for my spacious chamber in the boarding house. I wanted to put distance between us and the frustrated demons in Castropiero.

The slaves down in the cellar were called out, carrying sacks of goods pilfered from the pleasure house. The pregnant girl was wincing and holding her belly, and I feared she would drop the babe right on the street.

I led them through the dark lanes, supporting Lexander as best I could. The houses were tightly shuttered and not a lantern burned. A hush lay over the city as we waited for the Cileans to land.

When we finally made it to my room on the canal, and the bar was dropped on the door behind us, I let out my breath. With ten of us inside, we were a tight fit. But the slaves put the blankets on the floor, giving Bene the bed with Eshter to watch over him. The mother-to-be fell asleep instantly as her friend fussed over her. At least she wouldn't have the babe this night.

I settled Lexander by the window, then unlatched the shutters and swung them wide open. The moon had set, leaving only blackness. The water was as dark as the sky, with the waves reflecting the stars in rippled streaks. I dipped my fingertips, almost afraid to find out our fate.

But I felt nothing. I had been drained dry, too exhausted to understand the scattered images, a nightmare of blood and battle that leaped from one horrid sight to the next, distorted and incoherent.

"I have nothing left to give," I murmured.

Out of the darkness, Lexander spoke. "I'd say you've given enough, Marja."

I couldn't see him, but I could feel him close by. I closed the shutters and barred them, hoping they would not have to withstand a Cilean attack.

Lexander helped steady me when I sat down beside him. I realized he was feeling stronger.

His voice was low so the slaves couldn't hear. "During my brief moments of sanity in that cell, I hoped you would save me. I knew you could, if only you found out before they shipped me off to Stanbulin."

"Even then I would have come after you," I whispered. "I wouldn't let them take you."

"I'm fortunate that you are so capable."

I wished I could see his face. "You tried to halt me at every step."

He drew a deep breath. "No longer, Marja. I'll do whatever I can to help you. But clearly you can triumph on your own."

By the time I awoke the next day, the city was abuzz with the news. The Cilean fleet had come within sight of Veneto at daybreak. Panic had consumed the city as their sails appeared.

But strangely, the ships had come no closer. The winds had gradually pushed them away, until they disappeared over the horizon. The home fleet sped back to protect Veneto and the tips of their masts were reassuring in the distance as they patrolled the waters.

I knew the Cileans might prevail with the sea spirits eventually, but for the moment the Otherworld had sided with Veneto.

Most of the slaves were gone when I awoke, along with much of the salvaged goods. The pregnant girl had left with the others, probably because of Lexander. I couldn't blame them. They weren't sure what he would do once he fully regained his senses.

I took the remaining two slaves into the streets with me, leaving Eshter to watch over Bene as she did so well, and Lexander to recline in the open window. He was more alert but still tended to lose his balance when he tried to walk.

We paid an exorbitant amount for food. Shipping was disrupted by the lurking Cilean fleet. I refused to go anywhere near the pleasure house.

That night, the other two slaves sneaked away. I heard them go, but thought it was their own concern. We discovered in the morning that they had taken the rest of the coins and silver plate, leaving only Eshter's sword behind. Eshter was the sole remaining Castropiero slave.

"I'm sorry you didn't get your fair share," I told her.

"It's no matter." Eshter glanced at Lexander as if unsure if she should speak her mind in his presence. But Lexander had been most humble and ordinary in their discussions, allaying her fears. His obviously weakened state called out her nurturing instincts, and she brought him water and helped him to the privy just as she did with Bene.

Bene was lying in the bed, still in pain but awake. "What are we going to do now?"

"I must see the *doj,*" I declared.

Lexander's lips thinned. Of all my patrons, Domen Silvo had come closest to tapping the depths of my compliant spirit. Lexander must have seen that in him and instinctively known that I had given myself to him in every way. Except for my heart.

"He'll be glad to see me," I continued. "I'm sure he'll reward me with enough so you can go wherever you want." I knew nothing about Eshter but her name, yet I had trusted her to care for Bene. "Perhaps you'd like to return to your family?"

Eshter was already shaking her head, and judging from the look on Bene's face, he wasn't interested in going back to Frankish lands.

"You could live here," I suggested. "Veneto is the finest city I've seen."

Bene gave me a grin, only a shadow of his usual glee. "I want to stay with you, Marja."

I could see Lexander from the corner of my eye. "I'm going to find another pleasure house."

"There's a house in the Sea of Isles," Bene said eagerly. "I heard the master talking about it."

I faced Lexander squarely. "Do you know this house?"

"Yes, Tomaz was once master of House Allonis, on the island of Tremiti."

"Then that's where I'm going. What about you, Lexander?"

He hesitated. "I must go to Stanbulin to strike directly against Saaladet. That's the master house where slaves are evaluated before being shipped to my people," he explained to Bene and Eshter. "It will throw the houses into chaos if I can bring down Saaladet."

I knew where Stanbulin was located, having seen it on Etien's maps. "You have to go through the Sea of Isles to get there. Will you help me liberate the slaves of Allonis first?"

"I'll help you," Bene offered, with Eshter agreeing, "Yes, take me with you."

"If that is your wish," I told them.

Lexander turned away; he clearly intended to go alone to challenge the masters in Saaladet. But he was reluctant to let us take on a house without him.

"It would be better if we worked together," I said quietly.

"Are you sure you want to do this?" Lexander finally asked Bene and Eshter. "They may have heard about me and will be watching for us."

"We have to try," Bene said stoutly. Eshter looked uneasy, but she nodded.

So Lexander agreed. He didn't say a word as I prepared to go see the *doj*.

The *doj*'s anteroom was buzzing and the sentries took me directly in without announcing me. The *doj* broke into a smile, holding his arms wide. "It happened just as you said it would, Marja."

He hugged me close in front of his councillors, which startled me more than anything else he had done. It was a gesture of pure affection.

"The current was too much for them," the *doj* explained. "At last word, their fleet is retreating. Though I won't hold too much stock in that. We're readying a dozen more ships of war, newly purchased to join our defenses."

He led me through the side door into the spiral stairway so he could speak without his councillors overhearing. "You made the difference, Marja. Those ignorant fools in there claim it was tidal forces at work, but I know the sea. I've never seen her turn like that." He tucked a velvet pouch into my hand. It clinked with heavy coins. "You deserve every bit of my gratitude."

That was one thing I had come for. "And your enemies?"

His expression hardened. "The Cileans will live to rue the day they set their sights on Veneto. The Castropiero folk are being questioned, but they are reluctant to confess their secrets. When I am done with them, they will be executed. Their house and chattel were confiscated this morning. I will succor no spies in this city."

With that, I was done in Veneto.

He put his hand to my waist, making me tingle with anticipation. "You can wait in my private chambers, Marja. When I'm done here, we can celebrate our victory."

The *doj* was finally offering his trust in me, but I was reminded of the Frankish shipmaster. I had disliked running away from him, and intended that it should be different with the *doj*.

I sadly shook my head, trying to smile. "I'm sorry, but I must leave now."

His eyes narrowed. "Why?"

"You agreed from the beginning that I was free to come and go. I will return, but I don't know when that day will be."

"Day?" he asked. At my nod, he realized what I meant. "You mean to leave the city altogether."

"I go where I am called." I reached out to touch his arm. "I'm sorry to have to leave you. I love your city and I will see you always through the sea spirits. They will watch over you as long as you are true to them."

Doubt wavered over his face, as he considered how he could bind me to him. But I had been careful to remain beyond his control. "And if I say no?" he demanded.

I smiled sadly, knowing I didn't have to say it out loud—it would destroy everything we had shared.

He let out a pained laugh. "To have finally found such a woman, only to lose you! 'Tis most unfair of you to ask it."

I was touched and clasped his hand, but I could not bring myself to kiss him. I was afraid the passion would ignite between us. His eyes were anguished, and I don't believe it was simply regret for what I so freely gave him. He had been honest with me, and that meant much to him.

"Farewell," I whispered, slipping down the steps. At the curve I glanced up. He nodded stiffly, making no effort to stop me.

22

"This is my reward for helping the *doj* repel the Cileans." I poured the dozen gold coins from the purse into my palm. They slid together sensuously. "We can leave immediately."

Lexander pushed himself up. "Are you in danger?"

"I did the *doj* a great service," I retorted. "He has a high regard for me. But you're at risk, Lexander. The *doj* took Renata and Tomaz into custody. He would likely interrogate you, as well, if he had the chance."

Lexander retreated to don a pleated felt cap to hide his smooth head. With his torn and dirty clothing, he no longer looked like a master of Castropiero.

Lexander and I went to the wharfs along the main channel, where the merchants of eastern shipping docked. At my request, the *olfs* were accustomed to watching this area for the arrival of the winged ship from Stanbulin. Lexander also knew it well from his time as master of Castropiero. He had brought his slaves here twice a year to send them to Saaladet.

Everything had changed between us, leaving us both unbalanced. Lexander was cautious, watching every move I made. He never touched me or offered me his arm. There was an awkward constraint between us when we spoke. He acted as if he didn't know me, and he was carefully determining how best to deal with me. At night, we slept next to each other but never entwined as we used to.

With Bene, on the other hand, Lexander was quite gentle. He took care of him, and Bene delighted in his attention. In their short time together, they had developed a real rapport. Bene relied on him—and me—with utter faith and trust. It reminded me of how I used to be with Lexander. But I wanted Bene to rely on himself.

It felt as if there was too much left unsaid between me and Lexander. So I concentrated on our departure from Veneto, resolving to deal with everything else later. Lexander bargained for our passage to the isles with several shipmasters, switching dialects as needed. Chance had it that there was a ship that could take passengers leaving the next day that would pass through the Sea of Isles. For a good price, the shipmaster was willing to take us to Tremiti Island.

We decided to sleep onboard that night, and returned to fetch Bene and Eshter. I hired a palanquin to carry Bene, and once we reached the ship, Eshter bustled around, settling him in the snug cabin.

I lingered on deck gazing at the water city. I felt such a pang on leaving Veneto that it caught me by surprise. This was not my home, just as Helluland was not my home, but both places were special to me. I knew I would return someday.

"Marja, shouldn't you come inside?" Lexander stayed in the shadow by the door to the cabin.

"Why?" I was leaning on the rail admiring the gold flecks in the water cast by the lowering sun. The buildings floated serenely, with the sea mist softening every line and reflection.

"The *doj* does not release his treasures so easily."

"I won't let the *doj* stop me," I assured him.

"I wish I had your confidence." When I turned with a frown, his voice lowered. "There's the *doj* now. You mustn't be seen speaking with me."

Domen Silvo was striding up the dock. He had two sentries with him, and they crossed their spears to stand watch. The shipmaster emerged from his cabin as the *doj* climbed onboard, bidding his ruler a flustered welcome.

My breath caught. It would take but one word from the *doj* and I would be thrown in a cell along with the others.

Lexander was crouching down in the shadow of the ladder of the sterncastle. If the *doj* recognized him, we were all doomed.

I smiled in greeting as Silvo glanced around at the startled crew. "Are they treating you with respect, Marja?"

"Certainly, thanks to your generosity. Bene and I are being cared for well."

"Bene?" Silvo asked, without attempting to feign surprise. He was well informed that I had arrived here with a palanquin and several other people.

"Bene is my traveling companion. Would you like to meet him?" I led Silvo directly to the cabin. Lexander tried to wave me off, but I was not deterred.

As we entered, I announced, "Bene, this is our benefactor, Domen Silvo, the Doj of Veneto."

My eyes adjusted to the gloom to see Bene wincing as he tried to sit up, alarmed beyond all comprehension. Eshter backed into a dark corner, where her face couldn't be seen. She had chosen the most demure dress that the slaves had stolen from Renata, and I was certain the *doj* wouldn't recognize her as a Castropiero slave.

I hurried to Bene's side. "Lie back down." Over my shoulder, I told the *doj,* "He's been beaten badly. But this kind woman has been helping me care for him."

Bene's white face and the sudden sheen on his brow from his effort was not missed by the *doj.* "Forgive me for not rising," Bene mumbled.

"Don't concern yourself with that." The *doj* peered through the gloom of the cabin. "You are much younger than I had imagined. I thought that you two were . . ."

"Lovers?" I glanced at Bene.

"She would not," Bene declared, with very real vexation.

I put my hand on his hair. "Bene's like a brother to me."

He grabbed my hand and kissed it. "You are my savior, Marja!"

The *doj* nodded agreement. "That she is . . ."

I pulled the *doj* away, claiming Bene needed to rest. Out in the fading daylight, the crew and shipmaster were once again rapt with attention to see their ruler walking about their ship like an ordinary man.

Silvo turned to me. "Why must you go, Marja? The shipmaster says your destination is in the isles."

"I am called there," I said softly. "But we mustn't speak of that. I cannot reveal a sacred trust, just as I will never betray yours."

"You left too fast, Marja. I had to see you one last time."

"So you tracked me down and came to scare the mischief out of the shipmaster and his crew," I teased.

"Yes, but you let me this time," he pointed out.

'Twas true, I hadn't obscured myself with the *olfs* or tried to hide away. "Perhaps I wanted to tell you something."

He nodded. "Your words are always precious to me."

"Then listen carefully. I know more about your mother than you may think, for I am very much like her. You did not fail her, Domen. Your mother was not forced to accept Loranzo or their bond would not have lasted her lifetime. That kind of love is very rare, I have discovered. I believe she chose her lover, just as I chose you."

For a moment he looked like a boy, filled with pain and uncertainty. But understanding grew, and he nodded slowly.

He raised my hand and kissed it. He had never done so before. Without another word, he descended the ramp to the dock. The sentries proceeded before him, clearing the way for their *doj*.

After we set sail and Veneto disappeared behind us, Lexander still kept his distance from me. We were a dismal group for days on end as Bene recovered. Eshter often whimpered in her sleep, and she told me about some of the tortures that the patrons and masters had inflicted on them. Eshter's family had sold her against her wishes when Renata offered them too much to refuse.

But when Bene was finally on the mend, there was no stopping his irrepressible ways. He was worse than the *olfs* onboard, always dabbling where least expected. While he was still in a weakened state, he seduced his nurse, Eshter. After that, I often heard them rutting in the night or at first light.

One afternoon I came into the cabin to find Eshter down on her knees sucking his *tarse*. Her buttocks were exposed, with her skirt hiked up around her waist, and her bodice was lying on the floor. Bene was lolling back, enjoying it, his long curls falling into his eyes.

I quickly shut the door. "Don't let those sailors see you or you'll have your hands full."

Then I wished I hadn't entered, because they both smiled at me invitingly.

"Come join us," Eshter said, reaching out to me. She had a lovely hand and a dusky arm and rounded shoulder. I wanted to touch her, to see her black eyes close in pleasure and a slow flush infuse her rich skin.

Bene grinned, an edge of his old frustration tingeing his voice, "Yes, it's about time, Marja."

"Many thanks, but no," I demurred, opening the door a crack to slip back outside.

Bene let out a sigh. "She never will," he said to Eshter, whose disappointed expression made me feel bad in spite of myself.

I leaned against the rail, watching the waves and the undulating muddy line of the shore pass by in the distance. I longed for the simple release that pleasure could give. Bene was very tempting. Sometimes when he sprawled out on the bowcastle, his skin shining under the fierce sun, I wanted to sink my mouth onto his and abandon myself to desire. He was so good and true! But I didn't want to hurt him.

Eshter began to pursue me after that. She wasn't overt. She simply did things for me, ever attentive as Bene required less of her care. He began to make inroads on the sailors, and Lexander scolded him for rutting with at least one of the rough men in our cabin.

Eshter stayed by my side so I was never without a companion. She lovingly tended to my hair, helped me wash, and cleaned our clothes. I couldn't stop her. So I acquiesced when I normally wouldn't have cared about the filth involved in a sea voyage. The cabin was swept and the bedding thoroughly aired and beaten by our second day onboard.

I couldn't touch the water, but the ceaseless motion of the ship enabled me to commune with the sea spirits. I confessed how I had used the Cilean attack to betray Castropiero and free the slaves.

In return, they showed me the *doj* alone in the boat launch with his hand thrust into the water. He was calling to me, in the only way he knew how. I sent him my good wishes, though I didn't know if he could hear.

As we sailed southward, the spirits rewarded my confession with smooth seas and good wind. I saw plenty of raiders through their scattered images, but no ships ventured close to us.

As we passed into the Sea of Isles, the air grew warm and sultry, heavy with moisture. We joined a convoy of merchant ships in threading our way through the sage-green hills. The abundance of sheltering islands provided cover for raiders, so there was safety in numbers for the merchant shipping.

The shallow water was a brilliant blue-green and very calm. The people had darkened skin and curling black hair. Their robes flowed down to their feet, while the children ran about in brief tunics.

Our convoy stopped at an island to refill our water barrels. The hills were so steep around the bay that the houses marched up the sides. On top of a cliff stood rows of fluted columns. It had once been a structure, but the roof was gone, and the stones were bleached white like the rib cage of a great dead beast.

I was lured by the call of the land, intoxicated by the depth of time. Beyond the babble of spirits was an indelible impression of people living in this ordinary fishing village seemingly forever.

As we prepared to disembark, Lexander cautioned us, "You don't know the ways of these people or their tongue. Stay near me and all will be well."

"The *olfs* will help me," I reminded him.

My connection to the spirits seemed to make Eshter nervous. "Do we have to go?"

"You can remain here, if you'd like," Lexander agreed. "We won't be gone long. The convoy will be leaving at sunset."

"I want to get out and run!" Bene exclaimed. He gave Eshter a kiss on the forehead. "But you can guard the home fires, sweeting, such as they are."

"That purse is our greatest concern," Lexander said, referring to the coins the *doj* had given me. He had tucked the small bag into a crevice in the joint of a beam.

Eshter still looked confused, so I told her, "Do whatever you want."

"Latch the door behind us," Lexander advised. "And don't let anyone else in. Even the shipmaster himself."

I didn't have to hear the sound of the latch dropping behind us to know Eshter would obey Lexander. It was the duty of a pleasure slave to always please others. But she would learn, as Bene was learning.

We climbed down the rope ladder, the sun beating down on our heads. The heat raised a heavy stench on the waterfront.

Lexander bargained with shopkeepers for a basket of dried fruit and bottles of wine, getting a handful of odd coins in return for a gold one. He kept calling to Bene and me as we wandered around looking at things that were for sale—shaggy furs, pots glazed in red and black, and a herd of huge goats. Lexander bought a jug of goat's milk. I dribbled a bit for the *olfs* to taste. Bene quaffed his cup and asked for another. Lexander refilled the jug to take back to Eshter.

As part of his banter with the merchants, Lexander asked about the isle of Tremiti. They said it was a fair-sized island close to the eastern shores, ruled by a king who was loyal to Ditalia. That meant he paid homage to Kristna.

Then one of the *olfs* called me into a temple that was dedicated to the sun. It was warm and full of light. The floor was embedded with chips of stone, a mosaic of the rising sun between the islands and vivid blue waves. A fire burned on the altar, fed constantly by women who had dedicated themselves to the service of the sun god.

Bene and Lexander were not in sight by the time I emerged from the peaceful place. I descended through the sleepy town, lulled under the full warmth of the sun.

At the turn in the lane, I saw them sauntering ahead. Lexander had his arm around Bene, helping to support the basket on his shoulder. Bene laughed; then Lexander leaned over and gave him a rough kiss.

The casual intimacy of it struck me. Lexander never touched me anymore. He had agreed to help me, but nothing more. The first time he had desired me was when he realized I was a true submissive. But now I would no longer submit to him in every way.

There was nothing that could be done about our estrangement. My conflicted feelings over his betrayals didn't matter. As I had changed, so had his love for me.

As we sailed from the fishing village, the setting sun at our backs, I had only one thing on my mind. Lexander lingered on deck, leaning over the railing and sadly staring at the waves split by our passage.

Finally I approached Lexander and broke my silence. "Do you love Bene?"

"Love him? No. But he is endearing. He reminds me of so many young men who become pleasure slaves. Canille trained him well, nurturing his talents. I'm very glad that you rescued him so his spirit was not crushed by my people."

He was so admiring that he might well have said *Yes*. "Then why are you rutting with him? Unless you're seeking a new slave."

He shot me a pained look. "How can you ask me that?"

"I've refused Bene's advances since we left Montplaire. I won't let him serve me because if I do, he'll only continue to be a slave."

"Bene has grown a great deal since Castropiero. I wouldn't worry about him being too subservient. And I'm only one among several he ruts with. But you, now, you're another matter. You've withheld for too long—you're unattainable."

"What do you mean?"

"Remember the summer of your training, when I ordered you not to speak?" His voice lowered, as if sharing a secret only masters were taught. "I didn't touch you for moons. And then the first moment I did . . ."

I remembered how he had trailed his hand along my waist down to my thigh. His light touch had sent lines of fire ripping through my body. I had climaxed almost instantly. "Is that what I'm doing with Bene?"

"People always yearn for what they can't have."

"You think it was a trick that made me fall in love with you?"

"Certainly that was part of it." He nodded toward the stern. "I think you'll do Bene no harm if you have a roll with him. Maybe even together with Eshter. That should rub off a bit of your glamour."

I blinked. "I'll consider it."

I forced myself to walk away from him. Climbing down from the bowcastle, I went directly to our cabin. Eshter had lit a candle in the holder on the wall. She was snuggled in bed with Bene already. We had feasted early on the fresh provisions from the marketplace.

They looked so content. I wanted to feel that way, too. I missed holding my beloved, feeling adored and comforted.

"Is something wrong, Marja?" Bene asked. Eshter was ready to do my bidding.

I sat down on the edge of their bunk. They usually slept together, though there was another bunk above it. The other lower bunk was mine.

"I . . ." I couldn't quite say it. I touched Bene's leg through the blanket. "I want you."

Suddenly tears came. I was crying because I couldn't say that to Lexander. Not anymore.

Bene put his arms around me with Eshter hugging us both. "What's wrong, Marja?" Bene cried.

I had to laugh through my tears. This was no way to start! I wiped my eyes, pulling away slightly. "I'm being daft. Because I've wanted this for so long."

I leaned over and kissed him long and deep, the way I had imagined. He tasted good, and smelled of manly sweat and musk from rutting with Eshter.

Bene's face lit up. "Truly, Marja?"

I kissed Eshter. She was soft where Bene was hard, sweet and fragrant where he was tangy and sharp. They soon had my dress off and laid me back in the bed. They wouldn't let me do a thing. They caressed every part of me, rubbing out the tension, stroking heat into my flesh, and licking me into ecstasy. I drifted on waves of lust, and knew this was how delicious I made others feel.

I wondered if Lexander would come in and join us. But he didn't. He returned to climb into his bunk after all three of us were curled around each other, nearly asleep.

23

The island of Tremiti was a low, stony mound rising out of the turquoise sea. The exposed rock was white, like the buildings, with sparse vegetation along the coast.

"Allonis may have been warned about you," I reminded Lexander.

He adjusted the cloth over his head, cinched by a band. It was a common headdress among eastern folk, and concealed his distinctive smooth head. "I shall be very careful when I make my inquiries about the house."

He stared at the island intently. I could almost see him planning the attack in his head. He seemed impatient to get this over with so he could continue on to Stanbulin.

"You won't do anything without telling us?" I had to ask.

His mouth pursed slightly. "You still don't trust me, Marja? I suppose I deserve it."

With that, he walked away.

The shipmaster took us to the largest town on Tremiti. Knidos was on a tranquil, open bay. It was much like the fishing village our convoy had stopped at, only larger. The houses filled the steep hillsides and along the very top were clusters of ancient stone buildings with rows of white columns. Some were in ruins.

Once we stepped on shore, Lexander took charge. He kept a comforting hand on Eshter's arm, soothing her from time to time. She had been confined in the gloomy slave barracks of Castropiero for too many seasons, and the sleepy little town overwhelmed her.

Bene barely noticed. He was too excited, running ahead up the narrow, winding lanes. Cats sunned themselves on the whitewashed walls and on stoops; hunched old women wearing black scarves and skirts gathered like crows in the nooks and crannies, gesturing broadly as they spoke.

We took a room in a modest inn for traveling merchants. I lingered near the main door, where I could overhear the conversations, soaking up the language through the *olfs*. Eshter stayed in our room, relieved to retreat from the bustle.

Lexander refused to allow Bene to accompany him, so he ran in and out, exploring the neighborhood and returning with bits of food, describing the things he had seen. There were several small Kristna sanctuaries scattered among the more numerous shrines to myriad gods: rulers of sea, sky, and land. Even the bakers had their own patron god. As usual, the language barrier didn't seem to bother Bene.

Together we went to see the largest of the Kristna sanctuaries, not far upriver from Knidos. It was perched on top of a rock spire. Nearly a hundred clerics lived there, herding their goats and climbing the dangerous path up the cliff face while carrying supplies on their backs. It seemed that Kristna must be powerful indeed to command such an unassailable promontory. But I saw an *olf* tweak a cleric's nose on a whim, and another *olf* caused a cleric to lose his footing on the stones. Surely Kristna would not allow that if he ruled supreme on this isle.

The king, it seemed, had fallen on hard times. His old rambling palace was perched prominently on a hilltop. Columns had fallen down and the roof was riddled with huge holes. Clearly something was amiss here.

On Lexander's return, we all came together in our room. But Eshter was in tears and her swollen face showed that she had been crying for some time. Bene tried to comfort her, but she exclaimed,

"I can't help you! You should have left me behind in Veneto. I can't even go outside."

"Come with us," Bene offered. "We'll stay together."

"I'm too scared," Eshter cried out, almost angry. "I keep expecting those people to touch me, and then I'll freeze, like I always did, and let them do whatever they want to me."

"I'll make sure nothing happens to you," Lexander assured her.

"She doesn't need to be taken care of," I protested. "Eshter needs to find her own strength."

"If you act like a freewoman, then they will treat you as such," Lexander patiently explained.

"Free!" Eshter put her hands to her face. "What is that? If you all abandon me, I am lost."

We didn't have time for Eshter to come to terms with her ordeal in Castropiero. She had to be able to take care of herself. "If you can't be a freewoman, then be a freeman," I told her.

Eshter looked up in confusion. Bene snapped his fingers and pointed at me. "Like you did, Marja, traveling in disguise as a peasant."

"Nobody will pay any attention to you," I agreed. "You can go anywhere and see everything differently when you've become a different person."

Lexander glanced at me. "Indeed . . ."

"You mean act like a man?" she asked, almost appalled at the idea.

"Well, you're quite delicate, so you should try being a boy first." I smiled at her.

"What if someone realizes I'm a woman? What will they do to me?"

"People see what they expect to see," I assured her. "Try it."

"You should," Bene chimed in. "Marja was never challenged, and we went everywhere."

Lexander looked doubtful. I wasn't sure if it was my suggestion or the thought of me traipsing across the Auldland disguised as a man.

Eshter considered it for a few moments, then began to nod.

"Yes, I'll do it. You'll have to cut off my hair and get me some proper clothes."

"Surely there's no need for that," Lexander protested.

"Marja tied her hair back," Bene agreed. "Lots of boys do."

"Mine is too long." Eshter tugged on the dark strands that fell below her waist. "I want to feel different. I want to really be a boy."

"She's right." It would be a sacrifice to cut off her long shining hair, but it would be a fitting start to a new life. "I'll cut it for you, Eshter."

I loosened the thick braid and brushed it out with my fingers. Using Bene's knife, I cut off a long lock. It must have taken Eshter her whole life to grow her hair. Lexander grimaced as if he was about to protest again, to save her from herself.

"Did you find out where Allonis is?" I asked to forestall him.

"It's in Ovathi, an isolated village on the other side of the island. It's run by a guild that makes raw silk. The valley is filled with *mouro* trees that provide leaves for the silkworms to eat."

"Cloth doesn't come from worms," Bene protested.

"Silk does," Lexander told him.

I glanced over at my brocade cloak, lined with dark blue silk. The *doj* had also given me a whisper-soft dress made of green silk.

Lexander picked up one of the fallen locks of Eshter's hair. "Silk is as strong as iron, worth more than gold by weight. The king has granted the Katartarioi guild a charter to produce raw silk, and they chose that particular bay because it is easily defensible against raiders. Everyone in the village is part of the guild, caring for the worms, removing the silk from the cocoons, and spinning it into thread. Merchants buy the thread in bulk, and take it away to be dyed and woven into fabric."

"What about the pleasure house?" I asked.

"I discovered little and was wary of asking more. I don't want rumors to spread of my inquiries. We'll have to pose as merchants to get closer."

"Who will I be?" Bene asked eagerly.

"You and Eshter, since she'll be disguised a boy, can be part of my crew. We'll hire a ship to take us there, and you can blend in with the sailors and hear the talk on the streets." He held up a cautioning hand. "Discreetly, Bene. Do you understand? You can't go lurking around the pleasure house or asking people about Allonis. They may be watching for me."

Bene assured him, "I'll just listen and tell you what I hear."

I ruffled Eshter's hair to shake loose the cut strands. I had trimmed it close all around, leaving short bangs and exposing the dusky skin at the nape of her neck.

"How is it?" Eshter asked anxiously. "Do I really look like a boy?"

Renata's gown was too large for her, so she looked more like a child in her mother's clothes, far more vulnerable than confident.

"You'll make a fine sailor," Lexander assured her. "I trust you won't regret the loss of your hair."

Eshter shook her head uncertainly, rubbing her hand to feel it.

"What did you have in mind for me?" I asked Lexander.

He noticed my cool tone. "Women of beauty and youth don't travel around on a merchant ship. Perhaps you should pose as a sailor, as well."

"To use my talents to their fullest, I should be your mistress who accompanies you on your long trading trips."

Lexander set his lips together firmly. "No, that would expose you—" He broke off as I put my hands on my hips. "It's your decision, naturally. But if you act the part of a wanton lady, then you will be treated as such."

"My status will be low so I won't be a threat," I argued. "That may encourage people to speak before me."

"Perhaps," he conceded.

In the silence that fell between us, Bene ventured to say, "I think it's a good idea, Marja."

"Can you do it, Lexander?" I asked. "Play the role of my lover?"

Lexander went to the door, his manner more sardonic than I had seen since we had argued in Veneto. "Certainly. Let's go outfit our-selves for the grand performance, shall we?"

As we gathered together what we needed, I grew ever more worried that my disguise would not work. Lexander could hardly look at me; how could he convince anyone that I was his concubine?

Lexander took possession of my purse. "It will be safer from thieves. No man could take it from me."

It was reasonable enough, but his abrupt manner showed how tense he was. I said little as he bought the Eastern clothes that we would need to complete our disguise, even when he chose more de-mure robes and veils for me than I would have.

Eshter came along in some of Bene's castoffs, practicing her swag-ger and speaking in a deeper tone. She began touching the merchan-dise, rejecting everything with a curt shake of her head when the merchants suggested a price.

I was transformed when I changed into my Eastern robes, layer-ing the sheer fabrics for modesty. Along with a silk scarf over my hair, there was a small veil that curved over my cheekbones, concealing my lower face. I felt unpleasantly enshrouded.

Bene and Eshter donned rough, humble clouts, breeches, and shirts. But Lexander was magnificent in his white head wrap, red vest, and full pants that tied at the ankle. Instead of a sword, he wore long, curving knives on both sides of his belt.

After surveying the waterfront, Lexander pointed out a large galley of the kind merchants typically used. But I watched the ship-master's mate as he shouted orders and pummeled the crew to drive them faster, landing blows on their backs and shoulders with his stick.

I preferred a much smaller boat with a single sail, owned by two young brothers. Their love for their craft showed as they scrubbed the deck and stitched the sail. They would welcome the addition of more crew members, and there would be less risk if Eshter was discovered.

"We must take that one," I said, pointing to the smaller boat.

Lexander was already prepared to bargain with the shipmaster of the galley. "That one's too small. We couldn't possibly carry a load of raw silk in it."

I planted my feet and refused to budge. He walked a few steps away, then realized I was not coming. "Marja, be reasonable. That's all wrong for a merchant."

"Then our story must change. Because that is the boat we must take." I kept my voice low. "The crew on the galley isn't to be trusted."

Eshter shot a nervous glance at the larger vessel. "They're dangerous?"

I nodded. Bene protested, "But we have to pose as rich merchants. Why else would we go there except to buy silk?"

I thought of the Sigurdssons family and how shrewd they were. "The only way Lexander could prove himself is to actually purchase the silk. Do we have enough coins for that?"

"No," Lexander admitted. "In the end, our negotiations would have to fail."

"Then I think it's better if we give them something they don't have. That way we have some influence over the guild."

Lexander was intrigued. "What did you have in mind?"

I showed them the deep blue lining of my cloak. "We'll offer them color."

24

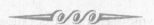

When we sailed toward the narrow opening of Ovathi Bay, I was the only one who had no doubt about our chosen path. Lexander was terse and paced incessantly; I'm sure he dearly wished the three of us had stayed on the other side of the island. Bene was unusually subdued and he kept shrugging his shoulders as if remembering Renata's beating.

Eshter was a serious and increasingly vocal boy. The two brothers accepted her without a murmur, much to my delight. Lexander cautioned Eshter to maintain her pose even if she was discovered by the brothers. "You must behave as if you truly prefer being a man," he told her.

"I do prefer being a man," she retorted. I knew then Eshter had chosen rightly.

A stout warship came out to meet us, tacking smartly against the wind. They demanded that we allow them to board, and Lexander graciously welcomed them. Down in the hold, they examined our sparse cargo of a small crate and two caskets. The crate held bunches of dried flowers and herbs that were used to make dyes, while the caskets were filled with pouches of ochre, cobalt, and crystalline minerals.

When the sentries found no weapons, we were allowed to follow them between the cliffs on either side of the passage. The cleft was not much wider than a large ship. Niches had been cut high into the rock where sentries were poised to attack. Their concern about raiders was so great that I wondered if we could somehow use that against the pleasure house.

The port official was waiting at the dock for us. His men searched the tiny cabin and cargo space of our ship again, including our personal belongings. Lexander had insisted that we maintain our roles down to the slightest detail, so we passed muster. Lexander had also supplied himself with letters of recommendation addressed to his new name, Mahali of Abund.

"What is your business?" the port official demanded.

"I've come to see the guild masters," Lexander replied.

The port official narrowed his eyes. "What is your trade?"

"I am a dyer," Lexander said with a bow and a flourish.

The man looked suspicious, but he agreed. "You can send a message with the boy."

It was not appropriate for me to accompany Lexander when he went to speak to the guild masters about setting up a dye works in Ovathi. Bene and Eshter set out to explore the village, but I was too conspicuous in my silk skirts and veil to walk about openly.

When twilight fell, I borrowed some of Eshter's breeches and slipped onto the dock. I had made friends with the *olfs* while I waited and several came along, willing to obscure me from sight. If anyone did see through my disguise, they would assume I was a local boy running an errand.

The village was filled with women using the distaff and spindle to twist and double fibers to make silk thread. Younger girls were bent over tiny cocoons, unwinding the long strands. The trees were carefully tended, and baskets of fragrant leaves were piled near a long shed where the tiny worms were cultivated.

But my concern was the pleasure house. There were only a few large houses positioned on the hilltops amid the folds of the valley. To examine each one, I had to scramble up through the scrub brush. Judging from the cries of a baby and the screaming laughter of children, the first house was clearly not Allonis. Nor the second.

The third house I climbed up to, scraping my knees and hands, was so quiet that it seemed almost abandoned. I crept into the garden at the rear and watched the glow from the kitchen doors, where a few servants were finishing cleaning up from the evening meal.

When a girl came out to empty a bucket of water, I slipped through the open door into a scullery. If any of the servants could see the *olfs,* then I would be discovered. But I had to find out if this was Allonis.

The *olfs* stayed close to me, showing from their reluctance that they were unaccustomed to entering this grand house. In every other way, it appeared idyllic. The servants chattered together comfortably as they concluded their duties, a good indication of the tenor of the house. The walls in the kitchen were painted with twining vines hung with fat clusters of grapes. The windows overlooking the garden were open to the ocean breeze blowing up the valley.

The kitchen was next to a dark courtyard, lined by slender columns. A number of doorways led off the courtyard, some closed.

In the far corner a few candles flared, illuminating people who were dipping and swaying in time to a rhythmic tapping. It was the slaves, dancing silently. The master snapped out orders in a basso voice, moving among them like a menacing shadow.

I slipped from column to column, staying within the darkness. A warm yellow light beckoned from a large room at the front of the courtyard. The walls were painted with pastoral scenes of trees laden with fruit and peasants working in the fields.

Inside a woman was seated on a cushioned bench, gazing out. Her smile was serene, and I realized she couldn't see the slaves dancing because of the number of candles that lit up her chamber. Her eyes were so dark that for a moment I thought she wasn't the mistress, but they sparkled too much to be human. Her hair was dark, short, and feathery, reminding me of Canille.

Suddenly the tapping stopped. By the time I turned around, the master was striding toward me. For a moment, I thought he saw me. I almost darted away, but I realized he was looking past me, at the mistress. I forced myself to stand firm, begging the *olfs* to continue hiding me in the shadows.

He walked by, blocking the light as he entered the chamber. On the other side of the courtyard the slaves were retreating through two doors. Some spoke together in low tones, warily watching for the return of their master.

The mistress silently rose and picked up one of the candles. She glided over to a small wooden door. With my heart pounding faster, I shifted to watch her, creeping as close as I dared.

The mistress opened the door to reveal a slave girl seated on a stool. She was naked, with her hands tied behind her back. Her ankles were pulled back so her legs were open, revealing her delicate pink nether lips. She couldn't see because of a black silk hood over her head, covering her face and tied at her neck.

The master and mistress didn't speak as they entered the small closet. The master looked sickly eager, like a rat sniffing for crumbs. Then the door shut between us.

I hesitated at the very threshold of the chamber. Surely I had seen enough to know that something very bad was happening to that slave.

But my feet carried me forward, stepping quietly across the rugs. Only one *olf* remained with me—it had ears on top of its head, like the numerous cats in the isles. I had to bribe it with the pick of my next three meals for it to stay with me.

I bent forward to see through the crack above the hinge. The mistress considered the slave thoughtfully, then brushed her fingertips against the girl's belly. A glitter caught my eye as the mistress moved away. She was holding a needle.

The girl jerked and trembled, trying not to move. The silk over her mouth moved in and out rapidly as she panted.

"What am I going to do this time?" the mistress asked in much the same tone as she would have wondered which wine to drink.

The girl didn't answer, though every movement cried out, *"No!"* She had been in this room before. I put my hand to my mouth.

The needle was tiny, yet wickedly sharp. The mistress trailed the tip over the girl's skin, flicking her nipples and making her squirm. When she slowly dropped the needle down to the girl's crotch, I held my breath.

"Do it," the master said harshly. He was flushed and his hand was moving on his *tarse.*

The mistress made a quick motion and the girl cried out as she jerked against her bonds. A thin line of blood beaded, then dripped into the dark hair over her nether lips. A searing echo of her pain shot through the *olf.*

In that moment, I also felt the slave girl's certainty of what would happen. The mistress would poke and scratch her until she was frantic, then penetrate her with a carved phallus that was worn with use. The master would pleasure himself, climaxing once or twice, while growling out encouragement to the mistress. Not even the slave girl's screams could make the mistress's expression change. She was dead inside.

The poor *olf* disappeared in a flash of light.

I backed out as fast as I could, choking on my tears, knowing my life depended on silence.

Only the brothers were on the boat when I returned, sleeping under the deck. I huddled in the stern as far from the dock as possible, sobbing. As soon as Lexander stepped onboard, he knew something was wrong.

He came to me, kneeling down and cupping my shoulder tenderly. "Marja, what is it?"

The words were ripped from my throat. "*Why*, Lexander? Why are your people so cruel?"

"You've been inside Allonis." He pulled his hand away as if scorched. "Did they see you, Marja?"

"No, the *olfs* hid me." For a moment, we had connected, but now it was gone. That made me feel even worse. "I know the gods have such great concerns that we're like ants beneath their feet. They trample us with no regard because they must. But what greater purpose does it serve for the masters to torture their slaves?"

"It serves no purpose but our own pleasure," Lexander said flatly.

I stared at him. "Have you no other desire?"

"Not here." Lexander shifted and started to stand.

But I put my hand on his arm. "I need to know why, Lexander."

He turned his head away as if he would refuse. Then he looked down at my fingers, resting lightly on his sleeve. "You don't want to know," he said roughly, but he didn't pull away.

I kept my hand on his arm, knowing my flesh would feel very hot to him, hoping he would reach out to me again. But he was closed off, guarded and distressed. "Tell me, Lexander. What makes the masters treat their slaves so badly? It could be the key to their undoing."

Lexander abruptly sat down beside me, dislodging my hand as he moved farther away. " 'Tis selfishness, pure and simple. You may not understand, but we don't have families as you do. We mature quickly and shun the kind of bonds you form. Maybe that's why we consider only our own needs."

"You don't have parents?"

His mouth twisted, but it wasn't a smile. "Not as you mean. A woman birthed me, but I met her only once and did not like her."

I couldn't imagine growing up without my mam and da. "And your father?"

There was a tremor in his hand as he adjusted his head scarf. I waited.

"Why must you ask me this?" he finally demanded.

"I'm trying to understand why your people hate us."

That caught him off guard. "We don't hate you . . . We use you for our own pleasure."

I shook my head. "Not always. The mistress of Allonis felt nothing while that slave girl screamed."

"Not all of my people are like that. Only those who leave our island become masters. We are the flawed ones, the unsociables and the disaffected. We are suited to the training because of our domineering or aggressive temperament, and are encouraged to go out and establish our own small kingdoms. We accept because we have nothing else."

"But, Lexander, everyone has faults and imperfections. Even the gods."

"You don't understand, Marja. My people embody perfection— we are the mold from which your people sprung. But you are blurred copies of what we once were. We are stronger and smarter, mastering the very currents of life that reside within. The best among us can move with a mere thought and command the elements at a great distance."

"I know. We almost died from the storm you conjured when we left Tillfallvik."

"I didn't cause that storm," he said irritably. "As I said, I'm flawed. I'm the last of my line. There will never be another like me."

That startled me. "You can't have children?"

"No." Bitterly, he added, "According to the whispers in Saaladet, each of the masters lacks certain traits and characteristics. We are good for nothing but to train toys for our betters. I always knew my work would not be valued even when I called out the best in a slave. Slaves are inferior and easily discarded."

I began to nod. "Now I understand why you hate us."

"I don't hate you—" he insisted, his voice rising.

I met his eyes. "You see your own flaws in us."

He shrugged as if he wanted to disagree. "We take out our anger on you, that's true. But my people consider you to be animals, creatures of our distant past. You don't hate a horse for being a horse."

I remembered how Ukerald had used me and the way Renata had relentlessly beaten Bene. "No, we're too much like you. You can't forget we're your children. We are *you* cast in a form that can sicken and suffer and die young."

He considered it as if he was searching for a way to reject what I had said. But he couldn't. "Perhaps you are our worst fear, just as I am my own people's worst fear. In truth, we are no better than you, just different. Why did I never see it before?"

"Because you believed them."

Bene and Eshter returned to the ship having spent too much time and coin in a sailor's tavern. They were eager to share everything they had heard, and had discovered that Allonis, the "house of pleasure," was legendary in the isles for its slaves.

Lexander stood up to distance himself from me, absently listening. His replies were short, as if he was much occupied. The *doj* had tried to control me after he had revealed himself, and I wondered if Lexander would try, as well.

But something remarkable happened. All the next day as we waited to hear word from the guild masters, Lexander's smile came easily, as if he'd been freed from a burden he had not known he carried. Even in the throes of passion, I had never seen him so suffused with simple joy. He took deep breaths of the fresh salty air, squinting into the sun, and he touched everything reverently as if he felt a connection to the simplest objects.

Bene and Eshter saw the change in him, too. They teased him and Bene even tried to tickle him under his open vest. Lexander threw him into the water and threatened a laughing Eshter with the same.

Despite the horror of Allonis, I felt a rare moment of peace. Now

I understood the masters. Despite their many differences, they were all obsessed with drilling perfection into their slaves, because they believed they were imperfect themselves. Lexander had never tried to reach his full potential because he was told he never could.

Now perhaps he would try.

Good news arrived; the guild masters had met and agreed to begin negotiations to establish a dye works in Ovathi. They would consider expanding their guild to include the dyers of "Mahali of Abund."

As a show of good faith, Lexander had been invited to their spring fete. "It's an important rite to ensure the health of their *mouro* trees," Lexander told us. "It shows they have accepted me."

"I'd like to attend," I said.

"Yes, the guild master said there would be a few women there, and that you would be welcome."

He was trying to please me. I reached out to touch him. "You have my thanks."

Lexander stiffened at my gentle caress. It was a reminder of his true feelings. But we needed to convince everyone, so I sternly put aside my sadness. I became very submissive, as he preferred, turning to him for suggestions on my garments and how to wear my hair. I feigned ignorance about the local customs I'd seen so he could explain them to me. Quite naturally, his masterful ways rose and he began to treat me as if I belonged to him. That would be good enough to convince the guild masters.

With Eshter's help, I was soon arrayed in a red silk robe that fell from one shoulder down to my feet. A silver chain was snug around my waist, pleating the fine material into hundreds of folds. Over my cheeks rested a white silk veil, nearly translucent, held up by a fine silver chain. It highlighted my eyes and barely muted the red of my lips.

As I stepped onto the dock, Lexander hardly glanced at me. He dutifully lent me his arm to escort me through the streets.

The guild house was not far from the docks. The darkened

ground floor was clearly a place of business. But up a curving flight of marble steps was a grand hall. Tables were set in a horseshoe shape, and some people were already reclining on the short benches. Though music was being played, it was difficult to hear because everyone was talking.

I picked out a few women amongst all the men. They examined me carefully, drifting among the guests and pausing to whisper to one another. Two had bared their breasts, indicating they were doxies for hire. There were no wives in attendance. I undid my veil as was customary inside.

The dinner began with the beating of a large gong. We took our seats in pairs around the table. Many of the guild masters were accompanied by younger men whom they caressed with casual familiarity. They continued to call to each other with outward good nature, but their comments were often barbed and pitched to be heard by the entire assembly. The laughter was loud and frequent.

Lexander treated me with utmost courtesy, touching me at all times to claim me as his own. My body responded to his caresses as if they were real, making my heart ache with desire. I spoke little, only when I was addressed, hoping my smile would serve instead. I was stared at intently by many of the men, and had to remind myself that they saw few strangers and were naturally curious about me.

Silence was finally called as the high guild master gave a long but rather perfunctory invocation calling on the blessings of the gods. A wide bronze bowl was carried forward and a sacrifice of *mouro* leaves, worms, cocoons, and heavy skeins of pale silk was burned.

The musicians struck up a haunting tune with a heavy, driving drumbeat. Servants hastily removed the bowl and tripod, as the guests gazed expectantly at the open end of the table. After a hushed moment, a dozen people entered and quickly took their places with their toes pointed and heads held high.

I recognized them. "It's the pleasure slaves," I murmured to Lexander, trying to hold my smile.

They began to dance, their hips swaying suggestively. They wore diaphanous tunics that displayed more than they concealed as the folds shifted. I had never seen dancing such as this—seductive and erotic. They flaunted their bodies as their eyes begged us to take them. They touched each other, tantalizing us with their pleasure.

I was enraptured. The *olfs* were spinning among them, feeding off the sensual effusions building in the air. The corpulent man lolling next to me urged a doxy to pleasure him in the crudest terms. She eagerly bent her head to satisfy him. Others were frankly touching themselves and their companions.

Lexander had gone very still next to me. Surely he would have to caress me. And I would have to please him in order to maintain our roles.

Suddenly I couldn't bear it. I couldn't let him touch me falsely. "I can feign illness so we can leave," I offered under my breath.

He didn't answer for a few long moments. "If you wish," he finally agreed.

I hardly had to pretend to be overcome by the heat. In a daze, I let Lexander support me as we got up from our bench and quietly went to the door. Many of the candles had been snuffed, leaving only the dancers illuminated, so we were hardly noticed.

But a woman stepped into the doorway. "Do you dislike the dancing?"

I put my hand to my head, sagging against Lexander as he hastily explained, "She is unused to the heat."

"Overcome by modesty, I would say."

I recognized her voice. It was the mistress of Allonis. I tried to stop Lexander from stepping into the light of the stairs, but he dragged me forward thinking I was acting ill.

The mistress knew with one look that Lexander was a fellow master. They were so close there was no hiding the sparkling depths of his eyes. "It is you!" she declared.

He realized his mistake and tried to shove her out of the way. But she was ready for him, hiding the knife in her hand with her skirt.

She grappled with Lexander, pushing me out of the way so I staggered to one side. She jabbed at his heart with the knife, but he parried her expertly.

"Imposters!" the mistress cried as Lexander caught hold of her wrist. "They are in league with raiders!"

The guild masters hadn't noticed their scuffle, but they began to rouse themselves. Lexander wrested the knife from her hand and in a motion too quick to see, slashed at her neck. She fell back with a wordless cry, clutching at her throat. But she was still alive.

I grabbed hold of Lexander, stopping him from finishing her off. "We have to get out of here!"

He warded off the blow of the first man who came at us, then followed me as I ran down the steps. Commands were shouted for the sentries to seize us.

I called desperately for the *olfs* to hide us from their sight. By the time the sentries responded, we were concealed as we fled from the guild house.

I ran as I had never done before. Lexander pulled me along by the hand and we fair flew to the docks. The clash of weapons echoed through the streets behind us as the sentries advanced.

Lexander dashed up the dock, yelling, "Cast off, Bene! Cast off!" long before we reached the boat.

For a moment I feared that Bene and Eshter were not onboard. But Bene had the mooring rope loosened and the brothers were frantically raising the sail as we arrived. Lexander had warned them that we might have to leave at a moment's notice.

Lexander picked me up and threw me onboard. He gave the ship a mighty shove as he jumped onto the bow. Eshter was at the rudder, turning the ship away from the dock as the wind caught the half-raised sail.

I started to get up, but Lexander pushed my head back down. "Get down!" he shouted.

Something whizzed by overhead, and the sound of spears hitting the hull made me cringe.

"Eshter!" I cried, knowing she was most vulnerable in the stern. Without the *olfs,* on this moonless night, I could see nothing.

The sounds of impacts trailed off as Eshter called back, "I'm unharmed!"

Bene moved cautiously at my feet. The brothers had dived through the hatch for safety. Torches flared on the docks as ships were readied to follow after us.

Eshter called out softly, "Can anyone see where we're going?"

Lexander moved forward to peer through the darkness. I grabbed on to his arm. "We can't abandon the slaves!"

"We'll be killed if we don't leave," Lexander said. He began calling instructions back to Eshter to adjust our course. The brothers emerged to finish with the rigging, subdued by our sudden flight. "We still have to get past the sentries on the cliffs."

Everyone held their breath as our ship slipped through the cleft leading out of the bay. The sentries were concerned about ships entering, not leaving, and they made no effort to stop us.

Bene joined us with Eshter as the elder brother took the rudder, steering us into deeper waters away from the isle. "What happened?" he demanded.

"The mistress recognized me," Lexander said.

I stared back into the darkness, knowing I wouldn't be able to see a ship even if it followed us. We were so close . . . "We can't just leave the slaves behind."

"We'll need a new disguise before we can return," Lexander said.

"We'll come back later," Bene consoled me. "Like we planned to do with Montplaire."

We sat in silence, feeling the full weight of our failure. Everything had been going exactly as we planned, until that fete took a carnal turn.

Finally Lexander spoke. "I think we must first destroy Saaladet. That way we can cut off the flow of slaves with one blow. Then we can take our time picking off each pleasure house."

"I'm all for that," Bene agreed.

I felt as if we were abandoning the slaves, but Lexander was right. The pleasure houses were forewarned and they were strong. We had to find another way.

"Then Stanbulin it is," I agreed.

25

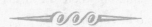

Five days later, the brothers sailed us through the narrow channel that joined two great seas. It was crowded with ships passing back and forth. At the innermost end of the channel was the city of Stanbulin, situated on a triangular point of hilly land with the sea on one side and an inlet of silver water on the other.

The tremendous ramparts that surrounded the city could be seen from far away. These walls surpassed every other structure I had seen, running the length of the waterfront. Massive square towers punctuated their breadth, and the tiny figures of sentries along the top made it clear their height was no illusion.

"There must be more than a hundred towers," Bene said in awe.

"Stanbulin is often attacked by warbands and marauders seeking its riches." The way Lexander surveyed the city reminded me that he had trained here, returning every two decades to receive his new assignments. He knew this city well.

There were gates piercing the wall here and there, with some opening onto small harbors. Each harbor was also walled off from the rest of the city, offering sentries the perfect vantage to attack a ship within. Bene and Eshter were frank in their admiration, but it was too foreboding for me. Masses of buildings covered the hills inside.

"Stanbulin is an ancient city," Lexander explained. "The gateway between east and west. You can find the finest of luxuries here and the basest of vice all wrapped in superstitious beliefs." To me, he added, "Kristna is powerful here, but there are many ancient gods whose worship is too strong to be supplanted."

Our small ship waited until a gate was raised in front of a public harbor. Soon enough we were waved through with flags so we could dock within the walls. I felt as if we were at the bottom of a well, unable to see yet the sounds of the city echoed oddly around us.

The brothers dealt with the dockmaster while we simply walked away. They would stay and take on supplies, if they were allowed. Our business with them was done, with all parties satisfied. Lexander had admitted the night before we disembarked that my choice had been sound—surely we would have been caught by the guild masters if we had taken the ponderous galley as he had wanted.

A broad shelf curved along the wall to an interior gate. Passing through, we were instantly thrust into a boiling sea of people, thicker than a swarm of bees. I grabbed Bene and Eshter's hands to keep from losing them.

After the tranquil villages in the isles, Stanbulin was stunning to the senses. It was an endless maze of walls, gates, stalls, and plazas spreading far into the distance. Along with packs of dogs that roamed around were beggars and cripples holding out their hands, following us as long as they dared and begging us for mercy.

Everywhere there were men sitting cross-legged on small rugs laid on the ground, often smoking noxious substances, adding to the stench. Some wore the long robes of the isles and wound cloth tightly around their heads. Others wore baggy pants embroidered in a rainbow of colors or brocade tunics that were closed with silk frogs. Most of the women tied dark veils over their hair and faces, revealing only their eyes through a narrow slit. Those dark eyes followed us, curious and exotic.

The words were as varied as the people. I heard a scrap of Frankish and was happy to see a few of the short, curly haired people. But Bene didn't notice them in the din.

The most prevalent tongue was spoken with a rapid sibilance. They used gestures to convey nuances with the turn of a hand or tilt of their head. I called to the *olfs* so I could understand what was being said, and concentrated on picking up as many practical words as possible, my tongue shifting around the strange sounds.

Bene and Eshter couldn't understand any of the shouts aimed in our direction, though the *olfs* told me that some were meant to admire my beauty. My veil was sheer, the only kind I could bear, and that seemed to grant leave for anyone to gaze upon me. Eshter strutted happily beside me in her boyish attire.

We gaped at everything, especially the strange animals—monkeys like skinny, brown *olfs* with hands as cunning as our own, and four-legged beasts of burden with long curved necks and a hump in the middle of their backs. The buildings were unusual, with red tile roofs and slender towers thrusting into the sky. Lexander pointed out monuments erected near the wells in public plazas—obelisks and marble statues painted in bright colors, celebrating great events or rulers in the past.

As we entered one plaza, Lexander stopped abruptly, holding us back. There was the clash of swords ahead and suddenly boys appeared from everywhere, dashing past us to escape the plaza.

"Is it a battle?" I cried as we ran back down the street.

Lexander turned into a twisting lane that led uphill. He made sure we weren't being followed before relenting his pace. "They're conscripting soldiers for their next campaign. The emperor died in the summer, after losing several cities along the coast to the sultan. The empress fights on with her new husband. It's tradition to gather men from the streets to fill out the empty ranks." He glanced at Bene and Eshter. "They'd take these two, and there's little I could do to stop them."

Subdued, we three were less inclined to gawk or stray far from

Lexander after that. The line between his brows showed his concern as he hesitated at a crossroads. "There's no help for it: We'll have to go through the slave market to avoid the conscriptors. Don't draw attention to yourselves. There may be masters from Saaladet here."

We entered the slave market through a high arch. Within were more twisting lanes that were partially covered by canopies. Evil twined among these walls, leaving me breathless. None of the *olfs* came along despite my pleas.

The market consisted of open stalls set within the nooks, and doors that opened on to chambers lined with rich tapestries. Women, men, and children were crouched down together or lined up with their heads bowed, waiting to be bought.

We passed a rough group of men with a tragic air, corralled in a wooden enclosure. They were nude to reveal the wounds of their *castrati*. Lexander said grimly, "Eunuchs are quite prized for their administrative abilities. The old emperor even relied on his sister's valet to lead his war campaigns."

There were hundreds of slaves of every race and age in the market. The enormity of it overwhelmed me. None of these people deserved to be enslaved.

At the end of the lane was a round building, the front half open with only pillars for support. Under the dome was a raised platform with crowds of men gathering below. At the top of the wooden steps was a table where several men sat writing on parchment. The back of the platform was crowded with people, some carrying whips while others were bound.

A woman stood at the front of the platform. She bent her head and reluctantly dropped her robe to reveal herself. She was full fleshed and unblemished, as if she had known only a life of ease. The men below began shouting out, raising their hands, as an older man in a saffron robe pointed from one to the other.

The woman was near to tears from being exposed. Her hands trembled and her head turned away. It incited the men who were bidding for her, and their cries grew more insistent.

Lexander hurried us past the auction. I wondered if any of those turbaned men were masters from Saaladet.

As we had agreed, Lexander took us straight to the master house. It was adjacent to the inlet of water that separated the city of Stanbulin from the rest of the countryside. The hills became cliffs along the water's edge.

As we approached a rounded butte, Lexander pointed up. "There's Saaladet, the master house."

Buildings were carved directly into the cliff face. There were four levels with the floors intersecting oddly as they followed the natural undulations of the promontory. Scraggly plants grew in the crevices among the rubble. On the low foothill in front of the cliff were a few small structures.

A wall encircled the base of the butte, sturdy enough to repel attack and topped with tall iron spikes. I doubted even Lexander could surmount it. "It looks like a fortress."

"It is." Lexander's expression had shut down, revealing nothing.

Lexander acquired a room on the top floor of a hostel close to the city wall. Through the lattice over the window, we could see the rooms of Saaladet cut into the cliff. Lights shone forth, but only a few people went down the slanting path to the city gate and the private harbor beyond. Unlike Castropiero, the master house did not entertain its neighbors.

In the privacy of our room, Lexander declared, "The only way is for me to poison the masters."

I stared at him. "Surely there are other options, Lexander. The masters must have made enemies in this city."

"The empire is in turmoil, Marja. Their lands are under siege by the sultan's warbands, which keep winning every engagement with their horse troops. And the empress just married a general few have trust in. From the reports I heard in the isles, I expected to see the sultan camped outside the wall. You'd not convince the great sanctuary of Kristna itself to care about Saaladet right now."

"You want to kill as many of the masters as you can," I said flatly.

"Yes, at the same time. It's the safest way. For that, I need poison."

Eshter was taken aback. But Bene was grinning as if unduly excited by the idea. "How will you do it?"

"I'll douse the wine with it. The masters are the only ones who drink wine."

"What about the servants? You don't think they drink the wine?" I remembered the kitchen servants in Vidaris taking sips from the open bottles.

Lexander waved that off. "The wine will mask the bitter taste."

"Will you bribe the wine seller?" Bene asked.

"No. I must do this myself. Poison is available here, though it will be expensive to get as much as I need."

I shook my head, disliking everything about his plan.

"We tried it your way with Allonis, and it didn't work," Lexander told me. "Saaladet is far more powerful than any pleasure house."

"You'll be recognized," I told him. "It won't be safe for you to go in."

"I can take care to avoid everyone on my way to the storage rooms."

It couldn't be that easy. But Bene clearly believed him. He offered, "I could pose as a slave and do it for you."

"This is not Montplaire," Lexander told him. "Slaves are kept confined at all times."

"I can imagine," Eshter murmured.

"I must go in alone," Lexander insisted.

"How can you get inside?" Bene cocked his head, examining the master house through our window. "We could go over the back of the hill and lower you down."

"It's been tried before, but never with success. My people guard Saaladet well." Lexander glanced at me, unwilling to say more in front of Eshter and Bene. His people had special powers when it came to protecting themselves.

"The gate is the problem," he continued. "The keepers know

who can enter. But there's also a sea gate, which lies between the walls that open into the harbor." Lexander pointed, and we could just see the top of one of the massive towers. "That gate is normally lowered so ships can't enter. I think it's possible to swim underneath, though it will be difficult without attracting the attention of the sentries on the towers." He turned to me. "I thought you could ask for help from the spirits. I need to be concealed, as they did when you went into Allonis."

I tilted my head. "I would have to be with you."

Lexander frowned. "No, that won't work. Perhaps I can do without . . ."

"There must be another way," I insisted.

"It will take a few days for me to locate the right herbalist. If you can think of something better—"

At that moment, the floor began to move. The hanging basket tilted, then began to swing.

We all reached out to steady ourselves. I'm sure my eyes were as wide as Eshter's.

"What is it?" Eshter exclaimed, as Bene let out a whoop. He rocked on his stool, exaggerating the sensation. *Olfs* popped in, excited by our reactions.

Lexander watched the basket for a few moments. "A trembler. Nothing to be frightened of."

The ground seemed alive, heaving for a moment before settling back down to sleep. I was eager to see if some trace lingered behind in the ground. Lexander wanted to survey the sea gate of the master house, so we headed back down to the narrow streets.

Lexander spent all of his time tracking down herbalists, trying to find one who could discreetly provide what he needed. I put on dark enveloping robes that showed only my eyes so I could walk through the city unhindered. Bene had to remain inside because of the roving bands of conscriptors, and Eshter flatly refused to give up her boyish attire.

With the *olfs'* help, I picked up enough to know that the empire was teetering. Generations of emperors had spent their riches too freely, building rich palaces and public buildings. Despite the people filling thousands of shops, vendors, and cafes, there were complaints that trade had fallen off due to the sultan's raiders.

I soon found the great sanctuary of Kristna, rising like a small mountain in the midst of the city. It was capped with domes of ever-increasing size and surrounded by towering minarets. I followed the *olfs* inside, and was dazzled by the gold-covered arches and columns. The dome seemed to float on the air as if Kristna's hand held it aloft.

The city flaunted its wealth, making it a tempting target. The empress was fighting with the patriarchs of the city over her choice of husband, while the new emperor conscripted goods as well as men from the city to bolster his campaign against the sultan.

Stanbulin felt like a juggernaut that would crush me if I threw myself into its meshes. The master house seemed impervious to it all, complacent within their cliff like an island in a turbulent sea.

By the time Lexander asked me if he could use the last gold coins to purchase the poison, I had no other choice. The more he had discussed his plan with us, refining the details, I had accepted the inevitable. He was determined to throw himself into the pit and fight his own way out.

But I was going in with him. After gauging the distance, it was clear that he needed the help of the *olfs* to obscure the sentries' sight. He agreed that I would accompany him into the harbor as long as I left immediately thereafter.

So I gave Lexander the purse, and he at last returned with a large glass bottle. White crystals much like salt were sealed inside with purple wax. The *olfs* scattered as Lexander locked it into a casket. It was made from the seeds of cherry laurel trees and would cause the masters to appear drunk—excited, flushed, confused, and finally drowsy. Once they lay down, they would never get up again. I feared Lexander would be trapped by the flames when the masters died, but he assured me that Saaladet would not burn as the pleasure houses did.

The next morning, we woke to see Saaladet's sea gate pulled up high and a winged ship passing into the harbor. Lexander told us, "More slaves have arrived. Tonight will be the perfect time for me to go in. They always celebrate when they have fresh stock."

"I'm ready," I agreed. I had my own plan, unbeknownst to him. I wasn't going to run away. I was going to hide in the harbor, ready to help Lexander in case he needed it.

When full darkness fell, we pushed our new rowboat into the inky water. Lexander carried the poison in an oilskin bag along with fresh corks and wax to reseal the wine bottles. He also brought a flowing ankle-length robe such as the masters wore. I shucked off my enveloping layers, leaving only a brief chemise, before slipping into the icy waters.

I gasped from the cold. I had been communing with the sea spirits since we had embarked, but the shock of the water jolted me.

The lights on top of the city wall looked far away. Several *olfs* cast a helpful light, and Bene and Eshter were two pale faces leaning over us.

"Will they conceal us?" Lexander asked quietly.

At my request, the *olfs* darted off to cloud the sentries' eyes, hiding us from their sight. I could see their swirling presence on top of the towers. "They're doing it."

"Good, let's go." He began to swim noiselessly toward the city.

I followed him as fast as I could. By the time we were close to the sea gate, I was immersed in the spirits, warmed by the exertion and their protection. Lexander was barely breathing hard, treading water without a sound. The sentries were right above us, bathed in the glow of the *olfs*.

From the sea spirits, I began to feel the tug of the current at our feet. "We'll have to go underwater from here," I whispered. "Let the flow guide you."

We took a few deep breaths, then plunged under the water. I could barely see, and felt something brush my head as I ducked under the sea gate. The gate interfered with the current, causing eddies beside it and speeding the water up as it passed underneath. I shot into the harbor with hardly a bubble.

When I finally surfaced, I checked first to be sure the sentries couldn't see me. I was gasping as I tried to catch my breath, afraid that they would hear me. But there was no one in sight. The sentries must have been leaning on the outside of the wall.

Then I looked around for Lexander. There was only black water around me.

I silently swam toward the dock. The large ship was there with the broad sails tied up. There were also several boats with single masts including one the size of our rowboat.

I climbed onto the dock, a ponderous stone quay, staying in the shadows cast by the winged ship. While Lexander went up to the master house, I intended to hide inside the ship. The crew was kept outside of Saaladet's gates and would return only when it was time for them to depart.

I looked for Lexander, calling to the *olfs* to come help me. But none would venture into the harbor. The sea spirits also withdrew. The silence was ominous, as if pressure was building in the air.

Visions of Lexander getting trapped under the sea gate flashed before my eyes. I kept hoping he would appear, bag in hand, calmly prepared to commit mass slaughter.

I was concentrating so hard on the water that I didn't notice the people coming down the path until they were quite close.

"Don't you want to stay together?" a woman asked, keeping her voice low as if afraid of being overheard. I had come to associate the sibilant words with Stanbulin, and knew enough from the *olfs* to understand the ancient tongue somewhat.

"This is the only way," the man insisted. "They'll need to open another house in Danelaw."

I slipped over the edge of the quay to dive underwater, making a splash. Before I could take two strokes, someone jumped on top of me.

The impact drove my breath away. I choked as the master hauled me back to the wharf.

The mistress reached down to grab my wrist. She lifted me one-handed from the water as if I were a puppy. She could have easily snapped my arm.

They were mere shadows in the dim light, but they examined me closely. "Who are you?" the mistress demanded, shaking my arm. "How did you get in here?"

I pointed to the city gate, hoping to distract them from the water. "Stanbulin," I cried, trying to get the inflection exactly right.

The woman fired rapid questions at me, but I couldn't understand because she spoke too fast. The mistress declared, "Look at what she's wearing! She must be a slave. How did you get out here?"

I pointed to the city gate, growing more frantic, but they weren't going to let me go. They marched me up the path toward the cliff. My bare feet scuffed on the smooth rock as I tried to look behind me. I couldn't see Lexander anywhere.

The mouths of the caves were larger than they looked from the streets below. The sides were shored up with pillars and stone blocks lay in neat lines, masking the rough surface beneath. The floor was worn into shallow trenches from centuries of footsteps, smoothing the impervious rock.

It was dark inside, with lanterns covered in perforated shades marking each arched tunnel. As we went farther, the weight of the hill seemed to close in on me. There was something waiting for me here, something I had long sought to avoid.

I was thrust into a round room with a perfectly arched ceiling. It was proportioned to suit the height of the godlings. Though we were inside a cave, it looked like other chambers I'd seen in the city with thick rugs on the floor and carved wooden screens to hide the walls. Cushions lay in piles near some low tables. The lanterns cast colored specks of light all around the room.

Another master arrived. His head was perfectly smooth like

Lexander's, but his face was gently lined and his voice was husky with age, so he must have been very powerful. The old master grasped my hand, touching my soft palm, noting I did little work with them.

Then he stood back and ordered, *"Gesig!"*

It was impossible to resist. My knees buckled in spite of myself. I was down in the position of surrender before I realized I had betrayed myself.

"Take her to the cells," he ordered in the Stanbulin tongue.

The younger master lifted me effortlessly to my feet. He said something about the boat that had arrived today.

"That's what we shall discover," the elder replied.

I stumbled beside the young master, fear choking me. Where was Lexander? What would they do to me?

We went down a slanting tunnel that grew steeper at the end. Water was dripping and in some places the rock glinted with moisture, picking up the lantern light.

Then the master thrust me into a tiny alcove and slammed an iron grate shut in my face. The lock rasped and the glow departed with the sound of his feet.

In complete darkness, I felt around the walls. The cell was barely big enough for me to stand. I crouched down near the grate where the floor was somewhat dryer, listening. A high-pitched sound was rising and falling, and at first I thought it was wind howling through the tunnels. Then I realized it was distant screams.

I knelt there, petrified, expecting the masters to return at any moment to begin their interrogation. I eventually fell asleep clutching the iron grate. I kept waking to the sounds of rats rustling in the tunnel or when the screams grew louder.

For the first time in my life, I was not sure when the sun rose. I was blinded inside the rock, cut off from everything. There was no food, no water, only the damp, cold darkness.

And it went on.

I tried to reach out to the Otherworld, but I couldn't hear the waves of the sea, and the *olfs* never responded. The only voices I heard were demon's whispers, sighing that I would die in this rocky tomb. They urged me to give up and accept my demise. They sapped my strength and numbed my mind. I resisted, but I knew that they would win in the end, as they had won with those far down the tunnel who had gone mad.

Eshter had told me that Renata had once put her down in the well to punish her. Eshter had stood there all night crying, trying to keep from collapsing. Another slave in the house had become ill after being dragged from the well, and he was taken away never to return.

Now the cruel voices insisted that Lexander had used the well when he was master of Castropiero. He had put boys like Bene down there to sicken and die. I didn't want to face it, but it was true. How many slaves had Lexander hurt?

The longer I resisted the taunting of the demons, the more convinced I became that they had kept Lexander from passing through the sea gate. They lived off the godlings, and that bottle of poison would have ruined their lair. Surely these demons protected the godlings as part of some lethal bargain.

Along with their torment, I was plagued by my thirst. Hunger came and went, but my need for water only grew. My lips cracked and I resorted to licking the rocks, trying to absorb all the moisture I could. But it wasn't enough. I would perish if I wasn't released soon.

It was the inhumanity of it that destroyed me. How could I resist when there was no one to resist against? I mattered not in the least to them. They had forgotten me. I was alone, a scrap of refuse left for evil to toy with.

I clung to the hope of rescue. Lexander knew I had been captured by the masters. He knew about these cells.

But what if he had drowned?

As the last strength drained from my body, I passed in and out of awareness. There was nothing I could do to save myself. In my waking moments, I wanted only to avoid the anguish inflicted by the demons, taunting me with visions of Lexander abusing the slaves and pleasuring his consorts. I pressed my cheek and my palms into the rock, flattening my body against it.

Slowly, I released myself to descend into the rock, where everything moved on a different scale. The rock embraced my spirit and gave me some comfort. I had imagined there was nothing inside the rock but eternity, but spirits flowed through, moving so slowly that it took a very long time for me to connect with them. There was room in my mind for only one word, and I chose—*peace*. No need, no want, no desire . . . only rest.

I knew my *inua* would stay in the rock forever when my body died.

26

When I was at long last dragged out of the cell, I hardly knew my own name. A woman's voice asked in slow, distinct words, "Will you obey?"

I nodded, my tongue too swollen to speak.

I was given water to drink, and I clutched the cup with both hands so I wouldn't spill it. It was not nearly enough, but it revived me somewhat. They wrapped a short robe around me that tied at the waist. A young man was being pulled along behind me, while another was being carried.

I was so relieved to get out that I felt giddy and grateful, as if I were being rescued.

Going up several levels, we were taken to another iron grate, this one towering far over our heads. In the large, hollowed-out chamber beyond, people milled about. The masters thrust us inside, clanging the gate shut.

Some of the others rushed forward, and in the lantern light filtering through the iron bars, I realized they were slaves. There were nearly two score of them. Some were reclining on rugs and padded mats, while others crouched near the curved rear wall.

It took three of them to carry the well-built young man over to some bedding. They called his name uselessly. "Torr! Torr!"

I launched myself away from the grate, heading for the water bucket that my nose found before my bleary eyes could see it. The other boy who had also been pulled from the cells followed me. I wondered if it was their screams I had heard. It made me sick to think there might be other slaves still down in those cells.

We took turns drinking as much as we could. The slave-mates of the unconscious lad fetched water for him when they saw we were parched near to death.

I spotted some bedding and fell into it despite the protests of another slave. The words were staccato, with the full, rounded tones cut sharp, but I could understand her complaints. They were speaking my da's tongue, the language of my homeland. "That's *my* bed! You'll have to make another for yourself. . . ."

Several slaves were removed the next morning and they didn't return until our evening meal of dried fish and mashed roots arrived. I mostly slept, waking only to drink more water.

With their pale skin and long, yellow hair, these slaves looked much like my Noromenn kin. But they were from the cold north rather than my homeland. I could hardly understand their dialects, with the words so clipped and fast. They huddled close into groups, indicating the ship had picked up slaves from four different pleasure houses.

They were wary of me. Obviously I had not journeyed here with them. Each time I woke it was to the particularly shrill voice of Grete, the woman whom I had ousted from her makeshift bed. She was always asking me questions. I ignored her, refusing to answer until I could determine what to do. It had not been good fortune that sent me to Grete, for she was determined to unravel my mystery. Perhaps she would have hounded me regardless of where I had collapsed, for Grete was stridently intense about everything.

When the three slaves were returned, they were crying and trembling. Some of the others gathered round them, trying to help. One girl was inconsolable, crying so hard her face was swollen and red.

Finally Grete's attention was focused elsewhere. "What did they do to you, Ileana?" Grete demanded. But the girl could hardly breathe, much less speak.

One of the older boys pushed Grete away. "Can't you leave her alone?" His sneer reminded me of Sverker, my nemesis in Vidaris.

"I never . . ." Ileana cried hysterically in his arms. "I didn't know . . . Why? Oh, why?"

The girl was bleeding from dozens of tiny sores on her thighs. The other slaves who returned were similarly overwrought and exhausted, their robes stained with blood where they had been cut. One of the boys had rope burns on his arms, while the other held his head in his hands and simply moaned.

I pulled the blanket over my head.

A few days later, the masters had evaluated all of the slaves in the pen. Grete had returned speaking faster than ever, recounting the awful details of what they had done to her. Tears flowed constantly, but except for an odd gasping sob with every breath, she couldn't stop talking.

I put my hands over my ears, trying to block out her manic face and wide open mouth. I wondered if Grete had always been like this or if she had snapped. Everyone was terrified or defensive or both. There had been a fight among the boys from different houses, with flailing arms and vicious scuffling as the others screamed and tried to get away. None of the masters came to investigate and eventually they tired themselves out, more bloodied and bruised than before.

Then the masters came to take me away along with Torr and Hans, the slaves who had been in the cells. The three of us hadn't yet recovered from our ordeal. Torr could barely walk, but Hans tried to dislodge the hands of his captors. They held him tighter and their strength was such that Hans had no hope of breaking free.

They led us back down the rough-hewn tunnel, and I feared for a moment that we were going down to the cells again. But we were taken through a door in the rock. The thick wooden beams were heavy, and the door boomed as it swung shut. I'd heard that sound from the holding pen, but hadn't known what it was.

Inside were doors spaced along the tunnel until it curved ahead and I could see no farther. My hands were shaking. These were the only doors I had seen in Saaladet.

But the first chamber held nothing more frightening than a bath. The tubs steamed with water, delivered through a cunning pipe that passed through a hole in the rock.

It was eerily familiar, reminding me of when Lexander had first brought me to Vidaris.

Torr and Hans definitely needed a wash after their long ocean voyage. I was little better after the filth of the cells. The master and mistress who tended to us seemed accustomed to the worst of grime. They watched us scrub down, pointing here and there to encourage a more thorough job. As they did, they drilled us on the names of each body part. Lexander had taught us the slippery-sounding words in Vidaris, and now I realized it was the Stanbulin tongue.

The master and mistress provided other words in the ancient language, which I drank up. It was difficult to communicate without the *olfs'* help, and I wished I had learned more since arriving in Stanbulin. But the masters were primarily interested in concepts like "clean" and "dirty," and what to call the tub, soap, and brushes.

When I was finally glowing and my hair hung in long, damp waves, I was shown into another room.

I began to take deep breaths, preparing for the worst. Someone barked, *"Vordna!"* and I bent my knees, assuming the pose of deference.

"What is your name?" the master demanded in my da's tongue.

"Marja."

"Your house?"

I felt a tremendous sense of dislocation. A year ago in Vidaris, I had been ready to board the winged ship to Stanbulin when Lexander had saved me. I thought I had escaped, but now my fate had caught up to me.

I gave the name of a northern house I had heard among the slaves. I was determined never to reveal that I was from Vidaris, not even under torture.

But that was the end of their questioning. I had been dreading an interrogation about how I had gotten loose in their harbor. But they must have assumed it was an oversight by one of the masters that I had been left behind on the ship.

Instead, a master and mistress ordered me through the poses at a fairly rapid pace. While one master rapidly marked on a scroll with a black quill, the elder one made continuous comments as he circled me—my height, the shape of my breasts, the size of my buttocks, my hair and face. My unusual eyes garnered a lot of attention. None of the northern slaves had almond eyes like mine, but the masters did not question their own assumptions.

As they ordered me through another series of poses, they went slower, giving them time to run their hands over my waist and down my legs. As their fingers probed me, checking my mouth, ears, and nether parts, I was once again a slave. I could protest, rebel, and fight them, but they would win in the end. It would be easy for them. They could throw me in a cell and forget about me.

Whenever I tensed or stiffened, they became more insistent. They were going to do what they wanted regardless of my desires. The agony came from fighting them.

So I began to accept that I was a slave again. It was a terrible accident that I was here, but I couldn't fight it. Not now.

I sank inside myself, finding that unchanging core that was unaffected by circumstance. Whether I felt ecstasy or pain, it was all the same if I yielded. Only my acquiescence mattered.

They brought back Torr and Hans, and ordered us to pleasure each other. I was warmed up and their stimulation ignited my body. But both were resistant. Torr was a well-developed young man with broad shoulders from working in the fields. His eyes were bloodshot when he managed to open them, and his skin had a grayish cast. He had fared the worst in the utter blackness of the cell. It had broken him. Watching him move about as if he were an animated corpse made my skin crawl.

Hans was shorter and stockier, younger than both of us. Hans worried me. He was enthusiastic at times, but then he lapsed into anger and actually shouted at the masters. When he was focused, he became very intent. He licked and sucked on Torr's *tarse* for a long time, even though Torr clearly did not respond. When I tried, I got the same result.

The mistress brought out a stiletto. The point of the knife was sharp, with the light catching its beveled edge. She made me move from between Torr's legs and took my place. The two masters stood behind him, holding his arms.

She placed the stiletto against his chest. In the Noromenn's tongue, she ordered, "Obey."

As she flicked the knife, it left a short red line behind.

Torr was cut a dozen more times, but he refused to make a sound though his legs jerked each time. The shallow cuts filled with blood, and a few ruby beads dripped down.

Then they motioned for me to suck on his *tarse*. He didn't want it, so I almost couldn't. But if I refused, it would be worse for all of us. So I used every art I could to tease him into excitement.

Even when I managed to coax some firmness into them, neither Torr nor Hans could sustain themselves for penetration. Torr's *inua* was already gone, while Hans had become unbalanced. He laughed when the mistress cut him the first time, a chilling sound. His outbursts garnered him a bloody set of wounds on his chest and back.

After much frustration and fruitless effort, Torr and Hans were removed from the room. I was sweating and trembling from what I had seen and done. I was also smeared with blood, though I had not been cut myself.

The young master and mistress took their place with me. I performed every rite of pleasure that Lexander had taught me, as well as some I had never encountered before. The mistress sucked each one of my fingers as if they were tiny *tarses,* and then she ordered me to do the same with her. I dived in with abandon.

The session with my buttocks was quite extended, and I was ordered to service theirs, licking and probing with my fingers. The master had a cold response, but the mistress was lovely. Her name was Numian. She wallowed in the pleasure, reminding me at times of Ukerald's consort, Drucelli. I had never serviced Drucelli, but Numian had a similar sensuality in every glance of her sparkling copper eyes, half lidded with pleasure. She was short compared to the rest of her people, near my own height, a perfect miniature goddess. She herself likely believed that she was flawed.

Occasionally, the elder master ordered Numian or the master to do certain things. It was as if the masters were in truth slaves themselves. I tried to imagine Lexander rutting on command, but it was hard to conceive of him being subservient to anyone.

I quailed at nothing, but Numian began inflicting tiny cuts on me, to see if I would resist. In my heightened state, the sharp lacerations merely served to raise me higher into ecstasy, as I released everything else to the demands of pain. I accepted each cut without looking away or tensing when Numian raised the stiletto.

My sweat made the wounds sting till my breath came short. When they finally let me go, I stumbled and nearly fell as I collapsed to the ground, unable to hear what they were saying.

As I swam back, someone gave the order for *gesig,* utter surrender. I pulled myself into a kneeling position, my head bowed, feeling as if I were floating away.

They were testing me to find my limits. But they couldn't reach beyond mine. I wondered if they would kill me in trying. . . .

But they were growing eager, discussing me. I couldn't understand exactly what they said, but they had realized I was a true submissive. Lexander had been so eager when he discovered my nature that he had taken me right then and there. Perhaps he had thought of how pleased the masters of Saaladet would be when he sent me to them.

But I could not think about Lexander now. Only a slave could endure this.

The one word I heard repeated was "*Tantalis.*" It was a place of great importance to them. I wondered if it was the island where Lexander's people lived, that elusive place that had made him . . . the place that would destroy me.

When they finally carried me back to the pen, I was past all remembrance. When I awoke the next morning, Torr and Hans were gone.

Days later, Torr and Hans still had not returned. The slaves speculated that they had been deemed unsuitable and had been sold at the slave market in the city. I didn't want to say anything, but I feared they had been sent back to the cells after they had failed their evaluations.

The masters and mistresses regularly took us from the pen for their practice sessions and to pleasure themselves. Perhaps it was part of the evaluation to see how we interacted with our patrons. The slaves had no thoughts of resistance.

I was taken from the holding pen quite often. It seemed that all the masters wanted to try a true submissive. So I joined them in their luxurious chambers, lolling on the softest blankets, stroking them. They clinked their silver-tined utensils as they ate, disdaining to use their fingers, while I sat at their feet accepting their scraps. There was always more pleasure to be given and accepted. I lost count of how many I rutted with under the light-spangled lanterns.

The masters seemed to be on holiday, enjoying the luxury of the master house while they were being trained or waiting for their next assignments. But we slaves were like water always pouring forth from a spring. We were evaluated, then sent off to our new masters in Tantalis, with another batch of slaves soon arriving to take our place. What they did to us mattered not.

Everyone watched me curiously, so I remained docile and meek. But whenever I was in the holding pen, I tried to rouse the other slaves, to talk to them about breaking free. Yet no one would listen.

They thought I was mad. They were so beaten down that only a great shock would awaken them from their stupor. In spite of myself, I felt as if I were sinking along with them, with nothing ahead but more misery.

Hope of rescue had become a burden I could no longer bear. I had to force myself to stop imagining Lexander striding through the tunnel toward me.

Late one evening, I was removed from the pen by Numian, the mistress who had performed my evaluation. Numian decided to take her pleasure with me and a mistress who deferred to her. This mistress was even more beautiful than Numian, but she required constant affirmation. As I pleased her, I murmured compliments about her luminous skin, her fascinating eyes, and the sumptuous curve of her breasts. . . .

Numian laughed at us and directed the whole thing. On the whole it was pleasant. Since my evaluation, none of the masters had marked me, and the scabs from the cuts were almost completely healed. The slaves were actually grateful that they weren't being beaten every day.

I did not have to feign enjoyment with Numian. She was not even harsh when she pushed me back into the holding pen, unlike some of the other masters, who shoved us away as if we were unfit to be touched. Her hand was gentle as she guided me inside.

That gave me the opening I needed.

Numian was so lulled by my subservience that she didn't expect it. I grabbed her arm and jerked her toward me. She stumbled into the pen, catching on to the bar to stop herself. I threw my body against the gate, slamming it back into her. There was a sickening crunch as her head was caught between the gate and the bar.

The weight of her falling pushed me away. Numian lay there with the whites of her eyes showing and a blood stain slowly growing on the floor.

There was an outcry from the slaves, which I quickly stopped. "Hush, or they'll hear you! Do you want to be punished?"

"They're going to kill you!" Grete gasped.

"I'm getting out of here," I told them. "And you're all coming with me."

Some of the slaves protested and backed up against the rough walls, as far away from Numian as they could go. Horror was etched in their faces. I couldn't blame them.

"Come!" I ordered. "Help me hide her."

I picked up one of Numian's arms and pulled. At my repeated orders, a few of the boys stepped forward to help. They feared what would happen if Numian was seen.

When she was laid at the back of the holding cell, I put my hand to her mouth. There was no breath.

She was dead.

Panic almost overcame me. I might as well have killed myself. I could feel the pressure of the evil spirits trying to seep inside through my transgression.

But the rising questions from the slaves brought me back to my senses. I couldn't tell them that Numian was dead.

I covered the mistress with the rug, tucking it around her tenderly, murmuring, "I give this kill to you, evil spirits."

The demons infesting the master house eagerly snatched at Numian's *inua* as it drifted away from her body, empowered by the words of her executioner. But Numian's godling spirit would not be easily absorbed. I hoped their struggle would occupy them while we made our escape. I would have to deal with the consequences later.

I straightened up. "Listen, everyone! It's time to escape. I've done this before. I used to be a pleasure slave, too, but now . . ." I had to stop and swallow. "Now I'm free. I've been working with my friends to rescue you."

"We can't just walk out of here," Grete protested. "They'll kill us."

"Everyone's asleep," I insisted. "Besides, if we see someone, we can overwhelm them before they know it. Look how many of us there are."

Another slave unexpectedly spoke up. "Maybe it is possible." It was the boy who reminded me of Sverker, with his overbearing ways.

He held up a twisted length of cloth and snapped it. I could envision him putting it over a master's neck and choking him.

"Yes, and bring the water bucket," I suggested. "Grab anything that can be used as a weapon. If we pile on all at once, no one can stop us."

One of the slaves had pulled over a rug to hide the bloody smear on the floor. I forced myself to step onto it and swing the gate open. "Quietly now, let's go!"

I didn't get the rousing response I had hoped for. But when I stepped outside, one by one they slipped out. They weren't inspired by my words—none of them wanted to stay behind with Numian.

I didn't care why they came. I prayed that they wouldn't scatter at the first sight of a master. I would not give up without a fight, and I readied myself to commit more outrage.

I had entertained so many different masters that I had become quite familiar with the tunnels. After the first turn, I led the slaves downward, preferring to meet up with servants rather than masters. We could hopefully frighten the servants away.

Twenty people made a lot of noise even barefoot. They coughed and let out slight cries of fright whenever they bumped together. I let only the slave next to me carry a lantern, afraid the light would betray us.

We passed by archways and tunnels that probably led to servants' chambers and storerooms. Several large spaces were empty except for tables stacked to one side.

Then the tunnel angled upward. We intersected another passage-way from the masters' quarters. The scent of the sea was strong now.

We emerged into an astonishing room. The chamber was in the cliff face, open to the twinkling lights of the city spread out below. The ceiling was crossed by heavy wooden beams instead of rock.

The slaves spilled into the room. I ran forward to see if there was a way down. But there was only the cliff below us. After my fall off the Londinium wall, I knew it was too dangerous to jump down. I got my bearings and decided to go over and down one level to reach the entrance to the master house.

As I turned, a master sat up from one of the benches where he had been reclining. A mistress was next to him. We had interrupted them rutting. I had bedded both of them and knew their names, but I didn't want to remember that.

"Get them!" I cried, leading the charge. "Don't let them take you!"

I had farther to go than the others, so the slaves reached them first. Along the way they had picked up brooms and stools. Other slaves grabbed what was at hand. One brawny young man lifted a table and brought it down on the master's head. The mistress screamed, but the sound was abruptly cut off as she disappeared in a flurry of makeshift weapons.

I didn't have to do a thing. Once unleashed, I had to call off the slaves. The master and mistress lay shattered on the floor. I hated it, but I said nothing to diminish their blood lust.

I led them up the spiral stairs to the chamber above. The master house was a maze, but in the neighboring chamber, another staircase led back down two levels. I dashed through an archway and another corridor, finally emerging from the entrance at the base of the cliff. Ahead of us was the squat stone building surrounded by lean-tos and small sheds. My nose told me it was the kitchens.

In the lantern light, some of the slaves were blood splattered and wild eyed. Grete had a grip on Ileana as if fearing the girl would crumple to the ground in a panic.

"Put out the lantern," I ordered. The slave instantly complied, leaving us in darkness.

I led them around the kitchen, to the path down to the city gate. There were two lanterns lit there, casting a pool of light.

"There's a gatekeeper at the bottom," I hissed. "Don't let him stop us."

I was shouldered aside by the young men who had taken eagerly to my revolt. They were impatient to attack, incited to murder by how we had been treated.

The gatekeeper had no forewarning of us descending on him. He cried out as the slaves tackled him with an animal sound.

I pushed open the gate, letting it clash against the pillar. The lanterns hung high on either side, casting yellow light around us.

"Go!" I ordered the slaves. The path was too narrow for us to gather. "Wait for me down below."

I stayed behind to pull the boys away. They were kicking the downed gatekeeper with their bare feet. As the last one came through the gate, I heard someone jump down onto the path.

"Marja!" Lexander exclaimed.

I turned to see Lexander, looking quite astonished. Then his arms went around me, and it was real—his body hard against me, the smell of his skin, and his face pressing my hair.

In a rush we came together. His emotion was too great for words. He had been frantic over losing me, knowing what went on inside Saaladet. He knew because he had done it all himself—cut innocent flesh, used slaves for his own needs, and cast the ones who rebelled into the dank, dark cells to die.

But this was Lexander, my lover. He was fighting his own training and even his domineering nature to make amends for the harm he had done. He was destroying his own people with his own hands.

Just as I had now killed. There was no going back for either of us.

27

Lexander came to himself in a rush, remembering where we
stood. He grabbed my hand to pull me away.

I resisted. "I have to finish this. I have to stop them."

"Not now—"

I wrenched away from them. "Yes, now, before they realize we're
gone. Before they find their dead."

I went back through the gate, looking for an exposed rock surface.
Most of the steep hillside was cloaked with dirt and rubble.

"Marja, what are you doing? They must be coming."

"They will be soon." I put my hands on the cool naked rock in
the darkness beyond the reach of the lantern light. "Please, Lexander,
take the slaves away."

"You're coming with us," he insisted.

I pressed my body against the cliff, resting my cheek on the rock.
"Lexander, listen to me. I must do this now. Don't interfere!"

I closed my eyes and sank into the rock. I had to release everything—
my thoughts, my feelings, even the dreadful sight of Numian's blank,
dead eyes.

Then nothing else mattered but the spirits in the rock.

The demons pricked my mind, trying to distract me, but they

longed for more death. They had welcomed my sacrifice of Numian. Her *inua* would be forever trapped, theirs to torment. They were hungry for more. In some twisted way, I was their creature now, serving their needs, for I swore all of the deaths I wrought here would belong to the demons.

I took a deep breath and managed to descend below their wicked frenzy to the detached embrace of the rock. These ancient spirits wanted no stories or sacrifices. They moved far beyond that.

They knew me now, having let me dwell among them as I had slowly died in the cell. Only a powerful connection such as that would allow me to merge with them now. Though I had sensed the spirits deep in the rock in Helluland, where the land was old, and in Issland, where it was newly made, never had I been able to commune with them in this way, as if we were one.

There was room for only one word, one emotion, and I became its very essence—*move!*

It was torturous, as if my mind was tearing apart under the tremendous strain. I almost lost myself inside the rock that stretched deep beyond the hill into the surrounding land and down under the sea. I was part of something unfathomable, but a tiny seed inside me remembered, *move.*

I felt myself shift as if the lower half of my body was sliced away. The rock screamed with the reverberations, ringing through me, deafening me—

The path shifted, jolting me into awareness. I tried to continue, but I was being shaken. Something hit my thigh and the sharp pain cut everything short.

Lexander grabbed my arm. "Marja, we must get away!"

He dragged me a few steps as I tried to keep my balance. The earth trembled and slipped underneath me. Large rocks were bouncing down through the light cast by the lanterns.

But I couldn't walk. Every bit of energy had been drained from my body. The sky was brightening with the coming dawn. Had I stood there unmoving throughout the night?

Lexander picked me up and ran to the gate.

I could feel him staggering as a boulder hit his back, but he shielded me and kept on going. A dull roaring rose behind us.

I clung to him as the hillside collapsed. The sound grew louder as the rocks hit the high enclosing wall behind us. The evil spirits intended to claim me as theirs, along with the masters.

But Lexander kept on running and the ground gradually stopped trembling. Bells were ringing around us, and shouts filled the air as people appeared in the doorways and windows.

I finally let go.

The sun was shining on the wall across from me when I awoke, forming a latticed pattern of shadow and light. For a moment, I was not sure where I was. The air smelled of cinnamon, and the heat was intense despite the early hour. I had become accustomed to the damp chill of the caves.

I escaped! was my first thought. In my heart I had feared I was truly a slave. The sunlit air rushed into me, infused with the living scent of the sea. I was free!

As I rolled over, Lexander appeared in an arched doorway. "How do you feel, Marja?"

He was so concerned that I sat up before I was ready. I hid the slight queasiness that it caused. I could tell from the aching of my body that I had fought with demons as I slept. It was too soon to tell if I had been tainted by evil.

There weren't any *olfs* in the room. I tried to put it out of my mind. It seemed a petty thing to quibble with the price of freedom.

"Where are the others?" I asked.

"In various places nearby. There were too many of them for our old quarters, though Bene and Eshter are keeping a few of the more fragile ones with them."

I stood up, testing my limbs. I was sore everywhere, as if I had been squeezed in a vise. "Were any of them injured in the rock slide?"

"I sent them away with Bene long before that. He was watching nearby." Lexander reached out to help steady me.

Through his touch, he was open to me. Startled, I met his eyes.

Lexander had been there constantly, haunting the master house, searching for a way to get in. He had never left.

His detached expression couldn't fool me. He loved me, deeply and ardently. For Lexander, knowing what was happening inside the master house but being unable to stop it was the worst fate he could have been dealt.

"What happened to Saaladet?" I asked.

"You destroyed it. The whole side of the butte caved in. If it hadn't been for the surrounding wall, the debris would have crashed into the houses below."

"The rock answered me." I remembered how it felt to enter that endless plane, as if my very *inua* had transformed in connecting with the spirits. "All those hours it felt like only a few moments."

The masters were dead, covered in the rock. Along with the servants in their beds. No one who served in a place like that was truly innocent, but they hadn't deserved to die.

Lexander sat in front of the latticed window. The rays of light fell behind him, casting his face in shadow. The blue sky was a welcome sight. I had grown so weary of darkness.

"Forgive me, Marja," he finally murmured. "I could not get through the sea gate, though I tried over and over again."

That seemed like a long time ago. "It wasn't your fault, Lexander. The demons stopped you because of the poison you carried. Your people use them to protect Saaladet."

His eyes widened. "I didn't think that my people could interact with the spirits of your world."

"Perhaps these are your own demons. They were there, infesting the very rock. They fed off the pain and anguish. They even took the death I wrought." I took a deep breath. "I struck down one of the mistresses in front of the other slaves. It was the only way to force them to follow me."

"Surely you don't look to me for absolution." His misery was clear. "I'm worse. I lured young people into slavery, making them leave their homes and sending them away forever to be used and discarded without a thought."

There was a charged silence, broken only by the tinkling of bells hanging from the lattice.

"I'm sorry, Marja." His tone was desperate, as if he had been driven to his brink, just as I had. "I molded your will to answer to mine, even after I freed you."

"I thought of you often in there," I forced myself to admit. "I thought of how you must have been during your training, and as a master. The things you did to the slaves."

He looked at me as if I had struck him. "Yes. I've done everything you saw, everything you hate." He didn't take his eyes from mine. "That's why I left you behind in Danelaw, Marja."

"I thought you wanted to protect me."

"Yes, but even more . . . I couldn't let you see my people. Ukerald is not the worst of us. Yet he was everything I have been in my life. I have been vicious to slaves just because I was thwarted in my own desires. I had been that selfish, that mean . . . and I knew you would see it in me."

So that was why he had built a wall between us. "I've always known that, Lexander. You can hide nothing from me when we are together."

"You didn't know the full extent of my sins until you saw Castropiero," he insisted. "And now Saaladet. You have every reason for not loving me."

"That's never stopped me."

"I know," he admitted, in the raw tones of honesty. "You give so freely to everyone around you, Marja. I have no doubt you would love me, simply because I need you so much. But I have been a monster too long to take the role of master with you. If I admit the truth . . . it's better for you to keep away from me. When you found out I was not a man, you thought it would be impossible for us to love each other. I believe you were right. I should not have lured you back into my arms."

I stood up and went to him at the window. It was difficult for him to reveal himself to me. There was so little I knew about him, and yet I had delved as deeply as I could. Anything more would come slowly, as he discovered himself.

Standing in front of him, I put my hands on his shoulders. He was cool to the touch as all his people were. "I've loved you for so long, Lexander. Since that winter's day in Vidaris when I touched you and a tear slid down your cheek."

He went very still beneath my hands. "You saw . . . ?"

I slipped my arms around him, leaning in closer so I could whisper in his ear. "You were miserable that day, and I didn't understand. How could I? It was this, wasn't it? You were thinking of your people, of your part in what they do to us."

"The futility of it all," he agreed. "It filled me up, snuffing out all else. I cared for nothing. But you"—he put his hands on mine, holding on tightly—"you are pure, open to everything around you. You never dealt out suffering, though surely enough has been inflicted on you. Instead you stood stronger than ever to protect others." His voice broke. "You were there when I realized the waste my life has been, spreading such horror . . ."

My hands smoothed his chest as I gently kissed his neck, murmuring, "Then how could you doubt me now?"

I slipped into his lap, kissing him on the lips.

For a moment he hesitated, as if fearing that I was merely responding to his need. "Marja . . ."

I dug my nails in, drawing him closer to me. I would not let him go until he could hold himself back no further.

"*Marja,*" he murmured.

His arms went around me tightly. Our lips caressed each other—mouth, cheeks, neck—I needed to feel every part of him. He was urgent, fervent, holding me as if he would fight all the demons of the world to keep me safe.

"Oh, Lexander . . ." I breathed. It had been far too long.

I swung my leg around to straddle him, pressing my body against his. He was ready, already straining toward me, and I gave a throaty laugh as I released him. I, too, was ready for him.

I reached out to him as I did to the *olfs*. He was open to me, and he would be forever. I would never doubt his love for me again. I could feel it coursing through him, like his lifeblood. I was a part of him in a way I had not imagined, as if our *inua* were entwined.

As he entered me, pulling me against him, we joined together. I strained, my feet braced against the mat and my hands holding on to his shoulders. His hands were insistent, pinning my hips against him.

I knew his exultation at possessing me again. In that moment, he reveled in his nature, owning me completely. He could because I gave myself to him.

And when I thought we could reach heights never seen before, a burst of light and exhilaration filled the room as *olfs* suddenly appeared. The creatures wheeled about in the effusions we gave off, rocking together in ecstasy. I had not lost them in spite of all that I had done.

The *olfs* lingered after our prolonged lovemaking. Every time I thought we had done all we could do, one of use would rouse and tantalize the other into ecstasy over again.

We might have gone on well past sunset, but there was a knock at our door. I quailed inside, but Lexander rose and loomed reassuringly in the doorway.

Then Bene rushed past Lexander, kneeling down beside the bed. "Are you truly unharmed, Marja? The others have been telling me what the masters did to you."

"What does that matter? I got them out, Bene!"

Bene gazed up at me in admiration. "I knew you would, Marja. The slaves are so grateful. They want to tell you themselves. I've been talking to them, explaining some of the things you taught me. Most of them are eager to get out and see Stanbulin. I told them they have to wait until you say it's all right."

I tousled his hair, knowing I would have to bed him in the next couple of days before his adoration got out of hand. "Where's Eshter?"

"Waiting downstairs. We're going over to the master house. People have gathered there to examine the debris."

My smile faded. I had bargained with evil spirits, yet it appeared I had somehow eluded their hold. "I must see it."

When we reached the streets, Eshter was waiting and our greeting had a few tears sprinkled amongst our relief. Eshter knew what it felt like to be a woman in the hands of brutal masters. She wordlessly took me into her arms, comforting me.

As we walked through the narrow streets, I was glad the *olfs* came along. They lent brightness and color to the dirty streets and dour faces.

I held on to Lexander's arm as we walked. We both took comfort in touching each other.

As we turned down the lane, the butte rose in front of us. The top was much the same, but the front surface had sheared off, leaving a depression where once there had been a craggy promontory. The rubble sloped steeply down to the base, where the sturdy wall still held. The rocks were pressing the iron spikes outward, and in some places had bent them, spilling boulders into huge piles on the other side.

"The houses below are already evacuated," Bene told us.

"And the first good rain will bring down more," Lexander added.

People were climbing among the rubble, picking through it and pulling out things, like scavengers on a carcass. A long maroon and gold banner flapped in the breeze, with one end wedged under a pile of rocks. All those costly goods the godlings had collected to transform their dreary chambers were buried here. Only the precarious wall holding up the slope kept more people from coming to pick through the rocks, searching for gold and jewels.

A fight broke out over an object that had been found. I shuddered.

"I wouldn't touch anything from this place. The demons were trapped when the rock collapsed. They're waiting to be released."

Perhaps my own evil deed was trapped here along with the demons, inside the very rock I had moved.

The fight among the scavengers was growing vicious, and Lexander urged us away, toward the harbor. "Did any of the masters survive?" I asked.

"None have come forward," Bene said. "It looks like you caught them all, Marja."

Dozens of near immortals snuffed out in a moment . . .

I continued walking around the butte, past the gatekeeper's shed. Only the small peaked roof was exposed. The gatekeeper's body was buried by the rocks.

I looked out to sea. "Another winged ship with more slaves will be arriving any day now."

"What are you thinking, Marja?" Bene asked.

"Lexander is a master. He could tell the shipmaster to do whatever he wants. They wouldn't gainsay you, would they?"

"No, they would obey me," he said as if realizing it himself. "I could find out where the pleasure houses are on their route. But my people will eventually come to find out why the flow of slaves has stopped."

"Long enough for two or three ships to arrive?" I asked

Bene was grinning. "We'll have a warband! We could go back to Allonis and get those slaves out. And Montplaire, too."

Lexander and I exchanged glances. We had not been counting on help from the freed slaves, but perhaps it was inevitable that our little band would grow. Bene and Eshter certainly weren't going anywhere without us.

"We could do it," I told them. "We can find out from the shipmasters where the houses are."

"They'll take us there themselves," Lexander agreed. "The shipmasters will swear we're from Saaladet, giving us free rein to do whatever we want."

I glanced up at the sheared wall. "Your people may find it impossible to rebuild their slave trade."

"Once we're done, there will be no masters left who are willing to serve them."

I bowed my head to the inevitable. The masters must be fought and blood must be spilled to free the slaves.

"You've cut them off at their knees," Lexander told me. "Now we just have to finish what you've started."

I took Lexander's hand, feeling his cool strength supporting me. Bene and Eshter moved in close, eager to do whatever it took. In that moment, I knew we would succeed.